ENTER THE DARK HOUSE

A COLLECTION

LAURIE FARIA STOLARZ

ENTER THE DARK HOUSE

A COLLECTION

— BOOK 1 —

WELCOME TO THE DARK HOUSE

— BOOK 2 —

RETURN TO THE DARK HOUSE

HYPERION

LOS ANGELES NEW YORK

Welcome to the Dark House copyright © 2014 by Laurie Faria Stolarz
Return to the Dark House copyright © 2015 by Laurie Faria Stolarz

All rights reserved. Published by Hyperion, an imprint of Disney Book Group. No part of this book may be reproduced or transmitted in any form or by any means, electronic or mechanical, including photocopying, recording, or by any information storage and retrieval system, without written permission from the publisher. For information address Hyperion, 125 West End Avenue, New York, New York 10023.

First Paperback Edition, September 2018
10 9 8 7 6 5 4 3
FAC-025438-19270
Printed in the United States of America

This book is set in Arial/Monotype, Courier New/Monotype, Garamond MT Pro/Monotype, Palatino Nova Pro/Monotype, Univers Next Pro/Monotype, Weber Hand ITC Std/Monotype
Cover Design by Jamie Alloy

Library of Congress Control Number for
Welcome to the Dark House Hardcover: 2013023992
Library of Congress Control Number for
Return to the Dark House Hardcover: 2015006630

ISBN 978-1-368-04124-9

Visit www.hyperionteens.com

For those who face their nightmares
with eyes wide open.

Dear Readers,

First, thank you so much for picking up this book. It was inspired by a nightmare I had several years back. In my dream, horror fanatics from around the country eagerly awaited the sixth film in a cult-followed movie series. And though the famed director/producer/ screenwriter of the series felt the story was finished with the fifth movie, he decided to host a contest: Fans could submit their worst nightmares for the chance to meet him and see his confidential new film.

I dreamed that seven teens won, and that they were flown from around the country to stay in a lush and lavish house, with rooms specifically tailored to each of their tastes and interests. As the winners arrived, they couldn't have been more excited by the idea of meeting the director and seeing his new project.

That's where my dream took a dark turn. I don't want to give too much away, but let's just say there's a creepy amusement park and the winners' worst nightmares— the ones they submitted for the contest—come back to haunt them.

As I was writing *Welcome to the Dark House,* I loved exploring the word *nightmare,* both literally and metaphorically. And I loved, even more, that though each character seems on the outside to be so radically different from the next, when we get to the heart of what truly makes them tick, we see they're unified by dark secrets and old ghosts—that fear transcends outward appearances and personas.

I invite you now to enter the Dark House. Make yourself at home and enjoy the stay.

Many, many thanks!

Laurie Faria Stolarz

WELCOME TO THE DARK HOUSE

IVY JENSEN

I WAKE WITH A GASP, COVERED IN MY OWN BLOOD. *It's everywhere. Soaking into the bed covers, splattered against the wall, running through the cracks in the hardwood floor, and dripping over my fingers and hands.*

I touch my stomach, searching for a stab wound. My chest heaves in and out. I'm breathing so hard that it hurts—so hard that I wish for my lungs to collapse and my heart to stop.

I wish that he'd killed me along with them.

The moonlight shines in through the open window, enabling me to see.

I'm in my present-day bedroom.

It's six years later.

I'm seventy miles away from the crime scene.

There is no blood, only sweat. There are no hardwood floors, either. A shag carpet covers unfinished plywood. I reach down and run my fingers over the thick wool threads, just to be sure. Then I check and recheck my comforter, looking at it from different angles. It isn't pink paisley, like the one I had when I was twelve. This one's dark, dark blue.

And there are pale green walls.

And angled ceilings.

And there's an armoire in place of a vanity.

There are no music posters on the wall, nor is there a single reference to the soccer I used to play.

I'm seventy miles away.

It's six years later.

This isn't the same room.

There is no blood.

This was obviously another nightmare.

Still, I make sure of everything by switching on my night table light. I make sure of everything by going through these rituals one more time: by saying the alphabet forward and backward one more time, by touching the pendant around my neck—an aromatherapy necklace that was supposed to be a gift for my mother—one more time.

I'm eighteen years old, not twelve.

I dreamed about him again, because I fear that he'll come back for me one day and do to me what he did to my parents.

Six years ago now.

In a room unlike this one.

Seventy miles away.

SUMMER

Ivy

IT'S SATURDAY AFTERNOON, AND I'M SITTING IN Dr. Donna's office. I've been sitting here, on this same leather chair, surrounded by these same four walls.

On the same day.

At the same hour.

For the same reason.

For the past six years.

I'm not sure if it helps, but I never skip a session, because coming here gives me hope that one day I'll no longer live in fear.

Dr. Donna sits across from me. Her legs are crossed at the knee, as usual. Her beige leather clog bops up and down to the ticking of her mantel clock as she waits for me to say something. But coming here—doing this—is starting to feel like watching a rerun. It's the same episode on the same channel, with the same actors, saying the same dialogue. Again and again. And again.

DR. DONNA: So, what do you think?

ME: What was the question?

DR. DONNA: It's been six years, Ivy.

ME: Six years and my parents are still dead, and I still feel like I'm rotting away in purgatory, waiting for a killer to determine my fate. Will he come back and kill me today? Or wait until tomorrow? Or will he put it off until next year? Or perhaps he'll surprise me on the ten-year anniversary?

DR. DONNA: And maybe he won't come back at all. You've changed your name. You've changed your address. You've even changed your family.

ME: What choice did I have with that last one?

DR. DONNA: My point is that maybe he's done.

ME: That depends. Do serial killers retire? I think he's waiting for the opportune moment, watching me, studying my habits. Sometimes when I'm shopping in town or walking home from school, I can feel his eyes on me.

DR. DONNA: Do you still think he's the one who sent you the gifts?

ME: I don't *think*; I *know*. He knows what I like. He knows where I live.

DR. DONNA: You're not into makeup, Ivy. So, how do you explain that elaborate cosmetic kit?

ME: And how do *you* explain the paisley-covered journal, the pink soccer jersey, and the Katrina Rowe CD? My love for those things was apparent from my bedroom that night.

DR. DONNA: A lot of people like Katrina Rowe's music, Ivy. And the color pink, paisley designs, and soccer . . . all of those things are popular too . . . as are stars. . . . That star necklace pendant you received, it doesn't get much more generic than that. Anyway, my point is that perhaps a secret admirer sent you the gifts.

ME: Except I haven't played soccer in six years, nor have I listened to Katrina Rowe. And no one who knows me now has any reason to believe that I used to like either.

DR. DONNA: You haven't told a single person? Even in casual conversation?

ME: You still think I'm being paranoid, don't you?

DR. DONNA: I think you have a lot of fear, and I want to help you to defuse it. But I'm not sure what else we can do here. We've talked about that night. We've talked about your nightmares. We've gone over every possible scenario—good and bad—of what could happen in the future.

ME: I need to try something else—to learn to live *with* fear, rather than *in* fear. I mean, lots of people live with fear, right? They put down good money for it. They seek it out from the front row of movie theaters and on roller coasters. They wait in long lines for ghost tours and to go inside haunted houses. They don't let it control their lives.

DR. DONNA: Interesting point. So, how do you propose we get there?

ME: I need to learn from those people. I need to see fear the way they do.

Autumn

IVY

I DON'T KNOW HOW I BECAME A SUBSCRIBER TO THE
Nightmare Elf's e-Newsletter. I'm not a fan of the movies,
and there's no chance that I'll ever become one, but with a
subject line that hints at ridding my nightmares for good, I
can't resist rescuing it from my spam box.

TO: IVY JENSEN

FROM: thenightmare.elf@gmail.com

SUBJECT: LAST CHANCE—NIGHTMARES BE GONE CONTEST ALERT

NIGHTMARES BE GONE CONTEST*
ENTER FOR A CHANCE TO MEET LEGENDARY FILM DIRECTOR JUSTIN BLAKE AND GET A BEHIND-THE-SCENES LOOK AT HIS CONFIDENTIAL NEW PROJECT

Dear Dark House Dreamers,

Greetings from the Nightmare Elf.
I'm sending this note to say,
If you tell me your worst nightmare,
I can make it go away.
Submit your bedtime horror
in a thousand words or less.
Then I'll add it to my sack,
and you'll enter my contest.

— The Nightmare Elf

Guidelines: Describe your worst nightmare in a thousand words or less. E-mail it to: thenightmare.elf@gmail.com.

Prize: An all-expenses-paid weekend, including an exclusive, behind-the-scenes look at the never-before-seen companion film to the Nightmare Elf movie series, plus the opportunity to meet Justin Blake.

Deadline: October 31, midnight EDT

Click HERE for Justin Blake's Web site

IN MY HEFTY ELF SACK, YOUR NIGHTMARES WILL KEEP.
BETTER THINK TWICE BEFORE FALLING ASLEEP.

*Must be 18 years or older to enter.

I click on the link for Justin Blake's Web site. I've certainly heard his name before. Most of his titles ring a bell from movie trailers I've seen on TV—those I've tried to avoid with quick reflexes on the clicker.

There's a drop-down menu that lists some of his films and characters:

NOTABLE FILMS	STARRING CHARACTERS
Nightmare Elf	Eureka Dash, Pudgy the Clown, Piper Rizzo, Jason Macomber
Nightmare Elf II: Carson's Return	Farrah Noyes, Danny & Donnie Decker, Meg Beasley, Candy Lane
Nightmare Elf III: Lights Out	Susan Franklin, Max Tarple, the Kramer family (Steven, Lara, Montana, Blakely)
Nightmare Elf IV: Don't Fall Asleep	Eureka Dash, Pudgy the Clown, Janson Dailey, Jed Clive, Betsy Wakefield
Forest of Fright	Sebastian Slayer, the Targo triplets (Ted, Mario, Selena), Joseph Newburger, Frederick Linko
Halls of Horror	Lizzy Greer, the Targo triplets (Ted, Mario, Selena), Glenn Sullivan, Ava Murray

Night Terrors	Little Sally Jacobs, the Baker family (Josie, Carl, Diana), the Robinson family (June, Roger, Daniella)
Night Terrors II	Little Sally Jacobs, Peg & Jessie Miller, the Ernesto family (Thomas, Juanita, Paulina, Kai)
Night Terrors III	Little Sally Jacobs, Jonathan Sumner, Felicia Thomas, Jake Willoby, Reva Foster
Hotel 9	The Scarcella family (Sidney, Darcie, Phillip, Jocelyn), Paige Rossi, Matthew Julian
Hotel 9: Blocked Rooms	Sidney Scarcella, Darcie Scarcella, Midge Sarko, Dorothy Teetlebaum, Carmen Roberge
Hotel 9: Enjoy Your Stay	Sidney Scarcella, Robert Scarcella, Midge Sarko, Emma Corwin, Enrique Batista

I click on the first Nightmare Elf movie title and an elf pops up on the screen: a blond-haired boy dressed in a red suit, a floppy hat, green gloves, and boots that curl up at the toe. With his rosy cheeks and bright blue eyes, he's kind of cute on first glance. But then you notice the way his ears spike up to look like devil horns and the pointy sword that is his tail.

Below him, there's a link with background information on the series' legend. I click on it.

THE LEGEND OF THE DARK HOUSE

One summer, many years ago, the Tucker family went on a camping trip. Deep in the woods, they came across an abandoned cabin with dark clapboard shingles, nestled in a grove of trees. A wooden plaque over the front door read WELCOME TO THE DARK HOUSE, written in red crayon.

The Tuckers decided to stay in the cabin instead of setting up camp. During their stay, six-year-old Tommy began to hear a voice inside his head. He didn't tell his parents—the voice told him not to. Tommy became withdrawn and secretive, often sneaking off into the woods to an old, abandoned storage shed. He called it the nightmare chamber.

"Make sure to visit the chamber three times a day," the voice told him. "There, you will do important work."

The voice belonged to a ten-year-old boy named Carson. While staying at the Dark House three months prior, Carson died from a seizure during a nightmare.

With his beloved elf doll in tow, Tommy would use a rock to scratch crude images into the walls of the shed— images of people with missing eyes, bleeding mouths, and stakes jammed through their hearts. The Tuckers grew concerned with Tommy's behavior. At the dinner table, he wouldn't speak. He refused to engage in any camping activities, like hiking, swimming, or sitting by the campfire.

One morning, Tommy's father followed him to the abandoned shed and saw the walls. "Explain yourself," he demanded.

"Go to hell," Tommy replied in a deep, slow, creaky voice, per Carson's instructions.

After five days at the Dark House, Mrs. Tucker, so disturbed by her son's worsening behavior, announced that they were cutting their vacation three days short. That same night, she dreamed about a thief in their apartment back home. Tommy had been experiencing nightmares too—recurring visions of a pack of snarling wolves tracking him through the woods.

Carson, still angry that he had died during a nightmare, wanted others to share his fate. His spirit, unable to pass on, had become quite powerful. He could see into the dreams of anyone who stayed at the Dark House—and make their nightmares come tragically true.

Tommy was the first victim. He died before the Tuckers finished packing, mauled by a wolf lurking near the nightmare chamber. Weeks later, Mrs. Tucker was killed by an intruder in their home.

After the Tuckers left, only Tommy's elf doll remained. Carson giggled at the sight of it, delighted to have a souvenir. And so he decided to inhabit the doll, dubbing himself the Nightmare Elf. Into his bright red sack Carson would collect the frightful dreams of the Dark House's guests, overjoyed to eventually release their nightmares into reality, making room in his bag for more.

So let this be a warning to all you campers: if you happen across the Dark House in the middle of the night, feel free to stop inside, but do remember this: *IN HIS HEFTY ELF SACK, YOUR NIGHTMARES WILL KEEP. BETTER THINK TWICE BEFORE FALLING ASLEEP.*

IVY

TO: thenightmare.elf@gmail.com

FROM: IVY JENSEN

SUBJECT: Re: LAST CHANCE—NIGHTMARES BE GONE
CONTEST ALERT

In a thousand words or less, describe your worst nightmare.

Dear Nightmare Elf,

For the record, I'm not one of your Dark House Dreamers, nor have I seen even one Nightmare Elf movie—or any of

Justin Blake's films for that matter—but I've been receiving your e-newsletters for years now, and this last one caught my eye.

I guess you could say that you found me in a weak moment, because the idea of telling an elf my nightmare, and having him magically take it away, sounds pretty amazing right now, especially at four in the morning . . . not that I actually believe a word of your BS. But, at the very least, maybe writing about my nightmare and sending it off into the black hole of cyber-space will trick me into believing that it'll never come back.

So, here goes.

For the past six years I've dreamed that my parents are being murdered in their bedroom across the hall. I'm haunted by this vision because it happened, in real life. I was in my room, sleeping soundly—until I heard it. A thrash-ing sound across the hall.

I sat up, able to hear more noises: a gasp, a sputter, an agonizing moan. Then silence, broken by an unfamiliar male voice: "And now it's your turn. You won't feel a thing."

My mother screamed. "Please, no," she begged. "Don't do this. I have a—"

There isn't a day that goes by that I don't try to guess at her missing words: "I have an idea"? "I have something to tell you"? "I have a daughter"? "I have a wallet full of cash"? I'll never know for sure. Her voice was cut short with a thwack. Then music began to play. String instruments. An eerie blend of violin and viola that reverberated in my heart.

I grabbed the phone on my night table and dialed 9-1-1. "I think someone just killed my parents," I told the operator, hearing a hitch in my throat, hearing words come out of my mouth that no one should ever have to say.

"Where are you?" the operator asked.

"In my room, across the hall."

"Is the person still in the house?"

"I don't know," I replied, keeping my voice low. "I mean, I think so. In my parents' room."

"Okay, I have your address. I'm sending help right over. Can you tell me your name?"

My name? My mind scrambled. My pulse quickened. And suddenly I couldn't get enough air.

"Hello?"

"Ivy," I choked out. "Jensen. My name, that is."

"Okay, Ivy. Listen to me carefully now. Is there a lock on your bedroom door?"

I looked toward the door, no longer able to hear my parents.

"Ivy?" the operator asked. "Are you on the first floor? Is there a window?"

I couldn't answer, couldn't think straight. My hands were trembling so furiously, but still I told myself that I wouldn't drop the phone; I'd keep it firmly gripped in my hands.

But then I saw it happen.

In slow motion.

Falling from my fingers.

Bouncing off the bed.

Landing against the hardwood floor.

It made a loud, hard knock. I felt it in my chest. It stopped my breath, stunned my heart, shot an arrow through my brain.

My bedroom light was off, but with the door cracked open, the hallway light leaked into my room and he was able to see me.

"Good evening, Princess," he whispered.

His hair was long and silver, tied back in a low ponytail. His face was covered with stubble. He cocked his head and smiled at me; his lips peeled open, exposing a pointy tongue and crooked teeth.

We both froze, just watching each other, awaiting the other's move—like two wild animals in the night. His eyes were unmistakable: tiny, dark gray, and rimmed with amber-brown. They reminded me of a bird's eyes.

His gaze wandered around my room—my walls, my floor, my bed, my dresser—as if taking everything in. The paisley bed linens, the soccer banners, my fuzzy beanbag chair, all the Katrina Rowe posters hanging above my bed.

A few seconds later, his eyes fixed back on mine, and he smiled wider. "It's very nice to meet you," he said, over-emphasizing every word.

I wanted to throw up. Chills ran down my spine.

Sirens blared in the distance then. He remained in the doorway a few more moments before backing away slowly and fleeing our little yellow house with the white picket fence and the long brick walkway—the place that I'd always called home.

But I knew that wouldn't be the end.

It's now six years later. Those eyes are still out there. And I live in constant fear that the killer will come back for me one day.

In my dreams, he plunges a knife deep into my gut before I can rouse myself. My eyes flutter open, and I'm able to see him. Those birdlike eyes.

His lips peel open and he smiles at me, his pointed

tongue edging out over his jagged, yellow teeth. "You knew I'd come back, didn't you?"

He twists the knife—two full turns—before pulling it out to examine the blade. I touch my stomach, smearing blood on my palms.

That's when I finally wake up.

I haven't told anyone this, but sometimes I wish that he would come back, once and for all. At least then it would be all over.

SPRING

Ivy

I PUSH THE TIP OF THE BLADE INTO THE SKIN AND make one solid cut. The onion falls in halves. I rip the skin off one of the halves and make a series of cuts, trying to get the layers as thin as possible—a technique only attainable with the sharpest of knives and the precision of an Iron Chef.

I toss the onion shreds into my bowl and look up, nearly awestruck by Enrique's Italian sausage. It's perfectly plump and juicy, slathered in a red chili glaze and stuffed with paprika and oregano.

"Ivy!" my sister Rosie shouts. She jumps in front of the TV screen, distracting me from Enrique's stuffing technique.

Rosie is eight years old and in love with SpongeBob. "What are you doing?"

I'm elbow deep in ground pork shoulder and shredded onion. "What does it look like I'm doing?"

She peeks at the TV screen, where Enrique, also dubbed the Spicy Italian Chef (even though he's from Argentina), is dressed in a bib apron and a pair of heart-patterned boxer shorts (his usual TV attire). Though I'm fairly certain his tanned, rippling muscles are part of the ensemble as well. Enrique's explaining the merits of a chunkier sausage over a lengthier one (something about moisture retention), but I'm pretty sure the vast majority of female viewers—not to mention his growing number of male admirers—could care less.

"He's hot," Rosie says. "But shouldn't you be using a fork to mix that stuff?" She points her glue-encrusted fingers into my bowl, coming way too close for my culinary comfort.

"Get out." I swat at her. "Have you been eating glue again?" There are suspicious-looking globules stuck in the corners of her mouth.

"I want a snack," she says, avoiding my question. "And I also want you to read my tea leaves." She takes a jar of dried mint from the spice rack and smacks it down on the counter.

"I'm saving that for Willow's stomach."

"Willow can spend the night doubled over in pain for all

I care. She refuses to let me borrow her blush." Rosie's big brown eyes bulge out in annoyance—a teenager stuck in an eight-year-old's body, Elmer's glue included.

"You're too young for makeup. Go find something productive to do." I flash her my porkified palms in an effort to repulse her, but the porkiness doesn't seem to bother her one bit.

Rosie starts singing extra loud—*"tra la la"*—and flailing her arms, trying to block the TV screen. Meanwhile, Willow, my twelve-year-old sister, comes rushing into the kitchen, saying there's something in the living room that I just *have* to see.

"I'm busy," I tell her.

"Well, get *un*busy," Willow says. "Because Rain and Storm are at it again."

Rain and Storm are my ten-year-old twin brothers, and the reason that people take birth control. I can hear Rain's menacing giggle from the living room. Meanwhile, it seems I've missed at least three of Enrique's steps. He's pouring a cup of red wine vinegar into a separate bowl, but I have absolutely no idea why.

"Come on!" Willow shouts. "They're going to mess up the drapes."

I grab a rag to wipe my hands, moving from behind the

island. In doing so, I accidentally bump my bowl. It drops to the floor. Ground pork shoulder falls against the tile with a slimy thud.

"*Ewww,*" Rosie squeals, nibbling glue residue from her fingers. "I'm not eating that."

I hurry into the living room, where Storm and Rain stand with their backs toward me, facing the bay window. "Prepare!" Storm orders.

I hear an all-too-familiar zipping sound.

"Aim!" Storm calls out.

"Fire!" they both shout.

It takes me a second to realize what they're doing. Pee shoots out, hitting the two potted plants in the window, splashing against the soil, and spraying all over the window screens.

"Go to your room!" I yell.

"Well, you *did* tell us to water the plants . . ." Storm argues, still giggling.

"*Now!*" My tone must scare them, because they do as they're told.

"Enrique's all done," Rosie says, from the kitchen. I can already hear the theme song to *SpongeBob*. "*Now* can you get me a snack and read my tea leaves?"

Most other eighteen-year-olds would probably hate my life. But I honestly don't know what I'd do if it weren't for the distraction of this household. I was placed with this family by protective services after my parents were murdered. My foster parents, Apple and Core (self-renamed from Gail and Steve) were a stark contrast to that darkness. Once hippie environmentalists, who named all their children after something in nature, they now need to make a decent living. So, while they go off to work, I stay at home playing full-time nanny for zero-time pay as the eldest of their five kids. School is my only time off, but it's April vacation, and everyone's home.

And *speaking* of April . . . that's my real name, my birth name I should say. But my foster parents changed it to Ivy. We had a renaming ceremony, complete with floral head wreaths, a dip in the lake, and dancing around a fire. I can't say I minded. I wanted to be someone else. I prayed to be someone else. Except for my name, so far my prayers have gone unanswered.

Ivy

My cell phone chirps, announcing that I have an e-mail. I pull it from my pocket to check. It's a message from the Nightmare Elf, only this time it didn't go into my spam box. I click on it, remembering the nightmare contest I entered months ago.

TO: IVY JENSEN
FR: thenightmare.elf@gmail.com
SUBJECT: YOU'VE BEEN CHOSEN
2 ATTACHMENTS

Dear Lucky Dark House Dreamer,

**In my hefty elf sack, your nightmares now keep.
Better think twice before falling asleep.**

—The Nightmare Elf

YOU'VE BEEN CHOSEN

What: To attend an all-expenses-paid weekend, including an exclusive look at director Justin Blake's never-before-seen companion film to the Nightmare Elf movie series, plus the chance to meet Blake himself. Congratulations. Your entry was one of seven selected from over twenty thousand applicants.

Where: Stratten, MN, home of Stratten University. Winners will stay for two nights at a bed & breakfast, chosen specifically by the Nightmare Elf.

When: July 17–19

Transportation: Once your attendance is confirmed with receipt of your registration packet and release form (see attached documents), air and local transportation arrangements will be provided.

RSVP: To reserve your spot, complete the attached forms and return ASAP. Space is limited.

*NOW, WHAT ARE YOU WAITING FOR?
PACK YOUR BAGS . . . AND PREPARE FOR
THE SCARE OF YOUR LIFE.*

NATALIE SORRENTO

"THIS DISCUSSION IS OVER," MY MOTHER SAYS IN her 1950s cardigan with an angel pin poked through the fabric.

Did a discussion ever start? There's a smug smile on her face because she thinks she's putting her foot down, but the fact is that her foot—as well as her entire body—has been under my dad's thumb ever since I can remember. My mother doesn't have a single thought that she can actually call her own.

We're sitting at the dining room table. A vase full of tea roses separates us, marking our opposing territories: me against them, thorns against roses.

"You need to think seriously about your future," Dad says. Before retirement, he worked at a plastics factory making BPA-infested food containers. He knocked my mother up when he was in his late fifties—when he was married to someone else, too—and when my mother was twenty-year-old eye candy, working as a teller at the bank. "Do something meaningful with your life," Dad says, as if I could ever compete with Harris.

My brother Harris and I were the product of said affair—twins, born less than sixty seconds apart. Even then we didn't want to leave each other's side.

"This is a once-in-a-lifetime opportunity," I tell them. "My essay stood out over all the other entries."

"Exactly," Dad snaps. "You have potential, but instead you hide it beneath that costume of yours."

"You wouldn't forbid Harris to go," I say; the words come out shaky.

Dad's face blows up like a balloon with too much air. He hates it when I bring up Harris. He hates it when I talk, period.

Before he explodes entirely, I storm to my room, locking the door behind me. The e-mail announcing that I'm one of the winners is still open on my computer. I read it again, making sure that it's real—that it still says what I think it does. My parents can never take that away.

I gaze over at my bookcase, the shelves of which are filled with all of Justin Blake's work, including a copy of *My Nightmare*, his autobiography, in which he talks about feeling like a constant disappointment to his parents. I know that feeling all too well.

I move over to my dresser mirror. There's a desk blotter covering the glass. I take it down, careful where I look; I don't want to see my whole reflection right away. My pulse racing, I pull off my sweatshirt, trying to focus on just the Nightmare Elf tattooed on my belly. When I went to the tattoo parlor, I told the artist to make an extra bulge in the elf's sack for my nightmare—the biggest one of the bunch.

I grab an eyeliner pen off my dresser and, across my belly, beside the elf, I start to write the words *In his hefty elf sack, my nightmare now keeps,* but there isn't enough room. The letters are squished.

I turn sideways to scope out the space on my back. Justin Blake's birth date is tattooed at the very bottom, right in the middle of my underwear line, right below Pudgy the Clown's chain saw.

Harris thinks it was psycho of me to get a man's birthday permanently inked on my skin. But at the time that I got it— just after my mom and sister had girls' night out and "forgot" to invite me—it made perfect sense, because I couldn't thank God enough for placing Justin Blake on this earth.

I angle my back a little more toward the mirror and pull down my underwear to see the couple of tattoos on my ass cheeks: Little Sally Jacobs's skeleton keys and part of the Nightmare Elf's infamous catch phrase, "Better think twice before falling asleep."

Looking at all these tattoos now, I want to tell myself how ballsy I am—how ballsy I was to have gotten them in the first place. But the truth is, they were strategically placed. I could never have gotten them where my parents would see, just like I could never go against their wishes and accept Blake's generous offer.

SUMMER

SHAYLA BELMONT

FINALLY I GET OFF THE PLANE, BUT I'M SO FULL OF negative energy that I can't even stand myself. I'm starving. My muscles ache. The woman sitting next to me in coach wouldn't stop coughing toward the side of my face. Plus, she smelled like bacon, and not the hickory-smoked country kind, more like the kind that's micro-ready in thirty seconds. And, as repulsive as that is, the smell only made me hungrier.

Admittedly, I'd wanted to upgrade to first class, but primo seats are slim to none when you're traveling to East Bum Suck, Minnesota, population: twelve.

I know; I sound disgusting. And I know; I shouldn't complain. I mean, this is a new adventure with new people and new opportunities . . . right? Plus no one twisted my arm to come here. I'm here of my own free will, as part of the Shayla Belmont "make the most of every moment" mission to have a fun and fulfilling life.

This airport is minuscule. People from my flight disperse like ants from repellent. Do they know something I don't? Did I miss the memo on fleeing creepy airports at the proverbial speed of light?

A woman rushes by me, nearly knocking me over.

"Excuse *me*," I call out, suddenly noticing that her pants are way too short, exposing her socks—purple ones with bright pink hearts, just like my best friend Dara's socks. The coincidence gives me a chill.

I gaze toward the windows, but they're blacked out so I can't see. I look around for a security officer or for someone who might be awaiting my arrival, but unfortunately I find neither.

A gnawing sensation eats away at my gut, making me question whether I should turn back around and go home. Still, I grab my bag and head up to the car rental counter. An attendant stands there, but it appears as though things could shut down at any second.

"Can I help you?" the attendant asks. She's at least seventy years old with long white hair and the palest blue eyes I've ever seen. She keeps her focus toward the crown of my head, rather than looking me in the eye.

I run my hand over my hair, wondering if she's admiring my new do. I got my hair straightened at a salon in Chelsea, a place that actually knows how to work with black-girl tresses rather than frying them as crisp as the aforementioned bacon.

"Good afternoon," I say, putting on my best smile. "Someone's supposed to be picking me up, but I'm wondering if there's another level to this airport. Is there a separate waiting area?" I look around some more, but I don't see any stairs, or an escalator.

"Would you like to rent a car?" she asks. "I have midsize sedans or minivans."

"I don't actually need a car." I let out a nervous giggle.

"Are you sure? Because there's a free box of wild rice with every rental." She places a box of rice on the counter and grins at me like it's Christmas, exposing a bright blue tongue and teeth that have browned with age. "This particular grain is native to this area."

I take a deep and mindful breath, as would Shine, my current yoga master, who believes in practicing compassion and kindness rather than succumbing to frustration, judgment, and blame (a practice that proves particularly helpful while riding the New York subway). "Is it always this quiet here?" I ask, attempting to switch gears.

"Quiet?" Her eyes are still fixed on my forehead. Maybe she's blind or has an aversion to making eye contact.

I glance over my shoulder. Aside from the two of us, the airport looks pretty desolate. "Are things more bustling earlier in the day?"

She laughs and snorts at the same time. A spittle of blue drool rolls down her chin. "Have you forgotten where you are? Do you need me to show you a map? US maps also come free with your car rental."

"Wait, *what*?" I ask, utterly confused.

She continues to laugh at me; her eyes roll up farther—I can barely even see them now. There's just a bulging mass of glossy whiteness that reminds me of hard-boiled eggs.

My cell phone rings in my pocket. I fumble for it, but it falls from my grip and clanks to the floor. I pick it up, hoping it didn't break. "Hello?" I answer.

"Hey," Mom says. "You landed."

I move away from the woman, accidentally bumping into a post from behind. There's a phone attached, with a piece of mangled wire dangling out from the bottom, reminding me once again of Dara.

I try to push the wire back inside a hole in the post, but there's too much of it—at least four feet—and it won't all go in.

"Shayla?" Mom asks.

I gaze upward at a support beam. There's a hook sticking out, where one could attach the wire. I picture Dara hanging there, her feet dangling, those heart-patterned socks. Her eyes snap open and stare down at me. Her dark blue finger points in my direction.

"Shayla . . ." Mom calls again.

"Hey," I say, my heart pumping hard. I look away and blink a couple of times. "I'm not so sure about this place."

"Not so sure about Minnesota?" Mom laughs. "You've been to India and Ethiopia, for goodness' sake."

"I know. It's just . . ." I move toward the exit sign at the opposite end of the room. What once appeared like a teensy airport now feels like a major shopping mall. "It's different here."

"Well, of course it's different. You just left the city, *girl.*"

I hate it when my mom goes all homegirl on me. "That's not what I mean." I peer back at the support beam. Thankfully, Dara's no longer there.

"Then what?" Mom asks, finally sensing my unease. "Do you want to come home? Just say the word and I'll have something arranged in a matter of minutes."

"Hold on." I move through the exit doors. A shiny black hearse is parked right outside. The driver's-side door opens and a hot-looking guy steps out: midtwenties, airbrushed tan, and dressed in Armani.

"Shayla Belmont?" he asks, holding up my picture—the one I e-mailed with my contest forms. His smile is totally killer.

"Yes," I say. "Are you . . . ?"

"Stefan. And your chariot for the evening, compliments of Justin Blake and Townsend Studios." He opens the door to the backseat. "I hope you'll find things comfortable."

"In a hearse? Are you kidding?"

"I never joke about transporting dead people."

"Except last I checked I was still alive."

"For now, anyway." He winks. "We're waiting for one more person who was on your flight."

I peek inside the hearse, spotting an ice bucket with an array of beverages inside it. There's also a basket of cinema snacks (movie popcorn, Jujyfruits, Sno-Caps, and sourdough pretzels). "Thanks," I say, suddenly remembering my mother on the phone. "I think I'm all set," I tell her as soon as Stefan steps away to load my bags into the back.

"Are you sure? Where are you anyway?"

"I'm just getting picked up from the airport."

"Okay, well call me as soon as you get to the B and B."

"Will do. Love you."

"Love you too, Shay-Shay."

After we hang up, I take a seat inside the car, noticing a movie ticket stub with my name on it. I pick it up to take a closer look. It's actually a welcome note, congratulating me once again on winning, and signed by Justin Blake.

Stefan closes the door behind me and already any reluctance has melted away, replaced with an overwhelming sense of excitement for what's soon to come.

GARTH VADER

"HOLY FREAKING SHIT!" I SHOUT, ABLE TO SEE THE house in the distance.

The driver looks at me in the rearview mirror. "Is everything okay, Mr. Vader?"

Okay? I'm practically drooling. "This seriously can't be real."

"I'll take that as a yes."

The house looks just like the one from the movie: the dark shingled exterior, the shutter-covered windows, the plaque over the door affirming what I already know.

"Welcome to the Dark House," the driver says.

Goose bumps rip up my arms. It's all I can do not to bust out of the car while it's still in motion. A dilapidated shed— no doubt Tommy Tucker's nightmare chamber—stands in the distance. "Was this place built just for us?" I know for a fact that the movie was originally shot in Hampstead, New Hampshire.

"The house was already here, from what I understand, but it was recently remodeled for your arrival. You'll find that everything about this weekend has been created specifically for this occasion . . . specifically for you winners."

"Wow," I say. "It's definitely the perfect spot." In the middle of nowhere, surrounded by forest. On the annoyingly long ride over from the airport, I think we might've passed three gas stations and two convenience stores, tops.

I grab my bags from the back of the hearse and walk around to the front of the house. The plaque is in direct view now. It's an exact replica of the one from the movie, written in red crayon by Carson, the Nightmare Elf.

"Pretty remarkable, isn't it, Mr. Vader?"

I think the look on my face is agreement enough. I mean, where do I even begin?

All dressed up in his little suit and his little tie, the driver ushers me inside. Here's where things differ from the movie.

It's like walking onto the set of *The Real World*, the Dark House edition. The walls are paneled with wood, giving the place the illusion of a cabin, but the furnishings are anything but camp-like. There's a huge room with high ceilings. A wide-screen TV hangs on the wall, as does a life-size photo of the mastermind himself. "This is incredible," I say, thinking aloud, noticing how the carpet looks to be at least five inches thick.

There's a plateful of Nightmare Elf cookies on a table in the center of the room. I palm five of them and then look around for a check-in desk, stoked when I don't see one, psyched that this doesn't appear to be a B and B, after all. "Are we alone?" I ask.

"Two others have also arrived—Taylor and Natalie, according to my notes, but we can double-check with Midge."

"Midge?"

"Midge Sarko from *Hotel 9.*" He looks around, as if trying to find her, peeking down a hallway, and looking into another room. "She'll be looking after all of you this weekend."

I feel the smile on my face widen. Midge is the psycho chambermaid who collects her victims' fingers in the pockets of her apron.

"I'm not sure where she is, so why don't I show you to your room." He pulls a notepad from his pocket. "You're in room nine."

"Sweet deal," I say, grabbing a couple more cookies.

He leads us through the living room, past a screwed-up ceramic rooster sitting by the fireplace. Its bright yellow eyes must be connected to a motion detector because it crows as I walk by, *almost* making me jump. We head upstairs to room number nine. I step inside, completely jazzed by what I see. There's a drafting table in the corner with an art caddy stocked with pencils, charcoals, and painting stuff. Lining the walls are illustrations from some of my favorite artists, like Haig Demarjian and Virgil Finlay, as well as a few pieces I don't recognize. A poster of Captain Death Row, my favorite band, hangs over the bed. It's an illustration of Captain Death— his smiling skull with a gap between his two front teeth— sporting a bandanna and sunglasses.

There are two beds in the room. I'm tempted to push them together so I can be like Bloody Bathrow, the lead guitarist of the Masochistic Underbellies. I saw Bloody's place on a show called *Crash Pads*. He's got a custom twenty-foot wide bed that he calls his kitty ride.

Beyond the beds, on the far wall, are a bunch of high-end guitars—a couple of them with metallic red and gold paint jobs. I've never tried to play, but maybe Blake thinks that I should. "There's no way you're getting rid of me after just two nights," I say, thinking how jealous my dad would be.

55

"Shall I leave you to arrange your things?" the driver asks.

I've yet to catch his name and at this point it feels weird to ask. "Solid." I flash him the peace sign and stick out my tongue, Gene Simmons–style. If only it were covered in faux blood.

Once he leaves, I set my sketchbook down on the table and flop back onto my new bed. It's bigger than my naked mattress at home. Our whole apartment could probably fit into the living room and entryway of this place alone.

I stuff a couple of cookies into my mouth and look up at the ceiling. Another of Haig's illustrations stares back down at me. It's done in dark pastels: cherublike children sleeping peacefully in bed while a sharp-toothed demon with bleeding eyes hovers inches away. It's way cool. And these cookies are way delicious. I think I've died and gone to Dark House heaven.

IVY

"JUST AROUND THIS BEND," THE DRIVER SAYS. "YOU must be anxious to stretch your legs."

I'm anxious, period.

We turn off the main road onto a long dirt path, and finally I'm able to see a house in the distance. As we get closer, I spot a sign over the front door: WELCOME TO THE DARK HOUSE.

"Is this really the B and B?" I ask, feeling my stomach twist. There's no parking lot, not one other car. "Is anyone else staying here?"

He gives me a curious look. "Don't you recognize this place from the Nightmare Elf movies? This house was made to look like the real thing. Aren't you a fan of Justin Blake's work?"

"Of course," I lie, the light finally dawning. The accommodations are movie themed.

I retrieve my bags from the back of the hearse, picturing my parents' caskets—the cherry wood, the engraved crosses, the satin interior lining.

"Welcome to the Dark House!" a voice bellows, pulling me back to earth.

I turn to find a boy standing behind me. He's probably my age, dressed in layers of gray and black. His wavy dark hair is held back with a bandanna, and there are silver hoops pierced through his eyebrow, nostril, and lip.

"Are you one of the winners?" I ask him.

"That depends . . . was Justin Blake born in Knoxville, Tennessee?"

"Maybe?"

"*Errrh,*" the boy lets out a game-show buzzer sound, denoting my wrong answer. "The correct response would've been yes. And if you were truly a Justin Blake fan you'd have known where he was born, as well as which schools he attended, and where he now lives. I'm Garth, by the way." He extends his hand for a shake. His fingers are loaded with more sterling silver jewelry than I've ever seen in one place.

"I'm Ivy." I shake his hand, fully aware that my palms are cold and clammy. "I guess you could say that I'm a fairly new fan of Blake's."

Garth closes the rear door of the hearse before moving around to the driver's side window. "I can take things from here," he tells the driver.

As if I couldn't feel more uneasy.

Still, bags in hand, I follow him inside, relieved that it's not creepy like the exterior. A wide open space is furnished with an L-shaped sofa, velvety chairs, and eclectic antiques—an artful blending of color, texture, and style. There's a workstation by the far wall. Beyond it is a set of stairs, and rooms to the right and left. A large granite island separates the living room space from a state-of-the art kitchen so similar to the Spicy Italian Chef's that I almost have to pinch myself. "Is that a real Pompeii oven?" I ask, pointing at it.

Garth sniffs in my direction, evidentally too distracted by my smell—the scent of my essential oils maybe—to answer.

"Has anyone else arrived yet?" I ask, my anxiety mounting by the moment.

"Two chicks I've yet to see—one went for a walk, so says Midge, resident watchdog; the other won't open her door . . . at least not for me." He grins, as if the idea of that makes him proud. He leans forward to sniff the side of my face. "Is that A-positive I smell on you?"

"A-positive?" I ask, wondering if that's the name of a new perfume.

"Your blood," he attempts to explain. "It's type A, right?"

I don't know how to respond—or if he's even being serious.

"I'll bet you clot really well, don't you?" He winks. "No coagulation problems for you."

"Welcome!" a woman says, coming down the stairs. She's wearing a maid's uniform—a black dress with a frilly bib apron over it—and there are little-girl ribbons in her hair. "You must be Ivy," she says with a smile. "I was just turning down your bed. I know it's a little early, but I figured you all might be tired. I see that you've met Garth."

Garth appears distracted again. He moves away, down the hall, into another room, slamming the door behind him. The noise makes my insides jump.

"Everything okay?" the woman asks me. Her shimmery white hair matches her pearly teeth and the shadow on her lids. She reminds me of Southern Sally Cooks from the Food Channel.

I manage to nod, trying to get a grip.

"I'm Midge." She smiles wider, exposing a shiny gold tooth. "You need anything, you just call on me. So what do you say . . . Are you ready to check out your room?"

We go upstairs and down a long hallway. The floorboards creak beneath my step. "Here we are," she says, opening the door to room number two.

It's larger than I expected, with two full beds. A giant, life-size cardboard cutout of Julia Child is positioned at the foot of one of them. "Wow," I say, startled by the sight of Julia holding a raw chicken up by its legs.

"I take it that someone's a cooking fan," Midge says.

It's true. I've been cooking pretty intensely since my parents were murdered. Not only is it a distraction, but it also makes me feel in control—wielding knives; the excuse to cut, slice, grate, chop.

"Ivy?" she asks.

I go to take a breath, but the air gets stuck in my chest, deep in my lungs. I sit down on the edge of the bed and silently count to ten, wondering what the hell I'm doing here and what I was even thinking. I touch the aromatherapy pendant around my neck, telling myself to relax. I unplug the cork and close my eyes, breathing in the cedarwood oil, reminding myself of its ability to induce tranquility.

"Do you need some water? Are you not feeling well?"

"I'll be fine," I say, finally able to catch my breath.

"Well, as you can probably guess, the winners' rooms are tailored to each of your individual tastes and interests, based on the personality profiles that you filled out."

I gaze over at the other side of the room. It's Barbie pink and suited for a dancer, with a ballet bar and a rack of dance shoes. A cursive sign over the mirror reads *Dance with Me*. "Is someone else sharing this room?" I ask, spotting a leopard-print suitcase at the foot of the other bed.

"Yes. Taylor. You'll be meeting her soon. She just went out for a walk. It's such a glorious day, isn't it?" Midge opens the drapes wide, letting in the light. It's late afternoon, and the sun's orange glow sinks down through the tree limbs, casting a strip of light over my bed, illuminating a copy of Deena Diddem's latest book, *Dare to Diddem*. (Note: in Deena-speak, *diddem* means to throw together random ingredients from your fridge and pantry and end up with a tasty new dish.)

"Just a little gift from Mr. Blake," Midge says. "I assume you're familiar with Deena's work?"

Deena Diddem, thirty-three years old, born in Toronto, the only child of Chuck and Nancy, climbed the culinary ladder, starting her career in the prepared foods section of her local supermarket. She's now the Food Channel's number one–rated chef.

I take the book and open to a flagged page. Not only has Deena signed the copy, but she's also written me a note.

Dear Ivy,

A little bird told me that you're a big fan of my show. I'm so flattered. Thank you so much!
I also heard that you love to cook. Who knows, maybe one day our paths will cross. In the meantime, keep on diddeming! Best of luck!

Love,
Deena

I run my fingers over her words.

"You like?" Midge asks.

"More like *love*."

"Great." She smiles. "Now if you don't need anything else,

I'll leave you to settle in. You'll notice the itinerary for the weekend on the night table."

"Thanks," I say, reaching to take it, more excited about this weekend than I ever thought possible and more hopeful than ever before.

WEEKEND ITINERARY

FRIDAY

2–7 p.m.	*Dark House Dreamers arrive*
8 p.m.	*Creepy comforts dinner—dining room*
9 p.m.	*Final Cut—theater*
9:30 p.m.	*Ghoulish desserts—dining room*

SATURDAY

10 a.m.–2 p.m.	*A brunch to die for—dining room*
4 p.m.	*Hearse leaves for the set—lobby*

SUNDAY

9 a.m.–noon	*Dead End Brunch for any remaining survivors—dining room*
2 p.m.	*Hearse returns Dark House survivors to the airport—lobby*

PARKER BRADLEY

INT. ENTRYWAY, DARK HOUSE—DAY

ANGLE ON

WOMAN, 50-something, dressed up as Midge
Sarko, one of Justin Blake's most villainous
characters; a chambermaid from *Hotel 9*, who
kills her guests with household items (a
turkey timer, a toilet bowl plunger, soap
scum remover).

                    MIDGE SARKO
Welcome, you must be Parker.

                        ME
And you're obviously Midge. Anyone
ever tell you that you look just like
Tina Maitland, the actor who played
Midge in the movie?

I move CLOSER on the POCKETS OF HER APRON.
The curly handle of Midge's signature
paring knife sticks out—always ready
to slice off a souvenir finger for her
collection.

                    MIDGE SARKO
                      (winking)
Tina's just an actor. I'm the real
McCoy.

I lower my camera to shake her hand.

                    MIDGE SARKO
Sorry about your flight delay.

                        ME

What's an extra two and a half
hours on the tarmac, right?

                    MIDGE SARKO

Well, if it's any consolation, it was an
extra two and a half hours for your driver
too. He was already on his way to get you
by the time he learned of the delay.

                        ME

Bummer for him.

                    MIDGE SARKO

But lucky for us, because you're here
now. Come on, I'll show you to your room.

I follow Midge through the house, filming the whole way,
as the infamous swish-swish sound of her ass fills the loud
silence.

"Excited?" she asks.

"Are you kidding? I can hardly believe this is real." I found
out about this contest totally by chance doing research for
my film class; it was posted on a fan site for Justin Blake,

notable horror director/producer/screenwriter. The site was littered with photos of Blake, favorite movie clips, and tons of Nightmare Elf–inspired fan fiction. I'd forgotten what a cult following Blake has. I used to be a fan too, back when I first discovered horror and didn't know much about the genre.

Someone had posted an entry that read: "Want to meet Justin Blake and get a behind-the-scenes look at his new confidential film project? E-mail me: thenightmare.elf@gmail.com."

I sent an e-mail, figuring I wouldn't hear back. But ten minutes later the contest guidelines appeared in my inbox. And eight months later, here I am.

Midge stops in front of the door at the very end of the hall. "This is it."

I point my camera into the room just before mine, wondering where the other winners are, looking for something else interesting to shoot.

ANGLE ON GIRL

GIRL, 18-ish, sits on her bed, looking
down at her hands. There's a tiny bottle
between her fingers, hanging from a silver
chain.

CLOSER ON GIRL'S FACE

Brown eyes, heart-shaped face, long dark
hair. She's way too beautiful to be real.

The girl looks back at me and I'm totally
caught.

"Hey," I say, lowering my camera, suddenly feeling like a
creep. "I was just shooting my arrival."

My explanation sucks, and she knows it too. Her forehead
furrows as she looks toward my camera; it's half-tucked behind
my back, as if I could possibly hide it now.

"Coming?" Midge asks me.

I give the girl an awkward wave and then proceed to my
room. A king-size bed greets me, the cover of which has dozens
of hungry, open-mouthed eels scattered across the blue fabric.

"I guess somebody has a sick sense of humor," I say, zooming in with my camera, remembering the essay I submitted for
the contest.

"How's that?" Midge asks, evidently clueless.

A laptop station sits beyond the bed with one of those ergo-
nomic chairs—one that probably cost more than my car.

"Nice," I say, moving farther inside.

As if on cue, music starts to play. An old black-and-white movie cranks to life on a projector screen on the far wall. The quality of the film is grainy, but I'd recognize this scene anywhere: it's nighttime, there's a storm outside, and an unsuspecting couple falls victim to the classic stranded-car-by-the-side-of-the-road routine. *The Old Dark House,*" I say. Circa 1932, if I'm remembering correctly from my History of Film course. "How fitting for the weekend."

"Should I assume that things are to your liking?" Midge asks.

"Definitely." I aim my camera at the bookshelves lining the room. They're jammed with screenplays—what has to be at least five hundred of them.

"You'll notice that some of them have been signed," Midge says, following my gaze.

"Signed by whom?" I ask, noticing a copy of *Citizen Kane,* one of my favorite films of all time.

"It varies." She grabs a copy of *The Shawshank Redemption* off the shelf. "Sometimes the writer, sometimes the director. This one's been signed by Morgan Freeman."

"No way." I set my camera down to take a peek.

"Mr. Blake keeps quite a collection." She smiles wide, exposing a shiny gold tooth. "Now, if you'll excuse me, I have some dinner preparations to attend to."

Once she leaves, I continue to check out the screenplays. Cameron Crowe. Alfred Hitchcock. Stanley Kubrick. John Hughes. It's too good to be real. They don't even know me here, so how can they trust that I won't steal a few?

I grab the script for *The Silence of the Lambs* and then turn to sit on my bed, startled to find that I'm not alone. The girl from next door is standing in my doorway.

"I'm sorry to bother you." Her eyes search my face, as if checking to make sure that I'm okay with her being here.

"No bother at all." I mean, seriously? Holy shit.

"I'm Ivy." Her straight dark hair hangs past her shoulders, over a long purple sundress that stretches to the floor.

"Parker," I say, trying my best not to stare.

But she's not even looking at me now. Her eyes are fixed on the projector screen—on the group of people taking refuge from the storm. They're sitting around the dinner table at the Femm family estate. There's a pounding on the door.

Ivy's eyes widen.

"This is actually a pretty safe scene in the film," I tell her.

"Okay," she says, even though she's totally *not* okay. Her face is completely flushed.

I go to shake her hand, but she's holding her cell phone and we end up making a weird cell phone–hand sandwich.

"Sorry," she says. There's an awkward smile on her face. "I

need to call home, but I can't get reception, and I'm hoping it's just my phone's issue."

"Not just your issue. There's no reception here, at least that's what the hearse guy said, but he also mentioned something about a landline in the living room downstairs."

"Thanks." She smiles. There's an irresistible spray of freckles across her nose and cheeks. "I promised I'd call home when I arrived."

"Where's home?"

"Boston, just north of it. And you?"

"San Diego, just south of it."

"Wow," she says. "We couldn't be farther away from one another."

"Not for the next forty-eight hours we're not." It takes me a beat to realize what I've said—how cheesy it sounds—and my face flashes a thousand degrees of hotness.

Ivy notices, and her smile shifts to a smirk. She must find my embarrassment amusing.

"The last hearse is pulling up," Midge calls. "It must be Shayla and Frankie, the final two Dark House Dreamers."

"Do you want to go down to meet them?" Ivy asks.

Not especially, I think, wondering if she has a boyfriend. But I tell her I'd like to, anyway.

NATALIE

MY ROOM AT THE DARK HOUSE HAS NO MIRRORS. IT was the very first detail I checked. Instead, it's decorated with all-things Justin Blake: T-shirts, key chains, comic books, clapboards, the LEGO-constructed version of Hotel 9, and a collection of Pez dispensers of some of his most notorious characters.

The suit Justin Blake wore to the Oscars in 1999 hangs on a hook, opposite my bed. I reach into one of the pockets and find an old gum wrapper. I sniff the silver packaging. It smells like berries. I run the tip of my tongue over the paper, finally stuffing the entire thing into my mouth. I chew the wrapper down, imagining the gum between his teeth, flipping over his tongue.

I remove the jacket from the hook and slip it over my shoulders, picturing Justin Blake on the red carpet, waving to his fans. I wave too, moving to stand in front of a movie poster for *Night Terrors II*, imagining that I'm his date for the premiere.

The far wall, behind a spare bed, is wallpapered with maps and postcards from around the world. I'm assuming there's some Blake-flavored connection. There's also a director's chair, a rack of men's shoes (size eleven), and an assortment of hairbrushes and combs (perhaps for Blake's thick wavy hair), though I don't spot any residual hair strands.

I check out the chair. It's been signed by Blake. I run my finger over a spot where the ink got smudged. I sit down, feeling overwhelmed and undeserving. Why does someone like me get to be so lucky, when someone like Harris got such a raw deal?

I look toward the closet, wondering if there might be more clothing and collectibles inside. I hurry over and slide open the closet door.

A full-length mirror stares back at me. It takes me a second to realize the reflection on the glass is my own—that it isn't some Nightmare Elf monster.

Was my reflection always this horrible? My face so long? My legs this short? My hands so big? Could my skin be any more pasty?

Others have arrived. I can hear the sound of new voices, the clunking of suitcases, the trampling of feet up and down the stairs.

I whip off the jacket, double-check the lock on the door to my room, and wedge a chair beneath the knob. Sitting on the floor at the foot of my bed, I pull off my wig. There's an eight-strand wad of hair clenched between my fingertips. Who do I think I am to be wearing Justin Blake's jacket? Or chewing his gum wrapper? Sitting in his chair? Thinking about trying on a pair of his shoes?

Even Taylor could tell that I didn't belong here. "Are you going to be okay?" she asked, on our hearse ride from the airport. She didn't even know me. We'd sat on opposite ends of the plane, had only exchanged a few words since we'd landed, but still she could sense that something was off.

"I thought this was what I wanted." I turned away, faced the window, drew a heart on the glass in the steam from my breath. "No one knows I'm here."

"Not even your parents?" she asked.

I could see her reflection in the window glass. Her dark blond hair was pulled back from her face, accentuating her wide green eyes, her pinched nose, and her perfectly pouted lips. Perfectly balanced features.

"I just left," I told her. Packed my bags, called a cab, snatched some money out of my mother's stash in the oatmeal box, and bolted. My mother had told me to be ready by three, that we were going to see a new therapist. I said I'd be waiting. And I wasn't lying: I *was* waiting. My heart pounding, I stood in my bedroom window, gazing out at the street, anticipating who would arrive first—either her or the taxi I called. The winner would dictate my destination. The taxi won, and off I went, on automatic pilot, to the airport, through the check-in, and then onto the plane, shocked that I'd done it. Defied them. Defied Harris. And in such a major way.

"Wow," Taylor said.

I could tell from her tone that she didn't know whether to be happy or sad for me. I didn't know either. This trip wasn't like a secret tattoo that I could hide. There was no turning back, no concealing what I'd done beneath layers of dark clothing.

"We're here," the driver announced as we pulled up in front of the Dark House. "You two are the first to arrive."

Taylor tried to hide her smile with a nibble of her lip. I hated that I was spoiling her excitement. I wanted to be excited too.

Hours later, sitting on the floor, I wonder if Taylor has turned up; it seems she wandered off. Earlier, Midge forced her way into my room to see if Taylor might be hiding somewhere.

I rock back and forth, watching the room in anticipation, as if it might spring to life at any moment—as if I'm in the audience, waiting for the movie of my life to start. I yank the eight-strand wad of hair. The action feeds my blood, soothes my nerves, slows the fleeting thoughts through my head.

My hair strands stick in the creases of my fingers. I sprinkle them over the rug, imagining them like seeds that might one day grow into something healthy.

FRANKIE RICE

ONCE THE PLANE LANDS, THE OLD GUY SITTING next to me spills his pill-meds all over the floor. I should ignore it, but I help him out, exiting the plane a good ten minutes after everybody else.

The silver lining? I'm picked up by a Cadillac hearse. The platinum lining? There's a hot girl sitting inside it.

"Hey," I say, joining her in the backseat.

There's a huge-ass smile on her face, like we're long lost friends and she's been waiting to see me all day. "Hey back at you."

She's cute—*really* cute with insanely bright golden-brown eyes; they're framed behind a pair of square black glasses.

"I'm Shayla," she says, sticking her hand out for a shake. "Shay, for short."

"Frankie," I say, shaking her hand. "No shortening required."

"Too funny." She laughs, despite the lameness of the joke. "Were you on the flight from JFK, because I totally didn't see you? Where are you from . . . and cool bracelet, by the way. Is that a Celtic knot?"

"Yes. Just south of Richmond. And the symbol for infinity, actually."

"As in Justin Blake forever?" She giggles.

"Something like that." I smile. She's so unbelievably perky.

We ride to the place where we're staying, with Shayla chattering on the whole way about art, politics, books she's read, places she's traveled. I try to listen to most of it, but I'm so busy anticipating what it'll be like to meet Justin Blake—how I should act and what I should say—that it's hard to keep up.

Finally we pull up in front of the Dark House B and B. Some lady dressed up as Midge Sarko greets us in the entryway.

"It is *so* nice to meet you," Shayla says, jumping in front of me to shake the woman's hand. "What an incredible opportunity this is."

Other winners are already here. A guy comes forward to shake our hands. "Hey," he says. "I'm Parker."

I introduce myself and Shayla—not that Shayla needs any introduction. She's already pumping Parker for info, asking him where he's from and when he got here, tossing me to the side. "This weekend is going to be *so* super fun," she tells him.

A guy layered in dark clothes and silver jewelry is sitting on a couch. He looks up from his sketchpad as I approach. "Hey, man," he says. "I'm Garth Vader."

"As in Luke Skywalker's father?"

"Garth with a *G*," he says, correcting me, as if the distinction is even worth it. "My dad's a huge Star Wars fan."

"I'm Frankie," I say, extending my hand for a shake. "Where are you from . . . besides the dark side, that is?"

"Delaware," he says, immune to the joke. He sniffs his fingers after shaking my hand. "O-positive, right?"

"Excuse me?"

"It's a gift . . . my ability to sniff out blood type. You're O-positive, aren't you?"

"Cool trick," I say, unfazed to find someone like him here—someone who wears his inner freak on his sleeve. Still, as psycho as he seems, he's right about my blood type.

I peek at his sketchpad. Is it any wonder that he's doing a color sketch of a two-headed ghoul? A mixture of blood and puke spews out of the double mouths, pouring down like rain. The guy may be a walking cliché, but he's actually pretty talented.

"Hey, there," Shayla says, making a beeline in Garth's direction. Clearly this girl has a social agenda. She plops down beside him. "So, let's hear it: What's your story? Who are you and what was your worst-ever nightmare? Holy yum fest," she says, before he can answer anything. The girl is a complete spaz. There's a plateful of Nightmare Elf cookies on the table in front of them. "No wonder it smells like a bakery in here." She takes one, proceeding to tell Garth that she's from the West Village and that the bakery near her apartment is "out-of-this-world fabu-licious."

My gaze travels to a girl in the corner, talking on the phone. She reminds the person on the other end to take their medicine and brush their teeth.

"That's Ivy," Parker says, standing at my side now. "I'm not sure if you noticed it yet, but we don't get cell phone reception here, so if you want to make a call, you have to use the landline."

"No calls for me," I say with a smile. The last thing I want is to listen to my dad whine about how I deserted him with two engine rebuilds and three front axle replacements. "It's nice to have a couple of days off."

"Especially when those days involve a major movie legend, right?"

"Totally." I love that he gets it too.

"Shayla? Frankie?" Midge is standing at the kitchen island, mixing up some sort of green punch drink. "Would you like to see your rooms?"

"Hold on," Shayla says, looking around. "Is everybody here? Are we all the winners?"

"Everybody's arrived," Midge says, dropping a handful of fake black spiders into the punch. "But not everybody's in this room. Taylor, Ivy's roommate, went for a walk and should be returning shortly. And, Shayla, *your* roommate is already upstairs."

"And I haven't even met her yet?" Shayla springs up from the couch—this is obviously a national emergency. If she were only half as cute, her eternally perky demeanor might be annoying.

We follow Midge upstairs, but the door to Shayla's room is locked. "Natalie?" Midge raps lightly on the door.

Meanwhile, Shayla continues to chatter on, saying how pumped she is to meet her roommate, like this is the most exciting thing on earth. And I suppose it is. I mean, I'm pretty stoked too. And it's sort of cool to be with people who share that same vibe, rather than at the garage where everything is always a downer, where doom and gloom are as encouraged as cash payments.

"Do you need some help?" I ask, watching as Midge struggles with the key.

"The lock already turned," Midge says, "so I'm pretty sure the key works."

"In other words, the door is stuck?" Shayla asks.

"Natalie?" Midge calls again. "Can you open up? Your roommate is here and she'd really like to meet you."

"Maybe she's sleeping," Shayla says.

Midge frowns, like someone just stole from her collection of severed fingers.

"Let me try," I say.

Midge steps to the side, and I grab the knob, forcing my weight against the door. It doesn't budge. "There must be something propped up beneath the knob, on the inside." I take a step back to gain momentum and then lunge at the door. At the same moment, the door opens and I go flying inside, barely catching myself from falling on my ass.

A girl stands there. Black hair, dark clothing. Way too Goth for my taste, but you can tell that she'd be totally hot with her full lips and slanted blue eyes—that is if she'd stop shopping at Freaks "R" Us.

"Sorry," Natalie says. She tries to smile, even though it

looks like she's been crying. Her skin is blotchy and her eyes are red.

This is way too much drama for me, so I ask Midge to point me in the direction of my room. She nods to an open door, across the hall—room number nine.

There are two beds inside. I'm assuming mine's the one without all the crap—the heap of clothes and art supplies, not to mention the bloody skeleton poster hanging above the headboard. I recognize the skeleton. It's from the album cover of a heavy metal band from the '80s. The lead guitarist plays a Gibson Explorer.

I move to my half of the room, noticing six guitars set up on the far wall. There's a signature Eric Clapton Fender Stratocaster, signed by the man himself. There's also a Telecaster signed by Jim Root from Slipknot. "Holy shit," I say, under my breath. These must be worth a fortune.

Still keeping my eye on the Clapton, I venture to touch a '70s Black Beauty Les Paul Custom—the same model that Peter Frampton made famous with his album *Frampton Comes Alive*. The thing is an absolute stunner with its sleek black body and mother-of-pearl block inlays.

I reach for a Gretsch, beyond stoked to see that it's signed by Jack White from the White Stripes. Seriously, do I need to pinch myself?

"What color is your blood?"

I turn to find Garth there. This is his room too. "Man, you scared the crap out of me."

"What color is your blood?" he repeats.

"I'm pretty sure it's red, the last time I checked. Hey, are these your guitars, or do you know where they came from?"

"*Do* you check?" he persists. There's a screwed-up smile on his face, like he just ate his family for lunch. "Do you cut your skin open and watch the blood leak out?"

"Not lately."

"You do know that blood is actually blue, right? When it's inside the body, running through the veins. It isn't until you cut yourself open and the blood hits the air that it turns that red color."

"Except I'm pretty sure that's a myth," I say, thanks to Ms. Matthews, my science teacher back in middle school. This whole conversation feels pretty middle school, but I play along, trying to keep the peace. "The blue color you see in your veins, under the skin, is really just a darker red," I tell him.

"What do you say we put that theory to the test?" He wields his mighty pinky ring; there's an arrow point at the very end—one that could probably do some damage.

Out of the corner of my eye, I spot what appears to be an animal skeleton of some sort on the drafting table by the window.

"Like it?" he asks, following my gaze. His eerie smile grows wider.

I look away, unwilling to let his bullshit get the best of me, and resume checking out the guitars.

"It belongs to a squirrel that pissed me off," he continues. "Now, it's a source of artistic inspiration. My good luck charm. Would you believe that I got stopped in the airport for carrying it? Security questioned me for over an hour. They went through all my bags and asked me if I've ever had thoughts of hurting others. I missed my connecting flight because of them. I was supposed to have traveled with Natalie and Taylor . . . both of whom I've yet to meet, by the way."

"And I should give a shit about any of this, because . . ." I turn to look at him again. He may be super tall, but I can tell that I'm at least twice his size—that beneath all those layers of gray, there's the body of a scrawny seven-year-old kid.

A second later, there's a knock at the open door, interrupting us.

Parker's there. "Hey, you guys want to come check something out?"

"Absolutely," I say, returning the Gretsch to the rack, more than eager to ditch this freak.

SHAYLA

THE BOYS HERE ARE SUPER CUTE, AND I'M SUPER excited to get to know them more—to get to know *everybody* more—but my roommate is a buzzkill.

"I want to go home," Natalie says, sulking at the edge of her bed, her cell phone clenched in her hand.

"Nonsense," Midge tells her. "You're just tired and probably hungry, but that's nothing that some rest and a warm meal wouldn't cure."

"Try clicking your heels together three times," I joke.

But Natalie's not really the joking type. She stares down

at her clunky black boots (for the record, Dr. Martens originals). I feel kind of sorry for her—and not because of her lack of style, though that's pity rendering too. Having spent the last nine years at four different boarding schools, I've had my fair share of abrupt transitions and seen some nasty cases of homesickness. My best friend Dara's included.

"Maybe you could just give us a moment," I tell Midge.

"Sure," she says, but she seems unsure, as if Natalie is a delicate flower that I could trample with one wrong step. Thankfully, Midge leaves us alone anyway.

I sit down beside Natalie on the bed, noticing that her hair looks even gnarlier than mine does, *pre*-relaxer. It's like something straight out of a Tim Burton movie—big and dark and creepy and fake. I try to imagine how she might look if she'd fix her hair and shed the bag-lady clothing. I'd bet she'd be really striking. She has a model's facial bone structure: high cheekbones, a nose that turns slightly upward, and a perfectly pointed chin. Plus, her lips look naturally full and her skin appears virtually flaw- and pore-less.

"So, Miss Natalie, where are you from? And what do you like?"

"I actually prefer to be called Nat."

"As in the bloodsucking insect? News flash, bloodsucking is so five years ago," I say, still trying to keep things light.

"You don't have to babysit me, you know."

"I think roommate-sit would be the more accurate term, don't you?" I smile. "Now, tell me, what's with the dark cloud hovering over your sunny time here?"

She gets up and fishes inside her suitcase, pulling out a package of Twizzlers. "I just really miss Harris."

"Your boyfriend?"

"My brother. We're twins."

I can feel the bewilderment on my face, unable to imagine missing my booger-picking brother after five months, never mind five hours. "Well, you could call him, you know . . . on the landline."

"He doesn't want to talk to me."

"Why not?"

She opens the licorice package, twists a stick around her index finger, and gnaws on it like a baby with a teething ring. "I didn't tell him I was coming here. I didn't tell anyone, for that matter."

"So, your parents don't know where you are?"

"They probably have some idea. I mean, they know I won the contest. They just didn't want me to come. Harris didn't either." She swallows a mouthful of licorice before loading her fingers with a couple more sticks.

"*I* could call them," I offer, suddenly remembering that I

promised my mom that I'd call her, too. I flop back onto the bed and kick up my legs, admiring my checkerboard pedicure. "Not to brag or anything, but I *do* have a way with parents. It's one of my hidden talents."

"I don't think so."

"Are you sure?" I ask, making the checkerboards dance.

A second later, there's a knock on the open door.

It's Parker . . . looking even more amazing than he did ten minutes ago. If I didn't know better, I'd say he just stepped off the runway. I mean, holy hunk of hotness with his broad shoulders, tousled blond hair, chiseled features, and sea glass–worthy blue eyes.

"Come on," he says. "We're all next door, in Ivy and Taylor's room. There's something you'll want to see." There's a delicious grin on his face. He's just so incredibly yummy.

"Totally," I say, jumping up from the bed. But then I look back at Natalie.

She's turned away now, silently asserting a big fat no.

It's all I can do not to scream. "Just give us a few minutes, okay?" I tell Parker, faking a smile, and closing the door behind him.

"You should go," Natalie says, between bites of licorice.

"Why don't you come too? I mean, we're here to get to know everyone, *right?*" I spend the next eleven minutes telling her about my arrival at Winston Academy, the only black girl in a sea of fair-skinned blondes with names like Josie, Bunny, Kiki, and Coco. "But I had to eventually mix in and give people a chance. I couldn't just sit around sulking in my room all day."

Still, bag of candy in hand, Natalie moves to lie down on her bed, drawing the covers over her face.

I suppose I can take a hint. I leave her alone and hop next door. But, to my surprise, no one's in there now. I go inside, curious to know what Parker was talking about—what I so desperately needed to see.

Half of the room is decorated with cookbooks and food videos, not to mention a creepy cutout of Julia Child holding a slimy chicken carcass. *Classy.* The other half is baby-doll pink and suited to a dancer. I wonder which side is Ivy's.

I continue to look around, checking to see if anything appears off, finally spotting a rack of ballet slippers. They're all so pretty and delicate—like tiny works of art. Even though I'm not a dancer now, I used to take ballet when I was a kid— back when it was okay for little-girl ballerinas to be something other than white and emaciated. But sometime around the age of eleven, when I started to sprout boobs and booty, and when I decided to trade my frizz-ball hair bun for neat little cornrows, my ballet teacher suggested that my "look" and body type might be better suited to hip-hop, which totally squelched my dreams of being in *Swan Lake* one day. I haven't danced since, which Dara always thought was crazy. "You're an incredible dancer," she used to say. "Don't let someone else's opinion dictate your life."

If only Dara had taken her own advice.

I peer over my shoulder to make sure that no one's looking, and then I go to try on a shimmering white slipper, but I can barely squish my toes in, confirming what my ballet teacher was talking about: some of us simply don't fit.

I move over to the closet, noticing a stash of glittery costumes, hoping that there's one for Princess Odette, my favorite character from *Swan Lake*. I search the racks, eager to find one before someone comes in and sees me here.

There are costumes from *The Nutcracker*, *A Midsummer Night's Dream*, *Peter Pan*, and *Sleeping Beauty*, but I don't see any for *Swan Lake*. I take some *Nutcracker* wings, imagining myself as the Sugar Plum Fairy.

Then I spot something else. At the back of the closet. A streak of red on the wall.

I part the costumes to get a better look. Dark letters on the back of the closet spell out GET OUT BEFORE IT'S TOO LATE.

GARTH

"OKAY, WHO HAS THE SICK SENSE OF HUMOR?" someone shouts.

"Sounds like somebody's looking for me," I holler back, proceding down the hallway, wielding my mighty ax.

It was Shayla's voice. She's in Ivy and Taylor's room. There's a sexy little smirk on her face. "Did *you* do this?" She points inside a closet.

Before I can ask or see what she's talking about, the others come back upstairs. I swing the ax, picturing myself as Sidney Scarcella in *Hotel 9: Blocked Rooms* in the lobby scene, when poor Mrs. Teetlebaum ventures from her room in the middle of the night. But they're all so busy blathering on that they don't even notice.

"Ohmygosh," Shayla bursts out as soon as she sees Parker. "So, I was just checking out the costumes, and . . . wait, where did you get that?" She's looking at me now, referring to my ax. A curious smile sits on her lips. I can tell she wants to play too.

"In the bathroom. The blade was stuck in the wall—just a sweet little reminder of why we're all here."

"Is it real?" Ivy asks.

"Unfortunately, no." I sigh, scratching my head with the plastic blade. "But it's the thought that counts, right?"

I move into the room and take a peek inside the closet. The costumes are pushed to the side, exposing the back wall. "Get out before it's too late," I say, reading the flaming-red words. I let out a big fat yawn. "I mean, seriously, this is *it*?"

"Did *you* do it?" Parker asks me.

"If only I could take the credit." I step closer to examine the writing. Some of the letters have fingerprints in the individual strokes. But, I know my stuff. "It wasn't written in blood," I say, "in case that was a concern."

"This from the guy who thinks that blood is as blue as his balls," Frankie says.

"I don't really believe that blood is blue. I just wanted to see if I could convince *you* that it was." I smile, making sure to expose my pointy incisors, hoping to psych him out. "If this were *real* blood there would be droplets all over the floor. Plus, if it's been at least an hour since this was written—and I'm assuming it has—the blood would've had time to oxidize."

"Meaning?" Parker asks.

"Meaning, it would've browned by now. It's got to be paint or marker, or something else—a nifty corn syrup concoction, maybe." I lean in to give the writing a sniff, noticing a slightly glossy sheen. "It's still wet."

"So, I guess that rules out the theory that it was done by a former guest," Shayla says.

It's lip gloss. I'm sure of it. I can tell from the beeswax scent. I reach out to touch the stain. "On second thought, maybe it *is* blood," I lie, pretending to lick the smear from my finger.

Ivy lets out a shriek. She's way too easy to disturb. My dad would be all over her paranoid ass, injecting fake blood into her toothpaste tube, and other "fun" stuff like that.

"Oh my God! Remember that scene in *Hotel 9: Enjoy Your Stay*?" Shayla asks. "When Emma Corwin commits suicide out of self defense?"

"So that the killer won't get her." Frankie nods.

"After Emma slits her wrist, she dips her fingers into her

own blood and starts to write the word *help* on the window glass," I continue.

"Only she doesn't get past the letter *L*," Shayla says, finishing my thought. Her amber eyes grow wide. There's a certain smart-girl sexiness about her. Maybe it's the square black glasses. Or maybe it's the curvy situation she's got going on beneath that ridiculous housewife tracksuit.

"What if Taylor left us that message?" Ivy asks, still freaking out.

"You seriously need to be medicated," I say. "I mean, think about it: a bunch of Justin Blake horror junkies travel from all over the country to partake in a scary weekend. This sort of stuff is to be expected."

"Okay, but if it was only done in fun, then why hide it in a closet?" Ivy nags. "Why not put it out in the open? This message was done in secret. Maybe Taylor was hiding when she did it."

"Or maybe Taylor doesn't even exist," Frankie says. "What if this whole scenario was created just for our entertainment?"

"There's a movie like that," I say. "Name that film: a group of seemingly random kids gets invited to spend the night in a mansion that's rumored to be haunted, only, in the end, there's nothing random about how the kids were chosen. They were all handpicked according to their personality profiles—sort of like the personality profile that we all had to submit for this contest—and the entire evening of horrors was orchestrated by the hosts."

Despite the accurate description, their faces remain blank.

"It came out in 1997," I continue, giving them a hint. "It bombed at the box office during its debut weekend, but then hit a grand slam in video. Jeffrey Salter was the executive producer, two no-name actors played the leads, and the director was . . ." I hum out the theme song to *Jeopardy*, waiting for someone to reply.

"Errrh," I say, sounding the buzzer.

"Are you talking about *House of Red*?" Parker asks. "Because that actually came out in ninety-six, not ninety-seven. And it was directed by Henri Maltide and *co*-produced by Salter. Maltide was also listed as a producer."

"Okay, but Salter did all the work," I say, correcting him. "Including writing the screenplay, so let's give credit where credit is due, shall we? Oh, and PS, Taylor *is* real, or at least according to Midge she is. She was supposed to be on my connecting flight, along with Natalie, but I got bumped thanks to my pet, Squirrely."

"I'm not even going to ask," Parker says, grabbing his cell phone. He takes a few pictures of the writing.

"*Peek-a-boo,*" Midge sings, poking her head inside the room. "Was someone looking for me a few minutes ago? I was down in the basement and thought I heard someone call out my name."

Parker points to the bogus message. "We wanted to show you something."

A twinge of surprise forms on Midge's face, but then her expression morphs into a sheepish grin. "Beats me," she says, reaching into the pocket of her apron. She pulls out a handful of bloody fingers. They look eerily realistic, complete with dirty fingernails and hairy knuckles. She holds them out for show and then pops them into her mouth.

This woman is my new idol.

Ivy lets out a gasp, covering her mouth.

"Oh, I'm sorry," Midge says. "How rude of me. Would anyone like a juicy thumb?"

"I would," I tell her.

Midge fishes a hairless thumb from her pocket and hands it to me. I pop it into my mouth. It's bubble gum.

"Are you all hungry?" Midge asks. "Dinner's almost ready."

"Shouldn't we wait for Taylor to get back from her walk?" Ivy asks.

"Taylor phoned just a little while ago, while I was on another call," Midge explains. "She stopped at a diner on Highway 9."

"Is Highway 9 far from here?" Ivy asks.

"*Everything* is far from here." Frankie laughs.

"We already have a car out looking for her," Midge says. "So don't worry. Just come down to the dining room in fifteen minutes. I'll have everything ready."

"Sounds great." I blow out a bubble and pop it with my ax, more than eager to get this party started.

Once Midge and the others file out of the room, only Ivy and I remain. Ivy paces back and forth, completely lost in her own little world, not even noticing the fact that I'm lounging on her bed right now. Part of me almost feels sorry for her—I used to get scared like that too.

I take a deep breath, thinking back to the day my dad pulled me aside and taught me all about Leatherface. "Do you want me to teach you what I know?"

She looks at me, alarm on her face, as if surprised to find me still here.

"About the blood," I explain.

Still no answer.

"Blink once for yes, twice for no," I continue.

She blinks once—on purpose or by accident, I'm not quite sure—and so I get up and stand in front of the closet. "See the glossy sheen?" I say, pointing to the individual letters.

Ivy finally shows a pulse and comes over to join me.

"Now, get real close," I tell her. "Do you smell the beeswax? I think there might also be a hint of petroleum jelly."

"Are you a bloodhound?"

"It's my superpower," I say, only half kidding. I may not be able to detect blood type for real, but ever since I was little, I've had a keen sense of smell—sometimes *so* keen that it became somewhat of a handicap, forever distracting my attention. I failed freshman Bio because Mr. Bing reeked of mothballs. "Do you smell the artificial ingredients?" I ask her.

She shakes her head.

I lean in to sniff the letters again, and that's when I notice it.

"What?" Ivy asks, able to spot the confusion on my face.

I look around the closet, searching for the source, spotting a palm-size smear of blood in the corner, by the floor. I kneel down to check it out. It's had time to oxidize, but I can tell it's still fresh.

"What?" Ivy repeats.

"Just more of the lip gloss," I lie, sparing her the truth. It's probably just a fluke thing anyway.

IVY

THE DINING ROOM OF THE DARK HOUSE IS STRAIGHT from a magazine: plum-purple walls, velvet drapes, gold-framed paintings, and a mosaic-tiled floor. Parker's filming the space, doing a close-up of a portrait of a half woman/half feline dressed in a fur coat.

I sit with the others around a marble table lined with thick red candles. Parker takes a seat beside me and bumps his shoulder against mine.

"Everything cool?" he asks, probably noticing that I've been mute for the past several minutes.

Little does he know that there's a ball of tension wedged beneath my ribs, making it hard to breathe. "It's fine," I say, forcing a smile, wanting to prove to myself that I can do this. Getting scared is part of the process, I repeat inside my head, hoping the repetition will make it okay.

A crystal chandelier hangs down from a vaulted ceiling, illuminating our meal, which is kept hidden beneath silver dome covers. Midge lifts the covers, unveiling some of America's most popular comfort foods: mashed potatoes, mac and cheese, green bean casserole, fried chicken, and barbecue spareribs.

"Holy yum-ness," Shayla says. "This is totally the meal from *Nightmare Elf III: Lights Out.* Remember when that couple ran out of gas en route home from their road trip? They went to the Dark House for help, and the family that was staying there at the time—"

"The Kramer family," Garth says to clarify.

"—served this very same meal." Shayla spoons a mound of mashed potatoes onto her plate and then tops it off with a drizzle of gravy.

"Can I pass you something?" Parker asks me.

"I'm good," I say, taking a glob of mac and cheese, even though the thought of ingesting anything right now makes me feel sick.

"So, when do we get to meet Justin Blake?" Frankie asks, as Midge fills our water glasses.

"Tomorrow," she says. "Didn't you find the itinerary in your room?"

"I think I might've been too distracted by the Clapton Fender Stratocaster."

"Nothing but the best for our Dark House Dreamers." She sets a dinner bell in the center of the table. "If anyone needs anything, just give this here a jingle, okay?"

We thank her and she leaves the room, dimming the overhead lights as she goes.

"I have an idea." Shayla perks up in her seat. "How about after dinner we play an icebreaker game. Something to help us get to know one another."

I look over at Natalie, feeling bad that we haven't officially met. "I'm Ivy," I say, somewhat encouraged by her presence— that there might actually be someone here who's more freaked out than me.

The others introduce themselves as well. Natalie flashes a polite smile and then resumes eating her food in silence.

"How about we play spin the bottle?" Garth says, between bites of barbecue spareribs. He flashes us a grotesque smile, his teeth and lips thoroughly saturated with dark red goo.

Shayla laughs in response, making me wonder if there isn't

anything she doesn't find hilarious. "How about a Justin Blake trivia game?"

"Except I'd beat all of you in the first round," Garth says.

"Don't be so sure about that one. What year did Blake graduate from college?" Parker asks.

"He didn't graduate," Frankie says. "He never made it through sophomore year."

"No, but he did graduate from Wentley Vocational-Technical School," Garth says. "His father wanted him to become an electrician."

"That actually isn't right," Natalie says, peeking up from her chicken leg. "His father wanted him to become a doctor, but they ended up compromising on electrical work, and that was only because Blake's uncle was a master electrician, so Blake was pretty much guaranteed a job."

Garth pauses from licking his goo-covered fingers. His mouth hangs open, exposing a hunk of chewed up pork. "Holy crap. She speaks."

"She just doesn't speak *to you*," Frankie jokes.

I angle myself in Natalie's direction. "Were you and Taylor on the same flight here? Did you ride in the same car?"

"Yes," she says, poking a hole in the nonexistence theory. "Why?"

"Because Taylor is missing," I tell her.

"Not missing, just not *here*." Garth rolls his eyes.

"I know what we should play," Shayla says, snagging the conversation back. "How about a game of two truths and a lie?"

"I vote that we don't play any games," Frankie says. "Let's just talk like normal people."

"If only we *were* normal people," Garth says, baring his sauce-smothered teeth once again.

"What did everyone write about for the contest?" Parker asks.

The table goes quiet for several seconds until Frankie ventures to speak. "I wrote about the nightmares I had after my uncle died—about digging his body up and getting trapped underground, right along with him."

"There's a movie like that," Garth says. "About a guy who gets buried alive."

"There are at least *ten* movies like that," Parker says, correcting him. "The idea is actually sort of cliché."

"Were you and your uncle super close?" Shayla asks, turning to Frankie.

"Close enough, I guess," he says. "But it was seeing the burial that *really* messed me up . . . seeing his body lowered into the ground and planted inside the earth, like it could one day grow back to life. What made it worse was that my mom had left a few months before."

"*Left?*" Shayla asks.

"Yep." He nods, drawing a train track across his mound of mashed potatoes. "She packed her bags and never looked back. This was her bracelet, by the way." He flashes us a gold link chain around his wrist. "It was passed down to her by her father—my grandfather. And, one day, she took it off, fastened it around my wrist, and told me that I could keep it and that we'd always be together."

"The symbol for infinity," I say, spotting the elongated figure eight.

"Which is actually pretty ironic, considering that she took off that following week. Anyway, my dad hates that I wear it—says it's a complete slap in his face—which is why I got this." He lifts the sleeve of his T-shirt. *Rice & Sons* is tattooed on his bicep. "It's the name of my dad's auto repair shop. My brothers have the same one—proof of our loyalty. Needless to say, allegiance is pretty big in my family."

"*I* have tattoos," Natalie says.

"*Plural?*" Garth asks, his eyebrow raised. He gives her body a once over, but only her face and fingers are bare. "How many, where, and of what?"

"Seven. All over. And all for Justin Blake," she says. "I guess I have my allegiances too."

"To a man you've never met?" I ask, genuinely curious about her motivation.

"Is that somehow less acceptable than getting permanently inked to show a supposed loyalty to something that you don't even care about?" Frankie asks, obviously referring to his father's business. "Something that you kind of even resent?"

"You don't *really* have tattoos, do you?" Garth says, zeroed in on Natalie.

"Why would I lie?" she asks.

"I guess there's only one way to prove it." The menacing grin on Garth's face reminds me of the Grinch's after having just stolen Christmas.

"She doesn't need to prove anything to you," Frankie tells him.

Natalie looks at Frankie and a tiny smile crosses her lips. A second later, the lights flicker and go out, tightening the knot in my gut.

"It's just a scare tactic," Parker says. He nods toward the hallway, where the lights are still on. "I'm sure this weekend is going to be full of them."

As if on cue, his words are followed by the roar of

thunder—a hard, heavy rumble that reverberates in my bones. Even Shayla jumps at the sound.

I focus on one of the candles, trying to exhale my mounting anxiety, but my breath gets caught in my chest, and I let out a wheeze.

"Are you okay?" Parker asks, placing his hand on my shoulder.

My heart beats fast. My hands start to sweat. I can't seem to get enough air. "I need to go lie down for a bit," I try to say, but the words come out choppy.

"*Seriously?*" Garth asks. "You're one of the chosen, here for the party. Stay for the rolling credits, why don't you?"

I really wish I could, but right now I need to get away.

PARKER

I wait all of five minutes before going upstairs to check on Ivy. "Hello," I call, rapping lightly on the door.

She opens it. Her hair's pulled back. There's a thin veil of sweat over her forehead and neck. Somehow it makes her skin glisten. The bottle pendant that hangs around her neck dangles toward her cleavage.

I nod at the travel mug she's holding. "You got something strong in there?"

"It's chamomile." She smiles. "Want some?" She points to a tin full of tea packets.

"I've got all sorts of flavors and colors: red, green, black, gray, kombucha, oolong, dandelion . . ."

"Thanks," I say, stepping inside her room. "But I'm not much of a tea drinker."

"Really?" She gives me a surprised look, as if not drinking tea is as peculiar as bringing a stash of it along on vacation. She sits down on Taylor's bed and the vee of her dress opens ever so slightly, exposing three solid inches of plump ivory skin. "I'm sorry I freaked out down there."

"Don't apologize. I get it. Being here is making you a wee bit anxious."

"More like a huge bit."

"I mean, I know the message in the closet upset you, and that Taylor's absence really bothers you."

She angles toward the closet and her dress opens up even more. "The message is probably like Garth said—a scare tactic." She looks back at me, straight into my face. "Are you okay? Because if you want to talk about something else, I totally get it."

"Right," I say, but I have no idea what I'm agreeing to, and the confused look in Ivy's eyes tells me that she doesn't know either.

I mentally splash some water onto my face, noticing that she smells intoxicating—like lavender and chamomile. I take a deep breath, trying to picture this whole scene like a movie—*anything* to help keep myself focused.

INT. BEDROOM—NIGHT

One half of the room is decorated for a dancer, with ballet slippers and costumes; the other half is full of cookbooks. There are two full beds.

IVY, 18-ish and unbelievably cute, sits on one of the beds, wearing a dress that's driving me crazy.

I move to sit beside her.

                    IVY
          Taylor already started unpacking
          her stuff.

She motions to Taylor's leopard-print suitcase at the foot of the bed. It's unzipped. And the top drawer to Taylor's dresser is only half-closed.

                    ME
And?

                    IVY
And why would she start unpacking
if she were just going to bolt? I
mean, I suppose I get it. Maybe she
needed some fresh air and wanted to
regroup, which is totally understandable. I mean, I keep having to
remind myself what *I'm* still doing here,
and why I even came to begin with.

                    ME
Why *did* you come?

                    IVY
Why did *you*?

                    ME
For the networking possibilities.
I want to be a filmmaker one day.

                    IVY
Which explains the video camera.

                    ME
              (nodding)
I only end up using about five
percent of the footage. But still,
getting in the habit of filming
stuff—trying to get those perfect
angles—and then editing clips
together to tell a story . . .
all of that helps make me a better
filmmaker.

                    IVY
Sounds like you really love it.

                    ME
I do. And getting to meet Justin
Blake is a major step in the right
direction. Now, your turn.

                    IVY
I don't know.
              (a shrug)
I guess I entered this contest because
I really love horror.

                    ME

Right.

            (a smirk)
I should've known that from your
expression during *The Old Dark House*
movie. I think it looked something
like this.

I flash her my most frightful face, my eyes
wide and my mouth arched open in terror.

                    IVY

That obvious, huh?

                    ME ·

Do you want to be an actress?

                    IVY

Apparently I'm not a very good one if
you're onto me already. Can you keep a
secret? I hate horror. Like, I *really*
hate it. I don't get what the appeal
is . . . why someone would ever want
to be scared.

                    ME

Okay, so it makes *perfect* sense why
you'd want to enter this contest.

                    IVY

Really?

                    ME

Not really. (a grin) How did you even
find out about the contest?

                    IVY

The Nightmare Elf kept e-mailing me.
For whatever reason, despite many
attempts to unsubscribe, I'm on his
e-newsletter list, which means I'm
constantly getting updates about his
numerous contests.

                    ME

Does the Nightmare Elf even *have* an
e-newsletter?

Ivy lets out an exhausted sigh and then flops back onto the
bed, making it impossible for me to stay focused. I put my

mental video camera away, zeroing in on the silhouette of her body beneath the thin cotton sundress—her curvy hips, her narrow waist, and the soft mounds of her chest. It's almost too much to handle, and I don't quite know where to look.

"Ivy?" I ask, after several awkward seconds.

Her eyes are wide. She stares toward the open window. Her chest moves up and down with each breath, accentuating the sweet layer of perspiration on her skin. "What?" she asks, rolling onto her side to face me.

But I've suddenly forgotten the question.

She props herself up on her elbow, brushing up against something beneath the coverlet, by the pillow.

"What is it?" I move closer to get a better look.

Ivy pulls a cell phone from beneath the bedsheet. Like Taylor's luggage, the case is leopard print too.

"I assume that belongs to Taylor?" I ask.

Ivy's mouth falls open. "Why would she go for a walk and not take her cell phone with her?"

"Maybe she forgot it. I forget my cell all the time."

"Yes, but Midge said that Taylor called her."

"She probably used a pay phone."

"I think we should tell the others," she says.

"And *I* think you need to relax. Do you want some more tea?"

Instead of answering, she pockets the cell phone and goes for the door, leaving me even more curious about her.

NATALIE

IT'S JUST AFTER DINNER, AND WHILE SHAYLA,
Garth, and Frankie snoop around in the living room, I hang
back in the doorway, staring at the phone on the desk.

"Come on," Shayla calls out to Garth, pointing inside a
media cabinet.

Meanwhile Frankie checks out a photo album. "Anyone
want to see a picture of Blake at prom?"

They continue to look around. And then Shayla moves into
the adjoining kitchen, where she lets out a screech.

Frankie drops the album to go see what happened. I move
closer too, leaning over the kitchen island.

Shayla whimpers, like she's injured. There's something dark and hairy in her arms. Its body coils against her skin.

"I'm bleeding," she whines.

"Help her!" I cry out.

Frankie tries to assess the situation, but Shayla's crouched on the floor now, her body angled away from him. Garth steps closer and pushes Frankie out of the way. He grabs Shayla, pulls her up, spins her around, and finally we're able to see.

A rat.

A huge, hairy rat.

Its teeth are crusted red. Its mouth opens and closes. "Eek!" it screeches. Or rather, Shayla screeches.

I realize then it's a puppet—the most realistic rat puppet I've ever seen. Shayla's hand is poked into the belly, making the mouth gape open.

"Are you kidding?" Garth laughs. "Where did you find that?"

"In the sink, next to the bloody rubber arm sticking out from the disposal. And, yes, obviously I *am* kidding—kidding you, that is." Her eyes are teary with laughter.

"Payback," Frankie declares. "That's what this calls for, so you'd better watch your back."

"I guess three summers at performing arts camp paid off," she says.

Frankie grabs the rat and chases Shayla with it, making like it's going to bite her. Garth joins in too. He plucks the bloody arm from the sink, following right after them—out of the kitchen and into another room.

Leaving me alone.

I look back at the phone, and then take a seat at the desk. I start to dial, feeling the urge to pull just a few hairs at the nape of my neck. But I push the last digit before I do.

The number connects. I listen to the phone ring, picturing the receiver on the night table in my parents' room, sitting beneath my younger sister Margie's oil painting of Mom. The painting was a surprise portrait, done from Mom's high school graduation photo, and presented to my mother at the town art show, at which Margie won honorable mention and Mom dissolved into a puddle of jubilant tears.

The phone continues to ring. My head is about to explode. I can hear the rush of blood in my ears, making my temples throb.

Finally someone picks up. I hear a click. But no one says a word.

"Hello?" I say, gripping the phone tight. "Mom? Is that you? It's me. Natalie."

I can tell that someone's there. I hear a sniff and then a sigh.

"Mom?" I ask again, figuring that it's her, ever obedient,

forever subservient. My name should really be Apple, and hers should be Tree.

"I'm in Minnesota," I say into the receiver. "I took that trip . . . the contest one that I was telling you about . . . the one where I get to meet Justin Blake. Anyway, I know that you're probably upset, but . . ." My voice trails off. I can't finish the thought. Tears streak down my face.

"Just know that this trip—my going, I mean," I continue, "has nothing to do with you and everything to do with me. I didn't feel like I could give up this opportunity. Justin Blake has been a major part of my life, and I want to tell him—need to tell him, *personally*—how much his work has meant to me."

The truth: it's been my saving grace.

The first time my father told me that I was an accident, I wrote Harris's name all over my body with a ball-point pen— 311 times—convinced that his name would shield me from my father's words.

I went out into the street like that, wearing shorts and a tank. The neighborhood kids didn't know how to respond to me. Mrs. Watson asked if I was feeling all right.

"She's feeling just fine," my dad said, running out to get me. "Just kid stuff." He rolled his eyes, as if she could identify with him. And then he yanked me inside, dragged me into the bathtub, started the water, and threw a bar of soap at my head.

"You're not worthy of having Harris's name on you," he said.

I was ten years old; it was the year I discovered the *Nightmare Elf* and *Hotel 9* series.

A couple of years later, when I overheard my parents telling Margie how much they wished I was more like her, I found *Halls of Horror* and its prequel *Forest of Fright*.

Last summer, when the Riskins invited us to their daughter's lavish graduation party, I overheard my mother telling Mrs. Riskin that we'd all love to go. "But Natalie won't be able to make it," she added. "She'll be at sleepaway camp that weekend."

I didn't have sleepaway camp, but thank God I had the *Night Terrors* trilogy.

"Please, say something," I plead. "Tell me that you don't hate me."

I wait for several seconds, but still no one speaks, which makes a bubble form in my throat. It bursts out through my mouth, and I let out a thirsting cry.

"Natalie?" Ivy asks.

She's standing in the doorway. I wonder how long she's been there and how much she already heard.

"What happened?" she asks.

I close my eyes, picturing myself like a piece of paper inside a fire, getting lapped up by the flames, melted away in the heat. But then I realize: the phone's still pressed against my ear. The line's still connected. I never hung up.

Ivy comes and sits beside me. She takes the receiver and places it up to her ear. "Hello?" she asks. "Is someone there?"

Her face furrows, like she doesn't quite understand.

"*What?*" I ask, desperate to know if it's really my mom.

"They hung up," she whispers. "I heard the phone go click. That doesn't make any sense."

It actually makes perfect sense to me. What I've done— coming here against my parents' wishes—is unforgiveable to them. As angry as they've ever been at me, they've never completely shut me out. "I wish I could talk to Harris."

"And Harris is . . ."

"Huh?" I say, suddenly realizing that I said the thought aloud. I'm aching to pull out a couple of hairs by my temple, where there's an inch and a half of fresh growth. I've been resisting the spot for months. "Harris is my brother."

A bell rings somewhere. If only this were ancient times and the ringing signified my death.

"That must be Midge," Ivy says.

I venture to touch the area by my temple; it's on the opposite side from where Ivy's sitting.

"I think we're supposed to be meeting in the theater," she says.

I poke my fingers beneath the wig, able to get a solid grip on a few strands in the time that it takes her to blink. I give them a light tug—not too strong, just enough to feel a tiny jolt. "Go ahead," I say, nodding toward the door. "The others will be waiting."

"What are you thinking?" she asks, placing a hand on my back.

I stop. My heart hammers. I release the grip on my hair, unsure if I've been caught.

"You think I'm just going to leave you here?" She grins. "No way. I'm not going anywhere without you." Her words make me tear up again. I'm not used to showing emotion in front of anyone, and the fact that I am—and that she genuinely seems to give a shit—only makes the tears flow more.

FRANKIE

SHAYLA IS SUCH A TEASE, BUT SHE'S ALSO REALLY cute, so it's hard to get her out of my head. I chase her into a theater room with Garth close at our heels.

The room is huge. A large screen hangs down, covering one wall, and there are four rows of movie seats, complete with cup holders and chairs that tilt back. I sit down in one of the seats. Shayla sits down too. But she picks the front row, away from me. And Garth parks his ass down beside her.

I can't tell if he's into her too. Or who she might be digging. She seems to be in love with just about everyone and everything, which in one way is totally annoying. But in another way it's kind of cool. I mean, it beats being around a bunch of oil-skinned cynics who think they got a raw deal in life.

Midge comes into the room. "Everyone take a seat. I've got a special surprise." She jingles her bell, commanding our attention.

But then Ivy busts in, snagging it away. "I found Taylor's cell phone," she says, holding it up.

Natalie and Parker file in behind her.

"Wait, she doesn't have her phone with her?" Shayla asks.

"Taylor used a pay phone to call me," Midge says. "Now . . . can we get back to business?"

Surprisingly—because she seems completely neurotic—Ivy backs right down. While she, Parker, and Natalie take seats in the back row, I move to the seat beside Shayla, hoping she's glad that I did (and hoping even more that Garth can take the hint). Shayla smiles at me, and I don't know what it is—how cute she is or her constant cheery disposition—but I can't help smiling back, even though I know I should be playing it cool.

"So, let's get started," Midge says, a syrupy-sweet smile on her round, puffy face. "You may have noticed some sticky-wicky things happening here at the Dark House. I don't want to give too much away—that'd be like finding out what's wrapped beneath the Christmas tree before it's time to open the gifts. But, mark my words, there's more to come."

"Meaning that we can sit back, relax, and enjoy the show, so to speak?" Parker asks.

"Enjoy it all!" She extends her arms outward like she's one of the models on a game show, presenting a brand new car. "Welcome to the Dark House, where you've come to stay, and we hope you'll play!" She bares her teeth like a rabid dog. Her eyes look freakishly wild, like they might even be dilated—like she's about to hack off all our fingers.

Midge points at the movie screen behind her, the lights go out, and music begins to play. It sounds like an old-fashioned merry-go-round—that sort of orchestral tune that's supposed to sound happy, only it's creepy and warped, and the beat's forever changing, one second too fast, the next second way too slow.

The movie screen lights up. The merry-go-round music stops, and the room goes morgue silent. Shayla grabs my arm in anticipation.

"What's happening?" I hear Ivy whisper.

The number ten appears on the movie screen, accompanied by a loud, piercing blare that hurts my ears. The noise is followed by a male voice—one that sounds old-fashioned too, like the voice-over from an old black-and-white TV commercial: "This is a test of the emergency Dark House system," the voice says. "The coordinators of your stay here, in voluntary cooperation with the Nightmare Elf, have developed this system . . . *to scare you out of your mind.* But this is not an emergency. It is a test. And if you are to survive, you need to pass it. To pass it. *To pass it, to pass it, topassittopassittopassit.*"

The words repeat over and over, faster and faster. On the screen, the number ten starts flashing. It looks three-dimensional. It's almost too bright to look at, and my eyes start to water. The ten switches to a nine. Then an eight. And then the numbers count all the way down to one.

The voice stops. It's replaced by music. I recognize the tune from my dad's collection. I can't help but sing the first line in my head: *"One is the loneliest number that you'll ever do."* I haven't heard the song in years—since my dad stopped allowing tunes in the garage, saying they were a distraction, the cause of all our screwups. Listening to Harry Nilsson belt out the lyrics reminds me of how eerie the song is. The melody is haunting. This whole scene is fantastically creepy.

Garth is giggling like a schoolgirl. I peer behind me to look at the others. Ivy's digging her fingernails into the headrest in front of her. Parker's got his hand on her back. And Natalie's sitting on the edge of her seat, winding a strand of her straw-like hair around her finger.

The number one flashes on the screen. I close my eyes, but still I can see it inside my head, pressed against my optic nerves.

Shayla's grip on my forearm tightens. "Someone make it stop," she whispers.

I find her hand in the darkness and weave my fingers through hers. Part of me wants—just for her sake—for this whole head-trippy thing to stop. But another part wants it to keep on going, so I don't ever have to let go.

I clench my teeth, anticipating a crash. It comes in the form of a scream—a heart-ripping wail that sends chills straight down my spine.

The scream is followed by a heavy thud at the back of the room, like someone or something fell.

Shayla stands from her seat, letting go of my hand. The music shuts off. The lights come on. It takes a couple of seconds for my eyes to adjust—for the orbs and color splotches to fade away. Once they do, I look around, making sure that everyone's okay and accounted for.

Everyone is. Except for Midge. She's nowhere in sight.

In her place, seated on a chair at the front of the room, is a Midge doll: round face, happy smile, fluffy white hair held back with ribbons, and a maid's uniform with tiny fake fingers sticking out from the pockets.

Garth jumps out of his seat to grab it.

"Was that Midge who screamed?" I ask.

"I think so," Ivy says. Her face is as pale as my white Irish ass. "I mean, it sort of sounded like her."

"I really hope so," Natalie mutters. But she isn't talking to us. She remains seated, staring down into her lap, having a full-on conversation by herself.

"Lookie, lookie," Garth sings, showing off his find: a cord attached to the back of the doll. He pulls it and Midge's all-too-familiar voice chirps out: *"Cakes, cookies, and pies supreme, eat up well and get ready to dream. The Nightmare Elf would like to see what we fear and then make it be."*

"Make it be?" Ivy asks.

"That doesn't make sense," Natalie pipes up, apparently done talking to herself. "We've already submitted our worst nightmares, so why would we need to re-dream them?"

"It's not exactly Steinbeck, Scarecrow," Garth says, wrapping the cord around the doll's neck. "I wouldn't take it literally." He punts the doll. The head slams against the far wall. Fake fingers go flying. The guy has absolutely no respect.

"Don't you think we should go look for Midge?" Ivy asks.

"Not before dessert," Garth says. "A little finger-collecting bird told me that it involves maggots and a bloody fountain."

"Happy yum-ness." Shayla hooks her arm with his, totally leaving me hanging.

SHAYLA

IVY'S INCESSANT NAGGING MEANS WE END UP passing on the dessert table to do a superficial search for Midge. We call out her name, head off in various directions, and check out all the rooms.

In the kitchen, I open the pantry closet and pull a chain that turns on an overhead light.

Holy creep-fest.

Facing me is a man's head, on a platter, with an apple wedged into its mouth. It looks completely real: gray skin, bloodshot eyes, five o'clock shadow, and bluish lips. A trickle of something orange drools out of its mouth, pooling under its chin. *Ew. Icky. Blech.* I move closer to get a better look, just as the door slams behind me. The overhead bulb goes out, replaced by two beams of bright red light, coming from the eyes of the head.

I turn back to the door. The light beams shine over the words *It's too late to turn back now*, scribbled in crayon.

I go for the knob, but it's locked. I jiggle it back and forth, telling myself not to panic—that this is obviously just a joke. "Let me out!" I shout, pounding on the door.

I search the walls—what's visible in the red light—looking for a key or some trigger that might open the door.

A heart-patterned oven mitt is there. It hangs on a hook, reminding me of Dara. I slam my back against the wall, able to picture her hanging from the ceiling.

Her body wavers. Her eyes snap open. She glares at me, pointing her dark blue finger. "There's no way out," she says.

I shake my head. Beads of sweat form at my brow.

"You weren't there for me," Dara whispers. "And so now you'll pay."

I close my eyes, then look away, but still her image is there. Her bluish face, her chalky lips, the telephone wire around her neck, and those heart-patterned socks.

I pound on the door again. I kick it, smack it, throw my weight against it.

Finally it opens.

Frankie's there, holding a bouquet of plastic machetes. "Holy shit," he says at the sight of me. He drops the machetes and I crumble into his arms.

"I'm so sorry," he says, stroking my back. "I saw you go in there and thought it'd be funny." He smells like a gas station.

Still, I press my nose against his shoulder and suck up all my tears. "I guess you got your payback."

"We'll call it even, okay?" He takes a step back to check my face. "Any chance dessert will make it better? We're done looking for Midge—for now anyway. All we're finding are props." He picks up one of the machetes and pretends to jab it in his eye. "Let's go have some lemon-filled eyeballs and intestine-layer cake."

"Sounds good," I say, taking one last peek into the closet. The heart-patterned oven mitt dangles in the red light.

In the dining room we find a platter of brains, a tray of mucous macaroons, two dozen maggot-infested cupcakes, and a plate of creamy fingers. Everything's spread out over the table, surrounding a blood-chocolate fondue fountain.

"Seriously, how did they do that?" Frankie asks, focused on the fountain.

"With red and blue food coloring mixed in," Garth says, dipping a strawberry into the red stream. "I must say, however, this particular mixture is pretty impressive—a sophisticated consistency, made possible only with just the right amount of corn syrup." He takes a bite of his strawberry, letting the bloodred chocolate saturate his teeth.

"Gross." Ivy squeals.

"What's happenin', hot stuff?" Garth says, trying to sound like Long Duk Dong from *Sixteen Candles*, one of the greatest films ever. He waggles his tongue, exposing a barbell pierced through the center.

I let out a laugh—so loud that a weird hiccupping sound shoots out of my mouth. Garth laughs at it—at me. And we both end up doubled over as the others look on with blank faces, which just makes me laugh more.

"If Midge is supposedly missing," Frankie says, popping a lemon eyeball, "then where did all of these desserts come from? Who set up the table while she was busy disappearing?"

"Maybe she had time to set it up *before* she disappeared," Parker says. "It's all part of the plan, I'm sure."

"What plan?" Ivy asks.

"A plan in which, one by one, we all start to go missing."

Garth rubs his palms together and lets out a maniacal laugh.

Meanwhile, Natalie starts muttering to herself again. She obviously has *way* bigger problems than just a humdrum case of homesickness.

"Does your imaginary friend want some brain cake?" Garth asks her.

I stifle a giggle by feeding a chocolate worm into my mouth, happy that Garth's here. He's in this purely for the fun factor, which helps distract me from thoughts about Dara. "So, what was your nightmare?" I ask him.

He ladles some chocolate syrup into a bowl; it looks like blood soup. "I wrote about the nightmares I had when I was seven—after my dad had dared me to watch *Nightmare Elf*. I didn't want to, but he teased me into it."

"Weren't you scared to watch it?" Ivy asks.

"Sure, but with a name like Garth Vader, there really isn't much of a choice in life. You either learn to like all things scary or you end up miserable. If you're smart, you pick the first one."

"And your mom was okay with you watching it?" Ivy continues.

"My mom's at work most of the time. My dad's on disability for a bad back."

"Is she into horror too?" Parker asks.

"Negative, just like her B-type blood," Garth says. "If my mom had it her way, my dad would've dropped dead years ago, preferably from a heart attack following one of his twisted tricks."

"What kind of tricks?" I ask.

"Stupid stuff," he says, dodging the question like darts. "Anyway, my nightmare was of the typical horror-movie variety . . . getting lost in the woods, finding the Dark House, being chased down a long alleyway with villainous ghouls stalking after me."

"No big deal, then," Parker smirks.

"No big deal *anymore*," Garth says to clarify.

I study his face, wondering if his story is entirely true, or if there might be something more vulnerable beneath his seemingly resilient exterior—all his layers of dark, dark gray. "Well, if you ever want to talk about it more . . ." I say, suddenly eager to learn from him—to know how something that had caused him nightmares could wind up being something that he could fully embrace.

"Talk?" he asks, confusion on his face.

I nod, thinking about Dara. She'd wanted to talk too. If only I'd been more willing to listen.

GARTH

SHAYLA'S OFFER TO TALK TOTALLY TAKES ME OFF guard and I don't know what to say. What I *do* know is that I don't want her to see me like that—like someone who *needs to talk* and gets bothered by crap, and has to work out all his feelings.

Just because horror was initially forced on me doesn't mean that I didn't learn to love it, or that I need my head shrunk, or that people should feel sorry for me.

So, maybe my dad's a little messed up. Maybe he shouldn't have shown those movies to a seven-year-old, or made life for my brothers and me like a real-life horror: locking us in the basement for fun, putting red food dye in our milk, leaving us home alone so that he could prey on us like an intruder, waking us in the middle of the night made-up like a zombie or demon.

Embracing horror was a means of survival, and so far it's served me well.

After one more dip in the chocolate fountain, I suggest we head outside to continue our search for Midge. There are seven flashlights lined up on a shelf by the door. Clearly, Midge wants us to go outside. She also wants to remind us of Taylor's absence.

I open the door. It's perfectly black outside. Aside from a spotlight positioned over the door, the area is shrouded by trees; they even block out the moon. I click on my flashlight and lead the way, remembering that Tommy Tucker's nightmare chamber was several yards into the woods, but still visible through the trees. I walk away from the house, aiming the beam into the trees, trying to find a path that might lead to the chamber.

"Midge!" I call out into the night, feeling the rush of my adrenaline.

"Are you looking for the shed?" Parker asks. "And, if so, wasn't it on the other side of the house?"

"I know what I'm doing." A slight exaggeration.

"Are you sure about that?" Parker asks. "Or is the Force not quite with you?"

I let the joke slide off my back, too busy trying to eavesdrop on Shayla and Frankie. They're talking just behind me—something about Frankie's boy band back home. I can't tell if she likes him or if she's simply one of those girls who likes everyone and no one at the same time—who makes people think they actually mean something to her.

Finally I find a dirt pathway that leads into the forest. "Bingo," I say, pointing my flashlight far up the path, into the woods. But still I don't see the shed.

A few yards down the path, a rustling in the brush to the side of us sends a wave of screeches through the group. I aim my flashlight in that direction, but the rustling travels to the other side, producing more noises.

Whoosh.

Creak.

Snap.

I stop short to listen, but all I can hear is the sound of Frankie cracking up behind me. I turn to look at him just as he throws a rock into the brush, creating the source of the sounds. This guy is a total comedian.

"Midge," I sing. *"Come out, come out, wherever you are!"*

Ivy lets out a shriek. I pause and turn back again, but it's just more of her paranoia. Close behind her, Natalie's busy talking to herself, but she's smiling all the while, so apparently it's a good conversation. I wouldn't be surprised if this whole psycho-babbling bit of hers isn't fake—if she isn't trying to act like a Justin Blake–inspired character in hopes of landing herself a starring role in one of his future projects.

The back side of the shed comes into view. I turn to the others, angling my flashlight under my chin to light my face as I speak. "Are you prepared to enter Tommy Tucker's nightmare chamber?" I ask, using a throaty voice.

"Let me in, let me in!" Shayla cheers.

"Not by the hair of my chinny chin chin." I move around to the front of the shed, amazed at how authentic it looks—all boarded up and with a busted padlock on the handle, just like the real thing.

"Midge?" I call. "Are you in there?" I open the door and aim my flashlight inside as Ivy lets out a gasp.

There's a rocking chair set in the middle of the space. Seated on it, with its gloved hands neatly folded, is the Nightmare Elf doll. Between its legs is a single candle, positioned on a holder. Its flame flickers against the walls, casting a light on all of little Tommy Tucker's etchings.

"Holy shit," Frankie says.

My sentiments exactly.

With a permanent smile and bright golden hair, the Nightmare Elf is dressed in a tattered red suit, a Santa-like hat, and boots that curl up at the toe—exactly like the one in the movie. It's missing one eye from when Tommy plucked it out using a fork, just as Carson ordered.

"It has a lazy eyelid," Frankie says, squatting down for a better look. "Just like the real deal."

I nod, picturing little Tommy Tucker dragging the elf through the dirt, tying a leash around its neck, and throwing it up in the air.

Beneath the chair is a shiny black music box, just like the one that Tommy had brought along on his camping trip, the one he used to store his treasures. I open it up, shining my flashlight on Tommy's Silly Putty egg, remembering how he used the putty to make bubbles that snap.

"Will you play with me?" a high-pitched voice squeaks, nearly knocking me on my ass. I take a step back.

Ivy lets out another shriek.

It takes me a second before I realize that the voice was Frankie's. He's almost teary eyed from laughing so hard.

"Asshole," I say, though I now have a newfound respect for the guy.

I turn the crank on the music box and a familiar melody begins to play.

"'I'm a Little Teapot,'" Shayla says.

But the words are different. A little kid's voice sings them: *"I'm the Nightmare Elf, oh yes siree. Here's my hefty sack, ho, ha, hee hee. Fall asleep tonight and you will see. I'll take your nightmares and make them be."*

"Look," Shayla says, holding out her arm. She angles her flashlight over the goose bumps on her skin.

Frankie does the same, comparing the size of his goose bumps to hers.

"Let's play it again," Natalie says, taking the box from me.

I turn to check out the etchings. Words line the walls—*Die!, Torture!, Pain!*—as do sketches of ghouls, giant rats, and people with missing eyes and serpent tongues. "T. T.," I say, pointing out little Tommy Tucker's initials. Below his initials is a picture of a wolf. I run my fingers over the image, imagining that it's real, that Tommy once existed, and that this doll truly belonged to him.

There's a picture of the Nightmare Elf holding his sack of nightmares. A hand reaches out from the bulge in the sack, as though someone's trapped inside it, desperate to get out. The words above it read: *There's no escape.*

"So cool," I say, completely inspired.

"Except it isn't true." Parker's reading over my shoulder. "You escape your nightmares when you wake up."

"Sometimes," Ivy tells him. "And sometimes they haunt you even when you're awake."

"Care to share?" I ask, curious to know what she wrote about in her contest submission.

"Check this out," Parker says, nodding to the wall by the door.

Be careful what you dream is etched into the wood. Below it is a collage of our names and seven pictures: a snake, an ax, a bear, a tombstone, a broken mirror, a noose, and a pair of demon eyes.

"Anybody want to claim their pain?" I ask.

"The gravestone," Frankie says, pointing out the image at the very bottom. "That's obviously for my nightmare."

"These images are obviously from all of our nightmares," Ivy says.

"Which one is yours?" I ask her.

Ivy looks away, toward the door. She's obviously a tease too.

Parker points to the snake. "This one's mine," he says, coming to Ivy's rescue.

"The broken mirror is mine," Natalie says.

"Mine's the noose," Shayla mutters, turning away from it.

"And mine is the ax," I tell them. "Leaving only the bear and the eyes. One must be Taylor's, and the other must be . . ."

143

I glance at Ivy, but she refuses to look at me. "I'll bet my right nut your dream involves devil eyes. Am I right?"

"Leave her alone," Parker says.

"According to the mastermind, there's no escaping your nightmare," I continue, talking toward the top of Ivy's head. "No escaping those eyes." I inhale the musty air, reminiscent of the basement back home, wondering how the theme of no escape will play out this weekend.

I can hardly wait to see.

Ivy

"I FREAKED AGAIN."

Back in my room, I sit on my bed, nursing a fresh cup of chamomile tea with an extra shot of lemon balm. Parker sits beside me.

"And just so you know," I continue, "I'll probably freak at least a hundred more times on this trip. But I'm hoping that each instance of freakishness will feel progressively less intense."

"Do you mind if we rewind a bit?" he asks. "You never told

me why you entered the contest," he says. "Since you're not a Blake fan, I mean."

I bite my lip and gaze into his face. A lock of hair has fallen over his eye. I'd give anything to touch it.

"Trick question?" he asks.

Part of me wants to tell him the truth about my past. But I'm also afraid of what he'll think after I do. What will he think of someone who fears everyday that her parents' killer is going to come back for her?

"I thought it might look good on my college application," I lie.

"And where *are* you going to college?"

"Le Cordon Bleu. It's a culinary school in Paris."

"And the people at Le Cordon Bleu really give a crap about winning a contest to go see a horror flick?"

I feel my face turn red.

"Makes complete sense." He nods when I don't say anything. "I mean, I can totally see how that would rank right up there with participating in the French club or feeding the hungry at a soup kitchen. Now that I think about it, I seem to remember a special 'Contests Entered' section on my college applications—only with all the turkey-coloring contests I entered as a kid, and the Fourth of July toasted marshmallow–eating contests, I couldn't fit them all."

"Okay." I smirk. "You got me."

"Have I?" He bumps his shoulder against mine. The gesture sends a wave of tea over the rim of my mug, spilling into my lap. "Crap, I'm so sorry." He gets up to fetch a rag, just as Shayla taps on the door and comes in.

"More fat and sugar?" she asks, holding a plateful of desserts from downstairs.

Parker looks back at me, straight-faced, as if less than jazzed about Shayla's impromptu visit.

"Does Natalie want to join us?" I ask, both relieved and disappointed that she's interrupted my moment with Parker.

"Natalie's holed up in our bathroom right now," Shayla says.

"Because she isn't feeling well?" I ask.

"Who knows." Shayla inserts herself between Parker and me on the bed—the Fluffernutter to our two pieces of bread. "I tried to bribe her with treats, but she says she wants to be alone. She even took her pillow and a blanket in there."

I'm pretty sure that Natalie pulls out her own hair. I almost caught her doing it earlier, but then she moved her hand away before I could fully see. I was never into hair pulling, but after the incident with my parents I started pinching—the skin on my kneecap, mostly, until it was purple, and black, and blue, and yellow.

A rainbow of dysfunction.

My way of trying to cope.

According to Dr. Donna, pinching was my way of transferring my pain and anxiety. If that theory holds true, the method never worked. Because as hard as I may've tried to transfer my pain, I always ended up with more colors, rather than less stress.

"I can go talk to her." I get up and head down the hallway to Shayla and Natalie's room. The door is open and I walk inside, past Natalie's bed. There's stationery sprawled out over her coverlet—envelopes, cards, and letterhead. There's also a fancy feather pen.

"Natalie," I call, knocking on the closed bathroom door.

"I'm fine in here." Her voice sounds all nasal-like; I'm guessing that she's been crying.

"Will you come out . . . even for a little bit? We're all just hanging out in my room, feasting on spider brownies and brain cake."

There's a loud thud against the door. It sounds like she might've kicked it. I picture her big black boots. I peer over my shoulder at the stationery, wondering what it's all about, especially since we're only here for the weekend.

I turn away and move over to her bed. Lying on the pillow is an envelope marked with her brother Harris's name. I pick it up and look back at the bathroom door, still closed.

The envelope hasn't yet been sealed.

I open it up, trying to be quiet, my eyes darting to the bathroom door. Thankfully, it remains closed. Finally, I get the envelope open and take out the card. It's a note to Harris from Natalie.

Dear Harris,

I know you're angry at me. Ever since I won this contest, something that was supposed to make me happy, it's been nothing but misery— misery for you, for Mom, for Dad. And so it's also been miserable for me.

I know you didn't want me to come here. You made that clear from the start. But it's too late to change things now. If I could I would, because nothing is worth anything if I don't have you in my corner.

I keep trying to talk to you. I'm not sure if you're listening. But I don't think I can make it through this weekend without your voice.

Love,

Natalie

I return the letter to the envelope. She must've tried calling home again. Her brother obviously doesn't want to talk to her. Still, I go downstairs to use the phone, hoping that she was the one who made the last call.

I pass the dining area—still a mess from dessert—and move into the living room. The lights are off. I flick them on, noticing a sudden chill in the air. The window over the sofa is open. The sheers blow in the breeze.

I go over to shut and lock the window, suddenly feeling like I'm being watched. I peer over my shoulder. "Natalie?" I call, wondering if she might be lurking.

No one answers. The stairway looks empty.

I glance over at the kitchen—also empty. And then I look toward the main door, assuming that it's locked. I check anyway, wrapping my hand around the knob. It turns and my heart sinks.

What if someone broke in?

I lock the door and turn to face the room again. "Midge," I attempt to call out, but my voice is far too soft.

I take a few more steps, before coming to a sudden halt, feeling my whole body tense.

Someone's there. In the closet. The door is partially open.

I can see eyes through the door crack, watching me, locked on mine.

My chest instantly tightens. I hurry into the kitchen and grab a knife from the chopping block. I begin moving toward the closet. My fingers trembling, I hold the knife down by my side. My heart hammers. I can feel the sweat at my brow.

I whisk the door open with a thwack.

No one's there.

The closet is empty.

There's just an umbrella and a pair of binoculars.

I let out a breath and rest my head against the wall, feeling a giant wave of relief. I move over to the desk, grab the phone, and press redial. The phone rings and rings, but then someone finally picks up.

"Hello?" I ask, when no one says anything. "Is someone there?"

"Who's this?" A woman's voice.

"Is this Natalie's mother?" I ask.

"Who's this?" she repeats.

"I'm a friend of Natalie's and she's here with me now . . . in Minnesota . . . on the trip to see one of Justin Blake's films. . . ."

The woman doesn't respond.

"Anyway," I continue, winding the coil cord around my fingers, "she feels really bad about coming here. She knows that you don't approve."

"Well, she's right. Her father and I *don't* approve."

"Okay, well she feels really bad," I say, knowing I'm repeating myself. "And I know that if she could do it again—go back in time, I mean—she'd make a different choice."

"What did you say your name was?"

"Ivy Jensen."

"And she's talked to you about things?"

"Well, I know how she feels about her decision to go on this trip . . . and how she feels about Harris."

"She told you about Harris?"

"Actually," I say, noticing that my fingers are completely entangled in the cord now, "I think she'd like to speak to him. Did they have a fight?"

"You have no idea what you're talking about."

"Well, maybe their falling out is something you're unaware of, a recent argument, something about this whole contest trip perhaps . . ."

"Harris is dead."

Wait. *"What?"*

"My son was stillborn," she continues. "Natalie was his twin."

"Are you sure?" I ask, thinking how stupid the question is—not to mention how insensitive.

"I think I'd know if my own son had died. A word of advice: I'd be very careful around my daughter if I were you. Now, if you'll excuse me, I have to go."

"Careful of what?"

She doesn't answer. Instead, she hangs up.

PARKER

IVY FINALLY COMES BACK INTO THE ROOM, HER FACE just as pale as it was after finding the message in Taylor's closet.

"I take it that things didn't go so well with Project Natalie?" Shayla asks, searching through Taylor's shoe rack.

"I think that maybe we should get her some help," Ivy says.

"Help, as in calling the fire department to break down the door?" Shayla asks. "Because if that's the case, you have my vote. I'm all for getting a few more hotties in the house."

"Her brother is dead," Ivy says.

"Hold up," Shayla says, trying to squeeze her foot into

a ballet slipper. "Not the brother that she's been talking about . . . not her twin . . ."

"Harris." Ivy nods. "He died at birth." She proceeds to tell us about the letter she found in Natalie's room. "I know I shouldn't have read it, but it was just lying there, and I had so many questions. And, anyway, in the letter, Natalie was apologizing to Harris for coming on this trip."

I raise my eyebrow in suspicion. "She apologized to a dead guy?"

"Hold on," Shayla says. "How do you know that he's dead?"

"I called her parents." Ivy brings her bottle pendant up to her lips. "I pushed redial after she'd called them, hoping that her brother might pick up. But her mother answered. And when I mentioned Harris's name, she told me that he was dead."

"Why would Natalie write letters to a dead person?" Shayla asks.

"Maybe it's because she's deranged," I say, stating the obvious.

"It's not just letters," Ivy says. "She talks to him too. I'm thinking that Harris is the one she's been mumbling to."

"Okay, well, I'll second Parker's notion: the girl is totally deranged . . . and I am totally depressed." Shayla tosses the ballet slipper back at the rack. "I need to go find me some big-girl shoes."

Finally, she leaves, but now there's an awkward silence between Ivy and me. I want to pick up where we left off pre–Shayla's dessert invasion, but I also don't know how to get there. After a couple more beats of silence, I pick up my mental camera, trying to imagine this as a shot.

INT. BEDROOM—NIGHT

Ivy sits down beside me on the bed. There's
a plate of desserts between us.

                    ME
          That was really cool of you to want to
          help Natalie.

                    IVY
          Believe it or not, it feels good
          trying to help her. Somehow she
          seems even more messed up than me.

                    ME
          How so?

Ivy takes a spider brownie from the plate

and chews it down, bite after bite, making
it difficult to answer.

I eat too. But after six cream-filled
finger rolls, I get up and call cut inside
my head, frustrated that it seems Ivy no
longer wants to talk.

"Don't be angry," she says. There's a smear of chocolate in
the corner of her mouth. If this were a movie, I'd lean in close
and kiss it away. "I really like you," she continues. "And I really
appreciate how sweet you've been to me. But I don't want to
ruin your time here with my drama."

I sit back down and venture to take her hand. "You're
definitely not ruining my time. Whatever the reason that you
decided to enter Blake's contest, I'm really glad that you did."

She clasps her fingers around my grip and then peeks up
into my face. "Believe it or not, I am too," she says, causing
my heart to stir.

"So, then, can I ask . . . eyes or bear?"

"Huh?" Her face scrunches.

"The wall etchings."

"Oh." She looks away. Her face falls. "How about you tell
me about your snake, first," she says.

"It was actually an eel," I say to clarify, as if the distinction even matters.

"Okay." She smiles, looking back at me. "How about you tell me about your eel."

"I'd love to tell you about my eel," I smirk. "If I had an eel, that is."

"Excuse me?"

"Wait . . . that came out all wrong." I can feel my face changing colors. "I made the whole thing up—my nightmare submission, I mean. It was a work of fiction, inspired by something that happened when I was a kid at summer camp. I got caught in a riptide and almost drowned."

"And you had nightmares about it?"

"Not exactly, but it makes for good contest submission material, don't you think? Especially when you add in the getting-attacked-by-man-eating-eels part."

"So, you *lied*?"

"I embellished . . . and tweaked . . . and altered the facts. I'm a storyteller," I explain. "It's my job to alter the facts."

"I'll remember that," Ivy says.

"Well then, remember this: I never embellish, tweak, or alter the facts when it comes to the people I care about."

Ivy looks downward—at our hands, still clasped together—and a tiny smile forms on her face.

I look at the clock. It's almost eleven. "Hey . . ." I begin, hating the idea of leaving her alone. But before I can finish my thought, a scream comes from down the hall, slicing our moment in two.

I go for the door and peer down the hall.

Shayla is there, dressed up like Eureka Dash from the Nightmare Elf movies. "He stabbed me," she says, stumbling forward, holding her gut.

Garth comes from around the corner, dressed like Sidney Scarcella from *Hotel 9* in a suit jacket with tails and a blood-stained apron. There's a demented smile on his face.

Shayla tries to grab the wall for support, but ends up collapsing to the floor.

"Holy shit!" I shout, rushing into the hallway. I scoot down to assess her wound, pulling up on the hem of her blouse.

"Not so fast!" she hollers, slapping my hand away. "You have to at least buy me dinner first."

Both she and Garth start laughing.

"Die, you lowly peasant," Garth says, pretending to stab his plastic knife into her back.

Shayla sits up and runs a finger over her blood-chocolate-smeared stomach. "You guys totally have to check out the costume closet downstairs," she says, licking said finger.

Frankie peeks out into the hall, a guitar strapped across his chest. "Can you guys keep it down?"

"Good night," I say, returning to the room and shutting the door. Shutting Ivy and me off from the rest of them—for a little while at least.

We end up lying in bed—me on Taylor's and Ivy on her own—facing one another, with the lights kept dim. We spend the next couple hours talking about everything—about favorite ice cream and famous couples. And best movie kisses (for her, that scene in *Breakfast at Tiffany's*, when Holly and Paul share a kiss in the rain while "Moon River" plays in the background; for me, the upside-down kiss between Spider-Man and Mary Jane).

"Do you have a boyfriend?" I ask, surprised to hear the words come out my mouth.

"No." She bites back a smile. Her cheeks turn pink.

I wait for her to reciprocate the question, but she doesn't. "I should probably let you get some sleep," I say, feeling a major blow to my ego.

"Don't go," she says. Her eyes widen. "Let's talk some more."

"About what?" I ask, hoping she'll finally open up about her nightmares, but she asks me about favorite comic book characters instead.

Finally, around three a.m., after we've explored just about every topic, except the one she refuses to discuss—the one involving her contest submission—we decide to call it a night.

She slips beneath the covers and closes her eyes. I close my eyes too. But there's no way I'm going to fall asleep. I toss and turn, flip and flop, finally resolving to wait it out until morning and watch her sleep.

I could seriously watch her all night, admiring her inky-black lashes against her pale ivory skin, the curves of her body beneath the coverlet, and those raspberry-colored lips.

But then her eyes snap open and I'm totally caught.

"I can't sleep," she says.

"Me neither."

"Are you feeling anxious too?"

"More like restless," I tell her. "What are you feeling anxious about?"

"Would you mind holding me for a little while?" she asks, in lieu of an answer. "At least until I fall asleep."

My heart absolutely pounding, I move to her bed and lay down on top of the covers while she remains beneath them. She rolls over and I hold her, savoring the warmth of her back against my chest. She smells like chamomile and chocolate—like something I want to bottle up and wash all over me.

In the movie version of my life, I'd have met her someplace else—while vacationing somewhere tropical, maybe. We'd fall in love with both the island and each other, unable to part at the end of our stay. My favorite scene would be the one where the camera zoomed in as we kissed—in the ocean, while it rained—with the balmy beach air crushing against our skin like velvet. A kiss that would top both Spidey's and Holly's any day.

NATALIE

Ivy went through my stuff. I know she did.

I almost opened the door. My hand was wrapped around the knob. My mind was flashing forward to what would happen if I confronted her.

But I didn't, because it feels safer in here—more controlled, less influenced by time.

How long have I been away from home?

How long has it been since Harris spoke to me?

How long ago did I call my parents?

Sitting with my back against the tub, I look down at the

strands of hair collected on the bath mat, between my knees. Twenty-six.

One-hundred-eighty-two wall tiles. Forty-three floor tiles. Thirty-six tissues in the box. Ninety-two squares of toilet paper. Three bars of soap. Five travel bottles of shampoo. Two drinking cups.

Someone screams. The sound echoes the screaming deep inside me. I grab the hair strands and get up, unlock the door, and take a step outside. Shayla's out in the hallway. She's dressed like Eureka from *Nightmare Elf.* Garth is with her, dressed as Sidney Scarcella. They're both laughing.

I close the door, move over to the sink, and toss the hair strands into the basin. Ever since I left home, I've been itching for another tattoo: Harris's beating heart, right over my own. When I was ten and wrote his name 311 times on my body, and my dad told me that I wasn't worthy of having Harris's name inked on my skin, I believed him. I *wasn't* worthy.

But maybe Harris would think otherwise. Maybe it would even get him to start talking to me again.

I take off my T-shirt and remove the towels I've placed over the mirror, squinting my eyes to avoid the whole picture. I pluck a lipstick from my pocket and draw the heart right over my own.

It doesn't come out right the first time—too pointy at the

bottom, too narrow at the top. I wipe the mark and try again on the other side of my chest. But it looks more like a potato. I wipe once more and give it another shot. At least ten attempts later, my chest is covered in lipstick smudges and smears, and so are my palms. And the side of my face.

A floorboard creaks. Someone's here. Outside the door. There's another knock. "Natalie?" Shayla's voice. "I have to get in there. I made a bloody mess of myself—literally—and I need to wash up."

I ignore her and rip off my wig. My heart pounds at the image. I hate the way I look. I probably even hate it more than my parents do. My real hair, beneath the wig, is the same dark color. I dyed it. And pulled out big chunks—what started out as single strands. Now, it's long in some places and short in others, with a gaping bald spot in the back and a few smaller ones on both sides. Too noticeable without the wig. Too much to cover up.

"Hello?" she shouts, knocking again. Luckily there's a lock. "We called your parents, by the way," she adds. "We asked them about Harris. Can you guess what they might've said?"

Sure, I can guess. Did they say that I was crazy? That I talk to myself? That I'm a constant disappointment? Did they mention that I preoccupy myself with things they don't understand? That when Harris died eighteen years ago, the expectations for me were doubled? But who could possibly live up to the achievements of two people, particularly when one of those people is a baby who probably sacrificed himself for his twin before he was even born? But still, I've tried. I study hard. I get good grades. I volunteer at church. But that's nowhere near enough. And I don't know what else to do—I don't know what else I *can* do.

Shayla knocks again. "Come out here and I'll tell you what they said."

I run the faucet, hoping she'll go away. I pick at my lips—the dry skin—rolling it between my fingertips.

"I'll give you ten seconds," Shayla says, talking to me like I'm three. She counts aloud, pausing between each number.

Until she gets to ten.

I take a deep breath and grab a three-strander from behind my ear. I yank, feeling a wave of relief swim through my veins. I check out the strands. I got the follicles, too.

"She's going to come in," a voice whispers.

"Harris?" At last. My whole body tingles.

The bathroom door whips open.

Shayla is there.

She stares at my reflection in the mirror—my patchy scalp, my bloodshot eyes, and the red-lipstick smudges on my face, neck, and chest. Her lips peel open in revulsion and then retract back in what looks like remorse; they purse tight, her brow furrows. Her expressions aren't so much unlike my parents' when they walked in on me in the bathroom back home and saw my very first tattoos. Only, unlike Shayla, my parents' remorse had nothing to do with invading my privacy, and everything to do with my very existence. At least that's what I believe. At least that's how they make me feel.

FRANKIE

AFTER A MOSTLY SLEEPLESS NIGHT—BECAUSE I WAS anxious about meeting Justin Blake—I didn't end up nodding off until sometime around five a.m.

It's now after one and I'm just getting out of bed. I grab a shower, and step out of the tub, startled to find the words THERE'S NO ESCAPE written on the mirror, through the steamed glass.

I look around, making sure that I'm alone. And then I move closer to touch one of the letters, able to feel a thick coating of wax.

I'm seriously going to miss this place.

Once dressed, I head downstairs to look for Shayla, disappointed that she didn't come into my room last night while I was playing guitar, practicing the song I wrote for Justin Blake, inspired by *Nightmare Elf*. I brought along the sheet music, hoping to give it to Blake as a gift, but it'd be even more amazing if he'd let me play the song for him on the Slipknot Telecaster.

"Good afternoon," Ivy says, standing at the kitchen island. She's made some egg thing—a big casserole dish of it. There are also pans full of bacon and potatoes. "Midge still remains among the missing," she says. "I say *among* because Taylor's still missing too. But I thought I'd make some food anyway." She grabs a cantaloupe half and begins slicing it up with the precision of an Iron Chef—fast and furious, making perfectly symmetrical slices. She does the same with the other half, the blade so close to her fingers that I feel myself squirm.

"Yikes," I say, when she's finally done.

Parker's watching too. "Remind me not to get on your bad side."

I take a step closer to grab a slice, and that's when I see her. Shayla.

She stares at me from the living room sofa. My first reaction is excitement. But then I notice that the sofa's been pulled out to a bed, and that there are blankets strewn about. Garth sits up from a heap of them. They obviously spent the night together.

"Hey," she says, smiling at me, like it's no big deal—like she hasn't been openly flirting with me since the moment I climbed into that hearse.

"Hungry?" Parker asks them.

"Starving." Garth stands from the sofa and stretches his arms wide.

"Can somebody go get Natalie?" Ivy asks. "Everything's just about done."

"I'll go," I say, desperate for a moment to myself. I round the corner and let out a breath, trying to pull the invisible dagger out of my heart, but it's wedged in way too deep. I guess I'm not so used to letting myself get hurt.

After a few seconds, I climb the stairs. The door to Natalie's room is partially open. She's sitting on her bed, gazing down at her suitcase.

"Hey," I say, edging the door open wider.

"Did they tell you?" she asks.

"Did *who* tell me *what*?"

"The others . . . about me."

"Apparently not, because I have no idea what you're talking about."

"Neither do they."

"Translation?" This chick is so messed up.

"Was that you playing the guitar last night?" she asks, switching gears. "Because if so, you're really talented."

"Thanks. Do you play?"

"No, but my brother does. I really wish that he were here. He and I don't usually go more than an hour without talking." She keeps her focus toward her heavy black boots.

I glance down at my infinity bracelet, suddenly feeling sorry for her. "I know what it's like to miss someone."

"Are you talking about your mom or your uncle?"

"My mom," I say, impressed that she was so tuned in at the dinner table.

"Why did she leave?"

"I ask myself that all the time. I guess she didn't want to be married anymore, or didn't want to be a mom anymore. I don't know. I don't know if I'll *ever* know."

"Who wouldn't want to be a mom to someone like you?"

The comment takes me off guard and I can't help but grin. "My mom and I used to have a lot of fun together. We'd go for long walks. She'd point out different types of birds, plants, flowers, trees . . . everything was an adventure with her. Sometimes I wonder if it wouldn't have been easier for me if she'd died along with my uncle. Growing up, it was way worse knowing that she was alive—that she was choosing to be away."

"So, how are you able to go on?"

"Well, you can't stop living," I tell her. "Otherwise, we might as well be dead too."

"I just don't know what I'm supposed to do," she says. "I mean, I want to meet Justin Blake and see the movie. But part of me feels like I should go home early—like I don't deserve those things since I came here without permission."

"Give yourself permission. Live your own life, make your own choices. Because going home early—punishing yourself—isn't going to change the fact that you came here to begin with."

"Is that what you do . . . give yourself permission, I mean?"

"It's easier said than done," I admit, thinking about all the times that my dad's dumped on my plans by having me work overtime, and how I haven't exactly spoken up. "But I try to have my own voice—at least most of the time."

"Your own voice," she repeats. Her eyes grow big as if what I've said is gospel.

"Now, come on." I hold out my hand, confident that whatever's bugging her is more than just a couple of days away from her brother. "Ivy's whipped up an IHOP-worthy brunch."

Surprisingly, Natalie places her hand in mine and together we go downstairs.

SHAYLA

I SPENT THE NIGHT WITH GARTH. AND IT WAS really nice—until it wasn't. Until it got all awkward and I wanted to go back upstairs.

It happened like this: after the costumes, neither of us was ready to end the night. Frankie was playing a guitar right upstairs, and the music made it easy for Garth and me to sink into the comfort of the living room sofa getting to know each other better.

We spent much of the night in hysterics, which is exactly

how I suspected things would be. But soon things got heated, and I found myself cuddled against his chest, playing with the tear in his T-shirt—one long rip across his navel.

I could tell that he wanted to kiss me. The truth is, I wanted to kiss him, too—to feel what it's like to kiss someone who has a hoop pierced through his lip and a barbell through his tongue.

He moved a little closer and stared straight into my eyes. "Shayla?" he asked. His lips—that silver hoop—were just inches away from mine. "Do you ever go for guys like me back home?"

The truth is that I don't, but I sure as hell wanted to try. "Guys like *you*?" I decided to play dumb.

"Yeah, you know . . . dark, slightly twisted, not exactly the most popular."

"I go for all types of guys," I say, stretching the truth like bubble gum.

"Good." He was staring at my mouth now.

I closed my eyes, anticipating the kiss. Not two seconds later, I went for it. The hoop was cold and hard against my lip and had a slightly metallic taste.

The barbell made more of an impact. It teased against my tongue, glided across the skin—kind of nice at first, but then it seemed like he was working it too hard, trying to impress me with too much rubbing, which caused a nasty buildup of saliva.

I pulled away and flashed him a smile that told him that I liked it. "I'm really curious," I said, poking my finger through the T-shirt tear. "When you were talking before about your nightmare . . . How were you able to end up loving something that had once given you bad dreams?"

Evidently, I'd found the mood breaker, because his body language changed. He looked away. His jaw tensed. "I just did." He shrugged.

"Yes, but *how*?"

He straightened up on the sofa then, pushed me off him, and got up for more dessert. He gulped down a mouthful of chocolate and let it drool down his chin.

But this time it wasn't funny.

After that, we pretty much took opposite ends of the sofa, not really talking to each other. I was done with the fun and games, and apparently that's all he was willing to offer.

He and I are sitting at the dining room table now, pretending like there isn't a giant elephant in the room. Natalie comes to join us, with her own fleet of elephants in tow—none of which involves Frankie, though they *are* holding hands.

I busted in on her in the bathroom last night—thanks to

her letter opener—and saw some of what she's been trying to keep under wraps: some sections of her hair are shoulder length, while others are barely an inch long. She's also bald in spots—places where she must've pulled the hair out; there was a wad of strands in the sink. If all that wasn't disturbing enough, she was covered in lipstick.

I told her I was sorry and offered to talk, but in that moment she couldn't really speak, and I didn't know who was more shocked—me by what I saw, or her because I was seeing it.

Ivy takes a seat at the table, having prepared a feast. It's kind of annoying how good she looks in the morning, despite having no makeup on and her hair pulled back in an old-lady bun.

"I wish I could cook like this," I tell her.

"Thanks. It's sort of my thing." She seems far more relaxed than I've seen her yet.

"*I* need a thing," I tell her. "Traveling, I guess. You should see all the maps and postcards hanging on the wall in my room upstairs. Seeing them just makes me want to go everywhere."

"I'm surprised that *you've* even seen them," Frankie says. "You haven't exactly spent too much time in your room, have you?" He raises his eyebrow at me.

"What's that supposed to mean?" I ask, knowing what he's insinuating, but I'm not really in the mood for drama. My head aches. I need more sleep. One of the sofa springs dug into my hip last night, and now the muscle's sore. I rub at my temples, relieved that Frankie doesn't say anything else.

"So," Garth says, breaking the beat of silence. He leans across the table to Natalie. "Shayla tells me that your brother's dead."

"Seriously?" I let my fork drop to the plate. I mean, could he have any less tact?

"Is he the person you've been mumbling to?" Garth asks her. "Of course, I have my own theories on the subject."

"You don't know anything about me," she says.

"That's true," Ivy says. "We don't. But that doesn't mean we wouldn't like to get to know you."

"What's up with the mirrors?" Garth asks.

"Catoptrophobia," Parker explains. "A fear of mirrors and/ or one's reflection. It can stem from poor self-image or urban legends associated with the supernatural . . . like the magic mirror in *Snow White*, for example."

"And you know this because . . . ?" Garth asks.

"Because the lead character in the screenplay I'm working on has catoptrophobia. He was traumatized after watching his sister play Bloody Mary at a sleepover. You know, the game where you summon evil spirits to appear in the bathroom mirror."

"So, which camp are you in?" Garth asks, focused on Natalie again. "Poor body image or supernatural sufferer?"

"I just hate my reflection," she says, as if she belongs in another camp altogether.

"Is that why you cover yourself up?" I ask. "Which is completely ridiculous, by the way, because you know you'd be totally gorgeous, right?"

"Have you ever tried to talk to someone about it?" Ivy asks. "A therapist, I mean?"

"I'm the product of therapy, and you can see how well that's worked out," Garth jokes.

"Yeah. Me too," Ivy says.

"Me three." Natalie smirks. "Harris is the only one who understands me."

"Okay, but Harris is *dead*," Garth says.

"Not to me, he isn't. I don't expect any of you to get it, but he talks to me. I hear his voice inside my head."

"The voice of a dead man?" Garth grins.

"*I* believe that stuff," Ivy says. "I think there are people who can communicate with those who've passed on."

"For me, it's only Harris," Natalie says. "And he hadn't spoken to me since the moment I got on the plane to come on this trip, even though I'd been continuing to talk to him. But then, last night, in the bathroom, he whispered a little something."

"A little *what* thing?" Frankie asks. "You make him sound so real."

"He *is* real—*very* real to me."

"I wish I could communicate with the dead," I tell them. "My best friend Dara hung herself, and I have so many unanswered questions."

"What's your biggest question?" Ivy asks.

"If she knows how much I cared about her, I guess."

"Why wouldn't she?" Garth's eyebrow raises.

I shrug, feeling suddenly self-conscious. "Maybe because I wasn't exactly there for her in the way that I could've been. She was pretty much a social outcast at my school. And instead of constantly trying to defend her, sometimes I just played along. I mean, I know it wasn't right, but being with Dara became social suicide for me."

"But real suicide for her," Garth says, stabbing me with the truth.

"Why didn't people like her?" Natalie asks.

"There was no one thing." I shift uneasily in my seat. "She just wasn't into the same stuff that the rest of us were, and that kind of brought down the group."

"Stuff like what?" Ivy asks.

"You know." I shrug again. My face feels hot. "The whole social scene at school—trying to get invited to A-list parties and go to A-list clubs. Dara didn't care about that stuff. She'd even go out of her way to reject it. Like, if I snagged her an invite to a party, she'd arrive underdressed."

"Imagine that," Garth says, poking a finger through the hole in his T-shirt.

"But it's more than that," I say, remembering a wear-red-for-love fund-raiser party when Dara showed up in blue-jean overalls and insinuated that Amanda's family was gluttonous for owning three homes and four cars.

"It's really hard to explain, but she wasn't doing anything to help her situation," I continue, "which was really frustrating to watch. I saw her becoming more and more isolated. And I know I definitely should've done something, because I knew that behavior wasn't *her*. Dara was so much better than all of that. But I distanced myself instead."

"And so now you feel responsible?" Ivy asks.

"Not responsible." I swallow hard. "I just wish I'd have known how unhappy she was. I mean, I knew she was depressed, but I never pegged her as suicidal." I look around for a wall vent, wondering if the air conditioner is on, if anyone thinks it's as humid as I do. "Anyway, it happened a little over two years ago, and I still dream about it—about finding her body and about how alone she must've felt—but, unlike some of you, I didn't go to therapy. I discovered Justin Blake.

During the weeks following Dara's funeral, there were round-the-clock marathons of his films. And, since I wasn't really sleeping much back then, his movies were the perfect distraction to my own horror."

"Cheers to that," Natalie says, raising her coffee mug. "Justin Blake's movies: the very best form of therapy."

We all raise our mugs to toast. A moment later, a cuckoo bird comes out from its birdhouse-clock to alert us to the time, only instead of just making a simple chirping sound, it starts to sing: *"Greetings, Dark House Dreamers, it's almost time for fright. The Nightmare Elf promises to visit you all tonight."*

"Holy crap," Ivy mutters, panic mode returned.

"Only one more hour to go," Garth says, rubbing his palms together.

I want to share his enthusiasm, but suddenly I want to go home.

GARTH

THE HEARSE PULLS UP AT FOUR P.M. SHARP. I couldn't be more stoked. Shayla comes and stands beside me as we pile into the back. I'd rather she kept her distance. I'm really sick of her bullshit, pretending that she's all into me, only to want to get inside my head and excavate something that isn't there.

She ends up sitting between Ivy and Parker. "So, was anybody able to dig up the details on this confidential, *Nightmare Elf*–inspired film project?" she asks.

"It seems to be totally hush-hush," Parker says. "Everything online and in the trades says that Blake's filming in Beijing."

"Hence the confidential-project part," I tell them.

"Even this contest was on the down-low," Frankie says. "I couldn't find it on Blake's Web site, and when I went back to the fan site a week or so after I sent in my essay, the contest post was no longer there."

"Blake's peeps probably took it down, tired of reading all of the entries—over twenty thousand supposedly." I yawn. "Anyway, I'm sure Blake's chartered a private jet to fly him back to Beijing after the filming tonight."

"What are the odds that I'd be able to sneak myself onto that jet?" Shayla giggles.

"I'd say they suck pretty hard-core," I tell her.

She shoots me a dejected look, which honestly warms my heart.

We drive for more than two hours before pulling onto a gravel road, lined on both sides with trees. Parker takes out his video camera, rolls down the window, and starts filming.

"Are you lost?" Frankie shouts to the driver as we get thicker into the forest.

The hearse rocks from side to side as the terrain beneath us gets more unstable. At one point I'm not even sure if the car's width will make it through the trees. Branches scrape and poke the windows and doors.

"You know this is killing your paint job, right?" Frankie calls out to the driver.

Finally we reach a clearing, but the tree boughs overhead block out most of the light. The driver—the same guy who picked me up from the airport—puts the car in park and gets out. At first I think he must be going to check on the damage, but instead he opens the door. "It's a little too narrow to drive," he says. "But we can get there on foot. It's just on the other side of these trees."

"What is?" Parker asks.

"Harris says we shouldn't go," Natalie whispers.

"Your dead brother Harris, right?" I say, intentionally being obnoxious.

We follow the driver down the long narrow roadway. It's several minutes of walking before the entire area in front of us opens up.

It's like something straight out of a dream. WELCOME, DARK HOUSE DREAMERS is lit up in Gothic lettering, hanging above an entrance gate. There's also a Ferris wheel, a merry-go-round, and a ride called Hotel 9; with multiple pointed roofs, it looks like the hotel in the movie.

There's a tall iron gate that surrounds the entire area, keeping it from the public. It's got to be at least thirty feet tall. There's also barbed wire threaded through and around the rungs at the very top. "What the hell is this?" Parker asks.

"It was an old abandoned amusement park, from what I hear," the driver says. "But it's been revived just for you, the Dark House Dreamers."

"Okay, but I didn't sign up for an amusement park," Parker says. "I'm here to see a movie."

"Well, perhaps you should get your ticket." The driver motions to the gate. "But first . . ." He pulls what appears to be a red handkerchief from the inner pocket of his jacket, only when he opens it up and shakes it out, it's actually a red sack, just like the Nightmare Elf's. "Please deposit any cell phones, cameras, or video equipment inside here." He gives Parker a pointed look.

"You can't be serious," Parker says.

"I *am* serious." The driver smiles. "If you want to see the movie, you'll honor Mr. Blake's request to deposit your electronic belongings here." He gives the empty sack a shake.

"And if we don't make a deposit?" Parker persists.

"Then no movie and no Blake," the driver says.

Frankie checks his cell phone for a signal. "Still nothing."

"So, then, it's not like it even matters," Shayla says, checking her cell phone too. "Except I *did* want to get a photo of myself with Blake." She keeps a firm hold on her camera. "It was a birthday present last year," she explains. "Just in time for my two-week sojourn to Prague."

"Rest assured, there will be plenty of photo opportunities later," the driver says. "Now, shall we?"

I place my camera and phone down into the sack. Shayla and the others follow suit.

"Very good," the driver says, tying the bag closed. "Now, without further ado . . ." He pulls something else from his pocket—a remote control—and points it at the front gates. The doors open to the sound of music—the same whacked-out carnival tune that played back at the Dark House.

The merry-go-round begins to revolve. The Nightmare Elf's fat little face goes round and round at the top. I move closer, standing just inside the gate now. There's a roller coaster called Creeper Coaster and a giant tree house called Forest of Fright. A wooden cutout of Eureka from the Nightmare Elf movies—dressed in her peasant blouse and '70s jeans— stands in front of a snack shack, holding a tray full of fried dough and popcorn.

It's way too incredible to be real: the blinking lights, the music, and the images from his films, brought to life, like on a movie set. All of it is hidden—here—in the woods. And to think that it was just forty-eight hours ago that I was hanging out in my parents' basement, filling out applications to work at random gas stations and liquor stores.

"This place is unbelievable," I say. "I mean, if I didn't already think that Justin Blake was a creative genius, this pretty much seals the deal."

A flat-screen TV lights up a few yards in front of us. We move in closer. And that's when we hear it.

Clamp.

Bang.

Bolt.

The park gates close. The driver threads a chain through and around the bars.

"Wait, what are you doing?" Parker asks him.

"Enjoy!" the driver hollers. He gives us a soldier's salute before turning away, heading back down the dirt path.

There's static on the TV screen now; it's followed by a black background that keeps flipping.

And then I see it. On the screen. Justin Blake's face. It has a grainy quality, but it's unmistakably him.

"Hello, Dark House Dreamers," he says.

"Hello," Shayla shouts back, silently clapping her hands.

"I hope you all had a pleasant journey to picturesque

Hundley County," he winks, knowing full well how lame this area is, "and that you're all enjoying the Dark House."

"Definitely," Shayla cheers.

"So, now that you've gotten a slight taste of the weekend, let's see to it that you get a full dose of what you came here for. After all"—he leans in closer to the camera, and his pale blue eyes widen for effect—"you came here to be scared, didn't you?"

"Yeah!" Frankie shouts, pumping his fist.

Natalie stands in front of us all. Her hands are clasped together and she's mumbling to herself, most likely auditioning for a future role.

"Okay," Blake says, but the word actually comes out "o-*kee-ay*." There's so much static interference going on: a crunching sound in the background and an annoying buzz. Add that to the fact that the screen continues to flip, and that there's a perpetual zigzag that cuts through his face, and it's hard to get the full *him*.

"So, let's get down to why you're *really* here, shall we?" he asks. "You want a behind-the-scenes look at my latest project, don't you?"

"Yes!" I shout, clapping my hands. I give Parker and Ivy a sideways glance. They're hanging on Blake's every word, as if we're all going to be tested later.

"You told me your worst nightmares," Blake continues. "That was your ticket into the gate. And let me just say in response to that"—he leans in closer again, his eyes bugging out like a deranged serial killer—"revealing your biggest nightmare probably wasn't the best idea."

Shayla squeals in anticipation.

It's extra grainy on the screen. Blake says a bunch more stuff, but none of us can hear him. The audio's all out of whack. ". . . to face your biggest fears," he continues, but the words aren't in sync with his lips. The speed must be off.

A moment later, the screen goes black.

"What the hell?" I shout.

It fades back a couple of seconds later, but Blake is no longer there. In his place, hidden among shadows, is someone dressed up as the Nightmare Elf; I can just make out his bright red suit and the chubby cheeks on his elf mask.

"The reason you're here is far more paramount than just a behind-the-scenes look at my film," the elf says, in a voice that isn't Blake's. "This park is the set of my new movie. And you are my stars."

"Seriously?" Shayla asks; her inflated ego just got bigger. "We're the actors?"

"The camera's already rolling," the elf says. "So, enjoy the park. Walk around, have a snack, go on all of the Justin Blake movie–themed rides as many times as you like. A word to the wise, however: the Eureka Shrieker is a real killer." He holds the sides of his head.

Ivy looks like she's about to hurl.

"But . . . but . . . but," the elf continues, "before you begin, there's something you need to know. There are rides and challenges tailored for each of you, based on your essay. If you want to make it to the final cut, you—and you alone—will have to face your nightmare by going on that ride. Anyone who enters another Dark House Dreamer's nightmare will be unable to attend the rough-cut showing at the end with the *real* creative genius."

"J.B.," Shayla whispers.

The elf's voice goes grave-serious: "Find your ride and face your fear. Any problems, including if you chicken out, just use the emergency phones. Now, what are you waiting for?" He unleashes a maniacal laugh that impresses even me. The TV screen fades to black.

"Holy freaking shit!" I shout. "I mean, do you seriously get what this means?"

"We're going to be in a movie!" Shayla bursts.

"With no script, directions, or rehearsals?" Parker asks, already trying to poke holes.

"Sort of like the reality-TV version of a major motion

picture," Shayla says. "Has that even been done yet? Or are we breaking some serious new ground here?"

Tears well up in my eyes. An opportunity like this could honestly change everything for me—show everyone who ever doubted me. My dad is going to freak.

While the others point out some of the video cameras positioned around the park, wannabe–Linda-Blair Natalie runs back to the entrance gate. She looks outward, through the bars, wiping an invisible layer of sweat from her brow.

"What's wrong?" Frankie asks her, obviously buying her bogus act.

Instead of answering, Natalie struggles to get the gate to open, pulling at the chain and shaking the lock. "Harris says we're trapped," she shouts.

"And Harris is as dead as last night's dinner," I say, still thinking about those amazing ribs.

"It's hard to be trapped when there are emergency phones," Shayla says. "Plus, I thought he stopped talking to you."

"He's started again. *Remember?*"

"Well, tell him to shut up," I say. "Because we're here to be in a movie. So let's get to it."

Natalie turns away from the gate, and we all move deeper inside the park.

IVY

I'M PROBABLY THE ONLY PERSON HERE WHO ISN'T completely enamored with Justin Blake and/or his work, and yet watching him on the overhead TV screen just now, and listening to whoever it was dressed as the Nightmare Elf say that we need to face our fears . . . it felt like they were talking directly to me.

The others seem excited to be here. Garth smiles for the camera as he poses with a wooden cutout of one of Justin Blake's characters (some girl with a big floppy hat and bell-bottom jeans). Shayla hams it up, squealing and giggling extra loud, as she plays that game where you slam a mallet as hard as you can, trying to get a puck (in this case, the Nightmare Elf) to jump up and ring the bell at the very top. She doesn't manage it on the first couple of tries, but then Frankie takes a crack at it, sending the Nightmare Elf soaring; the elf's head slams against the bell, causing the latter to ring and the elf's tongue to stick out from the impact.

Natalie, on the other hand, has the hood of her jacket up now, even though it's at least eighty degrees. She's repositioned her scarf, too, so that it covers her mouth and chin. A pair of oversize sunglasses conceals her eyes. I gaze up at a video camera, noticing that she's positioned away from it. Being videotaped must bother her—the idea of seeing herself later on film. I don't want to be videotaped either—don't want to risk that my parents' killer might one day recognize me in a movie.

"So, what do you think?" Parker asks, standing at my side.

"I'm not really sure *what* to think. I didn't ask to be in a movie."

"What's wrong? Don't want to be a reality star?"

I wish I could read his mind to know if he's thought about last night, because it's been on my mind all day. He was so incredibly sweet, staying in my room, and then holding me when my anxiety got too big.

"Hey, come check this out!" Shayla says. She's moved

farther into the park, past a merry-go-round with evil-looking horses. There's another ride tucked behind it, but only the back side is visible: a yellow house with a picket fence.

I wonder if it's mine.

"It's the greenroom," Shayla shouts. "Come on!"

Movie screens light up around the park showing films by Justin Blake. I look back at the house, eager to get away from it. I follow the others to where Shayla is. It's a lounge area, set up with patio sofas and chairs. There are food coolers positioned about, as well as a couple of portable refrigerators.

"Seven chairs," I say, nodding toward a dining area, reminded of Taylor's absence.

"Over here," Frankie says, calling us to one of the rides. "Check it out. This ride goes underground." He points out where a tunnel burrows down into the ground and then comes out several yards later.

The rest of the Nightmare Elf's Train of Terror looks fairly normal—like a basic roller coaster—with individual carts that resemble the Santa-like sacks that the Nightmare Elf always carries. The elf's chubby face is positioned in front of the very first cart. His eyes are aglow, the pupils flashing red.

Shayla climbs into the cart at the very front.

"Wait, how do you know you can ride this?" Parker checks out the ride's signage—basically a board that lists rules about staying properly restrained—obviously heeding the Nightmare Elf's message that, in addition to our personalized nightmare rides, we're only allowed to go on rides that are based on Justin Blake's movies.

"This ride is E for everyone," Shayla says, suddenly a park expert. She peeks up at the camera and sticks out her chest. "An equal opportunity thriller." She blows the camera a kiss.

Garth jumps into the cart behind her. "You'll probably want to sit this one out," he says to Natalie. "I don't think Harris would approve."

Instead of taking his remark with its intended sarcasm, Natalie's face falls flat. "You're right," she says. "Harris wants me to find a way out of here." She looks around at the perimeter of the park in a halfhearted search for an exit. When she doesn't immediately see one, she climbs into one of the carts, careful to keep all her layers of shrouding intact.

"Shall we?" Parker asks, motioning to the two train carts behind Frankie's.

I climb inside the first one. Parker steps into the cart behind it. He presses the start button, on a post by the list of rules. Everyone's handlebars drop down, locking us into place.

At the same moment, the Nightmare Elf lets out a childlike giggle. *"Hold on to your chair,"* the elf sings. *"Because I'm ready to scare."*

Shayla, Garth, and Frankie cheer in unison.

I clench the handlebars. A motor starts up somewhere beneath me, under my seat. The train carts begin to coast into a tunnel, before spiraling downward into a deep, dark hole.

"We're going underground!" Shayla shouts.

The Nightmare Elf lets out another laugh. *"Too late to turn back now."*

My stomach drops. I lurch forward, feeling like I'm going to fall out of my seat.

One of us howls. Someone else lets out a scream.

Finally, the carts level out and proceed in a forward direction again. But still there's only darkness. "Parker?" I call out, but I can barely hear my own voice.

The wheels rip across the tracks, screeching over any other sound.

I grip the handlebar tighter. My teeth clench harder. I close my eyes, trying to breathe through my anxiety. I'm stronger than my fears, bigger than this moment. I inhale and then exhale, blowing out my negative thoughts, trying to return to a state of calm.

The wind blows at my face, through my hair. And, for just a second, I almost convince myself that this is actually kind of fun.

But then my cart comes to a sudden halt.

And the screeching noise stops.

There's just the pumping of my heart—so hard and heavy

inside my chest that I can hear it in my ears, can feel it in my veins.

The lights remain out. I can't see a thing—not the person seated in front of me, nor the hand before my face.

Is it over? Are we stuck? Why isn't anyone saying anything?

I can hear the sound of water trickling. A leaking pipe, maybe. I reach forward to touch Frankie, but there's just empty space in front of me. Our carts must've disconnected, or maybe they were never connected to begin with.

"Parker?" I call, hearing the tremor in my voice.

He doesn't answer. Instead, it's another voice that cuts through the darkness: a child's voice, whispering something, but it's far too faint to hear.

"Hello?" I call out.

I strain to hear, able to make out the words *victim* and *doomed*. Should I get out of my cart? Try to find my way out? Is it possible that my cart went off the tracks?

A light clicks on over my head, making me squint. Finally, I can see.

An image of two boys waivers a few yards away. They look freakishly real. Dressed in tuxedos, the boys have slick black hair and stark white faces. Their eyes stare in my direction.

"Hello?" I repeat, but no sound comes out. There's a sharpness inside my chest, making it hard to breathe.

Music begins to play—piano keys tap out the tune to "Three Blind Mice." *"Seven blind mice. Seven blind mice,"* the boys begin to sing. *"See how they run. See how they run. They think they can get away from me, but I have another plan, you see. Fall asleep in the Dark House and you will be, seven dead mice. Seven dead mice."*

They smile at the same time—dark red lips, bright white teeth—and begin walking toward me.

I pull on the handlebar, but it won't budge, trapping me in place. "No!" I shout. My forehead's sweating. My mouth turns dry.

I shimmy my hips, trying to work myself out. The handlebar's pressed into my gut.

Tears slide down my face, over my lips. The taste of salt. The sensation of spinning. I'm going to be sick.

The boys are inches away now, their fingertips within reach. I lean back, reminding myself that they aren't real, that this is supposed to be fun.

Breathe through your anxiety, Dr. Donna would say.

I call up some of her other favorite sayings too—even those that don't quite fit—in an effort to stay grounded:

Remember that sometimes our minds play tricks. Sometimes what we think is real is colored by our imagination.

Allusion is temporary—our brain's way of protecting itself and processing information.

You've been through a lot, Ivy. Post-traumatic stress disorder can do that; it can impair your ability to decipher what's real from what isn't.

The boys reach toward my neck. Tears continue down my cheeks.

"Should've gotten out when you had your chance," they sing. *"Now it's time to do the dead man's dance."* They begin to dance, kicking their feet right and left, their dark eyes staring through me.

Moments later, the engine roars beneath my train cart. I creep forward again, plunging through the hologram.

The cart climbs upward, finally soaring through a loop-de-loop. The tracks screech with every turn. Finally, I can hear the hollers and cheers of the others as I go barreling down another drop.

At the end of the ride.

Outside again.

I'm able to see.

It takes me a second to realize that I'm behind Parker, rather than in front of him. Frankie and Natalie's carts are reversed as well.

"It's about time," Shayla says, shouting back at me. "We've been waiting, like, a kagillion hours for you to come out. Okay, so more like five minutes." She giggles. "We all came out at different times."

I seriously have no words. My breath's gone. I can't speak. It feels like I've been run over by a bus.

"So, what's next?" Garth asks, already looking for the next thrill.

"Hold up," Shayla says, standing up, hands on hips, clearly for the camera. "I mean, was that intense or what? A ride that goes underground? All of a sudden my train cart stopped and music began to play with a little girl's voice singing about burying a body. I recognized the song, but I couldn't remember if it was in *Night Terrors II* or *III*?"

"It was in number three," Frankie says. "The song is called 'Flatline' by Klockwise Krystina."

"It's in the scene with the postal guy at Little Sally's lemonade stand," Garth adds.

"My cart stopped too," Natalie says. "But only for a second, and there were so many sounds: a motor revving, wheels squeaking, the Nightmare Elf's laugh, and that heavy metal music."

"Not to mention your dead brother's voice," Garth says.

"Wait, what heavy metal music?" Parker asks. "All I heard was whispering. How about you?" He turns back to me.

I shake my head, unable to answer. My whole body's sweating and yet I feel completely chilled.

"So, then after that first drop," Shayla continues, "we

must've all gone in different directions, and experienced different things."

While the others seem intrigued by that idea, I'm overwhelmed by it. I mean, if I thought this was hard—separating for just a handful of seconds—how am I possibly going to face the nightmare of my life on my own?

PARKER

AFTER THE TRAIN OF TERROR, WE REMAIN HANG-
ing out by the ride, comparing one another's thrill. Ivy is way
freaked out. Her eyes are red and she's visibly trembling.

"What did you actually see in there?" I ask her.

"Two boys," she says. "Dressed in tuxedos and singing a
twisted version of 'Three Blind Mice.'" She takes a deep breath
and then proceeds to describe a couple of kids that sound all
too familiar.

"Danny and Donnie Decker from *Nightmare Elf II: Carson's
Return*," Garth says, all but drooling. "Did they do the dead
man's dance?"

Ivy bites her lip and gives me a blank stare, leading me to assume that she hasn't seen the movie. I wonder if she's seen any of Blake's films. And, if not, what the hell *is* she doing here?

"Man, I love those Decker boys." Garth smiles. "The scene where they sneak off from their cousin's wedding and get lost in the woods . . ."

"Only to find the Dark House," Shayla adds.

"Their nightmares about being poisoned by aliens were epic," Garth says. "Anyway, sounds like I picked the wrong cart. All I got was a fan blowing at the back of my head and the Nightmare Elf's evil giggle."

"And all *I* got were some dancing shadows and the rattle of Lizzy Greer's shopping cart," Frankie says.

I look toward Natalie, who's fallen silent, and take out my mental camera.

ANGLE ON NATALIE

She's sitting on the ground, picking at the hair on her arm (just about the only skin that's visible). The rest of her is covered in clothes (long dress, high boots, zip-up jacket, scarf, and oversize sunglasses).

NATALIE
(catching me spying on her)
Harris won't stop talking now. He
keeps saying that it isn't safe here—
that we should find a way out.

GARTH
(to Natalie)
Just curious, but do they wear
straitjackets where you live?

Shayla cracks up in response.

FRANKIE
(rubbing his chin)
Hmm . . . I wonder if Dara would
think a comment like that is funny.

Shayla's face drops. Her eyes narrow. The
tension in the air thickens.

SHAYLA
Why would you say something like that?

                    FRANKIE
          Oh, I don't know. Maybe it's because
          you're fake.

                    SHAYLA
          Excuse me?

          She cocks her head, as though genuinely
          confused.

                    SHAYLA (CONT'D)
          How am I fake?

                    FRANKIE
          Are you kidding?
                    (grinning)
          Where do I even begin?

                    SHAYLA
          Give me one example.

                    FRANKIE
          Well, for starters, you claim to feel
          bad about not being there Dara,

and for just playing along when others
made fun of her. And yet it seems
you're just as insensitive now.

                   SHAYLA
Wait, where is all of this coming from?
Did I do something that hurt you?

                   FRANKIE
Forget about me. I mean, *seriously*?
You're so wrapped up in the World
of Shayla that you don't even have a
clue, do you? Think about it. Those
nightmares you have, it's like Dara's
haunting you, trying to subconsciously
get it through your head.

                   SHAYLA
Get *what* through my head? If I hurt
you, I didn't intend to.

                   FRANKIE
Forget it.
          (laughing, tossing his hands up)

I give up.

CUT TO:

While Shayla licks her superficial wounds, and Garth and Frankie saddle up for another ride on the Nightmare Elf's Train of Terror, Ivy and I move to a bench. The temperature's dropped and I can feel her trembling. I wrap my arm around her shoulder, unable to stop thinking about last night.

It was nice spending the night with her. I close my eyes, picturing us lying together in bed, her back pressed against my chest, the scent of chocolate in the air.

"Parker?" she asks, pulling me back to PRESENT DAY: EXT. AMUSEMENT PARK—DUSK.

She nods in the direction of the ride. Garth and Frankie have squished themselves into the fifth train cart—the same one that Ivy had.

"What the hell?" Frankie shouts out, smacking at the start button.

The ride doesn't seem to be working now; nothing's happening. And the lights in the Nightmare Elf's eyes have gone out.

Ivy rests her head against my shoulder and reaches to take my hand. "Thanks for being so sweet to me."

"It's easy being sweet to you."

"It'd probably be easier hanging out with the others—having fun like them."

"I want to be with you," I say, giving her hand a squeeze.

"Good." She smiles. "Because I want to be with you, too." And I have no idea if she means for the next five minutes or the next five years, but I don't even care. Because we're together right now.

NATALIE

"WHAT'S HAPPENING TO US?" HARRIS ASKS. "I FEEL LIKE WE'RE *drifting apart.*"

"You're just angry because I'm not doing what you say. I'm not your puppet, Harris."

At first I thought it was a relief that he was talking to me again. But I have a strong suspicion that most of what Harris has been saying since his silent treatment has been a complete and utter lie, his way of getting back at me for leaving home in the first place. He doesn't normally get nasty like this. It's only happened a handful of times—and only when he's feeling particularly strong about something—that he'll punish me in the few ways he can. If it isn't silence, it's his incessant talking, especially when I'm asleep to intentionally keep me up. But I don't hold it against him. He's stuck on the other side, living in a sort of purgatory. Sometimes I wonder if he isn't waiting for me. Other times I think that if I didn't feel so alone, he'd leave me for good.

I don't expect the others to understand any of this. I know that it sounds crazy. It goes against what we've all been conditioned to believe about death.

I tried to talk about my ability to speak with Harris in one of my sessions with Dr. Gilpin. But she responded by asking if I ever thought about hurting myself, which is basically shrink-speak for, "Do you fantasize about getting up close and personal with a noose and/or razor blade, plastic bag, exhaust pipe, coat hanger, railroad track, fill in the blank with your suicide method of choice."

When I told her no, she prescribed me more pills, which I thought to be ironic considering that pills can also be ammo depending on how many you take in one sitting.

"Body lice?" Garth asks.

It takes me a moment to realize that he's directing the

question at me, because I'm scouring my arms, trying to count up all the remaining hairs. I wish I had a marker with me. I wish he would mind his own business.

Though, I'll have to admit, it was kind of cool at brunch, when we were opening up about stuff, and when I told the group about Harris and my issue with mirrors. Cool . . . except for when Shayla said I'd be gorgeous beneath all my layers. Bullshit. I saw the expression on her face when she busted in on me in the bathroom door and saw my reflection. That was truth enough for me.

"Go to hell," I tell Garth. Unfortunately, the words barely come out in a whisper and he's already turned around. And I've lost count of arm hairs, which Harris finds hysterical.

I've tried to tell my parents that Harris talks to me, that he's been growing up right along with me. Every birthday I have is his birthday, too. Every holiday celebrated, every family dinner, every therapy session and test I take at school.

He's there. He doesn't leave me. It's as if his soul is alive inside of me.

Even his love of guitar. The first time I went to a concert— really an arts festival in town, where various bands came to perform—we heard this guy play an acoustic guitar. Harris got completely swept up in the beauty of it all—the notes, the rhythm, the emotion strumming from every chord. Shortly after, I asked my parents to get me an acoustic guitar. I took lessons for Harris. Kept the guitar tuned for Harris. Polished the cedarwood. Switched over to an electric when he asked. Practiced all my chords, memorized every song.

For Harris.

You'd think my parents would want to know that when our tiny bodies left the womb barely a minute apart—one of us crying and the other without breath—that we were still connected in spirit. But they won't hear any of it.

Talking to them about Harris only scores me more sessions with more therapists, more people trying to fix me.

I know it breaks Harris's heart. I know he'd do anything to be able to communicate with our parents using me as the go-between. Maybe then he'd be able to pass on. Maybe then his voice would fade.

The weird part? He doesn't normally tell me things I don't already know. Like, he'll give me his opinions, but because he never leaves me, he never reports news to me—until coming to this amusement park, that is. Ever since we got here, it's been one report after another from him about stuff he couldn't possibly know.

"I'm telling you the truth," Harris says. *"It isn't safe for you there."*

"I think you just want to ruin my time," I tell him. "You're angry, and you don't know any other way to express that anger."

"Sounds like someone's been spending too much time with shrinks."

"This ride is crap," Frankie shouts, still trying to get the Train of Terror to work.

I get up and move to stand in front of Ivy, angled away from the video camera. I hate that we're being filmed. When the Nightmare Elf dropped that bomb, I had to hold myself back from throwing up. But then I took a deep breath, pulled out a couple of hair strands, counted up all the water bottles behind the snack shack—thirty-three, plus twelve candy apples, sixteen bags of popcorn, forty boxes of Jujyfruits— and reminded myself that I still have choices.

I can choose not to watch the film.

It doesn't have to ruin my experience here.

It's obvious that Ivy's ride on the terror train was far more terrifying than any of ours, and that it's affected her in a major way. I can't help feeling jealous of that. What I wouldn't give to get distracted by fear, to have it sneak up and give me a rush.

"Hey, Natalie," she says, looking up at me. Her brown eyes focus in and she cocks her head to the side. For just a moment I wonder if she can see straight through me all the way to Harris's soul.

"It's all going to work out fine," I tell her, recycling a phrase that's been used on me time and time again. I know the response doesn't fit, and I know the words are shit, but it's all I can think of at the moment.

Her eyes narrow; she looks confused. "Okay, but didn't you just say that we needed to get out of here?"

"Harris said that, not me," I say, correcting her. "And I think he might've been lying. When he first says stuff to me, it sounds pretty convincing inside my head, but then, after I think about it, I have to question his intentions. Like, is he really being honest? Or just trying to ruin my experience?"

Ivy's face scrunches, confused, and I'm not at all surprised. I sound like a flake, like my word can't at all be trusted, when in fact it's Harris's word that's up for debate.

"Let's keep moving," Frankie says, standing just behind us now. There's a determined look on his face. "Time's ticking and I want to go find my nightmare ride. I didn't come all this way not to meet Blake."

"I'll second that," Garth says.

"And I'll third it," Shayla agrees.

Surprisingly, Ivy follows along, and so does Parker. I fall in line too, shrouding my face as I move past the cameras, once again trying to block out Harris's voice, despite how empty I feel in his silence.

FRANKIE

WE MOVE THROUGH THE AMUSEMENT PARK, PAST all sorts of games of chance. Lights flash. Bells ring. Metal music blares.

"Step right up," a deep voice calls out. It's coming from a mannequin: Sebastian Slayer from *Forest of Fright*, dressed in his overalls and work boots, with a pickax slung over his shoulder. He stands in front of a bowling game with his famous toothy grin. "Hit the pin and win, win, win. Easy as squeezy. I love bein' cheesy."

"I love being cheesy too," Garth says, giving the mannequin a thumbs-up.

"The voice is probably motion activated," Parker says.

I'd have to agree. As soon as Shayla goes to give the mannequin a high five, we hear Sebastian's snort of a laugh, making all of us laugh too.

Garth steps up to try a game called Dead Ringer, based on a game that I've seen at practically every carnival I've ever been to. Except, instead of trying to toss a plastic ring around a glass bottle, you need to throw a miniature noose around the neck of a Barbie doll.

There's got to be at least two hundred Barbies lined up: Biker Barbie, Studious Brunette, Zombie Barbie, Princess Barbie-with-a-unicorn-on-her-head . . .

Ivy, Natalie, and Parker try the game out too, all of them grabbing nooses and tossing them into the sea of Barbie hell. Shayla, on the other hand, retreats back, her face all pouty like someone just died. Still, she makes sure to angle herself at the camera so the world can see just how tormented she is.

"My money's on Hula Girl," Garth says, trying to hook the Barbie that's wearing the floral lei and grass skirt. He doesn't succeed on the first try, nor does he succeed on the fifth, but that doesn't stop him from snagging himself a plastic sword from behind the counter as his prize.

We keep exploring, stopping for a few rounds of Forest of Fright Skee-Ball (the faces of the Targo triplets are on all of the balls), and a game of Nightmare Elf on the Shelf, where you have to knock Nightmare Elf dolls off a fireplace mantel, using Christmas stockings filled with sand.

"Step right up," Slayer says. "Hit the pin and win, win, win. Easy as squeezy. I love bein' cheesy."

"I really want to get to my ride," I say.

Shayla quickens her pace to catch up to me. "You're so brave," she tells me, trying to suck up, as if I didn't just tell her off. "I'm such a wimp when it comes to face-to-face stuff—stuff outside the safety of a movie or TV screen, I mean. And, let's face it, that's, like, the *worst* possible quality for someone who's supposed to face her biggest nightmare, right? You totally should've seen me at *La Bocca della Verità*."

"Bocci dell *what*?" I ask.

"*La Bocca della Verità*," she says again, carefully enunciating every syllable. "You know, the Mouth of Truth." She looks at me with a concerned expression, like I'm supposed to have a clue or give a shit. "You put your arm in the mouth—the sculpture of a mouth, that is—and it bites off the hands of liars. It's in Rome," she says, still trying to jog my memory, like I've ever been out of the country. "In the church of Santa Maria."

"I'll take your word for it," I say. She's so people-dumb it's scary.

Finally, we reach the back end of the park. I look up at the gate; it's at least thirty or forty feet high. There are three video cameras pointed down at us from the network of barbed wire. While Natalie turns away from them, Garth steps right out in front.

"Who'll give me fifty bucks to flash?" he asks.

"How about fifty cents?" I offer.

"This ass has star potential." Garth undoes his pants, letting them fall to his ankles; evidently it was never a question of money. He pulls down his boxers, bends over, and shakes his hairy ass.

"Eww!" Ivy shouts.

Shayla, on the other hand, thinks it's the funniest thing ever. "Should I flash too?" she asks.

"Definitely," Garth says, drawing up his pants.

But she hops away, the tease that she is, and leads us farther into the park.

We stop to go on the Eureka Shrieker, which is sort of like the Round Up, only faster, with Eureka's screaming voice in the background, shrieking over the sound of a chain saw.

"That was crazy," Ivy says, coming out of the ride, her hand clenched over her heart. But I also catch a glimpse of a smile, so I think she kind of enjoyed it.

Meanwhile, Natalie's got a huge grin on her face, no longer

talking to herself or picking at her arm hair. And Parker's explaining to Ivy who Pudgy the Clown is (basically that Pudgy's the product of Eureka Dash's nightmares).

"And Eureka Dash?" Ivy asks.

Seriously, is this chick for real?

Shayla continues to lead the way, already onto the next ride. From the outside, Hotel 9 appears to be a haunted house. A sign at the entrance asks, ARE YOU READY TO CHECK OUT?, which is basically Blake-speak for "Are you ready to die?"

We enter through a cobweb-laden door, only to discover that it isn't a haunted house at all. A giant open area has been decorated to look like the lobby of Hotel 9, in all its Gothic glory: red couches, dark walls, gold accents, and fancy mahogany furniture.

"Sweet!" Garth says.

My sentiments exactly. There are seven chair swings that hang suspended from the ceiling. We each take a seat, and the swings spin in a circle as we fly around the room.

Shayla, Garth, and Natalie extend their arms outward, making like they're birds or planes. Clips from *Hotel 9* begin to play all around us—guests screaming, dishes breaking, the chandelier crashing down in the center of the lobby as Sidney Scarcella cuts the chain with a machete.

It's absolutely epic.

"Someone looks a little green," I say, noticing Garth's sour expression as we exit the ride.

"Well if I need to barf, I'll be sure to do it on your face," he says. "Not that anyone would notice."

"That's actually pretty funny," I tell him, way too pumped to get pissed.

We pass by a fun house and then stop in front of a ride called the Wild Thing. There's a huge stuffed grizzly standing in front of it—the kind you see at lodges in the middle of nowhere.

"The bear," Garth says, lighting up like a Christmas tree. "Care to claim your pain, *now*?" He looks at Ivy.

"It isn't mine," she says.

"Ho hum, it must be Taylor's." He sighs.

The bear towers over me by at least three feet. Its mouth is wide open, exposing sharp yellow teeth and a thick gray tongue. With its arms raised, it's mid-growl, as if ready to pounce.

I reach out to touch its fur and it lets out a loud, hungry roar.

"Holy shit!" I yell, jumping back.

Ivy yells out too. But the others laugh, including Natalie, who also lets out a Sebastian Slayer–worthy snort.

I look beyond the bear, at the ride. There's a tent set up,

as well as a campfire, and some lawn chairs. Behind the tent, there's a network of trees and brush, like a forest. A trail cuts through it, reminding me of the path we took behind the Dark House, when we went to look for Midge.

Garth pokes his toy sword into the grizzly's gigantic stomach. The bear lets out another roar, but Garth doesn't so much as flinch.

"Let's keep moving," Parker says.

"Not before we do the *Wild Thing*." Garth starts singing, swaying his hips, and flailing his arms. He looks like he's having a seizure.

"Ride your own wild thing," I tell him. "This one isn't yours."

"Well, aren't you a fun poker," he says, pointing the tip of the sword into my bicep—again, and again, and again. I'm tempted to tear it out of his hands, but I clench my teeth and turn away, refusing to let him get to me. We move past the Wild Thing ride and make a sharp turn. Finally, I see my nightmare. I'd recognize it anywhere.

Graveyard Dig is set back from the other rides, beyond an iron gate. There are headstones lined up in rows. Some look ancient, tilted to one side or leaning slightly backward. Others are in the shape of a cross.

There's a king-size bed in the middle of the cemetery. There's also a dresser, a night table, and a closet. It's supposed to be my parents' room.

"Is this your ride?" Shayla asks.

I nod, feeling the color drain from my face.

"Batter up," Garth says. He's absolutely loving this.

Admittedly, I'm dreading it. Standing just outside the gate, I spot a rusty mailbox beside the lock. I open the lid. The action sets off a voice—one that's slow and deep, and laced with static and clicking: "Welcome, Mr. Rice. Are you ready to dig?"

Chills ripple down my back.

Garth scoots down to check out the box, pressing his ear against the side.

"Mr. Rice?" the voice asks. "Are you ready to dig?"

"You bet," I say, trying my best to sound brave.

"Use the key inside this mailbox to unlock the gate and your closet door," the voice continues. "Take the flashlight, too. You'll need it."

"Are you okay to do this?" Shayla asks me.

I reach inside the mailbox for the key and the flashlight. "Sure," I say, looking out at the graveyard and thinking of that day, thirteen years ago, when I saw my uncle buried. I click on the flashlight, my fingers jittery.

"Good luck," Parker says.

I unlock the gate and close it up behind me. It locks automatically with a deep *clink*.

Shayla stares at me through the bars. "It'll be over before you know it." She gives me a thumbs-up and flashes me a silly smile, still trying to get back on my good side.

"Just do me a favor," I tell her. "If I don't come out in fifteen minutes, come and get me, okay?"

"What are you talking about? Of course, you'll come out."

"Just promise me," I say, remembering how I passed out at Uncle Pete's burial. If I passed out inside this ride, who knows when I'd come to.

"I promise." She smiles, beaming like it's her birthday.

I turn away so she won't see my lip twitch any more than she already has, and then I head straight toward the closet.

Spotlights shine over the cemetery, highlighting some writing on the bed. A line's been spray-painted down the center of the mattress. On one side of it, it reads, *Mommy?*

"You're doing great," Shayla says.

I trip over something. A rock slab. I swipe the fog from in front of my eyes, but more fog fills the space. I navigate my way through it, using the flashlight to show the way. Finally, I find the closet door. It's surprisingly heavy, and I have to use both hands to unlock and open it.

I step inside. The door swings shut behind me. If I thought it was dark before, it's nothing compared to now. I try the knob; it's locked. I shine my flashlight around the perimeter of the space. The room is about the size of a small bathroom—much bigger than my parents' actual closet—but the floor is covered in carpet, just like the real deal.

In the corner, on the floor, sitting beside a shovel, a phone rings. I pick up the receiver, noticing an extra-long coil cord; it drags against the carpet. "Hello?"

"Good evening, Frankie." A male voice.

"Who is this?" I wait a couple of seconds before trying the knob again. It twists left and right, but I can't get the door to open.

I move over to the phone base and push the lever to hang up, trying to get a dial tone. The phone is dead.

I point my flashlight at the wire; the beam shakes with the tremble of my hand. The wire's stuck in a wall crack. I give the wire a tug, only to find that the end's been severed. This isn't an actual working phone. There's no real outlet. Nothing's plugged in.

The phone rings again. Four rings, five.

I pick it up, able to hear breathing—and suddenly I feel stupid. I mean, why am I bothering with the phone? And yet, I know his voice came from the receiver. I look at the earpiece.

At the same moment, I hear laughter—it's coming from the receiver again, only this time it sounds farther away.

I hurl the phone at the wall, unable to think straight. The phone smashes. I position the flashlight on the ground, angled in my direction so that I can see. And then I grab the shovel, determined to bust the door open. I wedge the blade into the door crack, beside the knob. The wood makes a creaking sound, but everything remains intact. I try again, jamming the blade deeper, but still nothing gives.

After several more attempts at trying to break the lock, I toss the shovel to the ground. My flashlight beam shines over the blade.

And that's when it hits me.

I look down at the rug, remembering how, in my nightmare, I raked my fingers over the carpet, thinking that it was my uncle's plot site, convinced that there was a phone ringing inside his casket . . . my mother calling at last.

On hands and knees, I scour the rug in search of a seam, feeling my fingertips burn from the friction. At last, I find a spot where the rug's been cut. I peel away a corner section. Beneath it, there's a two-feet-by-two-feet wooden panel on the floor with a shallow metal handle. I pull up on the handle, feeling a surge of excitement.

A ladder leads underground. I grab the shovel and flashlight and begin climbing down, my adrenaline peaked. It's dark at the bottom, but there are spotlights placed about, helping me to see.

I'm in a giant underground room, dug out of the dirt—like an abandoned mine. There's a wooden frame with strapping overhead and along the walls, holding the space together, so it doesn't come caving in.

There are headstones lined up in rows with a single red rose placed at each site. Tarantula-shaped trees border the graveyard, just as I described in my essay.

I look beyond everything, trying to assess how extensive the space is—if there might be a network of underground tunnels. But the lighting only goes to the edge of the cemetery. Beyond that is total darkness.

A blue teddy bear with no mouth and only one eye—just like the one I had when I was five—sits propped against a headstone. I grab it and make my way toward the back row, where there's a gaping hole in the ground.

There are two headstones behind the hole—the only ones without roses. One of them reads PETER RICE, my uncle's name. The other stone has a skull etched into the surface. There's writing beneath the skull, only it's too small to see from this angle. I move closer and scoot down, able to see: FRANKIE RICE engraved in the granite. Below my name is my date of birth—followed by today's date.

The sight of it freaks me out.

I look down into the hole. It's at least five feet deep and eight feet long and wide. A phone rings, again. It's coming from inside the hole—buried beneath the dirt. I point my flashlight, but I can't see a phone. I crawl forward on my hands and knees, trying to get a better look. Nothing. It must be buried pretty well.

Still holding the shovel, I slide down into the hole, ignoring the tiny voice inside me that says it's going to be a bitch to climb back out. The dirt is dry and powdery around me. It crumbles like a landslide, creating a pile at the bottom.

Still focused on the ringing, I aim the blade of the shovel into the dirt, knowing what I have to do. It feels good to dig—like in some weird-fantastical-surreal sort of way, I've been given a second chance to answer the call I missed thirteen years ago, when I couldn't wake up from my nightmare. What awaits me on the other end of that line?

My forehead is sweating. The muscles in my shoulders ache as I get deeper into the hole, on one hand driven by the ringing, on the other hand maddened by it. It's getting louder with each shovelful of dirt. I dig faster, sweat dripping from my forehead. About eight feet deep now, a dusting of dirt gets into my eyes. I drop the shovel to wipe my face.

At the same instant, I hear it. A clamoring sound: metal hitting something hard. My eyes stinging with dirt, I grab the shovel and continue to dig, finally finding the source.

A dark mahogany casket. The phone must be inside it. With trembling fingers, I dust it off and open it up. The hinges whine.

There's the phone.

There's Uncle Pete: a skeleton lying on a bed of creamy satin, dressed in a navy blue suit and a red tie. There's a watch around the skeleton's wrist. The strap is braided like his actual one. I slip the watch off and turn it over in my hand, feeling its weight. The back is blank, unlike my uncle's, which was engraved. The difference is reassuring, but still I feel like I'm going to be sick.

The phone rings and rings. It's tucked beneath Uncle Pete's arm. I pick it up and click on the receiver. "Hello?" I answer.

"Did you find your teddy bear?" a woman's voice asks.

"I did," I say, looking around for it.

"You'll always be my special boy," she says. "Frankie and Mom. Mom and Frankie."

Mom. The word has become somewhat foreign to me over the years. It feels weird to hear it directed at me now.

"Why did you leave?" I ask, unable to help myself.

There's silence for a moment as I wait for her response.

"Did you find your teddy bear?" she asks again.

I search around some more, inside the hole. No bear. "I must've left it above . . . outside, I mean. Should I get it?"

"You'll always be my special boy. Frankie and Mom. Mom and Frankie."

The receiver still gripped in my hand, I scurry to climb upward, out of the hole, to get to the bear. The dirt is powdery and light. The walls break apart beneath my grip and I fall to my feet.

I jump up, using the pile of dirt as leverage.

My fingers graze the top of the hole. Still holding the phone, I try to struggle up farther, but then something in my shoulder pops. A throbbing ache. My bicep quivers. I slide down again.

I get up and plunge my foot into the wall, but I can't get a good foundation. My foot falls away as the dirt slides down.

"Help!" I shout. The phone slips from my grip. I scramble to pick it up. A dial tone plays.

My one-eyed bear comes flying into the hole, landing on Uncle Pete. I can see a network of wiring above, just beneath the wood-strapped ceiling. A spotlight shines over it all, giving me a view of a pulley system. A giant bucket inches across it. Someone must be up there.

"Hello?" I call out.

The bucket wobbles from side to side and then turns over completely. Dirt comes raining down—on top of my head, surrounding my body. I try to wade through it as I struggle to get back on the wall, to work my way to the top. But the pulley continues to crank forward and soon another bucket appears. Fresh dirt comes pouring in, knocking me down against the coffin. I fall to my knees.

"Wait!" I shout. "I need help. Someone get me out of here!"

The skeleton's covered now. Dirt gets in my mouth, my eyes, my nostrils, my ears. The dial tone turns into an off-the-hook buzz, and then it becomes muffled by dirt as more of it comes piling in.

I crawl out from a heap. For just a moment, I think I've got a solid grip on the wall, only to realize that it's the floor. I'm turned around, upside down, unable to see, completely in a panic.

Just then, I hear someone running. I can't tell where it's coming from—if it's above or below me.

More dirt comes, weighing me down. Lying on my stomach, I struggle to turn over. But it's like a giant pig pile with me at the bottom. I can't move. I can hardly breathe. *Please,* I pray inside my head.

I don't want to open my mouth. It's already full of dirt. I try to move my leg, but there's too much weight on top of my limbs. And still I feel more dirt coming down. *Please,* I pray some more, but I'm not sure if anyone's listening.

The last thing I hear is the muffled laughter of the Nightmare Elf.

Giggle.

Giggle.

Giggle.

SHAYLA

I COULD TELL THAT FRANKIE WAS ANXIOUS. HIS LIP started twitching and his face lost all color. I'm feeling anxious too. I haven't been to a cemetery since Dara died, and Frankie's Graveyard Dig is bringing me back to that day.

I remember how people kept coming up to me: Dara's parents, her relatives, teachers, mutual friends, those I didn't know, faces I'd never seen before. They offered tissues, a place to sit, shoulders to cry on, someone to talk to.

"You were her one and only true friend. Please, Shayla-honey, you have my number; feel free to use it."

"You must be devastated to have lost such a close friend. You two were like inseparable sisters."

"Please, Shay-Shay, if you need anything, don't hesitate to ask."

Their kindness was too much to bear, but I didn't deserve any of it, and I wanted to feel all of it—all the pain, every bit of the heartache.

What Frankie doesn't know is that I *am* affected by her death. And that I *do* feel bad about the way things played out. My nightmares don't need to tell me anything, because deep down I already know. Deep down I've always known. I wasn't a true friend, but that didn't mean she had to die. And it doesn't make me responsible for her death. As guilty as I sometimes feel.

I could see Dara slipping deeper into depression, spending more of her time alone. I thought that maybe I could be friends with her in secret, when nobody else was around. But then Dara's parents announced that they were getting a divorce and she needed me full-time. Even though my heart told me otherwise, I wouldn't make myself available to her, except for when it was socially safe. Obviously no one at Dara's funeral had been aware of any of that, otherwise they wouldn't have bothered with me.

The fog in the graveyard is thick, making it impossible to

keep track of Frankie. "I promise," I call out again, hoping that he hears me.

I'd made a promise to Dara, too. Just before she transferred to my school, over hot fudge sundaes with candy canes sticking out, we made a whipped-cream-with-maraschino-cherries vow to always be there for each other, no matter what.

Parker peers through the bars. "Frankie, how's it going?" He squints hard, trying to see through the clouds of fog.

But Frankie doesn't answer. There's a deep *thwack* sound, like something heavy hitting against a slab of wood.

"He must be inside that shed," Ivy says.

I look around at the headstones, wondering what this ride could possibly be—maybe a mind challenge of some sort or an underground haunted house. I pull up on the lid of the mailbox, half expecting a voice to say something, but it remains silent.

Ten minutes later and I'm feeling completely restless. Natalie and Garth appear to be restless too. While she paces back and forth, Garth won't stop squawking about his growling stomach.

"I gotta eat," he says, finally heading off to find food.

I walk around the perimeter of the gate to where Ivy and Parker now stand, on the other side of the ride. The back of the shed is in full view. "Frankie?" I call.

A moment later, there's a ringing sound, like someone's phone. It's followed by music from *The Wizard of Oz*. "Ding dong! The witch is dead!" Only the music isn't coming from the graveyard.

I turn to look out into the park. Garth is at the nearby snack shack. Amusement park rides continue to bing, blink, and blare—only none of the sounds seems to match the *Wizard of Oz* tune.

"Where's it coming from?" Parker asks.

Ivy takes her bag from around her shoulder and holds it up to her ear. "Here." She squats down, dumping the entire contents of her purse onto the ground. But still there's nothing to explain the sound.

She fishes inside an interior pocket, finally finding the source. A cell phone. With a leopard-print cover.

"It's Taylor's," Ivy says. "I forgot that I shoved it in here."

"Well, answer it." I squat down beside her.

Ivy clicks the phone on. "Hello?" she says, switching over to speakerphone mode.

"Who is this?" a female voice asks.

"Ivy. I mean, that's my name . . . Ivy . . . Jensen." Ivy makes a face, realizing that she's not exactly killing it on this call.

I hold out my hand, silently offering to take the phone from her.

But then: "How did you end up with my cell phone, Ivy?" the girl asks.

"Taylor?" Ivy's eyes widen with alarm.

"Yes."

"You left it," Ivy says; her hand begins to tremble. "When you went for a walk . . . you left it behind, in our room. I'm your roommate for the weekend—at least, I was supposed to be."

"Except I didn't go for a walk, Ivy. Please tell me that you aren't at the Dark House right now."

"I'm not," Ivy says, locking eyes with me. "We're at an amusement park."

A couple of seconds later, Garth approaches, holding a piece of fried dough. He takes a giant bite. "Shit, this crap is cold," he says, spitting it out for the camera's sake.

I shush him, nodding to the phone, and Parker pulls him out of earshot. Meanwhile, Ivy is on the verge of panic. Her chin quivers. There are hives all over her neck.

"Who brought you to the amusement park?" Taylor asks. "Is it part of the contest? Are you alone or are others with you?"

"Where are *you*?" Ivy asks. Her phone-holding hand continues to shake.

"If the park is part of the contest," Taylor says, "then you're in serious danger."

"Wait, *what*?" Ivy's face goes flush. Her breath starts to quicken. Her eyes widen and her face is flushed. She looks like she's going to faint.

I grab the phone from her.

"Listen to me," Taylor continues. "Get out—*now*. If it isn't already too late. Didn't you get my message?"

I click off the speakerphone option and stand up. "What message? The one in the closet or—"

Before I can get the latter question out, Taylor is already talking. But there's another voice too. Maybe there's a crossed line, or maybe Taylor isn't alone. There's static on the phone, making it hard to hear.

I move away, searching for the hotspot, blocking my free ear.

"Do whatever you can," she tells me.

"Whatever I can to *what*?" I attempt to ask, but only part of the question goes through. The call is dropped.

"Crap!" I shout.

I start to look up the recent calls when I hear a banging sound come from the graveyard. "Frankie," I say, my voice barely audible. I look at my watch. It's been twenty minutes now and he still isn't out.

And I've broken yet another promise.

GARTH

FRANKIE'S BEEN INSIDE HIS NIGHTMARE RIDE FOR a while, which tells me that it must be pretty decent. Meanwhile, everybody's freaking out, including Parker, who tries to explain why I should give a shit that Taylor called her own cell phone.

"Seriously?" I ask him. "The only thing I give a shit about where Taylor's concerned is the fact that Ivy broke the rules by smuggling Taylor's cell phone in here. We better not be penalized for it." I look out at the park. It's dark out now and the glowing lights are mesmerizing.

"I think it's high time we go look for one of those emergency phones," Ivy says.

"Except there are no emergency phones." Natalie blocks her ears, as if she's concentrating on what's being said inside that screwy head of hers. The girl is such a fake. "Harris says that the Nightmare Elf was lying about the phones."

"I'll go check things out." Parker heads out into the park, donning his invisible bright red cape and superhero onesie.

"Now what?" Shayla looks down at Taylor's cell phone, clenched in her hand.

"Now we check out the goods. Any compromising photos loaded on there?" I ask.

She glares at me, like I'm the biggest asshole ever, which comes as a major relief. I'd rather she think of me as an asshole than as someone who's all about his feelings.

"Ever think that maybe the phone's been rigged," I suggest. "By the mastermind himself. My money's on Taylor's nonexistence. I'll bet she's not even real—just a bogus hoax to get us all worked up."

"But I met her," Natalie says. "We were on the same flight. We rode in the same car. She talked to me."

"Sure, Scarecrow. Just like your dead brother talks to you too. Nice look, by the way," I say, referring to her hood, scarf, and sunglasses. "Do you really think this crazy act of yours is going to score you more attention from Blake?"

"I'm not looking for extra attention," she says. "If I could, I'd hide from everyone."

"Well, I really wish you would," I tell her.

"Back off," Ivy says, shooting me a dirty look. Happily, I've made another fan.

"Don't be surprised if the phone miraculously starts working again," I say. "If so-called Taylor happens to call us back at some opportune time. Remember in *Nightmare Elf IV* when Eureka's walkie-talkie only seemed to work when she was alone? It was all so plotted."

"Oh, and PS," Shayla says. "Frankie still isn't out yet, and it's been thirty minutes since he entered the graveyard."

"Which means that Blake didn't cheap out on the rides," I say. "Frankie must be getting his money's worth, so to speak."

Shayla shakes her head at me—the same way my father does when he's looking at me like I'm dirt, which is pretty much a daily occurrence.

"If you wanted *Mary Poppins*, then you picked the wrong contest," I tell them. "You came here to be scared, remember? You do something stupid—like using the emergency phone to bring the hearse back—and you risk ruining this whole thing."

"I think I'll take my chances," Ivy says.

While she and Shayla head off to the supposed hotspot, and Natalie takes a seat on the ground, engaged in a full-on conversation with herself, I look back at the graveyard, jealous that Frankie gets all the fun.

IVY JENSEN

SHAYLA AND I SIT ON THE GROUND, TRYING TO GET Taylor's phone to work.

"There's still no reception," Shayla says, "which is totally BS. I mean, you were right here when it rang." She holds the phone up to see if that might help, and then removes the battery and snaps it back into place two seconds later. "The phone itself is working fine."

"Well, maybe Garth was right. Maybe the phone's been rigged."

"The last call received was from the nine-five-two area code," she says, looking at the phone screen.

"Is that near here?" I ask.

"Do I look like a walking Google search box? Maybe there's some clue in her pics."

I gaze over Shayla's shoulder as she searches Taylor's photo album. The same girl keeps appearing in each of the pictures, and so I assume that it's her. Taylor is really cute, with tousled blond hair like she just came from the beach, bright blue eyes, and delicate features. There are photos of her performing in plays, making goofy faces at the camera, and dancing at various recitals.

"I have to assume that she saw something at the Dark House," I say, "something that really freaked her out, because she left so abruptly, mid-unpacking, not even with her cell phone."

"So, you don't *really* think the phone's been rigged."

"All I know is that I wasn't even going to bring the cell phone with me," I tell her. "I'd slipped it into my bag, thinking that we might meet up with Taylor at some point. But the organizers didn't know that—that I'd bring it with me, that is; that I'd forget it was in my bag when we were depositing all our cell phones at the gate. They didn't even know that I'd find the phone to begin with—that I'd just happen to lie back on Taylor's bed and brush my hand against the covers in the right way. Don't you think that if they'd wanted us to find her phone, it would've been planted in a more obvious way?"

Shayla looks at her watch. "It's been forty minutes for Frankie." She tosses me the phone and then moves back over to the gate. "One of us needs to go in there," she says.

"'Not I,' said the fly," Garth says, between bites of sourdough pretzel.

"I don't want to go either," Natalie says, pausing from mumbling to herself.

"Then I'll go," Shayla says. "Somebody give me a lift."

"And what about the movie?" Garth asks her. "Or meeting Justin Blake?"

"I know." She nods. "But I promised Frankie that after fifteen minutes if he still hadn't come out, I'd go looking for him."

"Looks like you're twenty-five minutes late. So, why not make it an hour?" Garth laughs.

For once, Shayla doesn't laugh along with him. "I need to go in there," she insists.

"For all we know, Frankie's ride is already over," Garth says. "If he went underground, the exit could be anywhere—at any part of the park."

I look out at the park. A movie plays in the distance. A guy wearing a clown mask appears on the screen. He's got a girl cornered. It's nighttime and raining out. The girl melts down against a wall, begging him not to hurt her. But he sticks his knife in anyway. Her eyes bug open in shock, and then go completely vacant as her body falls limp.

Is that how my parents looked too?

"You're totally blowing it," Garth says, talking to Shayla's back.

Standing on two milk crates, she's climbed the graveyard gate and has her foot propped up on the top rung. She teeters there, trying to keep her balance.

"Are you sure you want to do this?" I ask her.

"More than sure." She jumps over. Her feet hit the ground with a thud, releasing a dusting of dirt into the air. She heads straight for the shed.

"That's it," Garth declares. "I'm done."

"With what?" I ask.

"With all of you, wasting our time, breaking the rules, and screwing everything up."

The fog machine has kicked into gear, shrouding Shayla's torso and feet, making her appear even farther away. "It's just hard to know what to believe," I tell him. "What's real versus what's screwing with our minds."

"That's the beauty of Justin Blake's work. And this is the

chance of a lifetime. I don't know about any of you, but opportunities like this don't normally happen in my world. In *my* world, all anyone ever expects is failure. But Justin Blake sees more to me than that, so I'm not going to disappoint him."

I bite my lip, able to hear the angst in his voice. I can tell he really wants this. But what I want is to go home. I look back out at Shayla. She's standing just outside the shed, but I can barely even see her.

"Harris says it's too late for her," Natalie mutters, peeking through the bars. "He says it doesn't even matter if she turns back now, because she already broke the rules."

"And what does he think that means?" I ask, still on the fence about her sanity.

"Twenty-six," she says, confidence in her voice. "Twelve rectangles, four ovals, seven crosses, and three squares."

"Excuse me?" I ask her.

Tears drip from the corners of her eyes, mixing with her thick black liner and making track marks down her cheeks. "Harris says there will soon be twenty-eight. And then thirty. And probably more. And probably more rectangles. All of them with roses. Except for two that have been freshly dug out."

"Okay, you're not making any sense."

"*No!*" she shouts, but she isn't talking to me. She covers

over her ears, as if lost inside her head. "That isn't true," she continues. "Don't say those things; it's all just lies."

"This whole Harris act is getting old." Garth yawns. "And so is all the bullshit drama. I'm out of here."

"Where are you going?" I ask.

The graveyard looks eerily vacant now. The fog machine has stopped again. A few residual clouds hover around the bed and dresser, but there's no sign of Frankie or Shayla. And Parker still isn't back yet.

"You're a smart girl. You can figure it out." And with that, Garth turns on his heel, leaving us in the dust.

PARKER

FADE IN:

EXT. AMUSEMENT PARK—NIGHT

ANGLE ON ME

I pass by a row of carnival games. It's
dark. The park looks nearly vacant. The
blinking game lights, coupled with their
binging-ringing sound effects, permeate

the stillness. I'm about halfway around
the entrance gate and still haven't been
able to find a phone, which is really sort
of ridiculous considering that they've
supposedly been placed for emergency
purposes.

I turn a corner, passing by more games. And
that's when I finally see it:

CLOSE ON AN ENGLISH PHONE BOOTH

It's about eight feet tall and three feet
wide. A checkerboard of windows forms the
front door panel.

I grab the handle. Lights start flashing right
away, forming a frame around eight Nightmare
Elf heads attached to the back wall.

There is no phone.

All the heads are the same: the Nightmare
Elf with his pointed ears, Santa-like

hat, and chubby face. But all the facial
expressions are different: one happy,
another sad. There's also a scowl, a glare,
and a puckering pair of lips.

VOICE RECORDING
Ring-a-ling-ding. Throw the ring for a
chance to ding-a-ling.

Is "a chance to ding-a-ling" carnival-speak
for a chance to use the phone? There's a
stack of plastic rings at the bottom of the
booth. I grab a bunch and stand behind a
designated line on the ground.

I toss a ring at one of the heads. It catches
on a hat but then falls to the ground.

VOICE RECORDING
Remember, if at first you don't
succeed, ring, ring again.

I toss another ring. This time it hooks
around the Nightmare Elf with the happy

smile. A bell CHIMES, announcing that I've won. I wait for something to happen, hoping that a phone will suddenly appear.

Instead the lights go out. The ride goes quiet. I linger a few more seconds before chucking the rest of the rings to the ground.

I'm just about to turn away, when I spot it, out of the corner of my eye.

CLOSE ON ELF THAT WAS FROWNING BEFORE

It now has a wild expression. Its eyes are wide; they stare straight out into space. Its brows are darted, and it's baring razor-sharp teeth.

I look up at an overhead camera.

                    ME
              (shouting at the camera)
          You think this is funny?

The elf doesn't move, nor does it blink.

I move around to the back of the booth.
There's a metal closet attached to the rear
panel. Someone must be hiding inside that
space.

                    ME
        Come out!

I kick at the metal sides and slam my fists
into the back panel. When still nothing
happens, I go around to the front again.

The elf's face remains with its wild
expression. I study it a few seconds: its
bright blue eyes, its waxy lips, its stupid
rosy cheeks.

PULLBACK TO REVEAL ME

I slam the door—so hard that the glass pane
BREAKS. I look back up at the camera.

ME

In case you haven't already figured
it out, I don't give a shit about
being in your stupid film. Cut my
role right now. I don't need this
crap. I don't need to meet you.

I wait for something to happen or someone
to come out. When nothing and no one do, I
head back to Frankie's ride.

CUT TO: NATALIE AND IVY, EXTERIOR GRAVEYARD
DIG.

NATALIE

"WHERE ARE THE OTHERS?" PARKER ASKS.

Ivy nods to the graveyard ride. "Shayla went to look for Frankie. And Garth took off, tired of waiting around."

Parker checks his watch. A look of concern crosses his face. "Did you find a phone?" Ivy asks him.

"Negative."

"So that was a lie," she says.

"Or maybe not," I argue. "Maybe whoever was left in charge of installing emergency phones never got around to it."

"You don't seriously believe that, do you?" he asks.

Do I? I can feel the confusion on my face. It must be catching, because Parker looks confused now too.

I move to sit on a patch of grass—away from their voices, so I won't be influenced. I close my eyes and try to concentrate on only one voice: mine. Except it's hard to know what I want, or what to think, when those things have always been dictated for me. Add that to the fact that Harris continues to tell me things he couldn't possibly know—about Frankie being buried and a blue teddy bear with a missing mouth—and it's hard to focus on the tiny voice inside of me.

In the end, I think Garth's voice is the most logical: we've all been given an opportunity here. It'd be foolish to throw it away.

I look over at Parker and Ivy, engrossed in conversation. "I finally know what I think," I say, moving to stand in front of them.

"Okay . . ." Parker still looks confused, his face twisted into a question mark.

"We need to find a way out of here," Ivy says.

"Without the others?" I ask.

"We haven't really gotten that far yet," she says.

"So, I guess you've decided to go with Harris's voice, then."

"That's right," Ivy says; her tone has softened. "I think Harris might be onto something."

"And I think he's trying to ruin our time here."

"And so what do you suggest we do?" she asks.

"Let's go on the rides," I say, feeling empowered to voice what *I* want. "We're here, so let's enjoy ourselves. Let's take advantage of this once-in-a-lifetime opportunity. Maybe we can try that terror train ride again—the one that goes underground. Maybe we can connect with Frankie and Shayla somewhere."

"We were thinking about that, too," Parker says. "But I'm not so sure we want to get lost in a web of underground tunnels."

"Especially in light of Taylor's phone call," Ivy adds.

"Didn't you listen to any of what Garth was saying? We're *supposed* to be afraid. This is *supposed* to be scary. We're at a horror-themed amusement park, where someone's filming a movie."

"I know." Ivy sighs.

"Then *what?*" I look out at the park, feeling slightly reassured that I'm not the only one who gets confused. The blinking yellow lights are nearly intoxicating, as is the smell of candy and popcorn. "Here," I say, pulling a long gray scarf from my bag. I hand it to Ivy, along with a spare pair of sunglasses. "I always keep extra stuff like this, just in case."

"What's it for?" she asks.

"Harris says you don't want to be recognized on film. Is that true? Are you already famous or something?"

Ivy's voice is gone now too.

"I don't want to be filmed either," I continue. "But I'll do just about anything to meet Justin Blake. So, I guess I'll see you guys later?" I turn away before they can respond, ready to go find my nightmare.

SHAYLA

LUCKILY, THE DOOR TO THE GRAVEYARD SHED IS open. I go inside, and the door swings shut behind me. I try the knob. It's locked.

"Frankie?" I call out, telling myself not to panic.

A lantern on the floor lights up the interior: wood-paneled walls and a carpeted floor. There's nothing else in here.

I pick up the lantern, spotting a cardboard tag attached to the handle with string. I flip the tag over, surprised to find my name printed across it. This lantern was placed here for me.

Someone must've had another way to come in here. I search the walls and the floor, knowing there has to be a hidden door somewhere.

At last, I find it—an area where the carpet's been cut away. Beneath it is a trapdoor. Someone's tagged it as well. *Welcome, Shayla* has been spray-painted across it. I touch one of the letters and a fresh smear of black comes away on my finger.

There's a small metal handle attached to the wood. I pull up on it. A ladder leads underground. I bring the lantern closer, trying to see what's down there, but it's too dark to tell.

"Frankie?" I shout. I look back at the door. Fog begins to seep in through the crack at the bottom. Part of me is tempted to pound on the door in hopes that the others will come get me out. But I begin down the ladder anyway.

Two rungs from the bottom, a bang crashes above. I startle and look upward. The trapdoor is still open.

"Hello?" I call out. "Frankie?"

No one answers.

I hurry back up the ladder, but before I can get to the top, the trapdoor slams shut. I push on it, but it won't budge.

I take a deep breath in an effort to quell the jangling nerves inside me. *What can this moment teach me?* I repeat inside my head—one of my yoga master's many life mantras.

I begin down the ladder again, also thankful for Garth's

logic: I've come here to be scared. I knew that when I signed up. Breathe in, breathe out. Remember that things are as they should be. There's no reason to panic.

Once I've reached the bottom of the ladder, I turn around, hoping to see Frankie. But there's nobody else here, and it seems I've reached yet another graveyard. Still, the whole scene is almost enchanting—in a Gothic, medieval-looking sort of way. It reminds me of a light show that my parents took me to in Scotland when I was twelve. There are dark trees with outstretched arms and twisted boughs surrounding the perimeter. Spotlights have been strategically placed on several of the limbs, illuminating the entire area and making everything look all aglow.

Just like outside, there are rows and rows of headstones—crosses, squares, and oval ones. Each stone has a single red rose lying in front of it, except for two stones in the back.

I meander around, recognizing most of the names on the headstones. They're characters from Justin Blake's films: Farrah Noyes from *Nightmare Elf II: Carson's Return*; Darcie Scarcella from *Hotel 9: Blocked Rooms*; Josie, Carl, and Diana Baker from the original *Night Terrors*—none of them lucky enough to make it into the next movie of their series.

I move to the last row—to the two stones without roses. I check the name on the larger stone—PETER RICE—unable to place it. Perhaps he's a character from one of Blake's earlier, lesser-known films. It seems that the two stones have the same plot site, leading me to assume that there's a crypt under there, which is actually quite appropriate considering that one of the occupant's names is Peter. Perhaps Blake was paying homage to Saint Peter, buried at Old Saint Peter's Basilica in Rome.

The plot area has been freshly filled. The dirt is darker, the mound is fuller, and there's zero growth (in this case, fake grass) sprouting from the site.

A skull is etched into the granite surface of Peter's sister stone; below it is writing, only the lettering is much smaller than that of the other stones. I scoot down to get a better look, hoping to find another message or maybe a clue as to where Frankie is.

The breeze rustles through the trees; making the wind chimes clink. The sounds help ease my nerves. *I'm being watched. I'm not alone. This isn't real. This whole scene has been created for the movie.*

I move the lantern close to the smooth polished surface of the stone, able to see Frankie's name with what I assume is his birthday and today's date. I blink a couple of times, knowing that this was done for cinematic purposes. But still my stomach twists, because the gravestone looks really real, really legit.

I struggle to my feet, spotting a shovel propped against the back of the stone. My heart tightens and I take another breath, wondering if I should start digging at Frankie's site, if that's what I'm supposed to do—if it's indeed part of this nightmare-challenge, especially with a name like Graveyard Dig.

I go to grab the shovel. But then I hear something. A crunching noise. It's coming from behind the graveyard border. I can't really see back there; there aren't any lights beyond this last row of stones, but I can tell that the space continues. The wood framing overhead extends into the darkness.

"Frankie?" I call.

More crunching; it's followed by a clanking sound. Keeping a firm grip on the lantern, I move in the direction of the noises.

With the lantern's glow, I'm able to see about five feet in front of me. There's a tunnel and a gravel-lined pathway. The sides of the tunnel are made of dirt, held in place by wooden strapping. Was this once a mine?

I call Frankie's name over and over, continuing through the tunnel. I recite the Gayatri Mantra from yoga class, still trying to hold it together.

I turn to look back, but there's only blackness now. The lights by the graveyard have all been turned off.

Another noise makes me jump: the shifting of gravel. Someone's moving in my direction.

"Hello?" I hold my lantern high.

A door creaks open somewhere in front of me.

"Shay-la?" a woman sings.

I don't move. I can hardly breathe.

"Come and find me," the voice continues.

My heart is pumping furiously. My hands are shaking uncontrollably. I'm here to be scared, I remind myself.

There's a trickling sound now, like water leaking from an overhead pipe. I walk deeper into the tunnel, able to hear a tiny whimper before realizing that it's mine.

"Do you remember our promise?" the voice asks.

I stop. This is part of my contest entry.

"You said you'd always be there for me," she says.

The voice doesn't even sound like Dara's. But whoever this is clearly represents her—or at least her memory—and I suppose that's why I'm here: to face Dara once and for all.

"Are you there?" she asks.

I begin moving forward again. A knocking sound goes straight to my heart. It sounds as if someone's rapping on a door. Maybe I'm supposed to answer.

Keeping the lantern high, I search the walls as the knocking becomes louder and more desperate, as if someone's trying to get out.

"Frankie?" I shout, wondering if it might be him.

Finally, I find a large gray door. The knocking comes from the other side of it. "Hello?" I call, looking down both ends of the tunnel—from where I came and to where I'm headed. Still, there's only blackness.

I wrap my hand around the knob, hesitating to open the door, half hoping that it's locked. But the knob turns without a hitch. The door creaks open. The air through my lungs stops.

It's dark inside. I lift my lantern higher. A light turns on—from the motion of the door—and I'm able to see.

A girl. A body. Hanging inside the closet. She's dressed in a long T-shirt and heart-patterned socks; her hair is in a sideways braid.

I drop the lantern. My hands fly up to my face. It can't possibly be real. The chalky lips, the dark eyelids, the bluish-gray skin. Telephone wire is wrapped around the neck, creating a makeshift noose. The wire is attached to a light fixture. A lightbulb hangs down from the closet's ceiling.

My head feels woozy and the tunnel starts to tilt. The body wavers too. Maybe the motion of the door disturbed it.

There's something in one of the hands. An envelope. A note for me. It's stuck to the skin with double-sided tape.

I take and open it, my mind unable to catch up to the written words: *You broke our promise.*

I step back, stumbling over my feet, wanting to get away, desperate to get back to the others.

The eyes snap open. And stare back at me. Dara's pale blue eyes, crying bloodred tears.

A scream tears out my throat. I back up more—away from the door, away from her, bumping into something behind me.

A red suit. Elf boots. A person is there. Wearing gloves, his fingers wrap around my throat.

"Your role has been cut, Ms. Belmont," he says. I can feel his breath against my neck.

His fingers tighten.

I try to let out another scream, but it sounds more like a wheeze. I'm choking. His fingers press against my throat. His hands wrap around my neck.

My feet are dangling now. I picture those heart-patterned socks.

My world darkens and swirls. More creaking sounds in the distance. It's mingled with another sound, another voice.

Dara's voice. Inside my head. She's crying out to me, thanking me for being there for her. At last.

GARTH

IT TAKES ME TWO LOOPS AROUND THE PARK BEFORE I finally find my ride. It's called Nightmare Alley, which makes perfect sense, seeing as part of my childhood nightmares involved walking down a long dark alleyway in the middle of the night, with Justin Blake's characters stalking after me.

The ride itself appears to be inside a building of sorts. Four giant walls have been erected, most likely to conceal what lurks behind them. I go inside and it's like I've died and gone to nightmare heaven. I'm in an entryway with walls that are at least ten feet high. They're decorated with illustrated murals of some of Blake's most well-known characters: the Nightmare Elf holding his sack of tricks; Lizzy Greer pushing a shopping cart and swinging her bloodstained ax; Little Sally Jacobs with the skeleton keys punctured through her eyes; and Sidney Scarcella from *Hotel 9*, serving a platter full of victims' ears—to name just a few. Word bubbles blow out each of their mouths: "If you dare." "Come play with me." "Ready to check in?" They urge me farther inside.

There's a bright red door in front of me. It's shaped like the silhouette of the Dark House. I open it, and the Nightmare Elf's mischievous giggle greets me.

It's dim inside. There are streetlights strategically placed down the long narrow alleyway—just far enough away from one another to keep the creepy quotient high. Bordering the alley are buildings and shops. I can tell they're all movie-set fake, assembled for the sole purpose of my nightmare, which makes this whole experience even more incredible than it is. I mean, if it wasn't cool enough that Justin Blake created this "ride," he created it just *for me*.

I close the door, and once again I hear the Nightmare Elf's giggle. *"Come out, come out, wherever you are,"* I sing, thinking how this whole scene reminds me a little of *Sesame Street*, but for horror lovers.

There's a handful of thumbtacks scattered on the ground.

I know they must've been tossed there by him, up to his corny elf trickery.

"Hey there, Darthy Garthy," the Nightmare Elf says. "Have you come to play?" The voice sounds just like it did in the movies, just like a little kid's. *"Garthy, Garthy, Go Barthy, Banana-fana Foe Farthy, Me My Mo Marthy, Garthy."*

I continue down the alleyway. Brick buildings sandwich me in on both sides. "What are you hiding for?" I ask him. "Come out here and get me."

Instead of showing himself, the elf continues to sing: *"I know your nightmare. I took it from your sleep. And whether or not you like it, it's mine, and mine to keep."*

I keep moving forward, spotting someone's foot sticking out from behind a Dumpster. A kid's shoe: bright red, shiny leather.

I inch closer, able to see that the shoe belongs to a girl. It's a hologram of Little Sally Jacobs from *Night Terrors*. I recognize her dark red pigtails.

Wearing striped socks and a purple dress, she's playing a game of jacks. She bounces a tiny ball and then snatches up a handful of the star-shaped pieces. There are droplets of blood on the pavement.

"Have you come to play?" she asks, keeping her face focused downward.

I open my mouth, shockingly at a loss for words.

Thankfully she fills in the blanks. "Did you bring me a piece of candy?"

I smirk, remembering how, in the movie, she was always looking for candy from strangers.

She starts singing to herself—that *"Frère Jacques"* song—and bouncing that stupid red ball of hers, collecting more jacks.

"No *parlez-vous français*," I tell her.

The jacks fall from her grip. The ball bounces away. Finally, she looks up. As expected, there are skeleton keys jabbed into the center of her eyes. Tracks of blood trickle down her cheeks. She goes to pull one of the keys out. The pulling makes a thick slopping-sucking sound.

I take a step back, bumping into a trash can.

The key is out of her eye now. "Want to play?" she asks. There's a happy smile across her face. Her lips and teeth are stained red. She stands and comes at me with the key, pushing it toward my face. *"Pansy, pretty girl, crybaby, sweet pea."*

A motor starts up behind me. I turn to look.

It's Pudgy the Clown wielding his chain saw. "Have you come to play?" he asks, giving the motor a rev. He comes right at me. His blade cuts across my neck.

I jump back, my heart pounding. I touch my neck. There is no blood.

It takes me a second to realize that the image is on a TV screen. It's three-dimensional and looks so real.

I move away, down the alley. Eureka Dash from the Nightmare Elf movies appears on the wall to my left. She's trembling; her hands shake. "He's going to come after us," she cries, tears dripping down her face.

On the other side of me, Sebastian Slayer from *Forest of Fright* is playing a piano in the middle of the forest. A severed hand and foot rest on top of the piano, right beside his pickax. He pauses from playing to look in my direction. "It's your turn next."

I want to think it's funny, but instead it makes me cringe.

A hologram of Emma Corwin from *Hotel 9: Enjoy Your Stay* is a few steps away. Using the blood from her self-sliced wrists, she starts to write *help* on the wall.

I stop, spotting something moving in the shadows, behind a Dumpster. Someone dressed up as the Nightmare Elf is slumped over Lizzy Greer's shopping cart. I approach him slowly, noticing the nightmare sack on the bottom rack of the cart.

Keeping his back to me, he asks, "Do you have any spare change?" à la Lizzy Greer.

The cart is filled up with soda cans. I know what's probably hidden among them—what Lizzy keeps tucked away.

"Spare change?" he asks again, without looking in my direction.

I start to move past him, but he pulls Lizzy's ax from the mound of cans and holds it up for show.

I take a moment to study him, wondering if he might be one of the drivers, but aside from his eyes, his face is completely covered with the elf mask.

Wearing his bright green gloves, he takes a cantaloupe from the carriage, sets it on top of the Dumpster, and chops it in two. The blade drips with juice and pulp. Cantaloupe guts plop onto the ground. "Enjoying your time at the park, so far?"

My pulse racing, I continue down the alleyway, able to feel his eyes burning into my back.

"Not so fast," he says.

I stop. And peer over my shoulder. Standing feet away, he straightens all the way up, and then comes at me with the ax. The blade slices through the air, missing my midsection by an inch, but still he manages to get my jacket.

I inspect the fabric, where it's been cut by the blade. "What the hell?" I shout.

"Didn't you come to play?" he asks.

I go to move past him again, but he grabs my arm, spins me

around, and backs me up against the brick wall. He's breathing hard and his breath reeks of coffee and oranges. He brings the ax high above his head, making like he's about to strike down.

I duck out of the way, pushing against him as I go. He lets out a laugh, as if my efforts are all a joke.

Straight ahead, a young boy appears on another screen. It's dark and he's in the middle of the woods, using a flashlight to find his way. "Craig?" the boy calls. "Paul?"

Craig and Paul are my brothers' names. The boy is supposed to be me.

A cabin comes into view. The Dark House. The sign is visible over the door. The boy knocks before going inside. There's a rocking chair with the Nightmare Elf doll.

"My name is Carson," the elf doll says, in his chipper voice. "Did you come to play?"

The boy begins to tremble.

I feel my stomach tie up in knots, remembering all those months I spent sleeping beneath the bed, praying that the Nightmare Elf would never visit my dreams.

The boy moves into a bedroom, tears sliding down his face. I want to tell him that it'll all be okay—that one day nothing will ever scare him again.

I turn away—it's too hard to watch—and follow the

alleyway as it turns a corner. There's an open door at the rear of one of the buildings. I go inside, able to hear the rattle of the shopping cart again.

I close and lock the door behind me, trying to catch my breath, reminding myself that this is all for the movie. A dim overhead lightbulb hangs down from a ceiling with peeling paint. A concrete staircase is to my left. Another door faces me. I'm assuming the door leads underground. I pick the stairs and climb them, two at a time, until I reach the staircase platform.

There's a deep clink sound. The door lock? Before I can turn to look, the lightbulb goes out. The door I entered opens. I can hear footsteps coming up the stairs. I search the walls, desperate to find a door handle or light switch.

Footsteps continue. "Garth," the elf whispers. "Are you ready to join the fun?"

I find a knob and turn it, relieved when the door opens and I can see again. The hallway's lit up. I close the door behind me, noticing that it's an emergency exit, and that it doesn't have a lock.

There's a long red carpet that runs down the middle of the hall. The walls are covered in thick, purple paper. There are gold-framed mirrors, slanted ceilings, and crooked numbers on all the room doors. It's like being on the movie set of *Hotel 9*.

I hurry down the hall until I reach the grand staircase—at least twenty steps high. It's framed in dark mahogany with balusters that look like evil serpents. Standing at the top, I look down at the lobby. More holograms. A group of kids in 1930s schoolboy garb—suit jackets, short pants, newsboy caps, and long kneesocks—play a game of Scrabble.

I look back over my shoulder, wondering where the elf is. The hallway remains empty.

Just then, a hologram of Sidney Scarcella enters the lobby. Wearing a butcher's apron over his bellboy uniform, he's carrying a pitcher of something dark. "More iced tea?" he asks the schoolboys.

They nod in creepy unison and he refills their glasses. I squint harder to see, accidentally brushing against the wall beside the banister. A picture falls—a family portrait of the Scarcellas. It tumbles down the flight of stairs. The glass inside the frame shatters.

"Garth, is that you?" One of the schoolboys stands. "Have you come to play?"

My forehead starts to sweat. I close my eyes a moment, noticing how unstable I feel on my feet.

"Garth, is that you?" the voice repeats. "Have you come to play?"

I scurry back down the hallway and try the knobs on a

bunch of the room doors. Most of them are locked, but the one at the very end opens. I go inside and lock the door. It's dark, but I don't turn on the light; I don't want the elf to know where I am.

"You don't really think you can hide, do you?" a voice asks. "I have eyes everywhere."

I turn to look. It's Pudgy the Clown again. He clicks on his chain saw and starts running toward me.

I slip beneath the bed, flashing back to when I was seven. Quickly the chain saw quiets and the room goes dark again.

There's a knock at the door and a scratching sound on the wall. I hold my breath, wishing I were someplace else, feeling a dull ache in my belly. I have to piss. I'm going to throw up. Acid travels up my throat, choking me.

I roll out from under the bed, able to hear more scratching—fingernails on wood. A lighter striking over and over. And a key in the lock, turning. I move toward the window, able to see a shadow moving with me.

I try to open the window, wondering where I'd land if I jumped. But it's locked. I fumble with the latch, the sound of knives carving—blades scraping against each other—behind me.

"Ready to check out?" a voice asks from the darkness.

Finally, I get the lock unlatched. I open the window, just as my pants fill with heat as I lose it on the floor, pissing all over myself.

I dive out the window, headfirst, telling myself there must be a safety net.

It takes my brain a beat to realize that I've landed, that I'm no longer falling, that the smack sound is my body as it hits the pavement. I'm still alive. A numbing calmness. Moments later I hear it: the rattle of a shopping cart.

On my stomach, I try to inch forward.

The rattle grows louder.

I can see someone coming at me. A pair of elf boots covered in dirt. But I can't speak, can't scream. There's a flash of red.

He reaches down to feel for a pulse in my neck. Despite the gloves, he's wearing a bracelet. It dangles in front of my eyes: gold, chain-link, with the symbol for infinity. Frankie's bracelet. "You tried so hard to change," he says, "but you're still a scared seven-year-old boy."

There's the glare of an ax blade, and a deep moan as the ax is raised high.

Ivy

AFTER THE OTHERS HAVE ALL DISPERSED, PARKER and I decide to abandon Frankie's ride—for now, anyway—to try Taylor's phone at the front of the park. We stand beneath the TV monitor, where Justin Blake first spoke to us. I push the talk button and hold the receiver at varying angles, but it still isn't getting reception. "We can keep trying in different parts of the park," I say, hoping to sound optimistic. I look toward the top of the gate, wondering how many bones I'd break if I jumped from the very top, and what barbed wire feels like when it enters the skin.

"What are the odds of digging our way out of here?" I ask, assuming the idea is nuts. But Parker looks at the gate for five full seconds and says it's worth a try.

We move over to it. I squat down and gaze upward, almost unable to see the wire at the very top—that's how far away it is.

Parker fetches a couple of plastic cups from a snack shack and hands me one. "Use it to shovel," he says, scooping up a mound of dirt.

I begin to dig, following the bars of the gate downward, into a hole. They seem to go on forever. I reposition, lying on my stomach, digging deeper into the ground.

"This isn't working," Parker says after about ten minutes. He tosses his broken cup and resumes digging, using his hands. The muscles in his forearms pulse. After about twenty more minutes, he steps inside his hole. He's almost up to his thighs, and still he hasn't reached the bottom of the gate. "It's like they knew we'd try to get out this way."

I sit at the edge of my ditch. "People are going to start to worry. Parents, I mean. Aside from Natalie and me, no one's called home yet—at least not that I know of, and it's been well over twenty-four hours now."

"Maybe we *should* venture underground," he says, nodding to the Train of Terror ride.

"No way." I shake my head. "Frankie and Shayla have both gone underground, and so far they've yet to resurface."

"We don't know that for a fact. Maybe they started underground but then followed a tunnel and came out someplace else. Let's face it, they could be anywhere—even beyond the gate." He nods to the forest.

I look out at the park. The actress on a nearby movie screen is running for her life. Naturally, she's in the woods, wearing heels instead of track shoes. She trips over a tree root and falls to the ground, letting out a sputtering noise that doesn't even sound human. She grapples forward on her elbows and knees.

I reach for my aromatherapy necklace, able to feel the girl's angst.

"What *is* that?" Parker asks, nodding to my necklace. He takes a seat beside me and our feet dangle inside my ditch.

"Cedarwood oil." I pull the cork out. "It helps induce tranquility and relaxation."

"Does it work?"

"You can be the judge."

"For real?" He goes to touch the bottle, checking for my reaction first.

I give him a silent okay and he moves in closer. His fingers graze my chest as he takes the bottle into his hand, sending tingles all over my skin.

Looking straight at me, he gives the bottle a tiny sniff. A subtle grin sits on his lips, as if he knows his effect on me. "I feel better already," he says.

"Me too." I smile—my first one in what feels like days.

"Was it a present from someone that I should know about?"

"It was supposed to be my mom's."

"Supposed to be?"

I bite my lip, wishing that I could take the words back. "Maybe we should go look for more hotspots."

He nods and gets up, steps out from my ditch, and dusts the dirt from his palms. I can tell that he's frustrated with me. I'm frustrated with myself.

"There's a gamesmanship quality here," he says, before I can apologize. "Survive your worst nightmare, get to be in the movie, get to meet the mastermind. Knowing Blake's work, I'm pretty sure we're not getting out of here until we do that . . . face our nightmares, I mean. The main character always confronts the villain before the end. The showdown is not only expected, it's mandatory."

"And I signed up for this because . . . ?"

Parker looks at me again, his eyes swollen and serious. "I don't know; you won't tell me."

I swallow hard, hating myself for being so guarded.

Yesterday, it probably wouldn't have mattered to me if he were upset by my secrecy. But today I'm upset too.

I don't want it to be like this.

"Let's get going." He extends his hand to help me up. I take it, feeling the warmth of his skin radiate over my face.

Parker notices and takes a step closer.

I try to glance away, but he forces me to look into his eyes by touching the side of my face. And making my heart pound. For just a moment I think that maybe he's going to kiss me. And, for the first time that I can remember, I actually want to be kissed. I want to believe that I can be just like every other girl, and not this person who's always waiting for the end.

Parker leans in a little closer and I stare at his lips—pale pink, shallow vee, slightly turned up at the corners. But before I can even feel his kiss, someone screams—a high-pitched shriek that severs the moment in two.

I turn to look. The girl on the screen—in the woods—is now running along a set of train tracks, while a dark-clothed someone follows behind her, keeping a steady pace.

"Let's go," Parker says. "We need to get this over with."

As we move toward the center of the park, a phone rings. I pull Taylor's cell phone out of my bag, but the ringing is coming from someplace else.

We follow the sound behind a row of Skee-Ball machines, startled to find a telephone booth.

"The emergency phone," I say, moving quickly to answer it. I push open the bifold door and grab the receiver. "Hello?"

"Who's this?" a male voice asks. "Wait, I think I might have the wrong number."

"No!" I insist. "Who is *this*? Who are you calling for?" I turn to look outward, spotting a first aid kit hanging on a nearby post.

"Is Max there?" the caller asks. "He left a message for me yesterday. Something about switching shifts. I'm just calling him back."

Parker comes and shares the receiver with me, his cheek grazing mine as we stand huddled in the booth.

"You have to listen to me," I say. "You have to help us. We're trapped inside an amusement park in the middle of the woods . . . someplace outside Stratten, Minnesota."

"Wait, so is Max *there*?" he asks.

Parker hangs up the phone.

"What are you doing?" I snap.

He presses the dial tone lever—again, and again, and again.

"What are you doing?" I repeat.

The dial tone never comes. Instead, the male voice is still

there. He's laughing at us now. "Don't think you can get out of here without facing your nightmare. I need those scenes for the movie."

"News flash: we don't give a shit about the movie," Parker says.

"Well, you should, because surviving your ride is the only way out—the only way the gates will reopen."

"And what if we refuse?" I ask.

"Then consider yourself stuck inside these gates." The phone clicks. He hangs up.

Parker takes my hand and leads me away from the phone.

"Wait," I shout, stopping short. "Justin Blake can't do this. I mean, legally . . . he can't."

Parker's eyes lock on mine; he needs no words for me to know just what he's thinking: this isn't being run by Justin Blake. "Let's go," he says, taking my hand again.

We round a corner and come face-to-face with a giant water tank. "Sink or Swim," I say, reading the name on the sign.

"This is mine," he says, the color suddenly drained from his face. "I guess it's my turn."

PARKER

I CLIMB A LADDER THAT LEADS TO A PLATFORM overlooking a tank of water. The tank is a perfect square, about twelve feet long and wide. The water is murky brown, making me think of my essay. Not only did I lie about the eels, but I also changed the setting from the ocean to a pond. Another thing I lied about, not being able to swim. The fact is that getting swept up by a riptide and nearly drowning prompted me to become a great swimmer. A national, competitive swimmer.

A sign on the wall says ARE YOU READY TO SINK OR SWIM? According to the directions, I'll need to stay in the water for one full minute. A digital timer blinks the number sixty. The clock will begin counting down as soon as I enter the water. Then, once a minute's up, a bell will ring, indicating that I've succeeded.

The directions also state that should I want to get out at any point prior to the required minute, I can push one of the many emergency buzzers located at the water's edge. At that time, the "ride" will stop and a diver will assist me in getting out. I spot the emergency buzzers right away; they're positioned just above the water line. The idea of them should be reassuring, but I have no reason to trust anything about this weekend. Plus, where are the divers?

"You're going to be freezing," Ivy calls up to me. She's standing outside the ride, at the bottom of the ladder.

"I'll be fine," I say, trying to sound optimistic, even though I'm beyond uncertain. I pull off my T-shirt and take off my pants, socks, and sneakers, leaving only a pair of boxers. I turn to look down at Ivy and give her a little wink to be funny.

Gazing back at the water, I try to imagine that I'm on the other side of the camera—that this is a movie with me as the lead, or that I'm a contestant on a new reality game show. But neither scenario seems to stick, because this is real; I am here;

I have to face this. My mental movie camera is temporarily broken.

I dive in. The water's cold, sending a shock wave through my body. Holding my breath, I plunge to the bottom. The tank is deeper than I expected—at least ten feet. Despite how much I don't want to be doing this, it's actually a relief to know that I lied—that no one can use a nightmare against me.

Once I reach the bottom, I kick off the cement surface and start to float upward. But then I feel it—something long and slick against my leg. I pop up, my head above the water now, and wait for what happens next.

Something sharp sinks into my calf. I struggle to swim to the side of the tank, unable to paddle fast enough. I reach down to feel the injured spot, just as something bites me again. My thigh this time.

I swim toward one of the emergency buzzers, my fingertips grazing the side of it, but I'm not close enough to push it down.

I fall beneath the surface of the water. My mouth fills up with muck. I resurface and spit it out. My skin's torn. My leg's bleeding. Spotlights shine over the water, enabling me to see the color red mix with brown.

I go for the buzzer again—this time able to reach it. I smack it, but it makes no noise. I punch it, slap it, beat it with my fist. Still nothing.

"Parker!" Ivy shouts. She says something else, but I can't quite hear her.

That's when I see them: long and black, cresting the water, coming at me.

Eels.

They're attracted by my blood. I duck my head and plunge, leaving the blood in my wake, hoping it'll be enough to satisfy them for now. But I can feel them swimming between my legs and biting at my feet. Teeth sink into the arch of my foot and I let out a howl beneath the water. My mouth fills up once more.

I kick the eel away, swim to the surface, and smack another buzzer. Still no sound. No divers, either. I look up at the digital timer. Twenty-two more seconds.

"Parker!" Ivy calls out.

"Stay down there," I tell her.

Fifteen seconds left.

Eels swarm at my wounds. I can feel the slickness against my skin. My hands bracing the sides of the tank, I try to lift myself out, but I'm bitten on the back of my knee. The pain radiates down my calf and I fall back in, slipping beneath the surface once more. Treading water, I try to swat the eels away. There have to be at least twenty of them in here.

"I'm coming up there," Ivy says.

"No!" I shout. I try to stay above the surface, but I keep

sinking deeper, my head spinning with questions. Will I ever make it out of here? How can this possibly be happening?

An eel swims between my legs. I grab it—it's at least four inches thick—and try to lift it out, but it's too heavy, too strong. It lunges for me, nipping at my side. An instant surge of blood.

I scream beneath the surface. Water fills my mouth. Something gets caught in the back of my throat, creating a choking sensation. I reach in to yank it out—a leaf. A piece of it lingers, making me want to gag.

Still, I fight to swim upward, feeling a tug at my thigh—teeth ripping through the flesh.

My hands hit something hard. I'm at the bottom of the tank, or maybe it's the side. I'm turned around, disoriented, having lost my sense of direction.

I somersault in the water, able to find my feet against a hard surface. I kick off with all my might, following the direction of my air bubbles as I struggle to reach the top.

Not quite there, I see something moving out of the corner of my eye.

Holy freaking shit.

It's a steel cover—just like in my bogus nightmare essay.

The cover expands the width of the water's surface, moving steadily across the top, closing in the tank.

Finally, I crest the water. I reach up to grab the ledge of the tank, hearing myself gasp. My lungs are aching. I can't seem to get enough air. The steel cover is only a few feet away, getting closer with each breath.

"Parker!" Ivy shouts.

The digital clock has timed out. Zero seconds left. I lose my grip on the ledge and fall beneath the surface once more.

The cover is within arm's reach. I swim upward and grab the edge of it, trying to hold it in place. My biceps ache. My forearms throb. The cover continues to push forward, closing me in, trapping me inside.

I swim to the side of the tank again. With one hand on the platform, I'm able to hoist myself up, gaining leverage with my elbow, and then with my knee. The cover grazes my foot as it seals over the surface of the water.

Up on the platform, I collapse into a mass of blood and throbbing muscles. The leaf's still stuck in my throat. I force it out, sticking my fingers into my mouth, hacking up a piece of a stem.

Ivy joins me on the platform. She rubs my back and tells me that it's all over. But it isn't. Far from it. Because now it's her turn.

NATALIE

GARTH'S RIGHT. WE'RE HERE FOR A REASON. AND IT'D be crazy to walk away from an opportunity this monumental. And so after he takes off to find his nightmare, I head off to find mine, despite what Harris says.

"You have to understand how much this means to me," I tell him. "Justin Blake has really been there for me."

"And I haven't?"

"Of course, but this is different. He was there for me in ways that you couldn't be."

"Well, then maybe you don't need me at all."

"That's not what I mean, Harris."

"Don't do this, Nat. If you don't listen to me ever again, listen to this: get out of there. If you don't, you just might join me . . . on this side."

I pull out more hair—from my eyelashes this time—wishing that his words didn't burrow so deeply into my heart.

I circle the park for a third time, still searching for my ride. We passed by it earlier, but I wasn't ready to go in at that point, especially with Harris's barking.

"Are you a little lost?" a voice asks, just behind me.

I turn to look. There's a movie screen there. On it is Little Sally Jacobs from *Night Terrors*, wearing a pair of pink sunglasses to hide her skeleton-key-punctured eyes. It's mid-scene and she's asking Mrs. Baker, a new neighbor, if she'd like to come inside the house for a glass of lemonade.

"You can meet my parents," Sally says, sweetening the deal. "Mama just made the lemonade this morning. She should also have some cookies coming out of the oven right about now."

This part of the movie—when the woman follows Sally inside—kept me awake for hours, because I knew just what would happen. And I was right. Mrs. Baker never came out.

I watch the scene for several moments before gazing around at the other movie screens scattered about the park: all of Justin Blake's films at various points in the story—some in the middle (Lizzy Greer chasing a streetwalker with an ax), others at the climax (Eureka trying to escape Pudgy the Clown, in some overhead ductwork). It appears that *Forest of Fright* just started, and the end credits are rolling on *Halls of Horror,* toward the center of the park.

At last, I spot my nightmare ride; it's called Mirrors of Mayhem, and it's basically a fun-house maze of mirrors.

It's dark as I approach. There's a blacked out door at the front. I climb the steps to enter, but it's locked.

"What the hell?" I shout, jiggling the handle and pushing my weight against the door panel.

Still, it won't open—even after ten minutes.

I scurry down the steps and circle the ride, searching for another way in, wondering if maybe there's some trick.

Finally, the "ride" lights up, as if by magic. Music pours out of it—a mix of organ and harmonica.

As I climb the steps again, the music grows louder, making it nearly impossible to hear Harris. Still, I know his voice is there. I can hear it, struggling over the music—like someone fighting to keep above water, only to end up drowned out by the waves.

I enter the walls of glass and the floor begins to rotate. I take careful steps, trying to avoid eye contact with my reflection by keeping my focus down. But it's absolutely no use. My reflection is everywhere—in front of me, beside me, cut in half, multiplied by five, as part of a giant mosaic of shapes. My Scissorhands hair, my crooked nose, my pudgy lips.

Arms too long.

Hips too wide.

Swollen skin from picking, plucking, pulling, pinching.

My face flashes red. In one mirror, I'm short and bulging, with stocky legs, a gigantic stomach, and a tiny head. In another mirror, I'm all stretched out and my face looks even longer than it is.

I try to turn around, to get out, but I'm already lost in the maze of my reflection. I shut my eyes and extend my hands to feel my way around so I don't have to look. But I manage to bump into the glass anyway—my cheek brushes against a corner of a glass panel. I open my eyes, catching sight of the brown mole on my upper lip. It looks bigger than I remember. Puffier than ever before. Is this another distortion mirror?

I turn away, smacking into another glass pane—my nose this time. My sunglasses fall off. Blood trickles from a nostril, over my lips, and drips off my chin, landing on yet another image of me—so much worse without the glasses, in the light. I'm standing on a mirror. Another droplet of blood hits the reflection below my feet.

There's more red—a flash of it reflected in the mirror. Someone's moving behind me, behind another section of glass. And yet I don't see a face. The image is too fast and fleeting. The redness whirls and ripples, as if the person's wearing a cape.

I turn, following the figure with my eyes. Finally, the image stops. I see a slice of red, perfectly still. I wait, breathing hard. My breath steams up the mirror, making an oblong stain against the glass, covering my forehead.

At last, I see who it is. The Nightmare Elf—most likely the same man who appeared on the TV screen when we entered the park, wearing a mask that has pointed ears, chubby cheeks, and curly blond hair. The mask is stuck in a perpetual grin; the forehead of it is shiny, as if it's somehow sweating too.

"You know why the elf is here, don't you?" Harris asks, ripping a hole in my heart.

Why is he so hell-bent on hurting me, on ruining this experience?

"What experience?" he asks. *"Is this what you call a fun time?"*

I hold my bloody nose. Where did my sunglasses go? I don't see them anywhere now. I keep looking for an exit. But, just one step away, I bump into a wall. The elf starts laughing. His head tilts back, jittering slightly, and he holds on to his belly. I sniff up the blood and extend my arms again, moving out from behind a pane of glass, trying my best not to cry.

The Nightmare Elf moves too. One moment I think he's in front of me, the next he's behind me again.

Then at my right.

And over to my left.

The reflections are too overwhelming. I'm standing in an alcove of a thousand mini-reflections of me. They make a checkerboard pattern, boxing me in, stealing my breath.

There's not much air. My chest feels tight.

A swirl of red dances around me and then does a cartwheel behind my back.

I try to get out of this alcove. I move to the side and then inch into what I think is another area, but it looks exactly the same; the checkerboard pattern surrounds me on all sides. I look up. There are mirrors there, too. And still more mirrors as I turn around—as if the thousand have somehow quadrupled.

Finally, the music stops. There's a rushing sensation inside my veins. I don't see the elf anywhere. There's just my reflection every way I turn.

I move out from behind a glass panel, but I'm blocked. There are mirrored walls all around me now, as if someone's locked me in.

I run my fingers up and down the panes, my breath fogging up the glass, wondering if there might be an empty space I'm not seeing. The Nightmare Elf giggles, but still I can't see him. I'm feeling more trapped by the moment. My throat constricts. I can't get enough air.

"I'm really sorry, Nat," Harris says. *"I wish you would've listened."*

I turn around and around as the floor beneath me continues to rotate. My head is dizzy. I stumble over my feet.

Suddenly, a wall goes black. I reach out to touch it just as a light clicks on inside it. The Nightmare Elf is there, on the other side. He waves at me with his glove-covered hand.

"He's come to watch you suffer," Harris says. *"The elf always appears at the time of death. After he steals your nightmare and uses it against you, he comes around to watch his dirty work play out."*

"Stop!" I scream. Blood spouts out of my mouth, from my nose, spraying the glass. I cover my fists with the sleeves of my jacket and then pound against one of the walls.

Nothing happens.

I pound harder, kicking the glass with my boot. The mirror breaks. But there's another mirror in its place, just behind it.

The elf laughs harder.

Harris begins to pray: *"Hail Mary, full of grace . . ."*

My heart beats faster. My pulse races harder. I start throwing my body against the glass walls, beating the panes with my fists, kicking as hard as I can.

Glass shatters, cutting into my skin, making everything red. Thousands of years of bad luck. I look up, just as a giant shard of glass slices downward.

IVY

PARKER IS REALLY BLEEDING. LYING ON HIS BACK, he's breathing hard, shivering from either fear or pure coldness. There's a bite mark on his side, two in his left thigh, and a few more on his calves and feet.

I take off my sweatshirt and blanket it over his chest, along with Natalie's scarf. "I'll be right back." I run down the stairs, round the corner by the phone booth, and see the first aid kit in the distance, hanging on a post.

Despite the blinking lights, the park feels vacant, especially without Parker by my side. It's quiet, as if someone's muted the volume, shut off the music, and pulled the plug on all the movie projectors.

The air is warm and thick as I move toward the post. Just a few yards away from it now, I hear something: the sound of footsteps, the crunching of gravel.

I stop and look around. Nothing.

I turn back to head for the first aid kit. There's a scuffing sound behind me again. "Who's there?" I call out.

No one answers.

An owl hoots in the distance as I grab the first aid kit. It's a metal box with sharp corners. I position it in my hands with a corner pointed outward, ready to use it as a weapon if need be.

I hurry back to the Sink or Swim ride and scurry up the stairs, two at a time, tripping on the tread at the very top. I kneel down by Parker's side, trying to catch my breath. "We'll get through this," I tell him.

I doubt that he believes me. I hardly believe myself.

Parker turns away from the tank, trying not to show too much emotion, even though his wounds are raw and weeping.

I pop open the emergency kit. Inside is a picture of first aid supplies. Otherwise, the box is empty. My heart clenches. My face flashes hot. I want to scream at the top of my lungs, but I hold in my emotion too.

I reach into my bag, grateful to have brought along a few

tea bags. Since his skin is already wet, I'm able to apply them directly to the wounds, placing one on the bite on his thigh, another on the bite on his waist, and then my last one on his ankle.

"What are you doing?" he asks.

"Tea contains tannins," I explain, pressing the tea bag against his ankle. His calf muscle flexes in response. "And tannins help clot blood. They also act as a natural astringent, which means there may be less chance of an infection." The golden hair that covers his legs appears slightly curly from the dampness. I wonder how it would feel against my skin. I swallow hard, trying to stay focused, noticing a large bite mark at the back of his knee. I flip one of the tea bags over to the fresh side and press it firmly against the spot.

Parker flinches from the pressure. "Lucky for me that you just happen to carry tea bags around in your purse."

"I think I may've mentioned that tea is sort of my vice."

"Sounds more like a serious problem. Should I be staging an intervention?"

"Surprisingly chipper for escaping a tank full of hungry eels, aren't we?"

"Are you kidding? If I knew it'd mean getting this kind of treatment, I'd have been eel bait hours ago."

I apply a bit more pressure to the wound. "You're a really good clotter, you know that?"

"Should I feel special, or do you say that to all your flesh-eating-eel victims?"

"You should feel special," I say, surprised by his persistence in flirting, especially all things considered.

I spend the next several minutes treating his wounds before I can no longer hold in the question: "What's happening here?"

Parker sits up and reaches for his clothes, his whole demeanor shifted—from somewhat optimistic to totally dismal.

"I mean, what would've happened if you hadn't gotten out of there?" I continue.

He pulls his T-shirt on over his head—over his smooth, tan chest. "I don't even want to think about it."

"Okay, but we have to think about it. You could've died in there."

"Bottom line: you shouldn't go on your nightmare ride."

"Is that why we haven't seen the others?" I ask. "Because they didn't make it out of their own nightmare rides?"

"Unless maybe they escaped?"

"And maybe Blake has nothing to do with this contest."

"There's no maybe there. I suspected that something was off as soon as we stepped inside those gates. When Justin Blake appeared on the screen, I could tell that it wasn't real— just a bunch of sound bites edited together. The real Justin Blake has too much to lose."

"So where do we go from here?"

"Tell me about your nightmare," he says.

"I want to."

"But what? My sexy bloodstained physique intimidates you?" He tries to stand, but the bites on his legs make him wince. He grabs his pants anyway, my cue to turn around.

A second later, I hear something drop to the ground. His boxer shorts, sopping wet. I can see them out of the corner of my eye. The sound is followed by the swish of jeans as he yanks them on.

"It's safe," he says.

Still sitting, I swivel around to face him. His hair is damp and tousled. The cotton of his T-shirt sticks to the muscles of his chest. And his jeans hug his upper thighs.

"Well?" he asks.

At first I think he's asking me how he looks. But then he sits back down, takes my hands, and tells me that I can trust him. "If it'll make you feel any better, I can tell you about a real nightmare that I once had."

"No more stories about eels?"

"No eels," he says. "When I was seven, I wandered off in a department store and couldn't find my mom afterward. I ended up in the boys' bathroom, crying in one of the stalls. Finally, a worker found me and brought me up to the service desk, where my mom was crying too. Anyway, for months afterward, I had nightmares about getting left behind in various places—on a road trip, at the grocery store, in the shopping mall—no matter how many times I made my mother promise that she'd never lose me again."

"Oh my gosh, that's so sad."

"Now, your turn. And keep in mind that nothing you say about your nightmare is going to freak me out."

"Don't be too sure about that."

"You're a lot stronger than you know," he says. "I mean, you made it here, didn't you? You entered this contest, you got on a plane."

"My parents were murdered," I tell him. "Six years ago. In their bedroom. I was home when it happened."

Parker studies my face, perhaps waiting for me to tell him it's only a joke. "Who did it?" he asks, finally.

"They never caught the guy, but they know he's a serial killer. He murdered a few other people before my parents, always playing music at the scene of the crime."

His faces furrows. *"Music?"*

"Scores from various horror movies—*Psycho*, *The Shining*, *Halloween*. He was a big fan of the genre. His killings—the style in which he did them—were copycat murders from the films. For my parents, it was the bedroom scene from *Haunt Me*."

Parker grimaces, perhaps picturing the scene. "I know that film."

"That's one of the biggest reasons I came on this trip—to meet people who love horror, that is. To learn from them. To see horror as a source of entertainment, rather than the bane of my existence."

"And how's that working out for you so far?"

"I'm cured, can't you tell?" I look at the tank. "Just when you thought it was safe to go back into the water."

"Jaws II, have you seen it?" He smirks.

"What do *you* think?" I smirk back. "Anyway, the guy who killed my parents, we made eye contact. I saw his face. And after everything was over, I had to change my identity and move in with a foster family. Natalie was right . . . I don't like being filmed. I don't want to risk that he might one day recognize me."

Parker looks down at our hands, still gripped together, and for five horrible seconds, I think he's going to let go. But instead he squeezes my hands tighter.

"His eyes have haunted my nightmares ever since that night," I continue. "I don't want to relive what happened."

Parker looks deeply into my eyes. Part of me wants so badly to glance away. But I don't, even as he breaks the clasp of my hands, and slides his fingers along my face, setting fire to my skin. "Do you want to hear what a nightmare would be for me *now?*"

"What a nightmare *would be?*"

"Going home after this weekend and never seeing you again."

"Seriously?" I ask, waiting for the punch line.

His eyes remain steady and somber. "Promise me that won't happen, okay?"

"I promise." I nod.

He runs his thumb over my lips, awakening every last nerve inside my body. My head feels spinny as his lips press against mine, feeding the aching deep inside me. His kiss is soft and sweet and salty inside my mouth. My hands move over the muscles in his forearms. Heat spills across my thighs and over my hips. I want so badly to crawl up right inside of him—into the part that knows no fear.

"Ivy," he whispers, once the kiss ends. He's slightly out of breath.

Meanwhile, my entire body quivers.

"You're right," he says. "We're going to get through this."

"Maybe we should wait the night out," I suggest. "It'll be sunrise before we know it."

"Except I don't think sunrise is going to get us out of here."

"So, then what do you suggest?"

"Keep looking for hotspots, keep trying to find a way out. And, in the meantime, try to focus on what happens after we get out of here." His pale blue eyes stare into mine, and once again I don't look away.

I don't ever want to look away again.

"There's so much about you that I want to know," he continues.

"Really?" I ask, almost unable to imagine the idea of anyone wanting to know me: this person who's seen too much, this girl who might still be in danger.

"Will you let me?"

I nod, unable to hold myself back. And so I lean in to kiss him again, almost forgetting where we are, and what we're doing here.

"I'm not going to let you go," he says, once the kiss breaks. "After the weekend, I mean. I think it's fairly safe to say that you're stuck with me. If that's okay, that is."

"Definitely okay."

Parker reaches out to take my hand, and together we move

down the stairs, beyond his ride, past a Forest of Fright Tilt-A-Whirl and a ride called Nightmare Alley. We round a corner.

And that's when I see it.

Again.

We passed by it when we first entered the park, only I wasn't quite ready to look at it then—not that I'm feeling particularly ready now.

My nightmare ride.

A small yellow house with a white picket fence.

"Ivy?" Parker asks.

I look toward the door, silently acknowledging the fact that I've been dreaming about my parents' killer for the past six years, and so when you stop to think about it—"I've given myself six years to prepare for this moment," I say.

"Don't do this." He grips my hands, as if trying to squeeze some sense into me.

I pull away, feeling a chill. "I have to," I whisper.

Keeping a firm grip on my mother's necklace, I begin up the walkway, anticipating what awaits me inside. Is it possible that I'll learn something about my parents? Or maybe about that night?

Parker calls out to me, telling me to shout if I need anything, promising to come looking for me if I'm not out in ten minutes.

The door swings shut behind me. A foyer light brightens the entryway. The layout of the house is different from my childhood home. The stairwell is on the left rather than the right, there's no hallway closet, and the walls are painted blue rather than covered with rose-colored wallpaper.

There are framed photographs on the wall. They're obviously different from the ones that had lined the stairwell of the real 3 Mulberry Road, but still the idea is the same. They're photographs of me, available online: a picture taken by the local paper at my eighth-grade graduation and a photo of me on a recent school camping trip.

My bedroom is to the right at the top of the stairs. My parents' room is on the left. Their door is closed. My head feels woozy. I reach out, my fingers trembling, to try the knob, but it's locked.

I head into my room and flick on the light, but it doesn't work. Only the dim hallway light seeps into the space. Exactly like that night.

I breathe in and out, trying to stay present in the moment, as Dr. Donna advises.

My room looks right: the pink paisley bed linens, the faux-fur beanbag chair, the soccer banners and Katrina Rowe posters.

I sit on the bed, flashing back to that night—awakening from a thrashing sound across the hall, then hearing a gasp, a sputter, and an agonizing moan. Those noises were followed by a stifling silence, interrupted by a voice: "And now it's your turn."

I pull Taylor's cell phone from my bag, remembering the phone receiver that I had that night—a cordless extension from the kitchen.

I dial 9-1-1, just as I did that night, knowing the phone won't work. And I'm right. It doesn't. Instead, a thrashing sound tears through the silence.

It's happening again. I'm twelve years old. I pinch the skin on my knee.

Music begins to play—a blend of violin and viola. I clench the bed covers, still trying to get the phone to work. But then it slips from my grip and falls to the floor. Bile fills my mouth. I swallow it down and take a deep breath, reminding myself:

I'm no longer twelve years old.

Parker is right outside.

The door to my parents' bedroom opens. The music grows louder. A man's there, dressed as the Nightmare Elf in a red suit and hat. He's wearing a mask. The elf's grin is frozen on his face.

"Good evening, Princess," he whispers. "It's *very* nice to meet you." The words send shivers all over my skin.

Unlike six years ago, there are no sirens in the background, no response to any 9-1-1 calls.

I clench my teeth, feeling a flood of emotion overcome me: fear, anger, regret. There have been six years of emotions before I got to this moment.

Before I got to this moment, I took self defense classes every Saturday morning. And slept with a kitchen knife under my pillow. And walked to and from school with a can of bug spray in my pocket. I imagined this very scene at least a thousand times, and yet it still feels like a dream.

A nightmare.

I mean, it can't possibly be happening, can it?

He turns the knife in his gloved hand. It's a six-inch, spring-spike, double-action blade, like the one that killed my parents.

I reposition myself on the bed, unfolding my legs from beneath me, and pressing my back up against the wall.

He moves closer. Standing over me, he pokes the tip of the blade into my neck. "You knew I'd come back, didn't you?"

The blade pokes deeper with the motion of my throat as I swallow. He cocks his head, studying my face.

I press my back harder against the wall. My legs bent in front of me, I kick outward. My heel plunges into his gut.

He stumbles back, but comes at me with the knife again, holding it at my jugular. "A quick incision is all it'll take. Just tell me when you're ready." He glides the blade across my skin. "Be a good girl now," he sings.

Just then, something pelts against the window. He turns to look and I grab his arm. I bring it up to my mouth and bite down through his sleeve, into his flesh. He lets out a wail. The knife drops from his grip.

I reach for it, but he snatches it away before I can get it. I move quickly, scrambling to the foot of the bed, struggling to get to the door. But he grabs my leg, holding me in place, slashing my ankle. At least four inches.

I tumble off the bed. My cheek smacks against the hard-wood floor. Lying on my belly, I search the room for something—*anything*—to protect myself with. I spot a metal ruler on the desk. I begin toward it, grappling forward on my elbows, but he steps on my hand, freezing me in place. The heel of his boot grinds down into my fingers, cracking the knuckles, burning the skin.

Parker shouts my name from outside.

"Your friend won't be able to get in," he says, standing over me now. "The doors are locked. The windows have bars. It's just you and me now, Princess."

I roll over to face him and he kneels down, pinning me

against the floor with the knife. I swallow, feeling the point of the blade cut into my skin, just above my collarbone. A trickle of blood runs across my chest, soaking into his glove.

Breathing hard, I look toward his waist, wondering if I could kick him again—if it'd make enough of an impact from this angle, or if exerting myself would only push the knife in deeper.

"Please," I whisper, able to hear the desperation in my voice, trying to think of something clever to say.

A giant crash sounds. I feel it in my bones, but it's in the room. The window broke. He straightens up to look.

I kick him—*hard*—plunging the heel of my shoe into his groin. He doubles over, letting out a grunt. The knife flies from his grip. I crawl across the floor and manage to grab it.

I get back on my feet, holding the knife out toward him, gripped in both hands.

He straightens up again. "Be careful with that, Princess." Standing just a couple of feet away, he approaches me slowly, his arms extended.

"Don't!" I shout.

He lunges at me. His hands wrap around mine as he tries to wriggle the knife from my grip.

"No!" I thrust the knife forward, plunging it deep into his side, in the space between his ribs.

He lets out a gasp. His eyes slam shut. He stumbles back.

I turn away and bolt out of the bedroom, closing the door behind me.

The door to my parents' room is open a crack. I push it wider, able to picture their room that night: the blood on the wall, over the bed, soaking the sheets, filling the cracks of the hardwood floors.

I cover my mouth, shaking my head.

"Ivy!" Parker shouts from outside, snapping me back to the moment.

I tear down the stairs, missing at least three of the treads toward the bottom. I propel forward, headfirst, somehow catching myself. I go to open the front door, but it's the kind that locks automatically. The lock doesn't turn. It seems to be stuck. I can't quite get my fingers to work right.

I can hear him upstairs. The clunking of footsteps, the thwacking of wood against the wall as he flings the door open.

Finally, I get the lock unstuck and flee outside, slamming the door behind me.

PARKER

EXT. IVY'S NIGHTMARE RIDE—NIGHT

A small yellow house with a picket fence
and bars on the windows. I'm just about to
throw another brick at the window glass,
when I hear something at the door—the sound
of a LOCK TURNING. The knob RATTLES.

Ivy comes flying out of the house, tears
streaming down her face. Blood stains the

bottom of her pants. Her leg's bleeding. A
sideways slit.

I drop my mental camera and pull off my T-shirt. I tear a
piece of fabric and wrap it around her ankle as a bandage.

"My bag," she says, checking her shoulder. There's nothing there. "I left it. I lost Taylor's phone." She looks back at
the house, just as a TV screen lights up behind us. The costumed Nightmare Elf appears on the screen—most likely the
same guy from the welcome video, the one dressed in the elf
costume.

"Greetings, Dark House Dreamers," he says. "Congratulations on facing your nightmares . . . *and surviving them*." He
releases a maniacal laugh. "Now, how would you like to see a
rough cut of the film? I do hope you'll enjoy it."

Numbers flash across the screen, from ten down to one.
The screen goes black, and then gets punctured by the image
of headlights. *Welcome to the Dark House* appears in red crayon.
The movie starts: there's a car driving down a gravel road.
Trees and brush surround the car on both sides.

The next thing I know, the name Ivy Jensen appears in the
credits. It's followed by my name and then Natalie Sorrento.
The car continues, angled toward us on the screen, before
finally coming to a stop.

"It's us," I say, able to see now that the car is actually a hearse. Ivy gets out and stares up at the WELCOME TO THE DARK HOUSE sign. More credits continue to roll: Frankie Rice, Shayla Belmont, Garth Vader, Taylor Monroe.

The film looks like it was professionally done, like whoever did it knows how to work a camera, but still, it's not Justin Blake's work—not the lighting, nor the audio, and certainly not the camera angles.

My bite marks throbbing, I keep one leg slightly elevated as I hold Ivy close, watching as our night at the Dark House unfolds. I've seen most of the content before, but some of it is new: a blond girl—who I assume to be Taylor—applying a thick coat of lipstick; Garth uncovering a splotch of blood in Taylor's closet; and Ivy watching me sleep—the same way I had watched her sleep. There's also a close-up of Garth and Shayla kissing, and of Frankie in the hallway, bummed that he's not the one she's with. We fade out on a back shot of Taylor as she flees the Dark House, into the woods.

Ivy huddles closer as we watch the scene where we enter the amusement park through the tall iron gate, as Shayla and Garth start cheering, and as we all stand beneath that first TV screen, where Justin Blake supposedly spoke to us. The shot dissolves on the tense expression on Ivy's face—the same one that's on her face now.

It's clear that the movie has been at least partially edited. I can tell by all the cutaways—each of us on the Nightmare Elf's Train of Terror ride, all experiencing different things.

Finally, we get to Frankie's ride. Anxiety bubbles in my stomach as Frankie enters the shed at the back of the graveyard. After a phone call fiasco, he finds a trapdoor and descends a ladder, going down to an underground graveyard.

He moves toward the back row, where there's a giant hole in the ground. The camera zooms in on a gravestone. Frankie's name is engraved in the polished marble. Beneath it are dates— what I'm assuming is Frankie's date of birth, plus today's date.

A moment later, there's a ringing sound. It takes me a beat to realize that it's coming from the movie. A phone's been buried; the ringing is coming from inside the hole.

Frankie climbs down into it, desperate to answer the call. He starts digging deeper, slinging the dirt with a shovel, creating a pile by his feet.

"Where's the phone?" Ivy whispers.

A coffin appears. A skeleton. A watch. The camera refocuses, angling on Frankie as dirt comes down on him from above.

Eventually burying him alive.

His screams have blades; they cut a hole in my gut. "Holy shit," I whisper, over and over again, almost unable to take it anymore.

Ivy's face is full of tears. She holds her aromatherapy necklace up to her lips.

The scene fades to black, and then we cut to Shayla. She found Frankie's grave. But then a noise startles her and she moves down a tunnel—what appears to be a mine—where she finds a body hanging in a closet; I can't tell if it's real. The camera angles on the Nightmare Elf. He approaches her from behind and lifts her up by the neck. Her feet flutter in the air as she struggles to break free. The last thing we hear from Shayla is the sound of her body as it drops to the ground.

The scene switches again. We're with Garth in his nightmare ride now. There are holograms and movie clips. Garth moves down a long, dark alleyway, dodging a dangerous encounter with the Nightmare Elf, trying to seek refuge in Hotel 9. The ride ends with Garth jumping out of a window. There's a close-up of him landing facedown against the pavement below. The Nightmare Elf appears again. The scene cuts just as his ax is raised high.

Ivy lets out a gasp that rivals mine. She's crying uncontrollably, her chest heaving in and out.

The scene changes once more. It's Natalie's turn now, but the film quality has changed. None of it looks edited. It's more like footage tacked on from surveillance video. Natalie's trapped inside a house of mirrors, pounding against the glass.

The mirrors eventually shatter and cut into her skin. Blood sprays everywhere. Natalie's screams are hoarse and desperate, I can feel them in my chest. But then I don't hear them at all. The silence is far worse than her screaming.

There's more footage too—of the disappointment in Ivy's eyes when Eureka Dash's scream interrupted our moment by the gate, of me entering the eel tank, and of Ivy and me kissing.

Finally, the closing credits roll. The screen goes black again. Then Ivy and I appear live, on the screen. The camera's on us.

"You've made it," the elf says. "The lone survivors, worthy of seeing the rough-cut. And now, as promised, I have a sneaking suspicion that you might be ready to leave the park. Am I right?"

"Where is he?" Ivy whispers, looking over both shoulders. She repeats the question, over and over, faster and faster.

"The entrance gates will reopen at the count of three," the voice says. "You will then have exactly ten seconds to get out. If you don't make it, don't despair; consider yourself a lead part in the sequel." He snickers. "Now, are we ready?"

I look in the direction of the entrance gates.

"One, two . . ."

Before he can get to three, Ivy and I make a beeline to escape. Keeping pace behind her, I hobble past a slew of games. Past the merry-go-round, the strong-arm challenge, and the Nightmare Elf's Train of Terror.

I hear the entrance gates unlatch. The doors begin to creak open. The bites on my legs are throbbing. The one on the back of my knee burns with each step.

Just shy of getting to the gate, Ivy's necklace falls to the ground, but she doesn't notice. I stop to pick it up. The bite at my side stings as I bend forward. There's a pulling-stretching sensation, and I let out a grunt. The pendant slips free of the chain. Sweat drips, stinging my eyes.

"Parker!" Ivy shouts.

I scurry to pick up the pendant, blood drooling down my leg and from my waist. And then I start moving toward the gates again, limping as fast as I can.

I trip and fall to my knees.

The gates have started to close.

Ivy's already free, already on the other side. "Hurry!" she shouts. She struggles to hold the gates open, but the doors are far too heavy. I see her getting dragged, using all her weight against the steel bars.

I get up and hobble forward, feeling my eyes fill with tears. I'm not moving quickly enough. There's no way I'm going to get there in time.

The gates lock shut just short of my getting there.

"No!" Ivy screams. Her voice echoes inside my head, bouncing off the bones of my skull.

I'm locked inside with no way out.

"We'll get you out of there," she says, grabbing my hands through the bars.

Meanwhile, I'm crying too hard for words, no longer able to hold in my emotion. The necklace falls from my grip.

"One of those underground tunnels has to lead outside," she says. "Or maybe we can try digging again."

"Just go," I say, shaking my head, knowing that she can't stay.

"I'm not going anywhere. Not without you."

"You need to get help," I tell her. "Then come back for me."

"I won't leave you," she insists, crying even harder now.

"You have to," I say, looking away, not wanting her to see what a mess I am.

Eventually, she picks up the necklace and places it back in my hand. "Hold on to this," she says. "Until I come back, okay?"

"Just promise me you'll come back."

She kisses me through the bars. Her lips are warm, her breath is hot. I can feel her tears on my skin, can already feel her absence in my heart.

"More than promise," she says, before kissing me one final time. After that, she turns on her heel, and escapes into the night.

AUTUMN

Ivy

I PULL DOWN THE GRAVEL ROAD THAT LEADS TO the amusement park. My car is compact and I'm able to pull up in front of the gate.

It appears that I'm alone. The sign welcoming me to the amusement park still hangs above the entrance, only it's no longer illuminated, and the words are slightly crooked.

I get out of the car. It's midday and the air is chilled, especially with the tree boughs shrouding the area. I go up to the gate, past the police tape that tells me not to. It's amazing how different things look in the daylight, no longer sparkly and alluring, but stark, drab, and haunted. I reach out through the bars, picturing Parker on the other side, the pleading look in his eyes, the tears running down his face.

I hate myself for leaving him here.

After I escaped and made it to the street, and flagged down help, called the police, and showed them where to look, it was two hours later and Parker couldn't be found.

The others couldn't either. Not even Frankie. When investigators went to dig him up, all they found was an empty hole.

The investigation turned cold quickly. The FBI believes whoever is responsible is smart, rich, and demented. The rest remains a mystery—a string of false leads and dead ends.

I look back at the welcome sign, thinking how excited everyone was by it. The statue of Eureka is still there too, only it's been blasted with a paintball gun. There are splotches of orange and green over her smiling wooden face.

This gated entrance area has been littered, too: soda cans, beer bottles, and snack packages strewn all over the ground— new and old Blake fans, desperate to get a taste of the "fun."

The sound of creaking metal startles me. The Nightmare Elf's Train of Terror must have a few loose hinges. The tarp on the snack shack rustles in the breeze. A set of wind chimes jangles.

A gust sweeps over my shoulders, blowing back my hair. I turn to get an extra scarf. But then I come to a sudden halt. I blink a couple of times, trying to make sense of what I see.

The Nightmare Elf doll. It's perched on the roof of my car. The same doll that we found in Tommy's nightmare chamber, with the missing eye and the dirty clothes.

My chest tightens. My mind begins to race. I look around—in the trees, down the road, beneath my car, in the park. But I don't see a single soul.

The gate creaks, making me jump. I turn to look. It's open a crack—just enough for me to slip through.

Music begins to play. The musical score to *Haunt Me*. The layering of violins, that haunting viola, the strum of the cello. It's coming from behind the merry-go-round, from my nightmare ride; I'm sure of it.

He's been waiting for me to come back.

I grab my keys, positioning the sharpest one—ironically, a skeleton key, just like Little Sally Jacobs's—between my index and middle fingers, ready to fight. And then I move through the gate and across the park, toward the merry-go-round, pausing at one of the horses. Its eyes are slanted and blue, reminding me of Parker's. Its golden mane is the same color as Parker's hair, too. It's crying bloody tears.

The merry-go-round music starts up, but it's so slow and tired that eventually it stops playing altogether.

But still the musical score to *Haunt Me* lingers—a pulsing beat that pelts against my heart.

The picket-fence gate in front of the house—my nightmare ride—opens and closes in the wind. I move to stand in front of it, reaching for my aromatherapy necklace, suddenly reminded that I gave it to Parker. I keep grabbing for it, forgetting that it's no longer a part of me.

I move through the gate. The front door is already open. Still gripping the key, I head inside and go to flick on a light. But it isn't working. The windows have been covered over, too. The only light is from the open door.

I keep it propped open with a loose walkway brick, and then I move up the stairs, past the photos. The music grows louder with each step. My skin feels hot. The key is sweaty between my fingertips.

Just a step away from reaching the second floor, I hear a scuffling sound. It radiates down my spine. My mother screams. The front door slams behind me. More sounds follow: a bolt locking, glass breaking. Did someone throw a brick?

"Ivy?" Parker's voice. It's coming from outside.

"Your friend won't be able to get in," another voice whispers. *Garth?* Where is he?

My adrenaline racing, I climb another step looking all around. Standing outside my parents' room, I wrap my hand around the knob, feeling my body tremble.

The knob turns. The door opens with a whine.

"Good evening, Princess," he says, his raspy voice speaking over the music.

It's my parents' killer. The birdlike eyes. The silver hair. He's got Parker in a headlock with a knife pressed against his neck. Wasn't Parker just outside? Is it possible that I heard wrong?

The killer smiles when he sees me, his head cocked to the side. "Welcome to the sequel."

I grip the key tighter. "I've been waiting for this moment," I tell him.

The comment takes him off guard. I can see it in the flutter of his eyelids, the swallowing in his throat.

Before he can rebound, I lunge forward, swiping at his face with the key. The motion causes him to release Parker.

I swipe at him again. This time I get his chest. He lets out a scream, but then I realize that I'm screaming too. I'm screaming as I cut him, as I stab him, as I plunge my key deep into his heart.

"Ivy!" Parker shouts, holding me back, taking the key, pinning my arms to the bed.

Someone else sits on my legs.

There's a hand on my forehead.

I wake up.

Parker isn't here.

It's Apple and Core, my foster parents. Rosie and Willow linger in the doorway, looking on.

I'm in my room. My covers are dark, dark blue. My walls are pale green and there are angled ceilings. A shag carpet covers the floor. And there's an armoire in place of a vanity. There are no soccer banners, nor is there a single reference to Katrina Rowe.

Apple gets up from my legs, sends Rosie and Willow back to bed, and then gently closes the door. Meanwhile, Core's got my knife—not a skeleton key—in his hands. My double-action switchblade; I've been keeping it beneath my pillow while I sleep.

Neither of them show alarm. Nights like this have been an all-too-regular occurrence—my subconscious wreaking havoc during my sleep, blurring the lines of reality, creating a mishmash of nightmarish visions from my nightmarish life. So far my parents have confiscated four knives and five keys, even though we were supposed to be playing by the "three strikes" rule.

Three strikes and they were going to check me in someplace,

afraid that I might hurt myself, terrified that I might hurt one of the others. I can't really say I blame them.

"You know what this means," Core says, sadness in his voice.

Apple nods, her eyes filled with tears. But instead of talking about the consequences now, she crawls into my bed and holds on to me for dear life. For just a moment, I forget that she isn't my real mother.

I face the window as she snuggles me close. The breeze filters in through the window screen, and I can hear the sounds from outside: the tinkling of backyard wind chimes, the banging of shutters somewhere, and the rattling of overturned trash cans.

The musical score to *Haunt Me* still plays in my mind.

I vow to make it stop.

I vow to find Parker.

EPILOGUE

IVY

I REACH FOR THE LARGE MANILA ENVELOPE HIDDEN beneath my bed—a package that arrived last week. With no postmark and no return address, I assumed it was another anonymous gift from my parents' killer, like the pink soccer jersey from two years ago. But then I saw that my name and address were written in red crayon, just like the WELCOME TO THE DARK HOUSE sign, and I knew that wasn't the case.

I open the envelope and pull out the winning essays. A note attached to the first one reads *See you for the sequel, Princess.*

As has become my my bedtime ritual, I begin to reread:

In a thousand words or less, describe your worst nightmare.

By Frankie Rice

At five years old, I was too young to be at a wake, but I was, and I saw the body. Dressed in a navy blue suit and a slim red tie, Uncle Pete was no longer as I remembered him: the funny guy at the end of the dinner table telling jokes. Instead, he was lying in a box with no reason to laugh at all.

I climbed up on a stool to view the casket and focused on just his hands, unable to bring myself to look at his face. Gone were the oil stains from working on cars. His hands were cleaned, polished, and powdered. If it weren't for the watch around his wrist—the same braided leather one that my dad has—and his long, callused fingers, I'd have sworn those hands weren't his.

Dad said that Uncle Pete had died in his sleep from accidentally taking too many pills. I hated pills after that. I hated even more that his death came only a few months after my mother had walked out without so much as a good-bye.

Later, at the burial, I was surrounded by rows and rows of headstones, perched over hundreds of dead, buried bodies—proof positive that happily ever after doesn't exist.

I watched as they lowered Uncle Pete down into the ground, and a wave of panic struck me. What if my dad died in his sleep? Who would I have then? For as long as I could remember, Dad had been taking pills from the little brown bottle beside his bed.

I folded to the ground, a broken-glass sensation inside my chest. Soon, no one was paying attention to poor Uncle Pete, covered in dirt. They were focused on me, the five-year-old nephew, as I tried my hardest to breathe.

I passed out and was rushed to the hospital. Doctors insisted that I needed therapy, attention, and rest. Dad laughed at the first two suggestions. And that last one was impossible, because that's when my nightmares started.

That night, back at home, lying in bed, I kept a firm hold of my teddy bear—the blue one with no mouth (the threading tore) and only one eye—so that it wouldn't leave me too. I tossed and turned for hours.

The phone ringing finally pulled me out of bed. I was convinced that it was my mother calling to tell me where she was and that the phone extension was buried underground, right along with my uncle. If I wanted to speak to my mother again, I knew I had to dig up Uncle Pete's grave.

I walked past a long row of headstones. The ringing of the phone grew louder with each step. Tarantula-like trees bordered the cemetery on both sides. They looked like they could spring to life at any moment and take someone else from me.

I got down on my hands and knees as the phone continued to ring. "Don't hang up," I shouted to my mother. "I'm going as fast as I can." I dug my fingertips into the dirt, desperate to answer her call.

The dirt came up easily at first, but around three feet deep, my fingers started to burn. Still, I kept going, my wrists aching, my shoulders throbbing. My heart pounded as I got closer—just a few feet more. I climbed inside the hole, using my heels to dig in too.

Finally I got to the casket. With trembling hands, I lifted the cover.

Uncle Pete's eyes opened. "Hey, champ. I really dig it that you dug me out," he joked.

He'd been buried alive.

I couldn't stop shaking. Sitting at the foot of the casket, teetering on the frame, I stablized myself to keep from tumbling forward.

"Thanks so much for rescuing me," he continued. "I suppose now you'd like to answer the phone." The phone extension was in his grip—in his powdery white hand.

I reached out to take it. At the same moment, Uncle Pete grabbed my arm and pulled me forward. I toppled on top of him.

The casket cover closed, locking me inside.

I woke up, out of breath, in my parents' bedroom closet. Two layers of skin had burned off my fingertips from digging into the carpeted floor.

The phone had stopped ringing by then, so I have no proof that it was my mother calling that night, but I have a strong suspicion that it was—that she wanted to say sorry about Uncle Pete.

I can't help but blame myself for missing that call—my one and only chance to get her back.

In a thousand words or less, describe your worst nightmare.

By Taylor Monroe

I should probably start off by saying that I hate camping— like, I really hate it. A deep-seated loathing that burrows to the depths of my soul. I'm not exaggerating, either. There's just so much to detest: sleeping in the woods, eating charcoal-blackened food, peeing in an outhouse, getting bitten by mosquitoes. I hate tents, dirt, greenhead flies, bug spray, lawn chairs, air mattresses, wild animals, and "Kumbaya" by the fire.

Of course, as luck would have it (please read sarcasm here), my parents insist that we go camping each year. This torture started at the age of eleven. I just turned eighteen (eighteen = a legal adult . . . and guess which legal adult will be exercising her right not to go camping this year). In case you haven't yet done the math, that's seven years of torture. Almost half of my life.

Don't get me wrong; I didn't always hate camping. That first year, I was really into it (or at least the idea of it). I had the dates marked on my calendar and I talked it up to friends, practically making myself out to be G. I. Jane, the star of the next hit reality TV show—one that has a wilderness theme. I was also packed and ready to go before anyone else in my family.

But then we got there and I discovered, much to my chagrin, that it wasn't at all like that episode of The Darkashians *. . . when the family drove a luxury RV two hours outside of LA to set up camp and spend the night.*

"Can you find us some long sticks?" Dad asked me on our first day there. He was standing by the fire, getting ready to make dinner, but he'd forgotten to pack skewers. "Six of them," he added.

With my mom and brother off swimming in the leech-infested lake, I had no other choice but to oblige. I abandoned my magazine and went up the trail, where we'd all hiked earlier in the day.

Trees and brush surrounded me on both sides of the path. With the sun sinking in the sky, peeking down through the limbs, I had to admit, the forest looked really striking.

I scanned the ground, searching for fallen sticks at least a couple feet in length. Maybe camping's not so bad, I thought, my mind flashing to the cute boy at the campsite next to ours. Maybe I'd ask him to toast marshmallows with us later. I smiled at the idea, and then reached out to snag a curved branch, catching a glimpse of something brown and furry in the corner of my eye.

I stopped to get a better look. Its eyes were watching me from beyond the tree, a stone's throw away.

A cub. So irresistibly cute, like something you'd see on the cover of National Geographic *or on that reality show* Super Cute. *The cub had a friend, who appeared to be cleaning himself off, licking his coat.*

I wondered if they were lost, but no sooner did that thought cross my mind than I spotted the mother. She emerged from some brush. And stared back at me.

My heart immediately sank. I didn't have time to react. There was a flash of fur, and the sound of a growl.

I was on the ground in seconds. The mother bear was on top of me, biting my arm, growling in my ear. Its razor-sharp teeth sank into my leg. It lifted me up and shook me from side to side, thrashing me around like a rag doll.

Surprisingly, I felt no pain. My body went into some sort of self-protective mode. I dropped to the ground, shielded my face, tucked into a fetal position.

But still the bear wouldn't let me go. It bit the corner of my mouth. Then my shoulder. And the back of my head. I could hear myself whimpering, could feel my body twitching. Its claws ripped through my T-shirt, tearing up my skin.

My vision was blurry, but I was able to peek around me. Blood was everywhere. I touched my shoulder, able to feel bone. I was sure I was going to die.

I reached for a rock, but it was beyond my grasp. I needed a few more inches.

The bear let out another roar before clawing at my side. I could feel my skin rip free.

"Dad!" I tried to scream, but the word came out a wheeze.

Still, Dad was able to hear me. He shook me awake. I'd been sleeping in my tent, having a bad dream. My magazine was on the ground beside me, splayed open to an article about bear attacks.

"Taylor, are you okay?" he asked.

I sat up, my heart pounding, my eye still blurred from my being pressed against the pillow. I collapsed into my dad's arms, feeling insurmountable relief.

He stroked my hair back and then started to pull away. But I refused to let him go. "Can you just hold me for a little while longer?"

"I'll hold you for as long as you want," he said, startled that I'd gotten so freaked. (For the record, I don't *typically scare so easily; I mean, hello, I entered this contest, didn't I?)*

Anyway, you'd think that after seeing how horrified his firstborn had become, he'd think twice about camping, right? No such luck.

In a thousand words or less, describe your worst nightmare.

By Garth Vader

I was seven years old when I got lost in the woods. It was during a camping trip with my dad and brothers. I woke up around two in the morning, needing to take a piss.

I grabbed a flashlight and walked down a dirt path, searching for the grove of trees, where my brothers and I had whizzed earlier in the day.

But I couldn't find it. Nor could I find my way back to the campsite.

"Craig?" I shouted, hoping to wake my brothers. "Paul?" Was this another one of my dad's tricks?

No one answered.

I hurried up and down the path, shining my flashlight over trees and brush, continuing to call out for help.

But no one came. And I was starting to panic.

Noises were coming from everywhere—sticks breaking, leaves shifting. Finally, after an hour of walking, I found a cabin. The windows were dark. Maybe the owners were sleeping. I shone my flashlight over the entrance. The words *Welcome to the Dark House* were scribbled in red crayon.

I knocked and the door edged open. I went inside, hoping to find a phone.

A voice cut through the darkness: "Have you come to play?"

A creaking sound followed. I aimed my flashlight at a doll. The Nightmare Elf, rocking back and forth in a wooden rocking chair.

The door slammed behind me. The lock bolted shut. The elf's smile widened.

Desperate, I ran into a room with an open door, hoping to find a phone.

Little Sally Jacobs was there, sitting on the floor, playing a game of jacks. "Do you want to play?" She looked up at me with skeleton keys jammed into her eyes. Blood trickled down her cheeks. She went to remove one of the keys—a thick slopping sound.

I hurried to the window, but it was locked, and I couldn't get the bolt to unlatch.

I turned back around.

Sally was there. "Leaving so soon?" she asked, coming at me with the bloody key.

I ran to the closet, closing the door behind me, and keeping my hand on the knob.

The doorknob twisted beneath my grip; she was trying to get in. I clenched my teeth and struggled to hold the knob steady, my wrists aching, my forehead sweating.

Finally the knob stopped moving. I placed my ear against the door, unable to hear a peep.

My pulse racing, I searched for something to protect myself, noticing a secret door at the back of the closet. I opened it. A long, dark alleyway faced me, surrounded on both sides by tall brick buildings.

I began down the alley, able to hear a rattling sound. I peered over my shoulder just as a shopping cart came into view. A woman in a big blue dress was pushing it.

Lizzy Greer from Halls of Horror. *She turned to face me, pulling a bloodstained ax from the heap of soda cans in her cart. "Have you come to play?"*

My body began to shake. I dropped my flashlight and tried to run past her, rounding a corner, spotting the rear door of Hotel 9. I tore through it and mounted a flight of stairs.

Someone was following me. I could hear the sound of footsteps, the creaking of a rocking chair, the bouncing of Little Sally Jacobs's ball, and the rattle of Lizzy's cart.

"Come play with us," their voices said.

I ran into one of the hotel rooms, locked the door, and hid beneath the bed. That's when I completely lost it—right there in the middle of my dream, I pissed on the sofa.

I used to get a variation of that nightmare a few times a week. Sometimes Pudgy the Clown would show up with his chain saw; other times, it'd be Sidney Scarcella wearing his butler's apron, or Sebastian Slayer in that scene where he plays the piano in the middle of the forest with severed body parts strewn about.

It was on my seventh birthday that I first saw the original Nightmare Elf *movie. My dad had dared me, saying that it was the only way I could prove I wasn't still a baby. Pretty screwed up, I know. But that's my dad for you.*

He and my brothers had watched a bunch more of your films that night. And me, being too chickenshit to go up to my room after seeing Nightmare Elf, *I brought a sleeping bag into the TV room so I wouldn't have to be alone.*

Keeping my head beneath the covers, I tried not to peek at the screen, even when my dad bribed me with money, candy, and days off from school.

But I also didn't want to be a baby. I wanted to make him proud—to this day, I've yet to succeed.

For a while, I was sleeping under my bed, paranoid that

346

the Nightmare Elf would take my dreams and make them come true.

The more fearful I became, the worse things got at home. My dad would call me pansy, pretty girl, baby, and sweet pea. He'd give me a baby cup at dinner and point me toward the girls' room when we were out in public. Finally, when I couldn't take his teasing anymore, I started watching more horror flicks—as many as I could get my hands on.

In the end, I grew to love horror just as much as my dad, probably even more because it became a part of my identity. Incidentally, in case you hadn't already noticed, I was named after my dad's all-time favorite villain—with one obvious adjustment, that is. He would've gone full out and named me Darth, but luckily my mom won that coin toss.

In a thousand words or less, describe your worst nightmare.

By Natalie Sorrento

I have nightmares about my reflection—about seeing myself, that is. They started two years ago, after my sister Margie caught me with my pants down—literally—after I'd just come out of the shower.

Standing naked, I was about to look at myself in the full-length mirror on the back of the door, but the steam from the shower had fogged up the glass. So I gazed downward at my thighs—at my very first tattoos. They were newly done and deliciously red and sting-y.

A moment later, the bathroom door whipped open. "Gross," Margie said, shielding her eyes from the sight of me. But still she was able to find my newly inked tattoos through the spaces between her chocolate-stained fingers. "What are those?" A megawatt grin formed on her face, like she'd just struck the blackmailing lottery. If only she'd wanted to blackmail me.

Instead, she went straight to my parents and pulled them into the bathroom. I'd managed to grab a towel, but my dad ripped it out of my hands. And they all stared, open mouthed.

At me. Naked. At my paunchy gut, my cottage-cheese legs, and the bloody tattoos on my thighs: Lizzy Greer's ax on one thigh, and the infamous door-with-a-peephole from Hotel 9 on the other.

I tried to cover up as best I could, cupping my hands over my boobs and crotch, while holding back hot, bubbling tears. But it wasn't nearly enough. And their expressions confirmed what I already knew. I was undeniably hideous. Deplorable. Hopeless. Regrettable.

Mom: "How did this happen?"

Dad: "If only . . ."

Ever since that day, I've avoided mirrors. I keep a desk blotter over the vanity in my bedroom. I close my eyes as I wash my hands in bathrooms. I never stand or walk too close to windows or glass doors, for fear of seeing a reflection. And I'm careful not to go into places that are known to have mirrors, e.g., hair salons, dressing rooms, department stores, and gyms.

I also avoid having my picture taken, including for class photos. I've ditched school on picture day for the past several years. Nobody's ever questioned it—nobody gives a shit that I'm not standing with my classmates, a fake smile across my zit-covered face.

Lastly, I keep myself covered—tattoos, wigs, sunglasses,

349

layers of clothing—so that no one has to see me. And so that I, in turn, never have to see the reflection of myself in anyone else's eyes.

But at night, I can't escape my reflection. I have nightmares about being trapped inside a maze of mirrors, unable to find my way out. With each corner I turn, my image gets uglier and more distorted—one moment short and bulging, the next stretched out and warped.

The images accentuate what's wrong with me: face too long, eyes too big, hair too frizzy, crooked nose, fishlike lips, hips too wide, waist too thick, chunky knees, pasty skin. In my dream, I try to run away from the images, but they're everywhere, chasing me, laughing at me. I move to the side—into yet another mirror—as if that one will make a difference. And it does. It's the worst image yet. It's the real me, in a real mirror—far worse than any distortion.

In a thousand words or less, describe your worst nightmare.

By Parker Bradley

Its teeth sank into my leg—a tearing, mind-blowing pain. Despite not being in the ocean, I thought it was a shark. But then its body crested the surface of the water, and I saw what it really was.

An eel—at least six feet long and five inches wide.

Its mouth arched open—dozens of razor-sharp teeth snapped at my ribs. I tried to get away, but it was too big, too fast. The next thing I knew, I was underwater.

In my mind, I screamed for help. In reality, I couldn't breathe, couldn't scream. Somehow I managed to paddle upward, and the eel lost its grip on my side. I started to move away. But then it bit my thigh—deep into the flesh— pulling me back under.

My mouth filled up with water. Everything around me turned red. Out of the corner of my eye, I saw something move over the surface of the water. An oil spill? A liquid of some sort? It was spreading like lava.

I broke through the surface again, able to see just what it was—not a liquid at all.

A steel cover extended over the entire width of the pond. The cover was moving closer, forming a lid over the water's surface. If I didn't get out, I'd be trapped underneath it.

More eels came, at least twenty of them, swarming me, tearing into my back, my chest, my legs, my feet. They pulled me under once more.

I looked up. The cover was above my head. I tried to push on it, but it wouldn't budge.

I paddled fast, chasing the edge of the cover, scrambling to get in front of it. But it was too late. The pond was completely sealed now.

I screamed beneath the surface of the water, this time able to hear my voice—a sharp, piercing wail that woke me up.

I was in the hospital, lying in bed, having a nightmare about something that had happened the day before. My legs were covered in bite marks.

A nurse was sitting beside me. "You had another one, huh?" she asked.

I nodded. It was my third nightmare that night.

"Those nasty dreams will fade with time."

If only that were true.

I had nearly drowned. It happened at summer camp,

when I was ten years old, after most of the other campers had already been picked up for the day. I was left waiting for my ride.

It was hot out, but since I didn't know how to swim, the counselors had forbidden me from going into the water. Even earlier in the day, when all of my fellow campers had free swim, I'd been given a squirt gun and a bucket of water, and told to keep cool.

But being the end of the day, the counselors had gone back to the office to clean up. So, I jumped right into the pond, and started paddling around. But no sooner did I get out chest-deep than I felt that first rip.

It took my brain a beat to catch up to the sensation. And when it did, I heard a yell, realizing it was mine. My voice. My panic. Like an out-of-body experience.

Water was splashing all around me—I was doing that, too—trying to get out, to get away.

But something still had my calf.

And clouds of red colored the water.

Eventually people came. There were sirens and flashing lights. Arms were reaching, pulling, tugging, twisting. Voices were shouting directives. All the fight I had was gone.

Months later, I did a report on eels in school. I learned that it's only in extreme situations that eels attack humans. Like, if the eels are feeding and someone gets caught up in the midst, or if the eels are caged and starved. Though somewhat reassuring, I haven't entered the water since. And I know I never will.

In a thousand words or less, describe your worst nightmare.

By Shayla Belmont

I was the one who found Dara's body. She'd hung herself in the closet, in her dorm room, at our boarding school—the same boarding school I'd convinced her to transfer to with the promise of cute boys, weekends in the city, and pizza-and-Chinese-food-flavored cram sessions.

Her feet dangled above the floor. She was wearing her heart-patterned socks—the same ones that we both owned from a trip to the mall months before when we'd bought matching pairs. Standing there, I had to wonder if she'd worn those socks on purpose, if she'd banked on me being the one to find her. Was that her way of forcing me to remember the way things used to be?

Her face was bluish gray. Her eyes were open, focused upward. The telephone wire wrapped around her neck had cut into her throat. I reached out to touch her hand, noticing that the blood from her arms had drained down to her fingertips.

That's when I knew for sure. It's when I felt my legs give way beneath me. My best friend Dara was dead.

I was nine years old when we met. It was at yoga camp in the Berkshires and we got partnered up by Saffron, the yoga master who insisted that Dara and I had the same karmic energy and were destined to be best friends. Little did I know that Saffron would be right. Little did I know that seven years of best friendship later, Dara would end up taking her own life. Where was her karmic energy then?

I've heard stories that your life flashes before you in those fleeting seconds before death. I wasn't physically dying in that moment, but emotionally I guess I was. Images of Dara and me raced across my mind: at thirteen years old, dyeing our hair green for St. Patrick's Day; dance parties in her basement; mini-makeovers in my bedroom; hot-fudge-sundae-with-whipped-cream pacts that we'd always be there for each other, no matter what.

I looked up at her face again. Her lips were chalky white, parted open, exposing the familiar gap in her front teeth, where she'd once stuck a Cheez-It to be funny. Her long orange hair was in a sideways braid.

The nightmares that I have about Dara are always the same—always me, searching for her. There's always a long, dark hallway, like in the resident dorm at night. I go to her room and open the closet.

And there's her body. Those heart-patterned socks.

Though, in the dream, her eyes are closed. And instead of fond memories flashing before my eyes, I'm haunted by those moments when I could've been a better friend. Like the time I left her teary eyed on my doorstep because I had dinner plans with Miranda and Gigi.

And the time I told her I was too sick to spend the weekend watching movies and giving each other mani-pedicures, as planned, because I'd been invited up to Bunny's ski house.

And then, just when things can't get any more hideous—and I'm unable to force myself to wake up—her eyelids snap open and she stares back at me.

"I thought we were supposed to be friends," she whispers, tears dripping down her face.

I open my mouth to tell her that we are friends, that she'll always be my best friend, but the words won't come out; they remain stuck inside my head.

Her arm raises up then, and she points in my direction with her dark blue finger. Her lips are pursed; her eyes are wide and teary. She's angry and sad at the same time. "You weren't there for me," she says. "You broke your promise. And now you'll pay."

Just when I thought my nightmares couldn't get any worse, I woke up to face the reality of my life.
—Ivy Jensen

RETURN TO THE DARK HOUSE

Dear Parker,

Years ago, after my parents were killed, my therapist thought it would be a good idea to write them letters—as many as I felt I needed to, for all of the things I wanted to share.

She told me that I should write the letters on special paper, seal them up in envelopes, and then mail them to myself, so that one day, years later, I could open the letters and see how much I'd grown.

The idea seemed stupid to me at the time. I was angry, confused, incapable of perspective, never mind growth. But I really don't know what else to do here, Parker. And so I'm going to write you letters, starting with this one, but not as a way to track my growth, and not because I think you're dead.

I'm just hoping to feel connected to you.

It's been almost two months since the Dark House, and in that time, the FBI has come up with only a few basic theories—or at least only a few they're willing to share with me. First, that aside from you and Taylor, all of the other contest winners were killed at the amusement park.

I don't think that's true. They have yet to uncover a single body. That theory is based solely on my testimony about the movie clips we saw just before my escape. Well, that and the amount of blood discovered at a few of the nightmare rides.

The second theory is that the person in charge has an unlimited supply of money.

I know, not exactly rocket science, right?

Everybody keeps telling me to move on. But how can I move any-where when you and the others are still missing? I know it may sound dumb, but after my parents' death, I never really allowed anyone to get too close—not my foster family, not one single friend—for fear that person might get taken from me too. But then I met you, and I broke all my own rules by allowing myself to be vulnerable and letting you in.

The time we spent together was the closest I'd felt to anyone in years. And, just as I'd always feared, you were taken from me too. But I'm going to get you back. And years from now when I open this letter, hopefully you'll be sitting right beside me, and I can share it with you for real.

Love always,

Ivy

LATE SUMMER

IVY JENSEN

My bedroom door creaks open, and the light from the hallway penetrates my room. I see his boot first: black wrinkled leather, soiled at the toe.

My gaze travels up his leg. He's wearing a bright-red suit, as part of his elf costume, along with a floppy hat and green gloves.

He stares at me in the doorway with his tiny, dark-gray eyes: they're rimmed with amber-brown; I'd recognize them anywhere. His silver hair is just as I remember it too—thick, shoulder-length, and wavy, tied back in a low ponytail, and with thin strands of black coursing through it.

"Good evening, Princess," he says. His tongue inches out of his mouth, between his crooked yellow teeth, in the creepiest of grins. He looks around the room—at my soccer banners, my music posters, and all of my touches of pink—before meeting my eyes again. "It's *very* nice to see you."

There's a cut on his face, just below his eye, extending four inches down his cheek. A trickle of blood runs from it, dripping onto my paisley bedcovers. Did my mom scratch him with her fingernails? Did Dad cut him with something sharp?

"Have you enjoyed the gifts I've sent you?" he asks. "The star pendant? The makeup kit?"

My fingers trembling, I reach inside my bag, searching for Taylor's cell phone. I go to click it on, only to discover that it's a calculator, not the phone.

The Nightmare Elf pulls a knife from the pocket of his suit and holds it out for show—a six-inch spring spike with a double-action blade. He brings it up to my neck, points the tip into my throat.

"Please," I whisper, pressing the back of my head against the wall, fighting the urge to swallow.

"Ivy!" Parker shouts. His voice is followed by the sound of glass breaking.

The noise startles me awake. I sit up in bed, out of breath, before realizing where I am.

In my room.

At the hospital.

A clock on the wall ticks. It's only four in the morning.

I touch my neck and try to swallow. It feels like sharp blades inside my throat. I must be getting sick.

Someone else must be up too. I can hear the sound of glass being swept, can picture the broken pieces entering someone's skin.

And that's when I remember.

I push the call button. "I need somebody to come in here!" I shout, despite the fact that my roommate is sleeping only a few feet away. I grab my notebook from beneath my pillow and write down the new clue, hoping I'm not too late.

IVY

THE TICKTOCK OF THE WALL CLOCK ECHOES THE ticking deep inside me. My very own personal time bomb, just a sneeze away from going off.

I pinch the skin on my knee, and feel the familiar cramp— a stabbing sensation at the base of my thumb that radiates up my arm, into my elbow, setting my nerves aflame. The cramping is what eventually gets me to stop pinching.

Not the bloodred nail marks in my skin.

Not the black-and-blue blotches over both kneecaps.

Not the shamrock-shaped patch of yellow (a bruise in healing) swimming in a sea of purple skin.

I think I might spontaneously combust if someone doesn't come in here within the next sixty seconds.

Ticktock, ticktock.

The medication isn't working. It's supposed to lighten and dull, but instead it seems to magnify. Everything feels brighter, louder, harsher, sharper.

I'm in one of the private meeting rooms. Sitting among white walls and metal folding chairs, at a laminate table with boogers and gum wads stuck underneath.

Because I started sleeping with knives.

Because Apple and Core, my foster parents, don't think I'm the safest person to be around.

Not safe for myself.

Not safe for any of my foster siblings.

I can't say I blame them. I honestly don't know what *safe* is anymore. I doubt that it even exists.

I drum my fingers against the table to drown out the ticking. My palm aches. The nubs of my fingers feel tingly.

Finally, there's a knock on the door. It creaks open. An officer walks in. Detective Thomas, local P.D. A major letdown. "I'd asked to speak with the FBI," I tell him.

"Nice to see you too." He nods a hello and takes a seat across from me. There are pouches beneath his eyes from lack of sleep. At least we have one thing in common.

I take my notebook from my lap and open it up to the first page. "There are some things we need to go over."

After only a couple of seconds of reading, he lets out a heavy sigh. His breath smells like Cheetos. "We've been through these details before, Ivy. I thought you had something new."

"I do, but first we need to review."

"We've already reviewed." He's looking at me rather than my notes. "We've also explored, dissected, examined, and revisited. Trust me when I say that we're doing all we can."

"Well, it isn't good enough."

"Ivy." His voice softens. "Leave the manhunt to us, okay? That's *our* job. Your job is to get better and then get out of here."

"Have you had a psychologist examine the winning contest essays?" I ask him. "Or analyze our personality profiles to determine how the killer chose us?"

"What do you think?"

"That's why I'm asking." I start flipping forward and backward through the pages of my notebook, pointing out charts and parallels I've drawn.

Detective Thomas indulges me by reading over a

chronology I wrote—my summation of what happened on the Dark House amusement park night.

The second worst day of my life.

But then he closes the cover and slides the notebook across the table at me. "Take care of yourself, Ivy. Get some rest and get yourself better. If we find out anything, we'll let you know." He gets up to leave.

"No!" I shout, getting up too. I flip the notebook back open and scramble to the page marked Unanswered Questions. "Did you find any of the people who helped set up the amusement park? Or how about the drivers who picked us up from the airport . . . or Midge?"

"The amusement park had been there for years." He sighs again. "It was abandoned and then revived for the Dark House weekend. The same goes for the cabin; someone made it look like the real Dark House. The FBI was able to find one of the drivers and he was brought in for questioning, but it seems he never met the suspect in person, only corresponded with him via text messages and e-mail. Those accounts have since been deleted."

"Okay, so what about all of the creepy voice-overs that were used at the park?" I point to item number seven on the list of unanswered questions. "Do we know the identity of those people?"

"Ivy . . ."

"It's a valid question."

"It's hard to find someone based solely on a voice—particularly a voice that none of the authorities heard. Need I remind you that all of the audio and visual equipment was gone by the time the officials got to the park? The people who were hired to do those voice-overs probably didn't even know what they were participating in—what the suspect's project was, that is."

"In other words, no one's contacted those people."

Detective Thomas holds up his hands, as if he wants to talk me down off an imaginary ledge. If only I could jump.

"Parker is alive," I snap. "He's going to star in the sequel. The killer is making another movie. What are you doing to stop him?"

"Get better," he says again, stepping back from the table.

"Doesn't anything I say mean anything to you at all?"

"Of course it does. I'm here, aren't I? You asked to speak to the authorities about a new lead in the case. I come all the way down here, and all you have are recycled clues, not to mention well-covered territory."

"The killer has a scar."

The detective's eyes widen as he studies my face, perhaps waiting for me to take the words back. When I don't, he grabs a notebook and pen from inside his jacket and sits back down. "How do you know?"

I draw an invisible line down my face with my finger. "I only remembered the scar recently. It's a diagonal mark that extends from just below his right eye to just above his jawbone."

"Hold on," he says, jotting the information down, "I thought you said before that he was wearing a mask during your nightmare ride. Did he take it off?"

I open my mouth to answer, feeling my face flash hot. A sickly sensation churns in my stomach. Acid burns a hole in my throat. I look back up at the clock—*ticktock, ticktock*—realizing what I've done.

"*Ivy?* Did he take the mask off?"

I shake my head, suddenly feeling like I've morphed into a little girl, caught for stealing from her mother's purse.

"Then how do you know about a scar?"

I bring a strand of hair across my eyes, as if it could possibly hide me. I take a deep breath and travel back in my mind to the instant that I remembered the scar—around four this morning, after having just woken up from a nightmare about my parents, about their killer, only he'd been dressed like the Nightmare Elf from the Dark House case. Parker's voice had called out to me (another Dark House detail). Plus, also in the

373

dream, I'd been searching for Taylor's cell phone (a third Dark House detail).

"Ivy?"

"I'm sorry," I say, shaking my head. "I'd been so swept up in the detail of the scar that I hadn't stopped to question it."

Thomas's furry blond eyebrows knit together in confusion; they look like caterpillars mating.

"I did remember a scar," I tell him. "But it was on the face of my parents' killer from seven years ago. You're right. The Nightmare Elf *was* wearing a mask at the amusement park. He never took it off." I breathe in and breathe out; there's tightness in my chest. "All of the nightmares I've been having . . . they've been colliding inside my head, bleeding into one other. Sometimes it's hard to decipher which details go with which case."

"Don't worry about it." He closes up his notebook. "Stress like this can wreak havoc on the brain . . . distort your sense of reality."

"But it *is* real," I insist. "The scar, I mean. I remember it distinctly. Isn't there a name for instances like this? Repressed memories or something?"

He gets up once again, not dignifying the question with an answer.

"Not yet," I bark, grabbing at the ache in my head. "There's

374

so much more to talk about. Did anyone check out the hardware stores within a twenty-mile radius of the Dark House? Here, I've located three of them." I pull a map from the back pocket of my notebook and open it up; it covers half of the table. "The red X is for the Dark House," I tell him. "The purple one is for the amusement park. The hardware stores are marked with blue X's. The green X is for the Horror House, a tiny one-room theater that's only open at night and only plays scary films. I was thinking that maybe the killer liked to go there."

"I wasn't aware that Internet access was allowed at this place."

"It's not. I've been working on this map since before I got here."

"What are the orange X's for?"

"Electronics stores where he might've purchased video equipment. Maybe one of the shop owners remembers him. Or maybe the shops use surveillance video. Or what about the real estate agent who sold him the Dark House?"

Detective Thomas stares at me with an amused expression, the corner of his mouth turned upward. "I'm impressed. But, as I've said before, you can rest assured that we've got all of these angles covered."

"What about Taylor then?" I persist. "What made her leave the Dark House early?"

"That's of no concern to you right now."

"*Tell me*," I insist.

"All you need to know where Taylor's concerned is that she saw something at the Dark House that alarmed her enough to leave. By the time investigators got to the house, they were unable to find that something."

"What was it? What did she see?"

"Ivy," he says yet again.

I hate my name. I hate my life. I stand in front of the door so he has no choice but to hear me out. "Why won't you help me?" A sob gets caught in my throat. "I mean, there has to be some reason."

"Some reason for what?"

"For why Taylor left. For why you're keeping key pieces from me. For why the two worst experiences of my life are melting together inside my brain, haunting me while I sleep."

Ticktock, ticktock. My whole body's sweating and yet I feel chilled to the bone.

"Step out of the way." There's tension on Detective Thomas's face, scrunched up on his brow.

I secure the knob in both of my hands, behind my back.

"I'm not asking you," he insists.

"Wait," I blurt, the answer finally clicking.

Thomas reaches behind me to grab the knob, but I widen

my stance so he can't. "You know you're only going to buy yourself more time in here, don't you?" he asks, lowering his voice. "What good will that do you or any of the missing victims?"

"Like you give a shit about any of us!" I shout. "You've already written them off as dead."

"You leave me no other choice." He goes to knock on the door, but I block his fist with my hand. "The killer knows where I live," I remind him, referring to the package I received just weeks after the Dark House weekend. It was filled with the winning essays of all of my fellow contest winners. I brought the package to the authorities, but with no postmark and no fingerprints, it was another dead end.

"You're safe in here," he says, pulling his fist away. He knocks on the door, right above my head. The sound echoes off the bones of my skull.

"No!" I shout, pushing myself against him—fists and arms and chest and head.

Because he won't hear me.

Because I have to make him hear me.

Everything that happens next feels like it's been set to fast forward—like I'm watching it on a TV screen, like it isn't actually happening to me.

The door whips open and I get pushed to the side. Two

nurses grab me from behind. They pull up my hospital gown, exposing my legs. Detective Thomas's eyes go straight to my knees—all bruised and swollen and purple and yellow—as a needle's stabbed into my thigh.

His face falls flat—the tension replaced by something else. Surprise? Repulsion? Pity? Remorse?

My slipper has fallen off. My heel catches against a floor tile. A layer of skin scrapes free. It takes me a moment to realize that I'm being dragged through the common room from behind.

People are talking.

Fingers are pointing.

A plastic dish falls to the floor with a clatter.

I'm brought into a room. My head hits something soft. A pillow. Cold sheets. What happened to my notebook? Where is my map?

Ticktock, ticktock. Another clock on yet another wall. But this medicine seems to do the trick, darkening my mind, dulling all of my sharp edges.

Until I can no longer hear the ticking.

Until all of my fight slips away.

NORTHBRIDGE
PSYCHIATRIC HOSPITAL

INCIDENT REPORT

Date and Time of Incident: 9/13, 3:30 p.m.

Patient Name: Ivy Rose Jensen

Age: 18

DIAGNOSIS

Post-Traumatic Stress Disorder, Depression, Anxiety Disorder

DESCRIPTION OF INCIDENT

(as reported to Amanda Baker, C.N.P., by Detective Clive Thomas)

Detective Clive Thomas had been in Private Meeting Room Two, per Ivy's request, to discuss details of the "Dark House" case in which she was involved. When Detective Thomas tried to leave the room, Ivy became hostile and began shouting at him. (Note: the shouting was heard in the common area of the hospital, as confirmed by Brooke Cantor, L.P.N.) Thomas reported that Ivy took hold of the doorknob and tried to keep him from knocking on the door. When he was finally able to knock, she shoved herself into him headfirst, and swung her arms at his face. Thomas reported that Ivy punched his jaw and elbowed his neck. At that time, nurses Dan Leiberman and Jonathan Zakum entered the room to assist.

PATIENT MEDICAL HISTORY/SHORT FORM

Adoptive Mother's Information

Name:	Gail "Apple" Jensen
Occupation:	Owner, The Tea Depot and the 24-hour Depot, Boston, MA
Marital Status:	Married

Adoptive Father's Information

Name:	Steve "Core" Jensen
Occupation:	Owner/General Contractor, Crunch Construction, Singham, MA
Marital Status:	Married

Maternal Mother's Information

Name:	Sarah Leiken
	Deceased at 41 years old
Cause of Death:	Homicide victim

Paternal Father's Information

Name: Matthew Leiken

Deceased at 44 years old

Cause of Death: Homicide victim

PATIENT'S DEVELOPMENTAL HISTORY

Past medical records for April Leiken (adoptive name, Ivy Jensen) show that April was the product of a full-term pregnancy and unremarkable birth. Neonatal is neither remarkable nor contributory, and developmental milestones for motor skills and speech/language acquisition occurred within average expectancies.

BEHAVIORAL PROBLEMS

(filled out by Gail Jensen, adoptive mother, upon hospital admittance):

Does your child currently have or has he/she ever had *(place an X beside all that apply)*:

Problems with sleeping	X
Appetite change or sudden weight change	X
Irritability or temper outbursts	X
Withdrawal or preference for being alone	X
Frequent complaints of aches or pains	(headaches) X
Recent drop in grades	N/A

(she's not currently in school)

Phobia or irrational fears	X
Difficulties separating from you	
Bouts of severe anxiety or panic	X
Repetitive behaviors (i.e., washing hands, checking locks)	X
Pulling out hair or eyelashes (pinching)	X
Talk to him/herself	
Have any imaginary friend	
Appear paranoid or afraid of others	X
Have any odd ideas or beliefs	X
Ever tried to kill themselves or others	

PAST PSYCHIATRIC HISTORY

After her maternal mother and paternal father were killed, Ivy saw Paula Laub, M.D. From the age of 9 to present, she's been seeing Donna Lamb, Ph.D.

Has your child ever been admitted to the hospital for psychiatric treatment?   No.

IVY

SHE'S HERE. SITTING AT A TABLE IN THE REC ROOM, in a chair that's way too small for her. Dr. Donna looks like a little kid.

"Hi," I say, in a voice that's just as small.

She doesn't hear me. The TV's too loud. *Wheel of Fortune.* I snatch the remote from the bookcase and lower the volume. No one who's watching seems to care, or maybe they just don't notice.

"Hi," I try again, taking the seat across from her. Somehow, despite the obvious change of space—not her stuffy office but the common area of a mental hospital—I still slip into rote routine, imagining this like a rerun on TV, suddenly wishing I could click away.

IVY: Thanks for coming to see me on such short notice.

DR. DONNA: Of course. I'm always here for you, Ivy.

IVY: So, I've been thinking a lot about the case.

DR. DONNA: Have you been thinking as much about healing?

IVY: It's him.

DR. DONNA: What's him?

IVY: The man who killed my parents, the Dark House amusement park killer . . . they're one and the same.

DR. DONNA: That's one theory that the authorities are working on.

IVY: *Excuse me?*

DR. DONNA: There are a number of theories, Ivy. The authorities are doing their job by looking into all of them. They want you to do your job too—by getting rest and getter better enough to go home. Don't you want that as well?

IVY: So, they've obviously been keeping secrets from me.

DR. DONNA: Do you think that rather the authorities don't want to burden you with the details of the case as you're trying to heal?

IVY: I think they owe it to me be honest, especially when I've been telling them everything I know, everything I remember. I mean, I'm part of this investigation too, aren't I?

DR. DONNA: This might feel like an injustice right now, but it's important to put things into perspective. Your disorder can often make feelings seem exponentially bigger, stronger, and more profoundly relevant than they need to be.

IVY: This isn't about my disorder. And my feelings *are* relevant.

DR. DONNA: Of course they are. That's not what I meant.

IVY: My parents' killer was a fan of horror movies. He re-created his favorite scenes from horror flicks for his crimes—just like the Nightmare Elf killer . . . the way he used Justin Blake's films as his inspiration for the Dark House weekend.

DR. DONNA: Okay, but why would your parents' killer go to all the trouble of organizing the Dark House amusement park weekend, holding a contest, and involving others if he only wanted to come back for you?

IVY: Because he wanted to make his own horror movie, and he needed more than one character. He handpicked all of us contest winners for his cast.

DR. DONNA: And how would he know that you, specifically, would enter the contest . . . someone who hates anything even remotely fear-inducing?

IVY: He kept e-mailing me his newsletters, ignoring my attempts to unsubscribe from his supposed list. He sent me contest opportunity after contest opportunity, awaiting the day I'd finally enter one of them. I told that to Parker—how I kept getting the Nightmare Elf's newsletters—and he seemed really confused. He never knew the Nightmare Elf even had a newsletter. None of the winners did. They all found out about the contest through various fan-flavored sites—places the killer must've posted once I'd finally entered.

DR. DONNA: You've obviously given this a lot of thought.

IVY: I have a lot of time to think in here.

DR. DONNA: What's that?

IVY: What?

DR. DONNA: On your palm and wrists. Don't try to hide it, Ivy. Have you been writing on yourself?

IVY: It's just my notes. The doctor confiscated my

notebook, so I have no other choice but to jot things down on my skin.

DR. DONNA: Why do you think he confiscated your notebook?

IVY: Because he's a controlling asshole.

DR. DONNA: Because he must've felt it was holding you back from getting better.

IVY: I'll be better once the killer's behind bars, once the others are found. To think the killer's been prepping me for years . . . sending me all those teaser gifts. The makeup kit for my theatrical performance, the star necklace pendant, because he wanted me to be his star.

DR. DONNA: And the soccer jersey and journal? Do you think that those things are related to acting and theater as well?

IVY: No, but they're just as important. They're clues that he knows who I am—before I was Ivy Jensen, that is, back when I was April Leiken, when I played soccer, and loved anything pink and covered in paisleys. Back when he killed my real parents.

DR. DONNA: Have you shared your theories with the authorities?

IVY: I'm done sharing with authorities. They've yet to help me with anything—not my parents' crime, not this one either. I need to figure things out on my own.

AUTUMN

IVY

It's six weeks later and I'm sitting in the same meeting room with the same ticking clock. But this time I'm not waiting for the police. And my palms and wrists are clean of ink. Plus my knees are no longer bruised, not that you can see them. I'm no longer dressed in a hospital gown. I'm able to wear my own clothes: my favorite sweats, my fuzzy slippers. I also got my bracelet back—six long strands of T-shirt fabric woven into a fishtail braid that winds around my wrist. The fabric is from Parker's T-shirt—the same one he wore on the Dark House amusement park night, the one he used to make a bandage for my ankle.

I touch over my heart, where my pendant used to dangle, reminded that he has something of mine too. My aromatherapy necklace. It'd fallen off as we were running to escape. One moment, we were fleeing the amusement park together, heading toward the closing exit gates. The next moment, Parker had stopped to pick something up. It took me a couple of seconds to figure out what it was.

That necklace was supposed to have been a gift for my mother. But she was killed before I could give it to her—just days before her forty-second birthday.

The necklace—a tiny bottle pendant with an even tinier cork, suspended from a silver chain—became my most cherished possession. Still, in that moment of trying to escape the park, I no longer cared about the necklace. I only cared about Parker—about him joining me on the other side of the exit gate. But time was ticking then too. The exit gates were closing. I strained my muscles, using all of the strength inside me to hold the doors open. But in the end, the iron gates closed with a deep, heavy clank, locking Parker inside the park.

And tearing my world in two.

At last, the door to the conference room opens and I sit up straighter. I smile—not too big, a closed mouth—and make direct eye contact as Dr. Tully comes in. He's older, mid-sixties, with hair like Albert Einstein and the tiniest glasses I've ever seen. He's the bigwig here. Patients don't normally meet with him, except upon admission or when there's a serious problem. Or just prior to exit.

He starts with small talk, asking me a few basic questions—about the weather and the food here, and if I noticed the full moon last night. I haven't missed a week of therapy for the past seven years, so I know just how to answer, lying straight through my teeth.

"I love the winter," I tell him. "My foster parents rent a place in Vermont and we go up on the weekends to ski. I can't wait to get back there." The truth: I've never been skiing. But my answer shows that I'm looking ahead, excited about life, not intimidated by the thought of spending time with family.

"The food here?" I flash him a sheepish grin. "Well, it's not exactly fine dining, especially for a food snob like me who wants to be a chef. Although, between you and me"—I lean in close—"the mac and cheese here kicks my recipe's butt." The lie nearly kills me, but the outcome is totally worth it.

Dr. Tully grins at my answer. I've shown him my sense of humor while, at the same time, conveying my aspirations.

And as for that magnificent moon: "Yes, I saw it. It was so big and glowing, like a giant snowball in the sky."

It's true that I noticed the moon. I'd have to have been an idiot not to, considering that a couple of the patients were howling at it. But it didn't make me think of a snowball. It made me think of Parker—made me wonder if, wherever he is, he could see it too.

The remainder of the interview is key, because he segues into the reason that I'm here: "How often do you think about the Dark House amusement park night?"

I swallow hard, trying to keep a poker face. The truth is that I don't remember what it was like to *not* think about that night. "I don't know," I answer, finally. "At least once a day. I no longer dream about it, though; and it's not the first thing on my mind when I wake up in the morning. I'm hoping that with more time—and closure—I won't think about it much at all." Breathe in, breathe out. *Ticktock, ticktock.* I keep my hands on the table, where both he and I can see them, resisting the urge to pinch.

"And what if you don't get that closure?" he asks. "What if the others aren't found and they never catch the person responsible?"

"I've been working on my own form of closure, trying to think up things I can do, ways I can help people, maybe talking to crisis victims . . . people who've had loved ones taken away from them. I don't know." I feign a shy smile. "Does that sound dumb?"

Dr. Tully leans forward. A good sign; my answer has piqued his interest. "It actually sounds very ambitious."

"I realize that. And I know I have a lot more healing to do before I can help others. But it's definitely in my long-term plans."

"Well, I think it's a great plan." He smiles, perhaps relieved by my newfound sanity and perspective—all thanks to Happy Hospital. "You've been through a lot in your lifetime—more tragedy than most people will ever know. It's healthy to think of that tragedy as a springboard to do good. Talk about your notebook, and your maps and charts. Are you still writing down all of your theories and trying to track the person responsible for the Dark House weekend?"

I shake my head, glad that he asked. "I threw all of that stuff away—not long after the doctor confiscated my notebook, actually. It was feeding an obsession and keeping me from moving forward. I can see that now."

"Do you still feel the need to help solve the case and find the missing victims?"

I shake my head again. "That isn't up to me. The FBI know what they're doing. My job is to get better and to get out of here." The very same words that Detective Thomas used on me.

"Well, you've certainly come a long way." He eyes me for

several seconds, studying my body language and nodding his head.

Meanwhile, I do my best not to swallow too hard or blink too often.

"I'd like to talk to you about the hospital's outpatient program," he says, finally. "It's important that you continue your therapy upon discharge."

I hold in my elation by squeezing my thighs together. "I'd like that."

"You'll be responsible for taking all of your medication. And should you ever feel overwhelmed, or overly stressed, or excessively anxious or fearful about anything, it's essential that you tell someone. Before your discharge, we'll establish a list of go-to people to call. How does that sound?"

"It sounds perfect." I flash him another closed smile.

In my room, I celebrate my get-out-of-jail card by packing up my stuff. While my roommate is at her group session, I move to the far wall by my dresser. I peek over my shoulder to make sure no one's looking in from the hallway, and then I scoot down by the heat vent and take off the cover. My notebook—a new one—is stuffed inside the duct. I snag it, replace the cover, and flip the notebook open to the back— to a letter I'm writing to Parker. The pages warm me like a blanket.

Dear Parker,

My mind reels, going over the details of the Dark House weekend, trying to come up with an answer—some unturned leaf, a magical pearl that might help to find you and the others.

Questions I wish I could ask you: Are you okay? The obvious: Where are you? Who's with you? Frankie, Shayla, Garth, Natalie? Will you ever forgive me for leaving you at the park?

Things I wish I could tell you: I miss you more than you know. I'll never stop looking for you.

Love always,

Ivy

Ivy

IT'S BEEN NEARLY FIVE WEEKS SINCE MY RELEASE from the hospital, and a lot of things have changed. For starters, I didn't go home to my foster parents. I moved into the basement apartment of Tillie, my foster aunt, just down the street. It's better this way. More privacy for me. Less potential danger for them.

For my entire life, no one around me has ever been safe.

"Aunt Tillie has a security system," Apple reminded me, zipping up my suitcase.

Without any of my things, my room looked like it belonged

in a hotel—like a place that one might inhabit for a limited amount of time, which, I suppose, is exactly what I did.

"This will always be your home," Core insisted, standing in the doorway.

I thanked them, hugged them, and told them I felt the same way. But, all the while, I couldn't help but feel an overwhelming sense of relief. Things would be easier on my own.

Another thing that's changed: I'm working now, full-time at the 24-Hour Depot, Apple's new restaurant in the center of town. I never did end up going to Paris for culinary school, as I'd been planning for the past three years.

I'm at the Depot right now, working the overnight shift, since it's not like I get any sleep anyway. One thing this job has taught me: I'm not alone in my insomnia. We have dozens of regulars who frequent this place, seeking camaraderie in their sleeplessness and solitude.

I pick up my knife, feeling an instant jolt of power, relishing the fit of the handle inside my grip. Using a soup bowl as a guide, I point the tip of the blade into a rolled-out sheet of dough and cut out a series of disks.

Gretchen, the hostess, pokes her head through the pass-through window, nearly knocking over a plate full of chicken-fried pickles. "Just a little FYI: there's a heaping hunk of hotness sitting at table eleven."

"I'm busy," I say, eyeing the trays full of pastry dough that I still need to cut.

"Suit yourself." She pops a pickle into her mouth. "Just trying to keep you in the know. Isn't that what you said you wanted? Candy and I have dubbed him the sexy squatter, by the way, because he's been nursing a cherry Coke and cheese fries for the past two hours."

I look up from my slicing. "Did you ask him if he wanted anything else?"

"Well, of course, I'm not an amateur." She rolls her big blue eyes. "But he says he's happy just sitting."

"Is he working on a laptop? Or waiting for someone?"

"No. And no. I already asked about that latter one."

"And you're sure it's been two hours?" *Ticktock, ticktock.*

She nods and pops another pickle.

The knife still gripped in my hand, I dart out of the kitchen. The dining area is sprinkled with customers—a mixture of regulars, some newbies, and a gaggle of college students pigging out after a party. "Where?"

"There." Gretchen nods.

Sitting at the corner booth with his back facing us, Mr. Mystery has slick dark hair and a leather jacket.

"A pretty fine specimen, wouldn't you say? And that's just from behind. Wait till you get the full-frontal view." She gives me an exaggerated wink, revealing a bright red heart stamped to her shimmery gold eyelid.

I slide the knife into my pocket, blade pointed downward, and then I make my way in his direction. "Can I help you?" I ask, standing at his booth.

He gazes up at me with dark gray eyes and a knowing grin. He looks to be about twenty-something with a tan face covered in stubble. "Well, hey there, Sunshine. When did you get here? I thought I'd have to wait all night."

"Do I know you?" I ask, my nerves ignited.

"Well, I've been coming in here at least once a week for the past few weeks, and you've been here each time, so I'd like to say that you've at least *noticed* me."

"I work in the kitchen."

"I know. I've seen you." He smiles and licks the salt off his fingers. "Through the kitchen window. Plus you're always coming into the counter area for something or other—with fresh plates and silverware or to give out samples of whatever you've been whippin' up back there. Am I right?"

"Do *you* know *me*?"

"I know your name. Does that count . . . *Ivy*?" He nods to my name tag, making my skin crawl.

I peer over my shoulder at Gretchen. Spying on me from the front counter, she gives me another wink.

"I wouldn't mind getting to know you," he continues.

I focus back on him, irritated that I don't recognize him from his past few visits. Has he been sitting with his back to the counter each time? Or maybe he's come in with other people? Though I'm mostly in the kitchen, it's true that I'm often in the counter area. I like to keep an eye on the people that come in, especially repeat customers.

I gaze up at one of our surveillance cameras, suddenly eager to watch the footage. "Why would you want that?"

"Oh, I don't know." He rolls his eyes, still grinning. "Have you looked at yourself in the mirror lately?"

"The mirror?" I ask, growing more confused by the moment. Does this have something to do with Natalie's nightmare essay? Her fear of her own reflection?

"Maybe it's because you're a princess," he says.

I give the knife a hard twist, feeling the tip tear through the fabric. "*What did you call me?*"

He looks around, as if someone could possibly help him now. "Did I say something wrong? I called you a princess."

"Who are you?" I demand. "How do you know me? Did someone send you here?"

"Wait, whoa." He leans back in his seat.

"How do you know about *princess*?" I snap.

"*Seriously?*" His mouth gapes open.

"Did you read my essay?" I continue. "Is it online somewhere I don't know about?"

"Okay, um, reality check?" He holds up his hands, as if to stop my words. "I have absolutely no idea what you're talking about."

"*Liar!*" I shout.

A moment later, someone tugs my arm from behind. I whip the knife out of my pocket, ready to fight.

It's Gretchen and Candy.

"Holy shit," Candy mutters, cupping her hand over her mouth.

That's when I notice.

The attention I've drawn.

The stir I've caused.

A couple of the college boys stand nearby, ready to pounce. Mrs. Sterling, who lost her husband six months ago and hasn't been able to get a full night's sleep since, sits at the front counter, staring in my direction.

I drop the knife. My face feels fiery.

"What the hell just happened?" Gretchen asks.

The boy who called me princess slides out from the booth. "Don't ask me. Ask *her.*" He nods at me, tosses a ten-dollar bill onto the table, and heads for the door.

"What happened?" Gretchen demands.

I look out the window, into the parking lot, watching to see which car is his—a Ford pickup, dark blue, tinted windows, trailer hitch on the back. He opens the door, climbs inside, and starts the ignition.

"I have to go," I mutter.

"Ivy?" Miko calls, poking his head through the kitchen window.

I know he's in the weeds right now, elbow-deep in night-owl specials, but I grab my coat from behind the counter. "I'm really sorry," I tell him. My car keys clenched in my hand, I bolt out the door.

IVY

BY THE TIME I MAKE IT OUT TO THE PARKING LOT,
the pickup is already gone. I drive down the main road, searching the streets. It's just after three in the morning and the glare
from overhead streetlamps cuts across my eyes, making my
head ache.

It's raining out; the droplets beat against my windshield.
The sound makes it hard to think. I turn down a narrow road,
following a laundry truck, only to discover that the street
is a dead end. The truck parks below a sign that reads SAL'S
CLEANING.

I look in my rearview mirror. There's a Dumpster behind me on one side and a stack of milk crates on the other—too narrow for a three-point turn. I go to put the car in reverse, but then I come to a sudden halt.

Someone's standing in my headlights, staring straight at me.

The laundry guy.

His driver's side door is open.

He smiles when he sees I've noticed him, seemingly unaffected by the rain. It drips down over his glasses, pastes his hair against his forehead. He looks about fifty years old.

I honk my horn, keeping my palm pressed against it. But he doesn't move. He just keeps on smiling.

I throw the car into reverse and start to back up, smashing into one of the milk crates. It crunches beneath my wheel.

I stop. And turn to look forward.

The laundry man is gone now. His driver's side door remains open. There's a bar across the rear door to the dry cleaner's; he obviously didn't go in.

I go to back up again, stepping on the gas, but the car doesn't move. The engine revs. My heart pounds.

It takes me a second to realize that my gear's in neutral. I shift to reverse. My tires screech as I back away, fighting to stay straight, rounding the corner, and returning to the main road.

I drive to the police station, knowing that Detective Thomas isn't in until six in the morning on Tuesdays. But I pull into the parking lot anyway and check my phone messages. I have three missed calls from Miko and a text from Apple.

I peek in the rearview mirror. My skin looks pale. My eyes are red and veiny. And my hair's in a messy heap of mousy-brown on top of my head. *So* far from princess-worthy.

I push the mirror away, pop a couple of my meds (several hours late), and then wait for Thomas's arrival.

Hours later, I wake up with my cheek pressed against the steering wheel. My neck aches. My mouth is dry. My cell phone vibrates against the dashboard.

The sun radiates through the glass, making everything feel magnified—the vibration, the brightness, my headache, the musty smell of my car.

I grab the phone and check the screen. PRIVATE CALLER. "Hello?"

"Ivy?" A female voice.

"Who is this?"

"Are you coming for us?" she whispers.

"Natalie?" I sit up straighter.

"*Are* you?"

"*Natalie?*"

The phone clicks. She hung up.

I climb out of the car and hurry inside the police station. Seated behind the dark glass barrier is Officer Squires. "Is he here today?" I ask him.

Squires lets out a sigh. He's sick of my dropping by here. I'm sick of it too. Before I left the hospital, I'd promised myself that I was done with the police, but ever since my discharge, I haven't been able to stop myself, clinging to my list of what-ifs: What if a clue I share helps find the killer? What if I don't say anything and the others wind up dead? What if going to the station just one more time means that I'll learn something new about the case? What if the police start seeing me as an integral part of the investigation?

Officer Squires pages Thomas, and within minutes I'm allowed through the door, inside the station, where the desks are lined up in rows. Officers are on the phone, surfing the Net, and talking in hushed tones. Detective Dearborn—the token female here—ushers me to the back, where there's a narrow hallway with interrogation rooms to the left and right. She leads me into the room at the very end, my least favorite; the window doesn't open. The interior smells like a locker room. I go inside and take a seat.

"Detective Thomas will be with you soon," she says. Her face reminds me of a Chihuahua's, with its beady eyes and pointed snout.

Thomas comes in a few minutes later. "Ivy . . . " he says, in lieu of hello. He closes the door and sits down across from me with a notepad and pen.

"She called me," I tell him. "Just now. She asked if I was coming for them."

"Okay, hold on, *who* called you?"

"Natalie." Didn't I mention that?

"How do you know it was her?"

"It was a private call, but it sounded like her."

He doesn't write anything down. "Did this person say anything else?"

"It was *her*," I insist. "Don't you think we should do something—tell someone?" *Why is it so hot in here?* I look around for a heat vent.

"How long did the conversation last?"

"A few seconds."

"A few seconds isn't exactly long enough to prove anything."

I know. It isn't. *Ticktock, ticktock.* I clench my teeth, feeling my skin begin to itch.

"There's more."

"Okay." His forehead furrows.

"There was a guy at the diner during my shift."

"And?"

"And he called me *Princess*," I say, proceeding to tell him how the guy had been hanging around the diner for more than two hours, and how it seemed he might've been waiting for me. "I'm pretty sure he was in his twenties. He had dark hair, hazel eyes, and he drove a Ford pick—"

"*And?*" Thomas asks again.

"What do you mean *and*?" I balk. "He called me *Princess* . . . just like I wrote about in my nightmare essay for the contest, just like the Nightmare Elf called me when he re-created my nightmare. Do you really think it's a coincidence?"

"I don't know. It could be."

"Would *you* call a complete stranger a princess?"

"Maybe if I were a twenty-something-year-old guy looking to flirt with a girl."

"It wasn't a coincidence. It was a warning. The killer's coming back for me again. He wants me to be in his next movie."

"We're not even sure there was a first movie—at least there wasn't one discovered."

"It exists," I snap. "I saw it. I lived it. The Nightmare Elf made us watch it." Our experience during the Dark House weekend was recorded; the killer was using that footage to make a feature film.

"Let's just say that this guy at the diner . . . his calling you a princess wasn't a coincidence . . . . .Maybe he found your essay online."

"It isn't online," I say, thinking how I wondered the same—how I asked the mystery boy if he'd found my essay on some site.

"Not that you know of." Thomas gives me a pointed look. "Maybe he's some die-hard Justin Blake fan, wanting to meet the girl who got away."

"Or maybe he came as a messenger," I say, "from the killer himself."

"Did he say anything else that might link him to the case?"

I shake my head and look away, almost tempted to make something up.

"Well, you don't need *me* to tell you that people are interested in your story, Ivy. In some way, you've become famous. A lot of Justin Blake fans would go to great lengths—including frequenting your place of employment—to meet you. To them, you're a real-life heroine."

"I'm hardly a heroine." Heroes don't leave others behind.

"Sounds like someone's being too hard on herself. Are you still taking care of yourself, getting the help you need?"

"If you're talking about outpatient therapy, then the answer is yes," I lie, knowing he has a point about the story's appeal. After the Dark House weekend, varied versions of the story spiraled out of control. Hard-core Justin Blake fans created videos depicting their own ideas of what happened. They posted them online, some even insisting that their films were the real deal. Last time I checked, there were more than two hundred phony films.

Also after that weekend, I started receiving prank phone calls (people claiming to be Natalie, Parker, and the others), as well as lame-o invitations and admission tickets to see the screening of numerous Nightmare Elf–inspired projects.

"Why isn't the FBI looking harder?" I ask him.

"They *are* looking hard. This *is* a serious case. We have five missing people and a potential killer on the loose. In my book, that's top priority."

"And in the FBI's book?"

"Would it make you feel any better if I had an undercover detective frequent your place of work? I already have cops staked out at your parents' and aunt's residences."

"It would make me feel better if we were on the same page—if you let me in on the investigation. I shouldn't have to hear from my therapist that my real parents' killer is a suspect."

"No one's excluding you, Ivy. We're just looking out for your best interest, as well as the best interest of the case."

"It's in my best interest to find the killer and find the others."

Detective Thomas studies my face for several moments, tapping his pencil against the pad, as if calculating his next few words. "Does the name Houdini mean anything to you?"

"Houdini, as in the magician?"

"As in the serial killer. He hasn't been active for a few years now. His crimes typically involve a magic-show theme. Like the Nightmare Elf suspect, he wears a costume and creates elaborate setups using lights, props, theater staging, video equipment. After he kills his victims, he moves the bodies; they don't turn up until months later, and when they do, it's in some showy, magical fashion."

"And the Feds think that he's the same person who organized the Dark House weekend? Do they have a concrete reason? Fingerprints? DNA?"

"It's just one of the many theories right now."

"In other words, no."

"We can't dismiss theories based on lack of evidence."

"Maybe you should take your own advice."

"Excuse me?"

"The Nightmare Elf's theme is horror, not magic," I remind him.

"Still, there are enough common threads to raise suspicion, especially since Houdini's victims fit the profile of your group: an eclectic mix of college-age students looking for a good time. The victims are often tricked into going to see a magic show; there's usually some element of winning a contest."

"What if the Nightmare Elf killer knew about Houdini and was trying to copy his style? What if he was hoping that you'd pin the Dark House weekend crimes on Houdini?"

"Ivy . . . "

"*What?*" I ask, able to hear the ticktock deep inside me. It throbs against my chest, echoing inside my brain. "You're wasting your time on any other theory that doesn't involve my real parents' killer."

"I've said it once and I'll say it again: leave the manhunt to the experts, okay?" He closes his notepad and tucks it inside his jacket.

"What about Taylor?" I persist.

"The FBI already spoke to her."

"So how come I haven't heard the outcome? Why did she leave the Dark House early?"

Taylor was supposed to have been my roommate for that weekend. She and Natalie were the first to arrive at the house. But not long after their arrival, Taylor left, in the midst of unpacking—without her bags, without her cell phone, without a word to Natalie that she was leaving. Later, we found a message in Taylor's closet, scrawled against the back wall: GET OUT BEFORE IT'S TOO LATE. I'm pretty sure Taylor wrote it—pretty confident that it was her way of trying to warn us.

"I need to talk to Taylor," I tell him. "We need to compare notes, fill in blanks, discuss each other's chronology . . . ."

"Whatever Taylor claims to have seen at the Dark House is of no concern to you right now."

"Can you arrange for the two of us to meet?"

Thomas leans forward, as if about to let me in on a secret. "You're what, three weeks out of a mental hospital?"

"Five weeks." I swallow hard.

"And how many times have you called and/or come to see me since then?"

"Four?"

"Try fourteen," he says, his voice softening. "Fourteen times in five weeks. Now, I know this must be frustrating, and it's not that I don't appreciate your input, but my advice for you?"

"Forget it," I say, getting up from the table. I go for the door, slamming it shut behind me.

TAYLOR MONROE

DOZENS OF DANCE RECITAL DRESSES HOVER ABOVE *my head. The tassels dangle into my eyes. The unsettled dust makes me have to sneeze. But I can't. I won't. I have to remain still.*

I'm hiding inside a closet, tucked behind the dancing bear costume from The Nutcracker Suite.

Someone comes into the room. I hear a floorboard creak. The sound of feet scuff against the carpeted floor. There's a sniffle and then a cough. Did someone open a dresser drawer? Is that my suitcase being zipped?

"I don't think she's in here." Midge's voice. "No, I already searched

it," she says, talking on the phone. "Yes, of course. That one's already done too. Are you even listening to me? I think she might've left."

The closet door slides open. The costumes shift forward and back. I'm at the far end, against the wall, about to lose my lunch. My hand is bleeding. The wound is throbbing.

"Wait a second," Midge says, still talking on the phone.

The costumes push forward again. Sequins poke into my eye.

"Come on, now. You aren't really implying what I think you are, are you?" she continues. "Well, then you can go to hell."

The phone beeps a couple of seconds later. I think she hung up mid-conversation. I hear the door shut.

My heart pounding, I grab the lip-gloss tube that's in my pocket and write the word KILLER *across the wall.*

"Taylor?"

I write KILLER *again, bearing down so hard that the tube snaps in half. Blood from my hand spurts over the rug.*

"Earth to Taylor Monroe," someone sings.

And that's when I realize . . . when I snap out of my daydream.

I look down at my notebook. The word KILLER is scrawled across the page. My pencil—not my lip gloss—has snapped in two. There is no blood; the cut on my hand has long since healed.

Chantel I-never-stop-playing-with-my-hair Coughlin, my resident advisor, is standing over me, twirling a curlicue around her finger. We're in the dorm lobby. At school. There are groups of students sprinkled about the space—doing their homework, sipping their coffee, texting on phones, and chatting among themselves.

"Holy embarrassing moment, Batgirl." My face fries with heat. I close up my notebook.

Chantel flashes me a polite smile, as if my nutty behavior is totally normal and doesn't warrant a snarky comment.

"I totally zoned out, didn't I?" I've been doing that lately, having flashbacks, getting cold sweats, murmuring to myself like some *Twilight Zone*–ish freak. "Lack of sleep does some funky stuff to people, doesn't it?" I fake a giggle.

"I have some good news," she says, straight-faced, all business, still curl-twirling. "It took some doing, but we were able to move your case to the top of our priority list."

"I have a case?" I ask, feeling the confusion on my face.

"A single room will be opening up sooner than anticipated. We should be able to get you in by the end of next week."

"Couldn't I just switch roommates?" I ask, pretty sure that I sound like a broken record. "It'll be kind of weird living alone. I mean, I came here to be with people."

"You'll love having your own room," Chantel says, bringing

a strand of hair up to her lips for a taste. "You won't have to worry about a roommate talking your ear off while you're trying to study, or having her friends barge in at all hours of the day and night while you're trying to get work done, or—the worst—eating all of your food."

"I practically have my own room *now*," I say, referring to Emily's absence. "And I absolutely hate it."

Emily and I were assigned as roommates, only she moved out (to crash on her BFF Barbie's spare futon) after only a few weeks into the semester, telling everyone that she couldn't possibly be expected to sleep in the same room as a killer.

"Plus, all of that barging-in-and-eating-each-other's-food stuff . . . " I continue. "It actually sounds pretty nice."

"You'll love it," she insists, voiding out my words with a jingle of her dollar-store bracelets; there are at least twenty silver bangles loaded on her arm. She lets them slide up and down her wrist as she talks—her own sort of background noise.

"Aren't there any other options?" I ask. "Somebody else who needs to switch roommates? I'd be happy to meet with them first. I mean, seriously." I feel my eyes begin to fill. "I'm not as horrible as everybody thinks. I was voted Most Popular in high school for three years in a row, for God's sake." My words sound stupid and desperate, and that's exactly what they are.

Chantel continues to stare at me, a plastic smile on her face, as if none of what I'm saying matters. *Jingle, jangle, jingle.* A second later, my own background noise kicks in: My phone rings in my pocket. I don't recognize the number.

"Go ahead and take it," Chantel says, as I'm about to hit IGNORE. "I have to run. I just wanted to let you know that everything is all set."

I try my best to hold it together as Chantel turns on her heel, joining a group of sorority pledges in the corner of the lobby (all dressed up like Elvis), leaving me without a say.

My phone continues to ring. I click on it to answer, eager for some love, even if it's in the shape of some nonexistent prize I need to claim: "Hello?"

"Taylor?"

"Yes."

"This is Ivy Jensen. We spoke on the phone once before . . . when I was at the amusement park . . . during the Dark House weekend."

"Wait, how did you get my number?"

"It was attached to your contest essay. It's sort of a long story, but the essays showed up in my mailbox one day. I really think we should talk."

"Okay, but I've already told the police everything I know."

"I realize that, but I was hoping that if we got together and compared notes, we could come up with some new ideas."

"Ideas for what? The FBI already has our testimonies."

"Well, I think that we can do better than the FBI."

The conversation falls silent. I don't know what to say, except that I don't want to talk about the Dark House anymore—about why I left, or what I saw, or what I could've done differently.

"*Taylor?*"

"We're not the police."

"Can we just meet and talk?"

I gaze out at the lobby of students. The group of sorority pledges attempts to serenade all of us by singing "Hound Dog" by Elvis, only it sounds more like *hedgehog*, which is so completely distracting.

"I'm really sorry, Ivy. But I've got a lot on my plate right now, and I need to stay focused on my studies."

"But people are still missing," she says.

"Okay, but aren't those people believed to be dead?"

"Do *you* believe it?"

"I don't have any reason not to. I mean, it's been more than three months, and there was so much blood everywhere."

"How about this reason: If you went missing but your body had yet to be uncovered, would you want people to stop looking . . . to just assume that you were dead?"

"I'm really sorry," I tell her again, still focused on the sorority girls and wishing that I were one of them. If this were before the Dark House weekend, there's no doubt in my mind that I would be.

"Can we at least talk on the phone, sometime when you have more ti—"

"I'm sorry," I say, cutting her off. "I just can't do this right now." I hang up before she can argue. And then I go back to my room and cry myself to sleep.

TAYLOR

A FEW DAYS LATER, CHANTEL SHOWS UP ON MY doorstep, asking me to move out of my room. "We were able to get you in even earlier than expected!" she announces, twirling a strand of hair. "Are your bags all packed?" There's a big, bubbly smile across her spray-tanned face, as if she's doing me a colossal favor.

"Oh," I say, for lack of intelligent words. "I'm actually in the middle of a Shakespeare assignment right now." I glance over my shoulder at the unopened books on my desk. "And I wouldn't feel right neglecting Romeo, considering how sucky his love life is. Can't moving day wait until the weekend?"

"I can help you," she suggests. "With moving, that is." She smiles wider. "The R.D. really wants this loose end tied up by dinnertime tonight," she says, looking past me, toward my side of the room—at all of my scream queen posters from *Scream*, *Halloween*, *A Nightmare on Elm Street*, and *The Shining*. Each poster features an exceptionally talented lead actress in the midst of a heart-pounding scene.

"I've been meaning to take them down," I say, with a nod to Neve Campbell. I don't know why I haven't already. "I used to be a little obsessed with strong female characters in cult-followed horror flicks."

"*Used to be?*"

"Yeah, you know, as in the past tense of the verb *be*."

Her face goes graveyard-serious, but I'm not sure she gets the dig. "No, I mean, has something changed since the start of the semester?"

Okay, um, *seriously?* "Just about *everything's* changed since the start of the semester." She knows that, so why is she asking?

"Someone said that you were a theater major."

"Dance and theater, actually. I love the idea of combining the two." At least, I used to love it.

"Like a musical version of *Psycho*? Norman Bates waltzing across the living room with his mother's cadaver."

"Talk about getting a stiffy," I joke. But I'm not sure Chantel gets that either, because she doesn't so much as grin.

"So, shall we get started?" she asks. "I'll bet between the two of us, we can get you moved in no time."

A group of girls on the floor lingers in the hallway, eavesdropping on our conversation. To them, I'm the girl who ran away and never looked back. The girl who's perfectly fine walking over dead bodies if it serves her in the end.

No one wants me here. I'm starting to not want it either.

A few more days pass, I have my new single room (down the hall, sequestered from everyone else), and people on the floor are buzzing about a mixer that's happening tonight at a fraternity house across the street from our dorm. Apparently, it's a big deal, with a live band *and* a DJ. And, P.S., you have to wear all blue. It's something about a blue moon tradition.

Girls in the dorm traipse around, trading blue clothing and borrowing one another's blue accessories. Once again, I'm sitting (lurking) in the lobby, by the soda machine, like a dirty old man in a lingerie shop. It's become my go-to spot, because at least while I'm here, though alone, I can still be surrounded by people.

A group of girls with blue wigs and Smurf-colored faces rushes by me. I'm pretty sure they're from the east wing, but it's super hard to recognize them, which sparks an idea.

I head upstairs and into the common bathroom. Just as I'd hoped, a bunch of blue stuff's been left behind—makeup, hairspray, body paint, glitter. I spend the next hour shrouding myself in shades of blue—my face, my hair, any visible shred of skin—until I can barely even recognize myself. The pièce de résistance: a tiara atop my head, only after just a few seconds of wearing it, I'm reminded of Sarah Michelle Gellar from *I Know What You Did Last Summer* (in the Fourth of July parade scene, just minutes before she's slaughtered by Susie's dad/the psycho fisherman), not to mention Sissy Spacek from *Carrie* (when she's voted prom queen and goes up on stage, adorned with a princess-worthy tiara, and pig blood gets dumped on her head).

And so I take the tiara off.

My nerves absolutely racked, I venture across the street to the party house. The door is unlocked; I go inside. The living room area is overflowing with blue people, carrying blue drinks, dancing to blues music, under bright blue flashing lights. I navigate to the punch bowl in the kitchen seeking a little liquid courage.

"Thirsty?" a boy asks me. He's dressed like one of the guys in the Blue Man Group.

"Very."

He ladles punch into a cup and passes it to me. "Freshman?"

"That obvious?"

"It's just that I haven't seen you around before."

"And you know everybody who goes here?"

"Just about." He taps his blue cup against mine.

"Maybe you just don't recognize me in my current state of blue."

"I think I'd remember someone like you—blue or otherwise." His dark brown eyes crinkle when he smiles; he's so unbelievably adorable. "I'm Jason."

"Taylor," I say, shaking his hand, stoked that I decided to come here tonight.

"My sister's a freshman here too. Do you know Barbie Reynolds?" He nods to my ex-roommate's BFF. I met Barbie on talent show night, just a few weeks into the semester. She smelled like roasted nuts and hated my rendition of the shower stall scene in *Psycho*—when Janet Leigh let out that delicious, blood-curdling scream.

"I don't know her," I say, quickly turning my back to Barbie, remembering how, after the talent show, she and Emily pulled me aside, acting all nice like they wanted to get to know me more, only to leave me feeling worse than I ever thought possible.

We'd gone up to Emily's and my room. They sat on my bed and started asking me all sorts of questions about the Dark House weekend, pulling others in from the hallway to listen to my answers—until it felt as if I were on trial, as if I were the one responsible for everything that happened.

"Okay, so, no offense," Emily began, "but ever hear of a thing called nine-one-one? I mean, when you realized the place was so messed up, wouldn't that have been, like, the logical thing to do?"

"Except I didn't have my phone with me at the time," I tried to explain. "I was hiding in a closet."

"In the same room that your phone was in, though, right?" Barbie raised an eyebrow at me. "So, couldn't you have just grabbed it?"

"Before you decided to bolt?" someone else asked.

Their questions made my head spin:

"Why didn't you wait in the woods until the others came?"

"Why didn't you warn the others before they went into the house? Weren't they expected to arrive just minutes after you left?"

"What took you so long to get help? Wasn't there, like, a 24-hour delay?"

"Do you think that if you'd acted sooner, the others could've been saved?"

"How can you even look at horror stuff now knowing that people are dead because of it? And because of you?"

There must've been at least twelve people in the room at one point. And, though they all had their questions, deep down they already knew the answers—or at least the ones they wanted to believe. Eventually, when I could no longer take it, I just rolled over in my bed, smothered my ear with a pillow, and stared at the wall, waiting for everyone to leave.

Emily stopped sleeping in our room after that night. Two days later, I was told I'd be getting a new roommate. The following afternoon, the plan had changed again; I was to get a single room (because no one wanted to be with me) as soon as something opened up.

"Too crowded?" Jason asks, evidently noticing that I've shrunken at least three inches in the last three seconds.

Before I can respond, someone bumps me from behind. Blue punch spills onto my back and onto the table. "I'm so sorry," the girl says.

Jason hands me a stack of napkins. "How about we go outside. There's a patio in the back."

"Fantabulous," I say, following him through the kitchen and out a pair of sliders. It's quieter out here—just small groups of people sitting about the yard.

Jason motions to a wooden bench and we take a seat. "Better?"

"Much."

"Not into big crowds, I take it."

"I actually love big crowds," I say, thinking about all of the dance competitions I've been in—hundreds of people watching my every pointe, chassé, and *rond de jambe*. "I'm studying to

431

be an actress, or at least I was, or am . . . or was. I don't know."
I let out a nervous giggle. "Let's just say that college has been a
big adjustment, and I'm questioning pretty much every aspect
of my life right now."

"Well, I hope that things are starting to clear up."

"Definitely." I smile. He's so irresistibly sweet.

We end up segueing to *his* big adjustment, two years ago,
when his dad's job got relocated halfway across the country
and he had to move, mid–senior year. "Do you have any idea
what it's like to have to move against your will?"

"I may have a slight idea," I say, thinking about my experience in the dorm.

"You're pretty cool, you know that?"

"Yeah, so are you."

We continue to chat about our hometowns and high schools,
about regular versus Double Stuf Oreos, and favorite TV shows.

But then someone yells out "Bombs away!" blowing the
moment to bits.

I look up. Barbie and Emily are standing on the porch
above us. There are a couple of boys with them too.

Before I can think to move, they all start hurling water balloons—a whole laundry basket full of them.

The balloons splash against a girl's shoulder, a boy's head,
and another girl's butt as she bends down to get her drink.

Jason jumps up and goes to grab a trash can lid for protection. At the same moment, I'm ambushed by water balloons. They drop down on my head and break on my face. Water shoots up my nose, runs down my throat, and I gag.

"What the hell do you think you're doing?" Jason shouts at them. He returns to my side. "Are you all right?"

I wipe my face—my eyes, my nose, my mouth—suddenly noticing that my palms are splotched with blue. My makeup has washed off.

"Holy shit," Barbie shouts, looking down at me from the porch. "That's the girl I was telling you about," she says to her boyfriend. "The one who let those people die."

"I should go," I tell Jason.

"Wait—no. Don't let those assholes get to you."

"Hey, Jason," the other boy shouts out, "I hear she's got a fetish for dead bodies. Ever do it in a casket?" Barbie and Emily erupt in a fit of laughter.

"*What?*" Jason asks; his face is a giant blue question mark.

I get up, still wiping my eyes, and move around to the front of the house. I cross the street and return to the dorm.

No one follows me.

TAYLOR

IN MY ROOM, I CLOSE THE DOOR AND MELT DOWN TO the rug. Blue-stained tears drip onto the shag wool fibers. How in the world did this happen? When did I become this hated person?

A few breaths later, I sit back up, startled by my reflection in the mirror on the back of the closet. My eyes are red. My lips are blue. My makeup is crusty, covering only patches of my skin. I touch the heap of hair tied up on my head, and suddenly my reflection changes—morphs into the red-haired girl from the Dark House, the girl who prompted me to flee.

The memory of her drags me back to that moment:

My hand's bleeding. I cut it. There's a nail sticking out from beneath the dresser drawer. I dart out of the room and head down the hallway. In the bathroom, I search the cabinets, unable to find a bandage. I wash the cut in the sink and then wrap it up in a paper towel. A three-inch slit. The blood isn't clotting. I need something more.

"Midge?" I call, back out in the hallway. Blood soaks through the paper towel and trickles onto the floor. I head downstairs, but the main floor is empty. Natalie and I are still the only ones here.

I move through the kitchen and open the door that leads to the basement, figuring that Midge must be down there.

It's dark. I run my hand over the wall, able to find a light switch. I flick it on. The door swings shut behind me.

There's a ladder-like staircase. Slowly, I begin down it, the light narrowing with each step. "Midge!" I call out.

Something brushes against my forehead. I swipe the spot, suddenly realizing what the something is; a pull cord hangs down from the ceiling. I give it a tug. My heart instantly tightens.

A life-size Nightmare Elf doll stands in front of me. The light shines over its porcelain face, exposing its wicked grin and rosy cheeks. I slap over my chest, feeling an instant wave of relief. It's just a doll. So, why am I feeling so unhinged?

"Midge," I call again, noticing a freezer chest in the corner—the kind that opens from the top with a lid.

A door slams somewhere upstairs. At the same moment, the Nightmare Elf doll flops to the floor, its face angled in my direction.

Holy. Freaking. Shit. I need to calm the hell down.

I look back toward the freezer, figuring there might be an ice pack inside it. There's a latch at the front. I go to pull up on it, but the lid's heavy—at least twenty pounds. I strain my forearms. Blood from my cut drips onto the latch and rolls down the front of the freezer. It isn't until I get the lid halfway open that I'm able to see.

The crown of a head—thick auburn waves, a part down the middle. Blue jeans, tan sweater, long beaded necklace. Gray skin, dark circles, eyes angled up at the ceiling.

A girl's body. She looks to be about fifteen or sixteen years old. My gut tells me it isn't real. But then I look at the arm—at the golden-blond hair sprouting from the skin, the spray of freckles extending from the elbow to the wrist, and the dirt and blood stuck beneath the fingernails from when she must've struggled—and I feel the room tilt.

Music starts playing. "Crazy Chick" by Robert Jango. The sudden rush of chords is like a freight train through my heart.

The girl's arm is bent upward in an awkward position. I go to move it down, but it's stuck—even when I try with both hands. The skin feels eerily real—smooth, supple. And there appears to be a paper cut on one of the knuckles.

"She's a crazy chick. She's so sick."

Eventually the music snaps me back to reality. I'm still in my room. Still looking in the mirror. The image of the red-haired girl is still staring back at me.

Is it a coincidence that someone is playing "Crazy Chick" just outside my room? Or do my dorm mates have me pegged just right?

I reach for my phone and search for the number. My pulse races as I wait to hear her voice.

"Hello?" Ivy answers.

"It's Taylor." I glance at the clock. It's four in the freaking morning. "Did I wake you?" *Duh*.

"I'm actually at work . . . the graveyard shift."

"I was thinking about what you were saying the other day, about how we should meet. I think it might be a good idea after all."

"Great. Your brother mentioned that you're in school on the East Coast."

"At Gringle, in New Hampshire, about twenty minutes outside of Nashu—"

"How about next weekend?" she asks. "I'm just outside Boston. I could drive up."

"I'll call you Thursday to confirm." I hang up and glance back at the mirror. The red-haired girl is finally gone.

From the Journal of E.W.

Grade 7, August Preparatory School

AUTUMN 1971

I hate it here. My grandparents think I'm in the way. That's why they put me here. I try to be good, but sometimes I just can't help myself, like when Olivia Kellerman was bragging about what a great biker she is because she can go really fast and then stop on a dime. So I rigged her brakes—tore the pads right off.

The next time she got on her bike, I bit my tongue, trying not to laugh out loud, but I couldn't help it, especially when she crashed into a tree. She screamed so loud. There was blood running from her leg. Served her right for being such a show-off.

Later, Nana figured out what happened. She found the pads in the pocket of my pants. She and Grampy say they don't know what to do with a kid like me who's always causing problems.

My mother didn't know what to do with me either. When my grandparents weren't home, she'd lock me in the laundry closet and then blast the TV really loud so she didn't have to hear me screaming.

Joke's on her, though, because she's the one who's locked up now. I guess living here is better than living with her, but not by much.

Ivy

"Ivy!" Gretchen shouts.

I pocket my cell phone, beyond excited that Taylor changed her mind.

"I needed that cheese omelet ten minutes ago," she says. "And where's my blueberry pancake?"

I pour egg mixture on one side of the griddle and pancake batter on the other. It's only four and there's already a morning rush. Orders line up like soldiers on the turnstile.

"You forgot the fruit cup on this one," Miko says, nodding to a bowl of oatmeal.

Over the past six hours, I've also screwed up on a pasta plate, the meatloaf special, and two French toast orders. Miko's been double-checking my work all week. Gretchen's been giving me the cold shoulder all night. My mom's been dropping in unannounced all month, no doubt in response to a pile of complaints about me. If I weren't the boss's daughter, I wouldn't have a job.

Finally, at six, my shift ends. I hang up my greasy apron, take a mug of dandelion tea into the far corner booth, and gaze out the window in search of a dark blue pickup. I've told Gretchen, Miko, and the others to be on the lookout, but the boy who called me princess hasn't been here since.

A clank sound startles me. I look up.

Miko's there, standing at my booth. "Sorry," he says, in response to my jolt. He places a plateful of waffles down in front of me. "Your favorite. Stuffed with strawberry goodness."

"Wow," I say, taken aback by his kindness. "Thanks. You're way too good to me."

"I know, but I'll let you make it up to me." He smiles, sliding into the seat across from mine. "So, is everything okay with you?"

"Fine, why?" I take a healthy bite.

"*Fine? Why?*" He gives me a pointed look.

I peer over my shoulder at Gretchen, who's spying on us

from the front counter. She's been crushing on Miko for months now, but he doesn't have a clue.

"You just seem really out of it," he says.

"You know who seems out of it?" I nod toward Gretchen. "I'll bet she could use a plateful of waffles too."

"I'm serious, Ivy. If we're going to continue working together—"

My phone vibrates. "Hold that thought." I pull my cell phone out of my pocket to check the screen.

An e-mail.

From the same Gmail account.

"This seriously can't be real," I mutter, shaking my head.

"What can't?" Miko asks.

The e-mail appears to have come from the same Gmail address as the Nightmare Elf's original account—even though that account was shut down. The subject line: Nightmare Elf e-Newsletter, Issue #208. The last e-newsletter I received— *pre*–Dark House weekend—was #206.

"Ivy?"

I click it open.

Dear Dark House Survivor,

　　Ready for the sequel?

　　Your leading man is too.

Best not to keep him waiting.

Click <u>this link</u>, see what to do.

To Be Continued,

—The Nightmare Elf

A curtain drops down inside my head, behind my eyes, making the room spin.

"What is it?" Miko asks.

Something touches my hand, and I startle. It's Miko—his warm fingers against my icy skin. There's a choking sensation inside my throat.

"It's happening," I tell him.

"What is? *Ivy?*"

I grab the knife from my plate. "I have to go," I tell him, sliding out from the booth and making a beeline for the door.

Ivy

I CLICK THE LINK AGAIN AND IT BRINGS ME TO YouTube.

The video is grainy, and it takes a second to see that there's a dark room and a metal folding chair. A pop of light highlights someone seated on the chair.

It's Natalie. She sits, angled sideways, shrouded in shadows. But still I can tell that it's her—dark clothes, clunky boots, black sunglasses, long, coarse hair. And the dark gray scarf. I'm pretty sure it's the same one she let me borrow—the one I used to blanket over Parker, after his nightmare ride.

"You can't see a face," Detective Thomas says.

I'm at the police station again, sitting in the same smelly interrogation room, only this time Detective Dearborn and Officer Squires are here too, looking on.

"Let's get this up on a bigger screen," Thomas says.

Dearborn leaves the room, returning just a few seconds later with a laptop. She sets it down, powers it up, and then takes my phone to copy the YouTube address.

The video begins on the larger screen, proving that size really does matter. There's so much more detail now. I'm able to see the contrasting squares of a tile floor. There's also a boarded-up window in the background.

Officer Dearborn adjusts the lighting and cranks up the volume.

"Hi, Ivy," Natalie says. Her voice has been distorted; it's deep, like a man's, and there's an electric current running through it. "As you can see, I'm still alive." Her legs are crossed. The toe of her Doc Martens boot bops back and forth in a strip of light; it's the clearest image on the screen. "I'm not the only one. But we can't get out of here without you."

I wish I could see her face—to see if her lips are all cut up from picking at them, like they'd been that weekend. Or if her eyes are as blue as I remember.

"Who is it even supposed to be?" Squires asks.

"It's Natalie," I say, as if it isn't completely obvious.

"Natalie Sorrento?" Squires asks, moving closer to the screen.

"It's her—same boots, same dark clothes, even the tone of her voice is distinct."

"What tone?" His face crinkles in confusion.

"The intonation of her voice, I mean, the way she pauses between words."

"*Shh.*" Dearborn places her finger up to her lips.

Natalie continues to speak: "Parker's here and he wanted me to remind you of something. Remember the story he told you? The one about his worst-ever nightmare? You told him that you'd never leave him, but still you did. Don't leave him alone again. Come find him, Ivy. Come be part of the sequel." Natalie leans forward, shifting slightly in her seat. In doing so, her hand dangles into the strip of light and we're able to see her bracelet.

Detective Dearborn hits pause, tracks back, and then hits replay, freezing the moment. The image is blurry, but it's also unmistakable.

"I can't really tell what it is," Thomas says.

"It kind of looks like a flower of some sort," Dearborn says, lightening the screen even more.

"It's a star," I blurt, able to see it clearly. "Just like the pendant necklace I received years ago."

"Could be a star." Dearborn nods. "Could be a lot of things."

"Was Natalie wearing a star bracelet during the Dark House weekend?" Thomas asks.

"Not that I can remember," I tell him. "But it's obviously a sign—the killer's way of communicating with me."

"It could also be a coincidence," Dearborn says. "Stars aren't exactly unique or unusual, at least as far as charms and patterns go."

"Maybe I'm getting old"—Thomas scoots closer to the computer screen—"but it looks like a pretzel twist to me."

"We'll have a videographer take a look." Dearborn pushes play again, but there's not much else to see. Natalie has fallen silent. There's just one more foot shuffle before the lights go out completely.

Dearborn clicks on the YouTube subscriber's profile. Movie Marvin's account looks pretty well established, with dozens of movie clips as well as a handful of videos he's made. Squires clicks on a video entitled WELCOME.

"Hey, I'm Movie Marvin," the boy on the screen says, "and I like to review indie films and make trailers, particularly in the horror or sci-fi genres. So, if you have something you'd like me to look at or a project you need a trailer for, feel free to message me."

"He can't be more than sixteen," Dearborn says.

"Could be another prank," Squires adds.

"No, this one's different," I insist. "The e-mail address is the same. Plus, the newsletter's issue number is 208. The last one I received was 206."

"Meaning that whoever sent this flubbed up the numbers?" Squires asks.

"No," I snap. "How did someone get so close to the actual number? I mean, off by just one digit?"

"First of all, after that weekend, the Nightmare Elf e-mail address was shut down," Thomas says. "But once an account has been deactivated, someone can claim that username under a new password. And, secondly, didn't one of the Nightmare Elf's e-newsletters appear on TV?"

He's right. It did. Soon after the Dark House amusement park weekend, the authorities went through my computer and e-mail accounts. The next thing I knew, the Nightmare Elf's e-newsletter—the one with the contest guidelines—was on the evening news for the world to see.

"Okay, so then how did Natalie know about the story that Parker told me?" I ask. "About his *real* nightmare." After Parker survived his nightmare ride—a tank full of hungry eels, based on the fictional essay he wrote to win the Nightmare Elf's contest—he told me that his real nightmare was based on an experience that happened when he was little . . . when he got lost in a department store and thought his mother had left him behind.

"That actually isn't clear." Dearborn backtracks to the spot and hits replay, making us listen again. "All this person says is that he had a 'worst-ever nightmare,'" she says.

"Didn't all of the winners have worst-ever nightmares?" Squires asks. "Wasn't that the whole point of the contest?"

"Okay, but I *did* tell Parker I'd never leave him," I argue. "How else would the person on the video have known that? Plus, she's wearing the same scarf," I say, pointing at the screen. "Natalie gave me that scarf at the amusement park. It got left behind."

"How can you tell it's the same?" Thomas asks.

"The color's the same. The fringe is too." The individual fringe strands appear to be an inch thick. "It's also big, like the one she gave me. I used it as a blanket."

"The Dark House weekend happened in July, didn't it?" Dearborn asks. "Was it unseasonably cold that night?"

"No." I shake my head. "Natalie gave me the scarf so that I could use it to hide from the cameras—so I could wear it to cover my face and head, that is. She knew that I didn't want to be videotaped; she could sense it."

"Sense it?" Squires asks.

"I'm not sure if Natalie was some kind of psychic medium," I attempt to explain, "or if she just had a special gift . . . but she could talk to her twin brother, Harris, even though he died at birth. He would tell her things, like that I didn't want to be recognized on film just in case my parents' killer might see me."

I swallow hard, knowing I sound crazy, able to feel the heat on my face. I venture to look at Thomas; he's studying my every blink, breath, falter, and flinch. Is he trying to decide if this is all a pile of BS? Or if I actually believe the BS? The thing is, I know he knows about Natalie's psychic claims. After the Dark House weekend, rumors spread that she was crazy, that she was never able to get over the death of her twin brother.

"Bottom line: virtually nothing on this film is clear," Dearborn says. "My guess is that it's a work in progress."

"Because it doesn't really say anything," Squires agrees. "Come be a part of the sequel, but where? When?"

"We'll look into it," Thomas says. "We'll do a full check on Movie Marvin. Natalie's parents will need to see the video too. Let's also get the e-mail and link over to the feds."

"I'm on it," Dearborn says, exiting the room with Squires.

"And then what?" I ask, stopping Thomas from ditching me too. "Will you let me know what happens? What checks out? What remains suspicious? What Natalie's parents say?

I want to be involved in this investigation. I *demand* to be involved."

"You already are involved—by bringing us clues, by keeping us informed. We, in turn, do our jobs by following up on potential—"

"What if *I* contact Movie Marvin?" I ask, cutting him off. "I could say I want him to create a video for me. We could arrange to meet. I could wear a bug. You could be staked out there too."

"Ivy—no. We're handling this. We're getting closer."

"You're only as close as my clues can bring you."

"We're grateful for your clues, but—"

"But you need me as well," I insist. "*I'm* the one he wants. Use me as a lure."

"Ivy . . . "

"Use me," I repeat.

He stares at me again, biting his lip, as if he's actually considering the option. "I can't," he says, finally. "We can't."

"Then I can't either. You're on your own, as far as I'm concerned."

And obviously so am I.

Dear Parker,

I still wear your T-shirt — the one you tore to make a bandage for my ankle. I wove it into a bracelet, using six strands — one for each letter of your name. I know that probably sounds overly sentimental (or just plain dumb), but right now, aside from hope, sentiments are all I really have.

I wear the bracelet around my wrist to keep you close — not that you're ever far from my mind. The other day when I was walking through a park, there was a mother looking frantically for her son, completely unaware that he was hiding behind a tree. I could hear the fear in her voice as she cried out his name.

Sometimes I cry out too. I'll drive somewhere secluded, roll up all the windows, and scream at the top of my lungs — until tears roll down my cheeks and the window glass fogs up.

At the park that day, I ran right over to the woman and pointed out her son's hiding spot. In that moment, I could feel her relief — like a million tiny snowflakes landing on my skin, sending chills all over my body.

I'd do anything to have somebody point out your hiding spot.

If only you were hiding.

If only it were that easy.

Love,

Ivy

IVY

A FEW DAYS HAVE PASSED SINCE I GOT THE VIDEO link of Natalie. It's early morning, after work, and I'm in my apartment, sitting in the dark, having purposely left the lights off. I used to hate the dark—used to dread the idea of not being able to see all that was around me. But ever since the Dark House weekend, I've forced myself to become acclimated to the things that used to make me uncomfortable— like horror movies, or at least Justin Blake's horror movies. I've seen every one now, have spent hours studying the plotlines and characters, asking myself questions. What is the appeal of

Justin Blake's work? How did the *Nightmare Elf* movie series become the inspiration for the amusement park rides? Do the answers lie in the dialogue? The setting? The themes? Or something else?

A knock on the door startles me. It's barely past six in the morning. I grab the baseball bat from beneath the sofa, just as I hear Apple's voice.

"Ivy? Are you still awake?"

I switch on a few lights and return the bat beneath the couch. "Hey," I say, opening the door.

Apple's holding something that looks like a pie. "Quiche me," she says, kissing my cheeks, European style. "Cooking makes me feel all *je ne sais . . . comment allez-vous.*"

"*I don't know . . . How are you?*" I ask, responding to her flumped-up French.

"Okay, so I know you're on your own now," she continues, "not to mention a much better cook than me, but I can still attempt to be an overbearing mother."

"You're hardly overbearing."

She takes two steps inside the apartment and comes to a sudden halt. She looks around, her mouth gaping open. Most of my things are still in boxes. "I guess you've been keeping pretty busy," she says.

To her this place must look even more vacant than it did

before I moved in. I suppose that's understandable, because I'm feeling vacant too.

Apple makes herself at home by going into the kitchen. She opens the fridge and makes a face at how little there is inside it: a jar of peanut butter, a bottle of ketchup, and a few cans of orange soda. "Do you need me to take you shopping?" she asks, letting the door to the fridge fall closed. "Or you're more than welcome to come home for your meals, anytime you like." She fills the teakettle with water from the sink and grabs a knife to cut into the quiche.

"I'm fine," I tell her. "*Really*. I've mostly been eating at the Depot."

"Here, come, eat," she says, setting me up at the kitchen table with a napkin and fork. "The quiche is still warm. Do you want some tea?"

I nod to the tea and do as she says, sitting down at the table. The first bite of quiche is like a shock to my mouth, especially since it came from her, queen of the microwavable dinner out of a box. It's salty with feta, crunchy with zucchini, and semi-sweet with caramelized onion. "You didn't make this," I smirk.

"Sure I did. It's Miko's recipe, and I followed it to a tee."

"Seriously?"

"Seriously. I never lie about food."

"Well, then, I guess there's a first for everything."

"Exactly." She winks at me. "It's never too late to learn, grow, become a better person."

"No hidden messages there." I chew. "So much for subtlety, right?"

"Well, I've never been one for subtlety."

"Very true." I take a few more bites. The egg is cooked to perfection; the texture is creamy and fluffy; the crust is moist and buttery.

She sets a mug of tea down on the table. Chamomile. My favorite. "So," she begins, sitting down beside me, an invisible agenda hanging above her head. "I got a phone call from Detective Thomas. He said you'd been to see him recently. Something about a video."

"It was a video *link*," I say, as if the distinction is even relevant.

"How come you didn't tell me about it?" Her forehead furrows. The lines between her eyebrows deepen.

"If I told you about every weird thing that happened to me, neither of us would have time for work or sleep."

"Do you want to come home?" She reaches out to touch my forearm.

"No. I'm fine. I just didn't think to tell you."

"Well, I want to know about this stuff, okay?"

"Okay."

"I *mean* it, Ivy."

"Okay," I repeat.

"I hadn't even realized that you were still trying to assist in the case."

"Because I didn't want you to worry."

"I'm a mom, it's my job to worry, remember?" Her expression softens; the corners of her lips turn upward. "Anyway, Detective Thomas wanted me to tell you that he had the video link analyzed, as well as the creator's account."

"And?"

"And it was another false lead."

I clench my teeth, sensing a storm coming.

"You have to believe that the authorities are working very hard on this case," she says, raining down on the quiche. "Detective Thomas attests to that."

"And you're telling me this, because . . . "

"Because he said that when you left the station you seemed really upset."

I take another bite to avoid having to speak, unsurprised that this impromptu visit is about more than just quiche and kisses.

"He asked if you were still in therapy," she continues, as if this conversation couldn't get any worse. "And so I called the hospital to find out about your attendance at outpatient therapy."

"I'm sorry," I tell her.

"You haven't been to a meeting since discharge, have you?"

"I know. I suck. I'm almost surprised they told you."

"They didn't tell me. They're no longer allowed to share your medical information. But *you* just did."

"Oh." I'm caught.

"Oh." She fakes a grin.

"Thomas isn't going to call Dr. Tully, is he?"

"You're missing the point, Ivy."

"No. I'm not."

"The agreement was for you to go to outpatient and group therapy at least once a week each."

"I've been busy working at the Depot."

"If the Depot is keeping you from taking care of yourself, I'll cut back on your hours."

"Is Thomas going to call the hospital?"

"Honestly, I don't know. What I *do* know is that he's concerned about you. He doesn't want anything you're doing—research or otherwise—to negatively affect this case."

"Even if what I'm doing is more effective than their so-called leads."

"Ivy." She takes a deep breath.

I push my plate away, having lost my appetite. "I'll start going to therapy again, okay?" As if the seven years' worth I've already endured has done any good.

"Promise?"

"Pinky swear," I say, winding my pinky with hers. "I'll call them after I sleep."

"I'll hold you to that." She nabs a corner of my quiche crust.

"Now, I'm tired and I actually need to get that sleep."

"Fair enough." She gets up from the table, gives me a hug, and kisses the crown of my head. "I just love you, that's all. And I worry. And I want you to be happy. If anyone deserves a little happiness in this world, it's you."

"I love you too," I tell her, knowing she means well, but also knowing she doesn't have a clue how much this case means to me.

Ivy

MIKO AGREES TO FILL IN FOR ME AT THE DEPOT while I go see Taylor this weekend. It's no wonder that Gretchen has a crush on him. Despite my constant BS— storming off, screwing up—he couldn't be sweeter.

I pull onto the Gringle campus and drive past a rolling green lawn sprinkled with ivy-covered brownstone buildings. When I texted Taylor last night, I was relieved that she still wanted to meet. My parents think I'm at the Food Expo in Portsmouth. They didn't even flinch when I told them that I wanted to stay at the nearby Sheraton to take full advantage of the convention's offerings. They simply handed me the company credit card, excited to finally see *me* excited about something.

It's Friday night, just after nine. I park in the lot behind Taylor's dorm and go inside. The lobby is mostly dead, except for a couple of students playing a game of pool. "I'm here visiting Taylor Monroe," I tell the girl working behind the front desk.

"Wait, don't you go here?" She hands me a visitor form anyway. "Because you look so familiar . . . " She cocks her head and studies my face as if trying to place me.

I quickly look downward and begin filling out the form, not wanting to be recognized.

But then, "Holy shit, are you . . . ?" Her hand flies over her mouth. "You're Ivy Jensen," she says, checking the form. "The girl who escaped that screwed-up amusement park. You're, like, totally freaking amazing, by the way."

"I'm not. Really."

"What are you even doing here?" Her dark brown eyes widen.

"I'm here to see Taylor Monroe," I tell her again.

"Okay, but don't you totally hate her? Because I would. Someone who runs from a burning building without a call to the fire department to help the others who are still fast asleep inside. Instead, she just let them all go down in flames."

I can feel the confusion on my face. "Can you tell me where I can find her?"

"She's in room 27, on the second floor. You can use that stairwell. But call down here if you need anything, okay? I wouldn't let you go down in flames. I'm totally Team Ivy." She extends her fist for a bump.

"Thanks," I say, leaving her hanging, already making my way upstairs.

My heart pounds with each step. Blood rushes from my face, leaving me a little woozy. I reach the second-floor platform and breathe through the racing sensation, remembering that I haven't taken my meds. I swallow down a couple of pills with a swig of my water bottle, and then swing the door open.

Taylor is already there, standing at the end of the hallway. She looks so much different than the way I remember from the pictures on her phone. Gone are the pretty dresses and the megawatt smile, replaced by baggy sweats and a subtle grin.

"Ivy?" she calls out.

I quicken my pace, past several more rooms, until I finally get to her.

"Is that really you?" she asks, wrapping her arms around me.

My face gets buried in the strawberry-scented mass of her thick blond tendrils, but oddly it feels good—like hugging a long-lost friend.

The embrace breaks, and I take a deep breath, feeling a melting pot of emotion stir up inside me. "This just feels so surreal."

"For me too." She takes my hand and leads me inside her room.

My eyes zero in on her leopard print bedcovers. They match the luggage she brought to the Dark House, as well as the cell phone I found in her bed that first night.

"Everything okay?" she asks, following my gaze.

I nod and take yet another deep breath, willing my medicine to work.

"I'm stoked to finally meet you." She squeezes my hand and motions for me to take a seat on her futon.

I drop my bag and sit down, wishing I could relax. There's a sour smell in the air that makes me think of salad dressing. "How did you manage to score a single room?" I venture, opting for small talk. "I thought perks like that were only reserved for resident staff and upperclassmen."

"It's sort of a long story," she says, plopping down on the leopard print covers. "And not exactly my idea of a perk."

I glance toward her shoe rack, where she's got an elaborate stash of ballet slippers. "Are you studying dance?"

"Another long story—one that requires at least a few squares of chocolate to tell. Feeling munchy?" She gets up and grabs a supersize bar of chocolate from her shelf. She opens it up and breaks off a piece. "Help yourself," she says, passing me the bar. "God knows that I do."

"What changed your mind about meeting?" I ask, steering the conversation.

"My life has been utter hell here, Ivy." She lies back on her bed and stares up at the ceiling—at a poster that says DON'T WORRY, BE HAPPY. "But who am I to complain? I mean, I'm still breathing, right? Not all of us Dark House Dreamers can say the same. Nobody here lets me forget that."

"Okay, so you changed your mind about meeting, *because* . . ."

"Now *that* answer requires something salty. Hungry?" she asks, taking me off guard.

I look down at the piece of chocolate melting in my hand.

"Because I have a serious hankering for pancakes and french fries right now." She rolls over to face me. "Oh, but wait, you're a real foodie, aren't you? You probably have a way more sophisticated pal—"

"French fries and pancakes actually sounds perfect right now," I tell her, feeling somewhat hungry too, and more intrigued than ever by what she has to share.

TAYLOR

Ivy is intense—like a walking ad for Valium or something. She barely says two words on the walk over to the student center, but I can tell that her brain is going—I can see it in her eyes: wide, yet unengaged, as if she's someplace else entirely. Plus, she keeps fumbling with something in her pocket. Car keys? Spare change? A cell phone? A stress ball?

The student center is mostly dead at this hour—too late for dinner, too early for post-party pigging out. I point out the variety of foods—from Tex-Mex and pizza to a potato bar with over twenty different toppings. "Normally the potato bar's my *go-to*," I tell her, "but at this hour the cheese sauce tends to be lukewarm at best, and the bacon bits are fuzzy and chewy rather than crisp and crunchy."

Ivy and I are on the same snacking page, so I order us buttermilk pancakes from Tessa's Kitchen and a large fry from J.B.'s Grill—stuff a dancer would never normally eat.

"Here," Ivy says, trying to slip me a ten-dollar bill.

"Put it away. The sugar and carbs are on me this time— literally." I sigh. "Straight to my ass and thighs." I grab a handful of ketchup packets and syrup containers, and we take a seat by the windows.

Ivy is way prettier than the couple of snapshots I saw of her online: straight dark hair, big brown eyes, razor-sharp cheekbones, and full pouted lips—looks that any horror film director would kill for. She takes a teabag out of her purse (?!) and dunks it into a cup of hot water.

"And some people just carry breath mints," I joke.

"Want some?" she asks. "I have a whole tin."

"No thanks," I say, nodding to my Diet Coke.

We spend the next twenty minutes devouring our feast o' fat and catching up on each other's lives, *pre*–Dark House weekend.

"So, when did you become interested in Justin Blake?" she asks.

"Sometime around birth," I joke. "I think my rattle was in the shape of the Nightmare Elf. But it wasn't *just* JB's work that I was so obsessed with. I used to love *all* types of horror. It was my dream to be a scream queen."

"A *what* queen?"

"Scream queens. You know . . . women who star pretty exclusively in horror flicks. It's a whole niche market, and it seemed perfectly suited to me—with my background in dancing, and all—because, let's face it, I don't exactly fit into the whole dancer-rexic mold."

"What's that?"

"Rexic. As in *anorexic.* The girls here are way too hungry, which in turn makes them bitchy and uptight. They just don't get that dance isn't solely for the huffy-stuffy stage. I mean, what about *The Rocky Horror Picture Show? Repo: The Genetic Opera?* Or *Poultrygeist: Night of the Chicken Dead?*"

Ivy looks at me, her face funked up, as if *I'm* a chicken dead.

"Opportunities for multitalented scream queens are ample," I continue. "Not to mention that the pay is decent and the time commitment is way more manageable than mainstream film, theater, and TV, especially for those of us still in school. And, P.S., you don't have to be some mega-whoa-superstar actor who began her career as a baby in Gerber commercials. But I don't want to be a scream queen anymore, not even a dancing scream queen. That dream pretty much faded after I got here."

"Why? What happened?"

I poke a syrup-drenched fry into my mouth, wishing I had another plateful. "It's weird. My parents met in the service, both stationed overseas, both saw a lot of death. They always taught me survival of the fittest, that when you get knocked down you have to pick yourself up right after, and that it's always the strongest who survive. And so, whenever anything hard hit, I'd immerse myself in theater and dance, becoming someone else, forgetting all the tough stuff, telling myself any story I wanted. But 'survival of the fittest' doesn't exactly leave much room for heart. I mean, just look at where that mentality's gotten me. I have no friends. I've gained twelve pounds. And don't even get me started on my grades."

"Okay," she says, clearly not following, and I can't exactly blame her. I sound like a babbling buffoon.

"In some way, coming to this campus . . . it's been the worst couple of months of my life. But in another way, it's given me perspective. I mean, how am I supposed to move forward when I haven't dealt with my past?"

"And so is that the reason you changed your mind about meeting? Because I'm a part of your past?"

"Sort of ironic, isn't it? I mean, since we never really met before now. The scary part? After the Dark House weekend, it never even dawned on me to deal with what happened. Plus, I got so distracted by my five minutes of fame. By the time I arrived on campus, I was the quintessential 'it' girl—the one who'd been on television and interviewed in newspapers and magazines, the girl who got away. But it wasn't long before that five minutes of fame morphed into five degrees of shame. Now everybody just sees me as the girl who could've stopped everything but who royally blew it instead."

"And how do *you* see yourself?"

"Lucky to be alive, I guess. But also questioning who I am. A coward who only cares about herself . . . ? A girl who's okay being noticed as the winner in a losing game?"

"Or a survivor."

"Okay, but a survivor at what cost?" I gobble a few more fries. "Anyway. I used to research the horror movie market pretty hard-core, looking for opportunities to audition. That's when I saw the Nightmare Elf's contest. I thought it might be a nice stepping stone, getting to meet JB and all."

"Justin Blake?" Ivy asks, as if there's any other JB.

"Well, *duh*?" I roll my eyes.

"And now for the million-dollar question." She licks her syrupy finger. "Why didn't you stick around to meet JB? What made you leave?"

"The police didn't tell you?" I ask, feeling the surprise on my face. "I found a body. In the basement."

Ivy's fork drops to her plate with a clank and her eyes get saucer-big. The girl has serious star potential.

"I'd cut my hand pretty bad," I tell her. "And so I went downstairs to look for Midge, hoping she'd have a first aid kit. There was a freezer chest by the boiler tank. I opened it, looking for an ice pack. Instead I found a girl's body."

"What girl?"

"I don't know." I shrug. "The body was gone by the time the authorities got to the house, and the inside of the freezer had been torched—probably to destroy the DNA."

"I had no idea." Her mouth gapes open. She reminds me a little bit of Barbara Steele from *Black Sunday*, one of the most notable horror movies ever.

"Anyway, I gave the feds a full description of the body, but there hadn't been any missing-girl reports fitting that description, so I'm not really sure where things stand on that front. I'm not even sure if the police believe that the body was real."

"But you're sure it was?"

"Definitely sure." I nod. "I mean, I think it was. I'm almost positive, that is." I let out a nervous giggle. "It's just that there's been so much bogusness surrounding this case. Right after

469

that weekend, an anonymous someone thought it'd be funny to send me an invite to see the sequel."

"Do you still have it?"

"Negative. I gave it to the police. But I *do* have a weird video link that I can show you," I say, perking up. "I got it just today, actually—just a few minutes before you arrived. I didn't get to watch the whole thing, but it looks super dullsville: a family, a diner, a waitress with Mohawk hair and vampy makeup."

"Can I see it?"

"Sure," I say, spotting my evil ex-roommate and her plastic pet Barbie at the potato bar. I'd give almost anything to cast them in a slasher movie, where they'd be the overnight campers, and I'd be the deranged ax-wielding counselor.

Emily lets out a snort of a laugh when she sees me look.

"Who's that?" Ivy asks.

"Emily, my old roommate, with Barbie, her *new* roommate, aka the leaning tower of Leesa. I really hope they get the fuzzy bacon bits."

"What makes her a leaning tower?"

"Do you seriously need to ask?"

Ivy takes a second look, her eyes zeroing in on Barbie's double-D cups, made even more pronounced by the Betty Boop decal on the front of her top.

"Barbie got those implants for her eighteenth birthday," I say. "No joke. She tells everybody. I actually got to see them. One night, in our room, Barbie was like a cheesy five-dollar peepshow, answering questions about the procedure and whether or not her nipples still get perky. TMI?"

"Just a little."

"Sorry." I feign a cringe. "Then I'll spare you the details about the bounce-touch-buoyancy test a couple of the girls gave her. Anyway, the real tragedy? No one told Barbie that ballerinas are pretty one-dimensional. Oh, and P.S., her real name is Leesa; not Barbara or Bernadette, or any other elongated version of the B-word."

"Really?" Ivy asks, her face finally lightening up.

Barbie turns toward us. The words "You Betty I'm Single" are printed below the Betty Boop decal, making us burst out laughing.

A piece of chewed-up french fry shoots out Ivy's mouth, landing against the window glass. "Oh my g—" she whines, unable to get the word out. A weird hiccupping sound croaks out her mouth.

My eyes tear up. My stomach twinges. And that's when I know for sure—that Ivy is my kind of cool, and that we're destined to be close friends.

BACK IN MY ROOM, I SEARCH MY E-MAIL FOR THE video link in question. "It was sent from a JB superfan—at least I assume it was a superfan, because he or she was claiming to be the Nightmare Elf."

Ivy pulls up a stool and sits *thisclose* for the optimal view of my computer screen, dust bunnies and all. "How do you know that the sender was only *claiming to be* the Nightmare Elf, and not the *actual* Nightmare Elf?"

"For reals?" I shoot her a stupefied look. "Do you have any

idea how many JB fanatics are out there posing as the Night-mare Elf?"

"Eighty-two on YouTube. At least the last time I checked."

"Which was probably just this morning," I say, only half-joking. Finally, I find the e-mail, sandwiched between offers for long-lasting love and millions of dollars in inheritance.

"Holy crap," she whispers. Her mouth drops open, her eyes widen with urgency, and her brows dart up. If I didn't know better, I'd say she'd been a scream queen for years. "This link was sent to you in a Nightmare Elf e-newsletter," she says.

"And, once again, do you know how many supposed Nightmare Elf e-newsletters have been created since the Dark House weekend?"

"No," Ivy says, shaking her head. "I mean, the issue number . . . it's 207, the next one in the sequence, following the e-newsletter I got last fall."

"I'm pretty sure the JB fanatics have all of that information covered. They may have a fetish for blood, spew, guts, and gore, but still they're a pretty savvy bunch."

"No," Ivy persists. "I got an e-newsletter recently too. But the issue number was 208—the one after this one."

"Meaning?" I ask, feeling my head start to fuzzify.

Instead of answering, she takes the liberty of clicking on

the video link. As the movie loads, she practically salivates. Her eyes fixed on the screen, she nibbles her lip and leans in closer.

"Do you want a napkin?" I joke.

She shakes her head, oblivious to my sarcasm. The video starts. A seemingly ordinary diner appears on the screen. It's filled with seemingly ordinary people, eating less-than-appetizing food—a square block of gray something (meat?), a basket full of brown bread.

"There's no audio," I say, as if it isn't already obvious.

It appears as if the video's being shot from one particular corner, but then we move closer, focusing on the family—a husband, a wife, their perfectly pretty daughter. The daughter looks to be about twelve or thirteen, with long dark hair, held back with a bright pink headband.

The mom in the video puts her arm around Daughter's shoulder. Dad laughs at something Mom says. Daughter sticks her tongue out in retaliation at both of them.

"Total Snoresville, right?" I ask.

Apparently Ivy doesn't think so. She cups her hand over her mouth.

"*What?*" I insist. "Don't tell me that this lame-ass, B-rated video holds the magical key to Oz." I take another look, noticing that Daughter is wearing a pink shirt that matches her paisley headband, which coordinates with her pink and paisley wristlet. Way too tacky, but that can't possibly be what's got Ivy all upset.

A few seconds later, the movie fades to black and Ivy stands up. She's trembling. Her face is white. She looks like she's about to hurl. "It's him," she whispers.

"Whoa, wait, what's him?"

"I told them. I knew it." She turns away, headed for the door.

"Ivy—wait," I call.

She doesn't listen. She doesn't answer me. She simply grabs her bag and goes for the door.

Ivy

I RUN.

I run faster than I've ever run before—as far as my legs will take me. Down a stairwell, through the lobby, across a parking lot, past a soccer field, and up at least a hundred tiny steps.

Standing by a giant clock tower, I try to catch my breath, my lungs straining, my heart aching. A cold breeze brushes against my neck, sends chills down my spine.

The campus is sprawled out beneath me. The lights are on in several of the buildings, and yet everything appears vacant.

"Ivy?"

I turn to look.

It's Taylor. She comes and stands beside me, wipes my tears with the sleeve of her sweatshirt, and then wraps her arms around my shoulders. She smells like maple syrup. "It's going to be okay," she tells me. "You're safe here."

If only that were true. But things are not okay. And I'm not safe anywhere—not while the killer's still out there, studying me, directing my every move. He knew that I'd eventually reach out to Taylor, and that we'd compare videos, just like he knew how to get me to enter the Nightmare Elf's contest last year.

Taylor pulls me closer, and I rest my head against her shoulder. I can't stop shaking. My mind won't stop reeling. Why can't I remember what Mom, Dad, and I had been talking about at the diner that day? Or the reason that Dad laughed? Or what Mom said in response. The fact that I can't remember those things widens the hole in my heart.

"The campus is pretty at night, isn't it?" Taylor asks. "All lit up. Sometimes when I feel like running away, I'll come here and remind myself how lucky I am."

"Lucky because you got away?"

"Lucky for a lot of things, I guess."

"I wish I felt lucky too, but sometimes I wish that I'd died right along with them."

She pulls away to look into my face. "Don't talk like that. I mean, I know this'll probably sound majorly cliché, but you have your whole life in front of you. Plus, it's like you said before: maybe the others are still alive."

"I was talking about my parents. Sometimes I wish that I'd died right along with them seven years ago."

Her expression shows no surprise; she must've heard that my parents were murdered.

"I'm going to find the killer," I tell her.

"Wait." Her eyes slam shut. "Your parents' killer? Or the Nightmare Elf killer?"

"They're one and the same."

"Excuse me?"

"The person who organized the Dark House weekend is the same person that killed my parents. No one can deny it anymore."

Taylor makes a confused face—her lip snarled, her nose scrunched.

"I'm going to find him," I say again. *Ticktock, ticktock.* The ticking of the clock tower vibrates inside my chest. Only instead of rattling my bones, it's somewhat motivating, reminding me that time is of the essence and I have so much work to do.

IVY

BACK IN TAYLOR'S ROOM, WE SIT IN FRONT OF THE computer. The video is paused. The air feels stifling. There's a twisting sensation in my gut.

"That's me," I say, nodding toward the screen.

"Hold on, *what's* you?"

"The girl on the screen, at the diner. That was me," I attempt to explain. "Seven years ago. Those were my parents—the ones who were murdered."

"Wait, *what?*"

"I know it sounds crazy, bu—"

"Are you sure?" She fast-forwards to a spot where the camera zooms in on me—where I'm resting my head on Mom's shoulder. My face looks a lot thinner now. My cheekbones are sharper. My chin is more pointed. My hair is darker, straighter, longer. But still, my eyes are unmistakable—light brown, slightly angled, with somewhat droopy lids.

"Holy shit," Taylor says, looking back at me, studying my face.

"I remember the day this video was taken," I tell her. "I'd gone to a diner with my parents and we'd sat at that checkerboard table. I remember playing checkers with the jam and peanut butter containers. My parents were murdered just a couple of days later."

"Holy shit," she says again. "We need to show this to the police. I mean, do you seriously get what this means?"

"That the killer's been watching me for years."

"Exactly, which is, like, *crazy town.*"

"It may be crazy, but it's also what I've suspected all along. Even before the Dark House weekend, I'd be walking home from school or shopping in town somewhere and feel his eyes on me."

"And you didn't tell anyone?"

"Of course I told. My therapist knew. She thought I was being paranoid. She still does."

"Okay, so if this crazed killer has been watching you for

years—and wants you to know it—why would he send the link to *me*? Why not send it to you? I mean, to me it's pretty meaningless."

"Because he wanted us to meet. And he was willing to wait until we did—until the two of us got together and compared notes."

"But what if instead of sharing the link with you, I showed it to the police?"

"You didn't have time to show them, though, did you? Didn't you say you got this link just before I got here?"

"Minutes before." She nods.

I replay the video again, searching for a clue—some hidden message as to where the others might be. Unlike the video of Natalie, this one wasn't uploaded by Movie Marvin. It was posted to Filmeo, a site where filmmakers showcase their works-in-progress—only this one hasn't been made public. Words sit at the top of the screen: EXCLUSIVE VIEWING PERMISSION.

"He posted this just for us," I whisper, proceeding to fill her in about the video of Natalie.

"And so obviously the videos were made by two different people," she says.

"Not obviously. The e-mail address is the same. The Nightmare Elf at Gmail."

"Are you sure?"

I nod. "In the video of Natalie, she was wearing a gold bracelet with a star charm . . . just like the necklace pendant I received years ago."

"Wait, what pendant?"

"I've gotten a number of anonymous gifts," I explain, "ever since my parents' death." I click on the Nightmare Elf's Filmeo account. There's no other information listed about him, or any other videos posted. I click on the link to e-mail him. A form pops up, asking for my name and e-mail address.

"You're not seriously going to send him a message, are you?"

"If the person who posted this video isn't the real killer, he's at least had contact with him."

"Ivy."

"What?" I turn to face her again.

She's looking at me like I'm a full-on freak, her eyes bulging, her lips parted like there's something hairy in her mouth. "We have to show this to the police."

I ignore her and continue to type.

Dear Nightmare Elf,

If this is really you, what did I put on my plate on that first night at the Dark House, when all of the winners were gathered at the dining room table for dinner?

Yours truly,

Ivy Jensen

P.S. If you wanted to come back for me so badly, why did you wait so long?

I read the message over several times, thinking how silly that first part sounds, but also confident that it will answer my question. No one besides the killer, Midge, and the other contest winners would know what I put my plate; I didn't get that specific in my police statement.

I position my cursor over the SEND tab, my heart absolutely racing. And then I hit SEND.

"I can't even believe you just did that," Taylor says. "Did you e-mail Movie Marvin too?"

"I did, but I didn't get any response." Not from any of my e-mail accounts, not even when I posed as an indie filmmaker looking to have a trailer made. "I'm thinking it's because I showed that video to the police."

"We have to show *this* to the police," she says yet again. "I mean, we're talking about a major piece of evidence."

I clench my teeth and look away.

"Ivy? Okay, you're acting a little *One Flew Over the Cuckoo's Nest*—and not in a good way." She stares at my balled-up fists.

I take a deep breath, my adrenaline pumping. But somehow

I also feel calmer than I have in months, more confident than ever before. "I can't go to the police," I say. "The killer wants me to do this on my own."

"Well, um, *duh*. Of course he does—so he can chop you up into a million pieces and throw you into a sinkhole."

"I've given the police seven years," I tell her, "and what have they done for me so far? My parents are dead. Five people are missing and assumed dead, including a boy I really care about—the first person I've opened up to since my parents' death. What more could the killer possibly take from me?"

"Only your life."

I focus on the video again. It's paused at a close-up of my eyes, back when there was a spark in them—when I laughed, and had friends, and looked forward to tomorrow. "I've spent the majority of my life feeling dead, fearing death, or wishing I had died."

"This isn't a game, Ivy."

"It is to him. And he wants to play. But this time I refuse to lose."

"Okay, seriously? It's time for some tough love. Let's push the pause on the intensity button, shall we? We need to think things through."

"I'm intense for good reason."

"Okay, but too much intensity and people wind up storing chicken carcasses under their beds. Didn't you see

Girl, Interrupted? What you need is some Handyman Harry." She holds up a keychain doll: a bearded little guy wearing blue-jean overalls and work boots. She presses his gut to make him talk.

"Hey there, hottie," Handyman Harry says. "Do you want to see my big screwdriver?"

"What do you think you're doing?"

"Not what, *who*." She winks. "I won him during freshman orientation for having the loudest belch. The loudest boy belcher got Harry's sister, Handygal Harriet." Taylor follows up with a burrito-and-soda-worthy belch so loud that it almost sounds fake. "Pretty impressive, wouldn't you say?" Taylor continues to press the doll's belly.

A series of terrible pickup lines play out of Harry's mouth: "Hey, baby, how about we build a future together? We can start with my hammer and some nailing"; "Hey, angel, does your crack need some caulking?"; "Do your shrubs need pruning?"

Taylor pretends to make out with the doll—*with* tongue—finally shoving it down the front of her sweatshirt. "Oh, Handyman Harry!" she purrs, tossing and turning on the bed, her eyes rolled back, her body quivering.

I can't help but laugh, even though I don't want to. And the harder I try to stop it, the stronger my giggles get. My stomach aches as tears streak down my face. Ironically, this is the worst time of my life and yet I haven't laughed as hard in years.

485

From the Journal of E.W.

Grade 7, August Preparatory School

LATE AUTUMN 1971

I just found out that some kid who used to go here killed himself. His name was Ricky Slater, and I've been assigned to his old room. Tray across the hall says that I'm the first person to sleep in Ricky's room since the suicide. He said that the room had been closed off for painting and refinishing, as if that would make everything nice. Too bad it doesn't work that way.

Gramps once bought Mother a pretty yellow sundress, but that didn't change squat. That same night she crawled into my bed and told me a ghost story—about a twelve-year-old boy named Johnny who'd lived on our property a hundred years ago, and died when the house went up in flames.

"Johnny was an angry, angry boy because of it." I can still hear Mother's little-girl voice.

I was six years old, and couldn't sleep after that. When Mother saw how scared I got with Johnny's story, she made a habit of visiting my room each night with a different, more horrifying tale about him.

"He may have died that day," she'd say, "but he's still here, in this house. Ever feel someone's eyes on you when you're in the bathtub or reading a book? That's him. That's Johnny, watching, studying, learning all of your habits. He talks to me, you know. He tells me how angry he still is and what I could do to make him feel better."

I'd beg her to stop talking about him. Sometimes I'd even pretend to be asleep. But it didn't matter. She was there, every night, whispering in my ear, waiting for me to cry. Only then would she leave me alone, which in some way was even worse, because I'd look around my room—at my stuffed lion and the nutcracker doll on my desk—and think they were possessed by Johnny's spirit.

People are saying that this school is haunted by the ghost of Ricky Slater. I wonder if Nana and Gramps knew that when they signed me up, and if they might've even requested that I get Ricky's room.

I'll bet anything they did. They knew about my mother's nightly ghost stories, but they didn't do crap to stop them.

IVY

EVEN THOUGH I GOT A HOTEL ROOM, TAYLOR INSISTS that I stay in her dorm.

"Let's just sleep on stuff, okay?" She opens up the futon and dresses it in pear-patterned sheets. "We won't make any major decisions until after we get some shut-eye. Oh, and P.S. sorry if the cushions smell like pickles. Sometimes I get a craving, and one time I spilled a jar."

We wash up and get changed—me in sweats and her in lipstick-kiss-patterned footie pajamas—and then crawl into our beds. It's just after one in the morning, but instead of going off to sleep, Taylor rolls over to face me. "I'm really glad we did this—that you called me, that I called you back, that you came here."

"Because I'm so much fun to be with, right?"

"More fun than I've had in weeks, to be honest. Sad but true. I mean, no offense."

"None taken."

"And now inquiring minds want to know: Do you blame me too?"

"Blame you?"

"For leaving the Dark House. For not taking Natalie with me, for not hiding somewhere—in the woods, maybe—and trying to warn you guys as you arrived."

"A lot of people would've done the same," I tell her. "Escaped from the Dark House, that is."

"Would *you* have done the same?"

I bite my lip, thinking back to how scared I was that weekend. "Part of me thinks that even if I'd wanted to bolt, I never would've made it out of there. I would've been paralyzed by my fear."

"By the time Natalie even crossed my mind, I was already deep into the woods. That message I wrote in the closet—get out before it's too late—just tells you how much of a coward I was. It was done on a whim, while I was hiding from Midge. I'm surprised you even found it."

"But I *did* find it. And I never forgot it. I knew something about it wasn't right."

Taylor shrugs. "I should've done so much more."

"You did the best you could at the time," I say, channeling my inner Dr. Donna.

"It was a full day and a half before I was able to get help," she says. "After I escaped, I still wasn't in the clear; someone was chasing me in the woods."

"Did you see who that someone was?"

"No, but eventually, when I got far enough away, I hid behind a fallen tree, my cheek pressed against a sharp twig, trying not to move. I stayed like that for hours, exactly as you describe—paralyzed by fear. I didn't move again until daylight."

"On Saturday," I say to be sure. "The day we went to the amusement park."

"Exactly." She nods. "It took a long time to find the road, and even longer to get picked up. But I did. A couple of truckers found me. They didn't speak English. Neither of them had a phone. And I didn't want to risk having them stop their truck. I just wanted to get away. They brought me to a bus depot and paid for my ticket. I ended up in Minneapolis, where I called the police. But I didn't know where the Dark House was—not really. And I just kept thinking about all of you guys, wondering what was happening." She looks away, her eyes filled with tears. "It seems like all I've been doing lately is wondering *what if.*"

"But hindsight is twenty-twenty, right?"

"So you don't hate me?"

I get up from the bed to bring her a box of tissues. "Of course not. Far from it."

"Well, that's a relief, because I was so afraid to meet you."

I sit down beside her and blot her tears with a tissue. "Well, I'm really glad that we *did* meet—that you changed your mind about getting together." Because this is the closest I've felt to anyone since Parker. And it feels good to be the strong one for a change—even if it's just in this moment.

IVY

I WAKE UP TO A BUZZING SOUND. MY CELL PHONE vibrates against the floor. I have a new e-mail message.

I sit up in bed. It's three a.m. Taylor's still asleep. A smiley face sleep mask covers her eyes; the front of it reads HAPPY NAPPER.

I reach for my phone to check who the message is from. The brightness of the screen stings my eyes and I have to squint.

But still I can see it: the Nightmare Elf's name in my in-box.

My heart tightens. The phone slips from my grip, clanking to the floor, waking Taylor up.

She pulls down her sleep mask. "What is it?"

"He wrote me back."

She sits up, clicks on her night table light, and then comes to join me on the futon.

The e-mail's subject line reads TO ANSWER YOUR QUESTIONS. I click to read the message.

Dearest Ivy,

   How nice to hear from you. I trust this finds you well.

   To answer your first question, you didn't really put too much on your dinner plate on the night of your Dark House arrival, despite the feast that had been arranged—the very same meal served in *Nightmare Elf III: Lights Out*. The smallest mound of macaroni and cheese was all.

   Your other question intrigues me, but I think I'll answer it at another time.

   —The Nightmare Elf

I clasp my hand over my mouth, feeling my entire body shake.

"Is that true?" Taylor asks. "About the mac and cheese?"

"True." I nod. There's a sharpness in my chest, making it hard to breathe.

Taylor gets up to grab her laptop off her desk. Meanwhile,

493

I reach into my bag for a sachet of lemon balm. I hold it up to my nose, concentrating on its ability to soothe.

"What the hell?" she shouts, sitting beside me again.

There's an error message on the computer screen. Taylor tries refreshing the page—it's the Filmeo account; I can tell from the URL. But the video's gone. The account appears to have been deleted.

"What happened?" she asks. She goes back to the original e-mail message, copies the link, and then pastes it into the browser. But the error message is still there. "We should call the police. They might be able to trace the e-mail address—or the server, that is—to find out where this person's located."

"I'm assuming they're already doing that. I mean, they have the e-mail address from the Movie Marvin video." The police tried tracing the original Nightmare Elf e-mails from a year ago as well, only, for whatever reason, they weren't able to pinpoint a location.

"Let's just go talk to them." She gets up and returns to her bed, closing the laptop.

My phone vibrates again. It's another message from the Nightmare Elf. The subject line reads: RAIN, RAIN, GO AWAY.

I click to open it up. The words *Do you like a wet seat?* make my head spin.

"What is it?" Taylor asks.

I look up in her direction, but then my eyes fix on the window behind her. Rain pounds against the glass.

"*What?*" she persists.

I get up and bolt out the door.

TAYLOR

Ivy runs from my room—yet again. I follow her out—down the stairs and through the lobby—calling after her in my loudest whisper to avoid waking anyone up.

I push through the exit doors. Ivy is a good distance in front of me. There are streetlamps shining over the parking lot, but it's still hard to see. It's raining out. The droplets pelt my eyes, making me wish I had my sleep mask, or at least an umbrella.

Ivy moves like a contestant on *Supermarket Dash*, weaving

through cars (in lieu of store displays), trying to find her own car (instead of a prize-winning box of Cheerios).

"Ivy?" I call, once again.

She stops in front of a small dark sedan a couple of rows over. I hurry closer, able to see that the windows of the car are open.

She swings open the driver's side door and reaches inside to retrieve something from the seat.

"What is it?" I ask, standing right behind her now.

"My windows weren't open," she mumbles.

"Well, I should hope not. This isn't exactly Punta Cana. I'm freezing my ass cheeks off."

She snags a flashlight from her glove box and shines it over a bright red envelope. The front of it reads FOR APRIL, WITH LOVE, in black block lettering. "He's here," she whispers; there's a tremor in her voice.

I take the umbrella sticking out from the side door compartment. I open it up and hold it over us. Meanwhile, Ivy aims her flashlight all around—over cars, at windshields—before going to tear the envelope open.

"Hold up," I say, stopping her a moment by grabbing her wrist. "This is tangible evidence. We shouldn't even touch it. We should just bring it to the police."

She ignores me and continues to rip it open, her dampened fingers unable to work fast enough. Finally, she pulls out a card. "An invitation."

"To where?"

She reads it over, her jaw clenched, her nostrils flared.

"What does it say?" I ask.

She turns it over so I can see.

YOU'VE BEEN CHOSEN ONCE AGAIN

What: To claim your leading role as the star of *Return to the Dark House*.

Where: On set, at an undisclosed location.

When: Filming begins as soon as you're ready to commit to the project.

RSVP: Respond via e-mail within 24 hours. Include your phone number, and you will receive a call from the director with all the details.

PS: If you tell, your costars' roles will be cut.

"There's something else," she says, pulling out a 4 × 6 photograph. It's a picture of five dolls. They're all lined up against a crude cement wall: a guy doll dressed in dark clothes, with lots of silver jewelry; a girl doll with weird patchy hair and shrouded in dark layers; two more guy dolls (one holds a guitar; the other one reminds me of a surfer dude with his scruffy blond hair); and a pretty dark-skinned girl with a smiling face.

"These represent the missing contestants, don't they?" I say, more as a statement than a question.

"And if we want to save them, we have to go to this." She nods to the invite. "We have to follow his rules or else their roles will get cut."

"Meaning?" I ask, fearing I know the answer.

Ivy pulls out her phone and opens it up to the Nightmare Elf's last e-mail. She hits REPLY.

"Holy Hell!!" I pull her fingers away from the screen. "Haven't you ever heard of impulse control? Let's talk about this."

"What is there to talk about? Are you with me on this or not?" She raises her eyebrow, à la Tippi Hedren in Alfred Hitchcock's *The Birds*.

"By 'with me,' do you mean not calling the police?"

"By 'with me,' I mean saving the others once and for all." Ivy glares at me like a possessed vampire junkie on blood-flavored crack.

"Look—" I take a deep breath. "It's three o'clock in the morning. We're standing in the middle of a rainstorm, in the middle of a parking lot. And I'm not even wearing public-viewing-worthy PJs." I flash her the hole in one of my kisses, right over my left butt cheek.

"So . . ."

"So, let's go back inside, change our clothes, get some shut-eye. We can rethink things in the morning when we're not so saturated."

"Except that every moment we wait, the clock just keeps on ticking."

I wouldn't be surprised if she can hear the ticking inside her head, like a time bomb about to go off. "We have twenty-four hours to respond," I remind her. "So, what do you say we use at least six or seven of them? I can't be responsible for any decisions made before ten on a Saturday morning with a stomach devoid of home fries and sausage links."

My comment takes her off guard, and the tension in her face releases. Game point: I've won this round.

Ivy

I WAIT UNTIL TAYLOR NODS OFF BEFORE HEADING
out to the hallway. Sitting on the floor with my back pressed
against the wall, I stare at the photo of the dolls, desperate for
some clue. The background is dark. The dolls look vintage
with their wide, haunted eyes and their dirty, scratched-up
faces.

I check my phone, knowing I have at least a couple of
missed messages—two missed calls from Apple and a text
from Core telling me to check in. I text both that all is well at
the food fest.

The e-mail from the Nightmare Elf is up on the screen. I hit REPLY, thinking about all the other questions I might ask him: Why my parents? Is it true that my dad went superquick, like the medical examiner said? What were my mom's final words? And are Parker and the others still alive?

I run the T-shirt bracelet over my cheek, imagining that Parker can feel it somehow. The reply box still open, I type in my cell phone number. My finger trembles over the SEND tab. Should I? Shouldn't I?

Finally, I press SEND, feeling a wave of relief. Only now can I get some rest.

There's a vibrating sensation inside my palm; it jolts me awake. I open my eyes and sit up. I'm back in Taylor's room, on the futon. Taylor's still asleep in her bed.

The phone clenched in my hand, the vibrating continues. The screen says PRIVATE CALLER. I click it on, moving out into the hallway. The brightness of the overhead lights shocks my eyes.

"Hello, Princess." His deep-throated voice sends shivers all over my skin. "It's been a long time, hasn't it?"

My head whirs. There's a swirl of darkness behind my eyes, making everything feel hazy and thick. "What do you want?"

"Oh, but this isn't about what *I* want. This is about what

you want, isn't it, Princess? You gave me your number. You looked Taylor up. *You* reached out to *me*. I'm assuming that by going to such great lengths, you must really want to reclaim your role."

"My role," I repeat, at a sudden loss for words.

"You want to be my star again, don't you, Princess?"

I reach for the keys inside my pocket and run my finger over the sharpest one—not as pointed as a knife, but it has a tip, and manages to soothe. *I'm in control. I still have choices.* "Where are the others?"

"It's enchanting to hear your voice."

"*Where are the others?*" I insist.

"By others, do you mean your costars?"

"Okay," I say. There's a hitch in my throat.

"You'll have to see, my honeybee."

A door creaks open at the end of the hallway. Three girls emerge wearing matching heart-patterned pajamas. They're giggling as they move toward the stairwell, seemingly without a care in the world.

I look at the time; it's 7:32 a.m. "How do you know that I won't go to the police?"

He laughs—a cackling sound that reverberates inside my bones. "Because I know you, April. I've been watching you for a long, long time, internalizing your every choice. You were desperate enough a year ago to enter my contest, despite how scared you were by it, just to put old ghosts to rest. You're even more desperate now."

My breath stops. My skin ices over.

"Cat got your tongue?" There's amusement in his voice. "Do you miss your fine prince, my princess? Would you like to see him again? I have an inkling he might like that too."

"Is Parker still alive?"

"Not so quick, my sugar stick. I believe you'd asked me a question. Do you remember what it was?"

"Why did you wait so long?"

"Because you're like that fine bottle of wine just waiting to be uncorked. It would've been a waste to indulge too soon. One needs to be patient until things have properly aged and ripened. Alas, from the very first time I saw you, I knew you'd be the perfect star. I hope you'll be my star again."

"Will it mean getting to see the others?"

"So long as you keep things between us. Do I make myself clear?"

"How do I know they're still alive?"

"You don't. That's a leap of faith you'll have to take."

"And if I don't take that leap?"

"Then you'll never know if you could've done something, saved someone, silenced the screaming inside your head."

There's a jumping sensation in my gut, a rushing sensation through my veins. "What do I need to do? Where do I need to go?"

"Ivy?" Taylor asks. She's standing right behind me. The door to her room is open. There's a confused expression on her face.

I hold up my finger, asking for a second.

"Who are you talking to?" she persists.

"Just give me a minute," I insist, cupping over the mouthpiece.

"Holy shit. It's him, isn't it? You totally e-mailed him, didn't you? Even though we agreed to wait."

The phone clicks. He hung up.

Ticktock, ticktock.

Boom.

TAYLOR

IVY IS TOTALLY GOING TO BLOW. STILL, SHE ACCEPTS my invitation for fresh air. We go outside and walk across the footbridge, finally ending up at the rec hall—a favorite spot on campus. There are cushy chairs, snack machines, game tables, and an espresso bar with ten degrees of boldness (for those particularly rough cramming sessions).

Ivy and I gravitate to the espresso bar. She brews herself a #10, while I go for a #3 with extra cream and two packets of sugar, and we sit on a couch, overlooking the foosball tables.

"Look," I begin, unable to take her silent treatment for one more sip, "I get that you're upset, but I thought the deal was that we weren't going to do anything until morning."

"The killer was about to tell me what I needed to do."

"What you needed to do *to what?*"

"I'm sure he'll call me back. He has my number. He knows how to reach me." Her cell phone's clenched in her hand.

"We need to go to the police," I tell her for the umpteenth time.

"No," she barks. "You need to promise me that you won't."

"I can't." I sigh. "I've already surpassed my limit on screwups regarding this case."

"Give me at least a week."

"A week to do what?"

"Research." She pinches the skin on her kneecap. "I just want a chance to go through the clues on my own before turning them over to anyone."

"You do realize that pawing over physical clues is, like, number one on the how-to-sabotage-the-evidence list, don't you?"

"I know what I'm doing."

"Oh, right, because you binge-watch *CSI?*"

"The killer knows what he's doing too," she continues, ignoring my jab. "He's way too smart to leave fingerprints or DNA."

"Are you really willing to take that risk?"

"I think you owe me a week."

"Why? Because everything's all my fault? Because you obviously blame me too?"

"Because I'm asking *you*—someone who was able to dodge the worst weekend of my life, and arguably the worst weekend of the five other missing contest winners—to wait."

Her words are sharp. They form a knife that stabs into my back. "Three days," I say to compromise. "After that, I'm going to the police. And I'm going to tell them everything."

"Three days," she repeats, extending her hand to shake on it.

I give her a hug instead. Her arms wrap around my shoulders, but the embrace falls short of the one from last night when she first arrived—that palpable sort of connection.

"It'll all be fine," she mutters.

I know she's totally trying to bullshit me—that things are about as fine as fuzzy bacon bits—but I take her lie anyway.

From the Journal of E.W.

Grade 7, August Preparatory School

WINTER 1972

I can see a face inside my head: a blond-haired boy with freckles and a pointed nose. I roll over in bed. My shades are drawn. My heart is racing. There's still three more hours until people start waking up.

I reach for my inhaler, flashing back to cold sweats and panic attacks, sitting alone in my bedroom at home, with the door locked and the light out, able to hear noises out in the hallway—footsteps, door knocks, floors creaking, bells jangling.

My mind told me that it was Mother making the noises. I could hear her evil little-girl giggle, after all. But every other part of me was convinced that it was the ghost of Johnny, outside my bedroom, coming to get me.

I click on my night table light. Everything appears normal—dresser, desk, chair, bookcase, journal—but it still feels like someone's here. I lean over the side of the bed to check beneath it. Empty.

It's been like this all week. Whenever I close my eyes at night, I can see that boy's face. I asked the man in charge of the rooms if I could switch mine, but he said no changes—that if he changed one, then everybody would be asking. I wonder if my grandparents are paying him extra for that.

Last night, when I got up to check the door, I could've sworn the temperature in the room had dropped by at least twenty degrees. I tried the knob. A good sign: it was still locked. An even better sign: I was able to unlock it, unlike years before in my bedroom back home.

I closed the door, turned toward the bed again, and felt my heart come to a sudden stop. There was something sticking up from behind my pillow—some kind of paper. I moved closer to see what it was, thinking that maybe a page had fallen out from my journal or that I'd misplaced a handout from one of my classes.

I moved to stand just a couple of feet from the headboard, and the answer became clear. It was a page from an August Prep yearbook. I scanned the photos, somehow knowing what I would find. And I was right. There was a photo of the blond-haired boy with the freckles and pointed nose—the same boy that's been popping up inside my mind.

Ricky Slater.

IVY

IT'S FORTY-EIGHT HOURS LATER, AND I STILL haven't heard back from the killer. And so I've been searching online, trying to find images of the dolls from the photo. Does he own them? Where are they from? What year were they made? What are the chances that I can find them together as a collection?

Dr. Tully called about an hour ago, reminding me about our outpatient therapy deal, which I took as a definite threat. And so that's exactly where I am—in the hospital parking lot, having just exited my car. I step through the doors of the mental health wing just as my phone vibrates in my pocket.

I check the screen: PRIVATE CALLER. My heart instantly clenches.

"Are you coming?" a girl asks, holding the elevator open for me.

I shake my head and click on the phone. "Hello?" I cover my ear and move toward the exit door, looking back out over the parking lot. "*Hello?*"

"Good evening, Princess." His voice sends a shockwave through my body.

"What do you want?" I ask him.

"This isn't about what *I* want, remember? Are you alone?"

I look back over my shoulder, just as someone emerges from the stairwell and then moves past me through the exit doors. "Sort of."

"Sort of isn't good enough, Princess. Go someplace private."

"Okay," I mutter, heading outside. I cross the road in front of the entrance, and then hurry across the parking lot, fumbling to retrieve my keys from inside my pocket. I go to get back inside my car, but the doors are locked. I jam the wrong key into the lock before finding the right one.

Back inside my car, I lock the door behind me. "I'm alone now," I tell him, all out of breath. The overhead streetlamps shine through my windshield, making me feel exposed. My head aches. I haven't taken my meds.

"Good, because our conversations should only be between the two of us. Do you understand that, April? One word to anyone else—any lofty plans to conspire with the police—and your costars will be cut. Do I make myself clear?"

"Very. I get it. It's just you and me. What do I need to do? Where do I need to go?"

"I've actually come to you. Do you have paper and a pen?"

I reach into my bag and pull out one of my many notebooks. "Okay."

"I trust that you'll keep these notes between us as well. One wrong move . . . "

"If you wanted to keep things so private, why did you contact me while I was at Taylor's?"

"You're a very smart girl, you know that?" His voice is soft and slow.

"She wants to go to the police."

"But I'm sure you've convinced her otherwise. I know you, April. I can predict your every move. And if you ever let me down, I'll find out and simply adjust accordingly. I always have a plan in place—an insurance policy that safeguards myself against disloyalty."

"You don't deserve loyalty."

"I may not deserve it, but still you're extending it to me, aren't you? By keeping our little secret. You must really want to see your costars."

"Where do I need to go?"

"Drive northeast on Route 87 from Sturbridge, Maine. Get off at exit 4 and take a right on Chelsea Avenue. Park in the lot behind Chalmers Chocolate Factory."

I write everything down, almost unable to imagine going through with any of these plans.

"When you get to Chalmers," he continues, "cross the street to the bus stop and take the number 452 going south. Get out at the Lancaster Road stop. You'll see a field; cross it."

My pulse races as I scribble down his every word. This is just too surreal. It can't possibly be happening.

"When you come to the other side of the field, there will be a small boat attached to a dock," he says. "Use it to cross the lake. Look for a tall maple tree with a yellow scarf tied to the branches. There you will find further instructions. Goodbye for now, my princess."

"Wait," I stammer. "When am I supposed to go there? When do I need to do this?"

"*The sooner the better to see a fine letter.*"

"A fine letter?"

"Don't wait too long. *Ticktock. Ticktock.*"

The ticking's inside me as well, clouding over my mind, making everything feel urgent, broken, dire, desperate.

"This offer is only available for a limited time," he chides.

"How limited?"

"By the count of one, my honeybun." The phone clicks. He's hung up.

IVY

I SPEND THE NEXT COUPLE OF HOURS DRIVING around, trying to sort out my manic thoughts. I pull over a couple of times—to respond to a text from Apple and then to answer a call from Core: "Therapy went fine," I tell him.

"Are you on your way home?"

"I'm spending the night at Candy's, from the Depot. She broke up with her boyfriend and now she's a wreck. She asked if I'd stay the night." Even though I no longer live at home, I know that he and Apple check up on me. They notice when my car isn't parked in the driveway.

"Aunt Tillie should be back from her trip on Monday," he says. "But you know that if you ever get lonely, you can always come home."

"I know. And thanks. I'll call you in the morning."

We hang up and I recheck my screen. Miko sent me a text: "You looked out of it this AM. The flu? I made chicken soup. LMK if I can drop it off."

Everyone's looking out for me. I have such a cheering squad on my side. And yet I feel so desperately alone.

I rest my head against the steering wheel, resisting the urge to bang it. What did the killer mean when he said "by the count of one"? One day? One week? It couldn't possibly have been one hour. He would've said if there was that much of a ticking clock . . . *right?*

In the same vein, I doubt he'd give me one week. Too much could happen in such a lapse in time—I could devise too much of a plan, become distracted, get others involved, or even change my mind.

It's one day. I'm sure of it. Just enough time for me to pack up some stuff and come up with an excuse for being away.

I drive onto the Gringle College campus and park in the lot by Taylor's dorm, wondering if coming here wasn't a big mistake.

It's raining again. The droplets pound against the glass, making it hard to see. I pull out my phone and call Taylor's number.

"Hey," she answers.

"I hope I didn't wake you."

"Are you kidding? I never go to bed before eleven; there's way too much goodness on TV, and speaking of . . . have you seen this week's episode of *Relationship 9-1-1?*"

"I doubt it."

"Wait, are you okay?"

"I'm fine, why?"

"I don't know. I guess you sound a little lost."

I look at my reflection in the window glass—tired eyes, pasty face, hair pulled back in a messy braid. "You'll never guess where I am right now."

"Paris? Sitting beside a hot French guy at some chic café? In which case, why are you calling me?"

"I'm right outside your building."

"Seriously?"

My breath fogs up the window. In the condensation, I write Parker's name.

"Um, *hello.* Earth to Ivy."

"I'm here. I mean, I'm *really* here. I can see the entrance doors to your dormitory," through the letters in Parker's name.

"Well, then what are you waiting for? Get your spontaneous ass up here."

"Okay," I say, relieved by her cheery disposition. Just hearing it, despite the darkness—in the car, in my heart—my spirits lift.

TAYLOR

I OPEN THE DOOR OF MY ROOM. IVY'S STANDING
there. Her clothes are wet. The mascara has run down her
cheeks. "Get in here," I tell her. "Let me find you some dry
clothes." I fish an acorn-pattered bodysuit from my basket of
clean clothes. "Feeling squirrelly?"

"Why do you have that?"

"Because sometimes I feel like a nut."

She can't help but smile, despite how deflated she seems.
Meanwhile, I continue to dig, finally finding a ho-hum pair of
sweats. "These good?"

"I'm actually fine," she says, twitching from the cold.

"You look about as fine as the monster zit on my forehead." I force the sweats into her arms and point her to the bathroom down the hall.

She comes back only a few minutes later, all changed, and sits down on the edge of the futon. "He called me again."

"He, as in our resident psychotic killer."

She nods. "He gave me directions—for what I need to do, for where I need to go—to find the others."

"And where *are* the directions?" I ask her.

"I'm keeping them someplace safe."

Translation: *I don't trust you enough to say.* "There's no place safer than with the authorities," I tell her.

"He wants you to join me too—the killer, I mean—to find the others, to star in his film."

"Did he actually say that?"

"It was more of what he *didn't* say."

"Call me crazy, but there's something about the words *killer* and *join* in that gives me the heebie-jeebies."

"This could be your opportunity," she says, "to right the past, to show everyone you're not selfish the way they think."

"The only opportunity is the one that involves calling the police. It's nutty that we haven't already." I mean, yeah, it sucks that I've become a social leper, but I'm hardly willing to risk my life to change that.

"You promised me three days."

"And so I'm obviously a total idiot."

"You made that promise because deep down you know I'm right. All the horror movies say so. The police are never the ones who find the killer in the end. They simply show up after the climax—after all the hard work has already been done."

The girl *does* have a point. But still, "I'm going to the police first thing tomorrow morning."

She stands up from the futon. Her forehead looks sweaty. "I'm sorry. It was stupid of me to come here. I just thought . . . " She lets out a sigh. "I actually don't know what I was thinking. To anyone else, this must seem crazy."

"Ivy—don't go." I stand up too. "I mean, truly don't go. Let's just drive down to the police and tell them everything we know."

"I can't." There are tears in her eyes. "I have to see this through—for my parents, for Parker and the others, and for myself. He'll continue to haunt me otherwise. I'll always be waiting for him to strike if I don't." She starts to go for the door. "I'm really sorry that I bothered you."

"Wait, are you kidding?" I move to block her from the

door. "You're not going anywhere. You're spending the night here—on my pickled futon. Harry wouldn't have it any other way." I grab Handyman Harry from a heap of random stuff on my desk. "He hasn't stopped talking about you since your last visit." I wink. "He's been dying to get you into bed."

Finally, Ivy smiles. I've cracked the code, broken through her wall. I grab an extra pillow and some blankets from the closet, and start making up the futon before she can try to weasel her way out.

Surprisingly, she follows my lead and settles into bed. I'm just about to slip on my eye mask when I notice that she's rolled onto her side, facing the wall, and that her shoulders are slightly jittering.

"Ivy?" I gaze over at Handyman Harry, knowing that we're so far beyond what even he is able to repair. And so I do the only thing I can. I get up and move to snuggle in beside her. I stroke her back, the same way that Darcy Conner did for me, four years ago, after the Starbound Dance Competition, when my ex-boyfriend Max dumped me for Paula Perfect Pirouette with the huge beaver teeth. "Do you want to talk some more?" When she doesn't answer, I pull a tear-soaked strand of hair from in front of her eyes. "We can just sleep on things for now." I wait until she falls asleep; only then do I go back to bed.

Ivy

SOMETIME AFTER SIX IN THE MORNING, WITH Taylor still asleep, I get up and write her a note:

Dear Taylor,

    I haven't had a lot of friends in my lifetime, but spending time with you, I can see how much I've missed. I'll call you just as soon as I can. Thanks so much for everything.

Love,
Ivy

I set the note on her night table, and then open the door to leave, accidentally catching my bag strap on the knob. The fabric makes a ripping sound.

I turn to look.

Luckily, she remains sleeping, her eye mask still in place.

I move down the hallway. The dorm is quiet at this hour. A cleaning woman in the lobby asks if I'm going for an early run, but I'm too uptight to answer.

It's still somewhat dark out. The sun is tucked behind a cluster of clouds, making the day feel even more ominous. I hurry to my car, get inside, and turn up the heat. Sitting with my head pressed against the steering wheel, I try to concentrate on just my breath, but it's balled up inside my chest, pushing against my ribs.

I check my cell phone. There's only twenty-five percent of the charge left. My fingers tremble as I reach inside the glove box and pull out my wool scarf. I unravel what's tucked inside it.

A knife. The blade is six inches long. The handle has a nice grip—slip-proof, hard plastic. I turn it over in my hand, reminded of its ample weight, assured by its curved tip.

Ticktock, ticktock.

I grab my phone and text Core that Candy's still in a bad way, and so I'll be spending the day trying to cheer her up. The mere idea that I could cheer up anyone should be a dead giveaway.

I text Candy next, knowing she has the day off: "Cover for

me if Apple calls. I'm at your place today, and btw I stayed there last night too. I'll explain later. Big thanks. XOXO." I power my phone down to conserve the battery, pull out my notebook, and flip open to the page with the instructions.

Route 87 is a two-lane highway that goes on forever. There aren't many people out this way. Maybe it's because it's still early. More likely it's because there isn't anything out here. He's sending me someplace desolate.

The early morning frost covers the road, making the pavement glisten. I peek in the rearview mirror a couple of times, feeling like I'm being followed, but the only cars on the road with me are so far back. Am I driving too fast? I look around for a speed limit sign. Sixty-five. My speedometer says eighty. I need to slow down.

More than two hours later and I finally reach exit 4. I take it and go right on Chelsea Avenue, spotting the chocolate factory immediately—a wide abandoned brick building with a crooked sign over the front entrance that reads Chalmers Chocolate, in what once must've been pretty red cursive. There's tagging along the side, and most of the windows have been boarded up.

I pull into the back lot and park, as instructed, behind the building. Aside from a tiny food market, a gas station/hotdog stand, and a drugstore that advertises check-cashing and lottery tickets, the area looks vacant.

The bus stop is across the street, just like he said. I peer down the road, able to see a bus in the distance, getting closer. I squint hard, trying to see what bus it is. As if by fate—my coming here, my doing this—the number 452 comes into view.

I stuff the knife inside my bag, grab my cell phone, and hurry across the street, knowing that I'm much more vulnerable on foot.

The bus doors open with a thwack and I step inside. There are only two other riders, neither of whom makes eye contact. I tell the driver that I'll be getting off at the Lancaster stop, hoping that he remembers my face.

I take a seat toward the front, reminding myself that it isn't too late. I can still call the police. Maybe they can hatch a plan; some undercover person who looks like me could go through the motions of getting to this very place. But then what if the clues end up being dead ends, once again? Would I get another chance?

I close my eyes, able to hear Detective Thomas's words darting across my brain, constricting the air in my lungs: *"You're, what . . . three weeks out of a mental hospital? How many times have you called and/or come to see me since then? Fourteen times in five weeks."*

Nearly ninety minutes later, after passing through miles of farm and conservation land, we reach Lancaster Road. I gaze out the window. There's nothing here.

"Are you sure this is where you want to go?" the driver asks.

"I'm sure," I say, able to feel the words in my chest—a sharp, jabbing pain.

I exit the bus. The doors fold shut. The air is cold. My breath is visible. The bus drives away, leaving me completely alone. I pull my phone out of my bag and power it back on. I have a bunch of missed calls from Taylor, not to mention twenty-two percent of my charge left—still plenty of juice to make a call. I look all around, feeling as if I'm being watched. The road is narrow. Woods border it on one side. On the other side is a grass field, just like the killer said.

Keeping the phone gripped in my hand, I begin across the field, headed for a rock wall, wondering what this area used to be. There's a dilapidated farmhouse that borders the field; its windows have all been boarded up. An old, rusted tractor, missing all of its tires, is parked in the driveway. There's also a windmill in the distance and an old barn.

Finally I get to the rock wall, but there's another field on the other side of it. I recheck the instructions; there's no mention of two fields, but still I begin across it. After about twenty more minutes of walking, I'm finally able to see it.

A lake.

A dock.

A small boat.

I check my phone again. I have twenty percent of charge left, but no bars. There's no reception. Should I turn back around? My brain tells me yes, but I move to the boat anyway and sit down inside it.

Using the tip of my knife, I scratch my initials into the wood as evidence that I was here. I should've done the same at the bus stop, should've left something behind on the bus . . . a bracelet, a lip balm.

The wooded land that surrounds the lake is thick and vast. I undock the boat, grab the oar, and start to paddle out, searching for a tree with a yellow scarf, keeping my focus on a grouping of trees directly across from the dock.

At last, I spot it. A long yellow scarf tied to a low branch. It flaps in the breeze, as if waving me over.

My shoulder aches as I paddle through the water at full speed. The front of the boat smacks into the land, propelling me forward.

I get out, tie the boat to a stump, and move toward the tree, searching for a clue.

The scarf continues to waver. There doesn't appear to be anything tied to it or written on the underside. I untie it from the branch, suspecting there might be a note hidden beneath the knot.

But there isn't. The scarf is clean.

I look down, between my feet. The ground's uneven. The dirt's been overturned. There must be something buried.

I crouch down and begin to dig, using a pointed rock. The dirt comes up easily. The muscles in my forearms throb from working furiously.

At last I find something.

The rock makes a clank sound.

There's a hard metal surface.

I continue to dig, lifting a box out of the ground. It's about the size of a carton of eggs, about the weight of one too. I jiggle it back and forth, able to hear the slight shifting of something inside.

My pulse races as I go to open the box, fumbling with the latch. I lift the lid; the hinges squeak.

There's an envelope inside. My name is scribbled across the front. I pick it up, noticing more envelopes beneath it—a whole stack of them—all with my name, all sealed, and all with the same handwriting across the fronts: block letters, slightly slanted.

I tear the top one open and pull out a sheet of paper. At first I assume that it's going to be further instructions.

But it's not.

It's a letter.

To me.

Dear Ivy,

I'm not really sure where to begin, except maybe with the obvious. There hasn't been a day that's gone by that I haven't thought about you at least a dozen times.

I worry that you didn't make it to safety. I wonder where you are and what you're doing, and what you imagine about the others and me. I also think about the status of things. Are the police close? Did they find enough clues? Did your nightmares ever stop? Or are they even worse now?

I replay the same scene inside my head: the one where the police bust in and find the others and me. You're there too, cutting my ropes, helping me up, leading me outside. I picture a bright blue sky, puffy clouds, fallen autumn leaves, and ambulance trucks in the distance with medics running toward us.

And I picture you: your lips pressed together with concern; your eyes tearing up with relief; your hands wrapped around mine, almost unwilling to let me go. Again.

I wish that I could see you, and hold you, just like I did in your room that first night. I miss you, Ivy. A lot. And so I'm writing you this letter, and I'll write you a bunch more—as many as I have to—to remind myself of hope. It's easy to forget it exists—at least it is for me right now.

Love,

Parker

I reread the letter, my heart pounding, my body quaking. This seriously can't be real. It must be part of a setup.

"Ivy?" a voice calls from behind me.

I turn to look, startled to find Taylor.

Still wearing her sweats from last night, she has a confused expression on her face. "What are you . . . ?" Her voice trails off. "You just left. Again." She stops from speaking to study my face.

I open my mouth, wanting to answer, desperate to ask my own questions too: What is she doing here? How did she find me? Did she get instructions from the killer as well? But instead of saying anything, I remain silent, the words stuck in my throat.

Taylor's eyes move to the metal box, and then to the hole I dug, and finally to the letter in my hand. And that's when something in her brain clicks. Her eyes soften. The muscles in her mouth loosen.

She gets it—maybe not the "*it*." But she gets that something big has happened. And that's obviously "it" enough.

She comes and wraps her arms around me without another word. Meanwhile, I'm crying so hard now—and not just because of the letter, but also because of her kindness—that I have virtually no words left.

From the Journal of E.W.

Grade 7, August Preparatory School

WINTER 1972

I shouldn't be awake. It's the middle of the night, but something startled me and I sat up in bed and looked all around.

There are numbers on the wall, in front of my bed. Big, small, tall, fat. Numbers. Scribbled. Glowing in the dark. Making my muscles twitch.

I click on my night table lamp. The numbers disappear right away. Relief. I can breathe.

Should I turn the light back off? No. I don't want to know if the numbers are still there.

I've been waking up every night. Each time it's something new: whispering, laughing, knocking, the creaking sound of hinges. Sometimes I'm not fully awake and think that it's Mother trying to scare me. But then I remind myself that she's locked up for good, punished for setting the house on fire with me inside, trying to blame it all on the ghost of Johnny.

Sometimes I wish that I'd burned to death that day. Other times I feel like I am on fire—like every inch of me is singeing, and that no amount of water will make me feel normal. Whatever normal feels like.

I don't want to go to sleep anymore. I lie awake in bed, feeling like a little kid again, back home, shaking beneath the bedcovers, reaching for my inhaler, hating and wanting Mother both at once.

I told the man in charge of the rooms about all the weird stuff that's been happening, but he said it was probably just my imagination, that a lot of the kids complain about the same kinds of stuff.

I asked Tray across the hall if weird stuff happened to him too. He said that one time he heard knocking on all the walls of his room, and that he now sleeps with the light on. I will too. I also have a statue of Mother Mary, a prayer candle, and some rosary beads. I stole it all from the chapel when Father Pranas wasn't looking. I hold Mary tight as I close my eyes for bed, praying that Ricky won't come, but he always does, just like Mother. She always came too, bringing stories of Johnny along with her.

TAYLOR

IVY'S FACE IS FLUSHED. HER BODY'S SHAKING. There's a tear-soaked letter clenched in her hand. I pry it free, more than curious to know what prompted such a reaction.

The letter's from Parker—*major* reactor. "Do you think it's real?" I ask, ever the pessimist.

"How did you find me?" she asks, in lieu of an answer.

"Easy. You woke me up. I followed you here."

"*What?*" She looks confused, like I'm speaking in special code.

"Okay, so maybe it wasn't *that* easy, now that I think

about it. By the time I got out to the parking lot, you were already pulling away. Normally I'd have just turned around and gone back inside, but let's face it: you were acting like an escaped mental patient last night—and not in a cute come-eat-Checkers-with-me sort of way; more like in an I've-got-a-fresh-pack-of-razor-blades-at-the-ready kind of way. Bottom line: I couldn't *not* follow you. You're just lucky that I happened to have a full tank of gas."

"You followed the bus too?"

"I followed the bus, I followed your car."

"But you didn't try to stop me?"

"Believe me, it wasn't for lack of trying. First of all, I called you, like, a bagillion times, but it kept going straight to voicemail. And then you were driving so fast that I nearly lost you twice. And PS, you ignored my honking. By the time I pulled into Chalmers, you were already boarding the bus, and I was sixty minutes over trying to snag your attention. My curiosity was way too piqued at that point to interrupt you on your mysterious mission. I was determined to see just *where* you were headed and why. I totally thought I was bagged once you got off the bus, but I was able to pull in behind an old boarded-up barn. It was kind of exciting, actually. I felt like Veronica Mars."

"Did you cross the fields?"

"Well, um, yeah." I feel my eyes grow big. "I'm *here*, aren't I? Of course, I didn't go on foot. While you opted to walk, I drove—at least as far as I could, that is. I ended up taking a road that wrapped around the side of the field, keeping my eye on you the whole time, Ms. I'm So Hyper-focused That I Don't Even Notice When People Are Following Me. Not exactly the best quality for someone who claims to have killers after her, FYI. Anyhoo"—I pause for a breath—"I parked my car somewhere around that rock wall. I was almost tempted to try phoning you then, but I left my cell in my car and didn't want to risk losing you by going back to get it."

"He's still alive," she says, nodding to her box of buried treasure.

"Right, because dead boys don't write letters. The whole transparency thing makes it nearly impossible. It gives new meaning to the expression 'can't get a grip.'"

"I'm *serious*," she scolds me. "It sounds like the others are alive too—or at least some of them."

"How do you know that these letters are really from Parker? That this isn't someone's warped idea of fun?"

"Just look," she says, handing me another letter.

Dear Ivy,

The person who's taken me found a bunch of the letters I wrote to you. He ripped up a couple, kept a few, and then encouraged me to write you more—with a number of stipulations, that is.

At first I felt a spark of hope, picturing you someplace safe—like inside your bedroom, snuggled beneath the covers—reading them. But when I stopped to really think about it, that hope morphed into something else—fear, anger—because I figured he'd be using the letters against me somehow. Or, worse, against you.

I'm supposed to tell you that if you want to see me or any of the others again, you have to come here and find us. I wish that weren't the plan. I wish I never had to write that sentence. I hope you'll never have to see it.

> Be safe, Be smart, Love,
> Parker

I look up from the letter. "The boy has a way with words, doesn't he? But can he also make a decent breakfast?"

"He's being told what to write," she says, ignoring my attempt at humor.

"Not everything. Plus, it sounds as if he started writing to you on his own—like it was his idea to begin with."

"I've been writing to him too." Her face turns pink, seemingly in love with the idea that they're both on the same letter-writing wavelength (despite the fact that people are missing—ahem, *assumed dead*—and that we're standing in the middle of nowhere).

She spends the next several minutes poring over more letters—until I can't take it any longer and have to ask the obvious. "So, what *is* all of this? What does it mean?"

"It means, this is it. The real deal. I'm going to find the others."

"Like, *now*?" I ask, the light finally dawning—the remote location, Ivy's sense of urgency, the freaky phone call she talked about last night.

"Now," she says, her eyes completely focused, blink-less, as if there isn't a doubt in her mind.

"Ivy?" I shout. "I mean, holy freaking freaksterville. This is crazy."

"No." She shakes her head. "Crazy is not taking this

opportunity. Crazy is blowing it by telling too many people. Crazy is knowing that a killer is after me and doing nothing about it."

"Crazy is *this*," I snap.

She goes to open another letter, but I stop her before she can, snatching the entire stack, and thus revealing the hidden jewel.

A handheld tape player sits at the bottom of the box. "Jackpot!" I declare, picking it up. I push EJECT to pop out the audio-cassette. Scribbled across the front are the words PLAY ME.

Ivy takes the tape and studies the label, looking at it from different angles, as if it's an alien object dropped down from outer space. After a few moments, she puts it back in and pushes PLAY. The tape is staticky at first, adding to the whole creepy vibe.

"Hello, Princess," a voice seeps out, cutting through the static and making the surreal *real*. "I hope this finds you well. If you've come this far, I'll assume you'll travel a little farther. Do you see the path that cuts through the woods, not far from where you're sitting?"

"Right there." Ivy points.

"Take it," he says.

"Wait, how does he know that we're sitting?" She looks all around.

"It's a tape," I remind her. "He's assuming that you're sitting. I wouldn't overanalyze it."

"When you come to a swamp area," the male voice continues, "the path will fork. Go to the right."

I grab the recorder and push PAUSE. "We seriously need to think things through, because let's just say, for argument's sake, that you continue to indulge this psychopath by playing his twisted game. Then what?"

Ivy responds by taking the recorder back. She gets up and begins down the path, leaving me in the proverbial dust.

"Um, *hello*?" I call out. "You're not bailing on me, are you? Particularly after I followed you here and hiked around a lake, sans boat, sacrificing my brand-new pair of Uggs."

Ivy turns to face me again, gazing down at my sacrificial boots. "What do you mean?"

"I mean, I'm coming with you," I say, before I can think twice about it.

"Excuse me?" she asks, as if I'm speaking in secret code again.

I stare out into the woods, flashing back to that day at the Dark House, scurrying past Natalie's room, and then climbing out a window and fleeing into the woods without ever looking back.

"Taylor?"

"Who else is going to tip you off to all the standard cliché horror gimmicks? I'll be able to smell the evil clowns and menacing elves from a mile away."

Ivy studies my face in anticipation, as if a giant anaconda might come bursting out of my mouth. "Are you sure?"

I nod, unsure, and she comes and wraps her arms around me. Her body quivers like the leaves on the trees all around us. And suddenly it seems so obvious—why the killer chose her in the first place.

"You're, like, the quintessential scream queen," I tell her, taking a step back. "The girl who fights for the good of others, despite the consequences; whose bravery trumps her fears."

"Bravery or stupidity?"

"I'm not like that," I tell her. "That's the difference between you and me."

"Except you *are* like that," she argues. "I mean, you're here, aren't you?"

I shake my head, fairly confident that while she's the heroine, I'm the character who thinks she's smarter than everyone else but actually gets slaughtered en route to escape.

Somehow despite knowing that, I follow her down the path.

Ivy

TAYLOR AND I TAKE THE PATH THAT CUTS THROUGH the woods, walking for what feels like miles. I know she doesn't want to be here. And part of me wants to tell her to go, but I hold that part in, grateful to have her with me.

"Hey, aren't we looking for that?" She points to a swamp.

I nod and push PLAY.

"Once you find the swamp," the voice says, "it'll just be a little bit farther."

I push PAUSE again, my mind reeling with questions. How long will it take for someone to find my car behind the chocolate factory? At what point will my family contact Candy and figure out that I lied? How long after that will the police go into my e-mail to put all the pieces together?

"Ivy?" Taylor's several steps in front of me now. "We're going the right way, aren't we?"

I wonder where she's parked—if it's in a spot that has cell reception, if someone will be able to trace her phone's whereabouts.

"Are you still with me?" she asks.

I nod and push PLAY again.

"I'm really excited to see you, Princess." His voice is soft and deep; the words come out slowly. "Very soon now. Just keep on walking."

The path narrows. There are tall, vine-like bushes on both sides of us. The tops of them form a ceiling above our heads, and we have to keep ducked.

"What's he saying now?" Taylor asks.

The path winds left and right, forming a maze. Branches stick out in my path, pulling at my hair, scraping against my cheeks. I try to keep up, but Taylor quickens her pace, hell-bent on getting to the end.

"Just a little bit farther," the voice reminds us, as if talking in real time.

Several yards in front of me, Taylor lifts a branch and peeks outward. "Holy shitster!" she declares, cupping her hand over her mouth.

"What is it?" My heart sinks.

She waves me over, still keeping her eyes locked on whatever's out there, beyond these shrubs.

I move slowly, my heart pounding.

"Are you there yet, Princess?" The soft purr of his voice sends shivers all over my skin.

I join Taylor, by her side, and gaze upward. A huge, Gothic-looking building sits in the distance behind an iron gate. With multiple pointed roofs and a cobblestone courtyard in the center, overgrown ivy crawls up the sides of the building, twists around the front pillars, and clogs up a chimney. "What is this place?" The windows have been boarded up, but both the gate and entrance doors are wide open. "Someone wants us to go inside."

"Of course they do," Taylor says. "Come right in, step right up, and you too can drop off the face of the earth, just like your fellow contestants."

"You don't have to come with me," I tell her. "I'll understand if you don't."

Taylor nods, perhaps considering her options.

I try to stay focused, wondering what this building once was. A rich person's home? A castle? There isn't any graffiti or tagging, so either no one knows the building's here, or nobody comes out this far.

"It must be ancient," she says, pointing toward the entrance. There are gargoyles over the door, looking down at the front steps. There's also a garden gazebo and what appears to be a chapel attached to one side of the building. "Maybe it was once a convent or monastery," she guesses.

The building itself sits in the middle of a sprawling field, with woods just behind it. There's a dirt path that branches out from what was probably once a driveway, but there are no roads that lead here.

"Welcome," the voice says on the audiotape, making me jump.

"Kill that thing, will you?" Taylor snaps.

I click it off and reach into my bag. I wrap my hand around the knife, reminding myself of my mission. I'm here to save Parker. I'm going to find the others.

"Now what?" Taylor asks, as if this is just some random stop on an errand list.

"Now we go in."

"For reals?" Her teeth are clenched. She's itching her palm.

"I mean it," I tell her. "You can turn back. I won't be upset."

"Will you turn back with me?"

"I can't." I shake my head.

"Then how can *I*?" She takes a deep breath and starts toward the building.

TAYLOR

IT'S JUST AFTER TWO IN THE AFTERNOON, BUT THE sky is gray and the clouds hang low, making it feel much later. We move across the courtyard, passing by a huge water fountain with a basin that looks like an ice cream dish—rounded bottom, tulip top. Behind it, there's a sculpture of a curly-haired boy with a wide-open mouth. His blank eyes angle toward the ominous sky. This whole scene flashes me back to my Gothic horror days—when I was in love with anything Stoker-ish.

I reach out to take Ivy's hand, but she's got it stuffed in her bag. Her inky-dark hair blows back from her face, accentuating her pale (ghostly) skin and rose-colored lips; she reminds me a little of Allison Hayes from *The Undead*.

As we move up the front staircase, there's a tugging sensation inside my gut—one that tells me I should go back. I mean, seriously? The spooky house, the creepy gargoyles, the iron fencing, and the fact that we're in the middle of nowhere without cell phones . . . "This whole scene has got classic horror doom written all over it."

Ivy remains mute. She hasn't spoken in the last several minutes, and it's starting to freak me out.

The front doors appear to tower over us by at least three feet. Ivy stops a few steps behind me, her eyes hyper-focused, as if they could burn the place down with a single blink.

"Okay, this whole Carrie White routine has got to stop," I tell her. "Say something. I need to know that you haven't been body-snatched."

Finally she takes my hand, and together we inch through the entrance doors. There are hundreds of tiny candles scattered about the lobby area—on the floor, lining the walls.

"Someone's here," I say, stating the obvious.

She takes another step; a broken floor tile crunches beneath her shoe. The ceiling is broken too. There's a hole overhead, where there might've once been a chandelier. Mangled wires hang down from it.

Another eerie sculpture faces us on the back wall. It looks like it was done in limestone: a life-size woman reading a book, with children swooning at her feet. The children look possessed—tiny pupils, darted eyebrows, rounded faces, and dimpled cheeks. Beyond the sculpture is a grand staircase with wide steps and thick banister railings. I picture myself falling through the center, mid-ascent.

"So, maybe this wasn't such a nifty idea." I gaze back at the entrance doors, beyond tempted to bolt.

"What's that?" Ivy asks, nodding to a package at the foot of the sculpture. It's about the size of a shoebox and tied with a big red bow. Beside it is a hefty flashlight.

"A party favor?" I offer, trying to keep things light for the sake of my own sanity. I pick the package up and give it a shake. Something knocks around inside it. "Do you want to do the honors?"

"You can," she says, her hand stuffed inside her bag again.

I look back at the entrance doors once more, picturing myself leaving, trying to formulate an excuse. My fingers fumble as I work to untie the ribbon. I don't get the knot undone on the first few tries.

"Need some help?" Ivy asks.

"I got it," I say, finally pulling the ribbon free. I open the box and peek inside.

At the same moment, the front doors slam shut with a loud, heavy thud. The box springs from my hands, dropping to the floor.

"No!" I shout, going for the door. The sound of bolts locking echoes inside my brain. My heart tightens into a fist. The handle doesn't budge.

Music starts to play—the theme song to *Haunt Me*.

"Shit, shit, *shit*!" I shout, pounding on the door, knowing I totally blew it.

Tears fill Ivy's eyes. I'm crying too—on the inside, trying to hold it together. I'm so freaking stupid.

"This song," she mutters. "My parents. The killer played this just after . . ." She focuses back on the gift box.

I move to pick it up, revealing what's inside: a video camera— the kind that straps to your head. There are earphones attached, with another piece that curls downward for a mic, reminding me of a 911 operator. "Put it on," I tell her.

"You can't be serious."

"Look," I say, forcing the camera into her hands. "This isn't exactly *my* idea of fun, either. But since you came to play, don't you think you should follow the rules—at least to begin with?"

Ivy reluctantly slips the video camera on so that the lens shoots out from the center of her forehead and the headphones rest over her ears. The tiny voice piece hovers a few inches in front of her mouth.

"There's crackling," she says, signaling to her earphones.

I move closer and grab one of the earpieces to listen.

"Welcome to *my* nightmare, Princess," a voice plays, making my stomach twist.

"Are you ready to be a star?" he asks. "You survived *your* worst nightmare. Now, it's time for you to experience *mine*—a place that haunted me when I was a young boy. The cameras are rolling—except for your camera, that is. And how nice that you brought a co-star. Taylor Monroe, are you ready to reclaim your role?"

"Go screw yourself," I shout into the mic. I take Ivy's hand and give it a firm squeeze. "We're going to get through this," I tell her, trying to convince myself the same. I muster my best smile, pretending to be acting a role, telling myself this isn't real.

I thought *I* was jittery, but Ivy's trembling like a diabetic in need of Pixy Stix. Still, I click on her camera, really wishing I'd gone with my gut.

From the Journal of E.W.

Grade 7, August Preparatory School

WINTER 1972

I woke up to whispering. A boy's voice: "Find it. Get it."

If only I knew what the "it" was.

My mother used to tell me that Johnny's "it" was setting my grandparents' house on fire, just as he had done years before (to his house—the one that had been there before Nana and Gramps built their new one).

I grab my Mary statue. "Why?" I ask it, wishing Mary could explain all the stuff that's been happening: these visions and voices; seeing Ricky's face when I look in the mirror; and spotting him in the library, between stacks of books, with a noose around his neck.

Sometimes I feel like I'm in a movie—like none of this is real. But then I press Mary against my cheek, hard, until my teeth cut the flesh inside my mouth. The blood is real. All of this is real.

IVY

"I TRUST THAT THE CAMERA IS PROPERLY AFFIXED to your head." His voice in my ear makes my head feel dizzy. "Now I can see things from your point of view. Do you have any idea how exciting that is to me?"

I bite the inside of my cheek, imagining the camera like a ticking time bomb, about to go off. Taylor stands by my side, listening in, one of the earpieces turned outward.

"This building used to belong to August Prep," the voice continues. "The school opened in 1896. Thomas Shumacher, the owner of this estate, wanted to create a small, multi-aged academic environment that would cater to alternative learning styles and accept boys from all walks of life and with various areas of interest. I lived at this very boarding school, where five years prior to my admission, a student had committed suicide."

"Too bad that student wasn't *you*," Taylor says, speaking to the camera on my head.

"Parents pulled their sons from August as rumors about the suicide spread," the voice continues. "Many believed the building was haunted. By the time I got here, the number of students had dropped from forty-eight to just twelve. Do you believe in hauntings, Princess? Things that go bump in the night?"

"And now for the million-dollar question: Why does he keep calling you Princess?" Taylor asks.

I shake my head. I don't have an answer. There's a prickly sensation all over my skin.

"You'll have just four hours to save the others," the voice says. "In order to do that, you'll need to get through every challenge and follow all of the instructions."

"Every challenge?" I whisper.

"Every challenge has a clue," he explains, as if speaking directly to me. "If you want to find the others, you'll need to collect all of those clues. Now, let's begin. Proceed to room number two."

Taylor hands me the flashlight. She has her own—one of those mini keychain ones. She clicks it on and begins to look around, heading to the area behind the statue. There's a doorway to the right of a grand staircase. She pushes the door open.

We've found the kitchen. It's huge—like for a chef—with high ceilings, stainless-steel appliances, and a crumbling tile floor. Beyond the kitchen is a dining area with long rectangular tables. I angle my flashlight all around and catch something moving out of the corner of my eye.

To my left.

By the fridge.

I shine my flashlight at it, feeling my whole body tense.

"Holy shit," Taylor says, following my gaze.

A boy's face is there, on the fridge door. Blond hair, angry eyes, a scowl across his lips. The image is transparent, as if it's being projected somehow. I turn to look behind me, where there's a wall of cabinets. I open a few of the doors, wondering if there might be a camera hidden inside.

"It's gone," Taylor says.

I swivel back around. The image has vanished. But still I can feel someone's eyes on me. "Let's go," I say, leading us through the dining area.

We take a turn into a hallway. Candles help light the way—wall sconces positioned about five feet apart. I shine my flashlight over cracked walls with peeling paint and insulation peeking through the ceiling.

"Bingo," Taylor says, standing in front of an open door. She angles her flashlight at the number two hung on the wall.

I move to stand beside her, and peek inside the room. More candles light up the space; they're set atop elementary school desks lined up in rows. There's a portable chalkboard at the front of the room. The words WELCOME TO MY NIGHTMARE are scribbled across the surface.

"Remind me why I followed you here," Taylor says. "And why does it smell like rotting fruit?"

I take a step inside. A screen drops down behind the teacher's desk, covering the chalkboard. An old-fashioned film projector at the back of the room, just a few feet away from us, clicks on. The screen goes dark and grainy.

I turn to look at Taylor, just as the classroom door swings shut, nearly smacking her in the face. She jumps back, into the hall. I hear the lock turn.

"Ivy?" she shouts. The doorknob jiggles as she struggles to get back in.

I try the knob too. It doesn't budge. The door is solid wood; there are no windows to smash. My hands wrapped around the knob, I yank with all my might, my foot propped against the wall for added strength.

There's a clamoring sound in the hallway. A moment later, the knob pulls away in my grip. I go soaring back, landing smack against the floor.

"Are you okay?" Taylor asks.

I get up. My back aches. There's a clanking sound against the door on the other side. She's trying to get her knob back into place.

I try as well, aiming my flashlight into the hole; it seems there's a metal bar that I need to fit through a squarish space. After several seconds, I finally get the bar to slide in, but the door still won't open.

"Would you like a cookie?" a voice asks from behind me.

I turn to look. There's a girl on the projector screen. Little Sally Jacobs from Justin Blake's Night Terrors films. I recognize her right away: her dark red braids, her purple sundress, the skeleton keys jammed into her eyes.

She's holding a tray full of cookies. "This batch just came out of the oven." She smiles wide, despite the blood running down her cheeks. "I also have fresh lemonade inside my house. Want to come have a glass?"

The movie projector makes a click-click-clicking sound. Meanwhile, it's quiet out in the hallway now. I place my ear up against the door. "Taylor? Are you still out there?"

"*Hellooooo,*" Little Sally Jacobs sings. "I believe I asked you a question. Cat got your tongue? Or maybe *I've* got the cat's tongue." She giggles, pulling a short red tongue from behind her ear like a coin trick. The tongue wiggles between her fingers. She pops it into her mouth and swallows it down like candy. "*Yummy, yummy in my tummy,*" she sings.

"Taylor?" I call again, knocking on the door.

The image of Little Sally Jacobs darkens on the screen. The background behind her grays as well. It looks as if she's hidden in shadows. I can no longer see her face or features, nor can I tell that her dress is purple.

By the time the image lightens, it's morphed into a woman—someone much older than Little Sally Jacobs. Wearing a long black dress, the woman has her hair pulled back into a tight bun atop her head, and there are deep lines in her face.

"You're a naughty, naughty girl," she hisses. The lines in her face seem to deepen and multiply as she moves closer and her image becomes bigger. It looks as if she's moving out from the screen, as if this footage is three-dimensional.

She points at me, her finger waggling left and right, scolding me, forbidding me.

"Taylor?" I shout again, unable to recognize the woman. She isn't from one of Justin Blake's films.

"Go stand in the corner," she snaps.

I bite the inside of my cheek, waiting for the moment to pass.

"You heard me," she continues, moving into the center of the room, as if the image has morphed again, become a three-dimensional hologram. "As a student here at August Prep, you will do as you are told. Now, if you don't go stand in the corner, you won't ever get to see your friends. Is that what you really want?"

My mind starts to race. By *friends*, does she mean the other contest winners? Does it include Taylor too?

The woman has a cookie now. "*Mmmm,*" she says, moaning over its goodness. A trickle of blood drools out her mouth and rolls down her chin. There's an eerie grin on her face. "Oatmeal-raisin. Would you like a bite?"

I brush Parker's T-shirt bracelet against my cheek, reminding myself why I'm here.

She grimaces when I don't answer. Her eyes narrow into slits. "I'll tell you one final time," she says; her teeth are stained with red. "Get in the corner—*now!*"

I do as she says, moving to the far corner of the room, reassuring myself that there are still more challenges to tackle, more scenes in his movie. The killer's going to play with me for a while.

"Ivy?" Another voice.

I turn to look.

Natalie's there, on the screen. The hologram is gone.

"Where are you?" she asks, looking all around as if trying to find me.

My heart beats harder. My pulse races faster. Was this pre-recorded? Or is it possible that it's live, that she knows I'm here?

Her wig is off. Her hair's uneven—shorter in some places, longer in others. She's wearing the same clothes from the Dark House amusement park night—the layers of black and gray.

"You're probably wondering how I'm still alive," she says. "I saw the rough-cut version of the film. It looked like I died, didn't it? Like a giant piece of pointed glass fell on top of my head. But I was able to step back, thanks to Harris's warning, just in time. The glass landed on my foot—my leg, actually—right above my boot laces, hitting an artery." Staring straight into the camera, she kicks her foot out from beneath her dress. Her leg's been wrapped with a bandage. "There was a lot of blood, Ivy. I hope you never had to see it. Lucky for me, our elfin friend doubles as a medic."

Her face looks exactly as I remember it, if not a bit thinner: pale blue eyes, pointed chin, dark full lips. The background behind her has been blacked out, so I can't see where she is.

"My clue for you is April showers. Now, can you guess where you need to go next? I'll give you a little hint." She reaches into the pocket of her dress and takes out a tiny book. *"Shhhh,"* she hushes, placing her finger up to her lips. "There's no talking in here." She opens the book up to the middle and begins to read.

I nod, suspecting I know the answer to her clue.

"Oh, and before I forget," she says, moving closer to the camera, as if about to let me in on a secret. "If you're seeing this video, then you know that Harris has been right all along. He was right about the amusement park, wasn't he? And about your fear of being videotaped? So, know that he'll be right about this."

Huh?

"He has a warning for you too," she insists. "Don't let her out—"

Static cuts off her words, filling the room with an ear-deafening hum. I remain staring at the screen, not wanting to move, desperate for her to reappear.

But she doesn't.

And I can't—move, that is. My chest tightens. My head feels even dizzier than before. I clench my teeth and hold my breath, while the room starts to spin. I silently count to ten, waiting for the sensation to pass, remembering something that Dr. Donna used to say: "The physical side effects of the emotions that we feel . . . those are as temporary as the emotions themselves."

After a few moments, I'm able to squat down to the floor. I lower my head between my knees, hoping the rush of blood to my brain will give me a surge of stability and enable me to breathe normally.

"Ivy?" Another voice.

I can hear again. The hum has stopped. I lift my head—the room wobbles into place—and peer over my shoulder.

Taylor is standing by the projector. There's a remote control in her hand. "Are you okay?"

The door is open again. Both knobs are in place.

"I went to look for something to wedge into the door crack," she tries to explain. "But I couldn't find anything, and so I gave the knob another shot. Wait, are you okay?" Her face scrunches at the sight of me.

I can feel the panic all over my body—a cold, tingling sensation. But there's another sensation too. Hope? Gratitude? Is there a word that falls in between?

Because Natalie's still alive.

There isn't doubt in my mind now.

TAYLOR

IVY FILLS ME IN ON WHAT HAPPENED, LOOKING ALL around as she does—into the hallway, at the projector screen, over both shoulders, and in the far corner.

"Natalie's alive," she says. "It was her, on the screen. April showers."

"Okay, my head hurts."

"That's the clue. Natalie said it." Instead of shedding any additional light, Ivy moves out into the hallway, ever eager for more punishment.

I begin to follow, just as a door slams shut somewhere,

freezing me in place. There's a sound of footsteps—wooden heels against marble floor tiles. I can't tell which direction it's coming from. I look back toward the classroom, and then down the hallway. A few moments later the footsteps stop, but still my heart keeps pounding.

"There," Ivy says, spotting a sign for the library. It points us just a few doors down. "That's where Natalie said we need to go."

I follow Ivy inside, immediately struck by what I see. The names of all the contest winners (FRANKIE, PARKER, NATALIE, GARTH, SHAYLA, IVY, and TAYLOR) are splattered across the walls in dark-red paint. There are portraits of all of us too, done in a Renaissance style with rich colors and serious expressions.

While Ivy moves toward the portrait of Parker, I check out the one of Garth. His dark eyes are mesmerizing; I can almost feel them somehow, watching me, studying my every move.

The library is about the size of a gymnasium, with super-high ceilings and a monster fireplace that's big enough to stand in. There's a main circulation desk at the front, a baby grand piano at the back, a bunch of study tables in between, as well as rows and rows of books.

Ivy and I move to the reference desk—a thick mahogany island littered with the dust of broken tile. I aim my flashlight at the ceiling, where there's a hand-painted scene of seven sad-looking children sitting in a circle, all holding the same book.

"Creepy super freaky," I mutter, also noticing a three-tiered chandelier.

Ivy searches the desk, in hopes of finding another clue perhaps. "There's crackling again," she says, placing her hands on the headset.

I move closer to listen, bracing myself to hear his voice.

"Welcome to the library, Princess," he says. "The smell of fine literature lingers in the air, doesn't it? The notes of vanilla and nutmeg? The acidic scent that comes with paper and ink. Ricky Slater used to escape in here to read the greats: Hemingway, Poe, Keats, Proust . . . you name it. One thing most people don't know about Ricky, however, is that it was the voice in his head that he was really trying to escape—the one that told him how inadequate he was: socially defunct, unable to relate to those around him, even on those rare occasions that he tried. The reason *I* know all of this . . . as you can imagine, Ricky was a hot topic after his fatal departure, not to mention that I'm the one who found his suicide note—stuck in the pages of *Madame Bovary,* his most checked-out work. I want you to go find the note now."

Ivy stares at me, her mouth snarled open, as if there's a booger hanging out my nose.

"*What?*" I sniff.

"Do you believe in ghosts?"

"Well, *duh.* Ever see *The Amityville Horror* or *The Conjuring?* I don't mess with spirit shit."

As if on cue, music starts to play from an old-fashioned record player in the corner.

I go to check it out. It's one of those big, boxy players with the automatic arm and the vinyl disk that goes round and round.

A female voice sings: *"I've got my eye on youuuuuu, Sweet Cherry Pie. My eye's on youuuuuu, oh, no, I can't deny. Oh, Baby Boooooo, I'll be coming for youuuuuu."* Denise Kilborn's voice; she's one of my dad's favorite singers.

The rhythm is slow and haunting. It's being played at the wrong speed. There's a lever at the top of the player. I move it a notch to fix the speed, but nothing happens. I click the power off, but still the machine plays—even when I smack the arm off the record, scratching the needle across the vinyl. The music is obviously coming from somewhere else.

I shine my flashlight all around, searching for a speaker. Instead I find two glowing red lights, two aisles over, in the stacks of books. The lights hover over a set of encyclopedias.

I move closer, angling my flashlight between the bookshelves, able to see that the lights are actually eyes.

They belong to a boy—the same one we saw in the kitchen, against the door of the fridge.

Ivy screams at the sight of him—a bloodcurdling wail.

I move to the end of his aisle. The boy looks freakishly real. He has a stark white face and blond hair, and is dressed in prep-school gear: khaki pants, navy suit jacket, leather loafers, striped tie. He's standing against the wall, staring in my direction.

I get even closer; I'm just a few inches away now. He looks about fourteen years old.

"Taylor?" Ivy's voice. She's standing behind me, at the end of the aisle.

There's a pile of books at the boy's feet and something metal gripped in his hand. He grabs a book off the shelf, opens it up, and plunges down with the metal object: a librarian's due-date stamp. The word DIE! appears on the inside cover.

He tosses the book, grabs another, and does the same; his teeth clench with the force of his stamping.

DIE!

DIE!

DIE!

He goes to take yet another book—a copy of The Masque of the Red Death, by Edgar Allan Poe. But instead of stamping, he pauses. His eyes zoom in my direction again, as if he can really see me.

The music stops. The boy's lips part. He's mouthing something, but I can't hear him.

"What?" I move closer.

"Get out," he hisses. A deep, angry voice.

A shiver runs down my spine. I take a step back, bumping into Ivy, letting out a gasp.

She pulls me away, her fingernails digging into my skin as she brings me back to the main area, with all the study tables. "Did you blow out some of the candles?" she asks me.

It takes my brain a beat to make sense of the question—to notice that while most of the candles in the library remain lit, the ones on the study tables have all been blown out. Tendrils of smoke linger in the air, as does the smell of sulfur.

"No." I shake my head.

"Someone's been here. With us."

No shit, Sherlock.

Her flashlight stops on a sign at the end of a row of stacks, denoting the call numbers of the books contained within.

"The Dewey Dummy Decimal System." I sigh. "Some evil librarian's idea of classification." I angle my flashlight over the card catalog—basically a hutchlike piece of furniture with a bunch of narrow drawers containing a bazillion tiny index cards. "Lucky for you I used to volunteer at my school library. The ball-busting, menthol-smelling librarian insisted that I learn Dewey, the old-school way." I open up the appropriate drawer, and sift through the row of cards, eventually finding the right one. "Gustave Flaubert's *Madame Bovary*," I announce, pulling the card out. "Eight-forty-three-point-eight." I move my flashlight beam over the series of call numbers at the ends of the rows of stacks, finally landing on the right one. "Bingo," I say.

Ivy takes the card and hurries in that direction—a couple of rows over from the DIE!-stamping boy. She squats down at the end of the aisle, running her fingers over torn, cracked spines. "It's here," she says, after only a few moments. *Madame Bovary* looks absolutely ancient with its wrinkled yellow pages, most of which are loose. Ivy flips through it, her hands trembling.

"Hurry up," I tell her, more than anxious to move on.

"Shhh," a voice says from behind, making me jump.

Ivy jumps too, and lets out a gasp.

An old woman is there, behind us, wearing a billowy white dress. She has long gray hair and the most wrinkled skin I've ever seen; the lines form tiny checkerboards. "Are you ready to check out?" she asks, her eyes rolled up toward the ceiling.

Ivy's in complete panic mode. She avoids the librarian's gaze, continuing to search for the note. But I remain looking at the woman—at the dark-red tears running down her face, getting caught up in those checkerboard lines.

The old woman's image wavers slightly, but just like the boy, she looks so real.

"I've got it," Ivy says. Her fingers tremble as she opens a folded up piece of paper.

The note has yellowed with age, but the words are still very clear.

Dear Reader:

I'm sorry for what I've done, but I couldn't bear listening to the voices anymore. They creep up on me in the middle of the night and sneak beneath my bedcovers to whisper into my ear. They remind me how foolish I am: foolish for waking up in the morning; foolish for going through the motions of the day; foolish for going to bed at night, only to repeat it all over again.

I'm haunted by other voices too: my parents, teachers, classmates, dorm monitors, the headmaster. Everybody telling me how I should act, should speak, should feel, should do in school.

"You should read this, not that."

"You should look up, not down."

"You should study harder, not longer."

"You should speak loudly and clearly."

"You should think twice before speaking at all."

My life is an endless black tunnel of "should." But what no one seems to realize is that I hate myself even more than they do, and that the voices in my head are the loudest ones of all. This is the only way I know how to silence them — this is my "should."

Love,
Ricky

"Holy shit," Ivy whispers.

"What's the clue?" I ask her.

Ivy looks back down at the letter, and then at the bookshelf.

"Are you ready to check out?" the old lady asks again. She starts to laugh—a high-pitched cackle.

Ivy drops the book. Pages spill out onto the floor.

I pick them up, along with the book, and flip the cover open to the front—to the spot where the checkout card goes. Ricky's name is there, on the card. "He signed the book out a bunch of times, which either means he was a really slow reader . . . "

"*Or?*" Ivy asks, champing at the proverbial bit.

"Or he was just really into horny, middle-aged French chicks."

"This isn't funny."

"Who's laughing? Beside Grandma Creepy, that is." I nod to the old lady. "Look," I say, doing a doubletake at the check-out card. "Beside Ricky's name . . . It says twenty-eight R."

She holds the card super close to her face, like an old man with cataracts. "It has to be a clue."

"Okay, but what does it mean? And how does it go with April showers?"

"April's my real name," she says.

"Since when?"

"Since before it had to be changed."

"Okay," I say, for lack of better words, assuming the name change must have something to do with her parents' murder. "And . . . you take a lot of showers?"

Before she can comment, the music starts up again: *"I've got my eye on you, Sweet Honey Bee. My eye's on you. There ain't no leavin' me. With me, you'll be, for all eternity."*

"Ugh," I moan, barely able to think straight, let alone crack the all-important code.

As we start toward the door, I hear something else—a turbulent clamor that stops us in our tracks, like metal tearing through metal. I cover my ears and look around, trying to figure out where the sound is coming from. A dusting of cement sprinkles down on top of our heads.

I look upward. The chandelier wobbles from side to side. I push Ivy out of the way just as it comes soaring down, crashing into a table, snapping it in two.

Ivy lets out another enviable scream, and we both hurry out of the library, my heart hammering, my nerves shot. And still that creepy Denise Kilborn music plays in the background.

NATALIE SORRENTO

HARRIS SAYS THAT I'VE BEEN HERE FOR MONTHS now, but I wouldn't be surprised if it's been closer to a year. I've lost track of time.

I'm cold, hungry. My bones ache. My muscles twitch.

Is Ivy really going to come?

Facing the wall, I tell myself that this isn't really a prison cell, that I merely climbed down inside a manhole and found myself a nice little alcove where I could be alone. *Being here is my choice*, I repeat inside my head. *Nobody made me come. Nothing's making me stay. I can leave whenever I want.* I grab a few strands of hair—nice long ones with lots of elastic. I give them a quick tug. The follicles look like snow.

I wonder what my parents are thinking, what the news is saying, if anyone cares. I can almost hear my parents now:

My mother: *"We tried to steer our daughter in the right direction, but she never would listen."*

My father: *"She was too obsessed with this Justin Blake person. Someone should hold him at least partially responsible for creating such cultish filth."*

Harris says that some of the contest winners are dead. I know I should believe him, but he could also just be saying that so I'll work harder at trying to get out.

There's a clank sound in the distance—metal against metal. He's back. The Nightmare Elf. He wears the suit from the movie, like some deranged fan, giving a bad name to all of Blake's true fans—like me.

The air down here is musty. The smell must be from all the storm drains, I tell myself, picturing a manhole cover, imagining myself lifting it off and climbing down a ladder.

I wind my finger around a clump of hair. More follicle snowflakes sprinkle down in the light. Christmas will be coming soon.

The Elf is getting closer: the sound of footsteps against the cement. I lie down and shut my eyes, so he'll think I've been good and taken all my pills. Hopefully he'll leave me a tasty present.

IVY

BACK IN THE LOBBY, I TRY TO CATCH MY BREATH, silently acknowledging what just happened: a crystal chandelier—so huge and heavy that it was able to break a table in two—almost landed on my head. And if it hadn't been for Taylor pushing me out of the way, it most definitely would have.

"Thanks for saving my life," I tell her.

She's sitting with her back up against the wall. Her head is in her hands. She doesn't look up.

"I'm sorry." I sit down across from her. "I never should've gotten you involved in all of this."

"It's not your fault." She peeks up in my direction. "I was the wise one who followed you here, remember?"

"But only after I showed up at your dorm, in the middle of the night, like an escaped mental patient," I say, remembering her words, as well as the pill container in my bag. I haven't taken my meds in the past couple of days.

"You're *not* really an escaped mental patient, are you?" There's humor in her voice, and yet her expression remains serious.

"No. They let me out for real—on the condition that I take my meds, do as I'm told, go to therapy, and stop trying to set myself on fire."

"*Seriously?*" Her eyeballs bulge.

"Kidding." The joke feels foreign in my mouth; I can't remember the last time I tried to be funny.

"Well, this is way more fun than, say, lounging around in bed or going to the mall."

"Now *you're* joking," I say.

"About hanging out in a creepy, abandoned building and being terrorized by a psycho serial killer trumping such activities as shopping and/or lounging . . . you're right; I *am* joking. But I wouldn't want you to go through this alone."

I hold her gaze a moment, wishing that, like the way I felt about Parker, I'd have met her someplace else, under different circumstances, and that we'd have had a completely normal shopping/lounging/stay-up-all-night-pigging-out-on-junk-food-and-talking-about-boys kind of friendship.

Instead of this.

I run my fingers over the copy of *Madame Bovary*; the suicide note sticks out between the pages. I read it a few more times, looking for some hidden message. But I don't find anything that goes deeper than the words themselves. "I wonder if any of this is even real."

"What do you mean? Which part?"

"All of it: the suicide note, the story of Ricky, the killer's nightmare, his going to school here . . . "

"Or if this is just a movie location, you mean? With us as the actors." Taylor looks directly at my strap-on camera and gives it the finger.

I gaze back down at the book and flip to the checkout card. The clue is written in black marker, just like the note itself. "Twenty-eight R."

"*R,* as in right," Taylor guesses. "Like part of a locker combination."

"I guess only time will tell." I fish my notebook out of my bag and open up to a fresh page. I scribble down both of the clues, as well as the phrasing "Don't let her out . . . "

. . . of my sight?

. . . of my mind?

. . . of this building?

. . . of my life?

Was Natalie/Harris referring to Taylor? Or Shayla? Or someone else?

There's a clicking sound coming from my headphones. "He's going to say something." I signal to Taylor.

She slides over to join me.

"Enjoying your time so far?" his voice pumps out. "Tick-tock, ticktock. Need I remind you that your time is limited?"

Taylor gives my video camera the finger again and then flashes me her watch. We've already burned an hour.

"I was in the seventh grade when I found Ricky's note," the killer says. "People had associated Ricky with *Madame Bovary*, since he'd always had the book in his possession, checked out seventeen times over his two-year stint at August. One might've thought he'd have gotten himself his own personal copy. But, in some way, Ricky liked the attention that came with always checking out the same book—a book about a cheating woman who took her own life, not so much unlike his own mother. At least that's how the rumor went. Alas, Ricky thought that his choice for the note's hiding spot was somewhat poetic, but instead it just proved futile, because no one ever thought to look there. A more obvious spot would have been someplace in his dorm room, left out in the open for all to see. I want you to fix his poor decision now. Find room F and place the note on his bedside table. Then turn off the lights and blow out the candles."

IVY

WE MOVE PAST THE LOBBY, IN THE OPPOSITE direction from the library. There's a long, narrow hallway with broken floor tiles and rotted moldings. I shine my flashlight along the walls, startled to find a series of photos taped to the crumbling plaster.

I angle my flashlight closer, feeling my heart pummel. "This can't be real."

"What can't?" Taylor asks. She's farther down the hallway now.

The photos look brand-new, printed on bright white paper,

with vibrant colors. I focus in on one of the photos. "It's him," I say, thinking aloud.

The clothes he's wearing are the same . . . all the layers of charcoal and gray. His hair is the same too: dark and straggly, held back with a bandanna. The photo was taken here. He's sitting on a bench with the courtyard fountain behind him.

"And I repeat: *What can't be real?*" Taylor asks, standing by my side again.

"It's Garth," I say, noticing the sharpness of his jaw.

She moves within kiss distance of the photo. "How can you tell? He's angled away from us. And, wait, where are his hands?"

"It looks like he's got them behind his back," I say, wishing that I could see them too—to recognize any of his silver jewelry. "See there, the way his shoulders protrude outward in an unnatural position. He could be tied up or handcuffed."

I shine my flashlight over the other photos. There's one of Shayla in the lobby, sitting against the wall. Though she's also positioned partially away from the camera, I'm able to spot the pursing of her lips and the flare of her nostrils; it looks like she might be crying.

The photo of Frankie is less clear. It was taken in the library, where he's seated at the piano. His hair has grown out over his eyes. His fingers look mangled and cut up. There's a scar across the front of his wrist. Was it always there? Do I remember it from before?

"Do you think this might be some sort of trick or illusion?" Taylor asks.

I close my eyes and flashback to the Nightmare Elf's video—the one that Parker and I were forced to watch before trying to exit the amusement park. It looked like Frankie had been buried alive. But in the back of my mind I've wondered, hoped: What if the burial was just a scene created for the Nightmare Elf's movie? What if Frankie was dug up and then revived immediately after the scene cut?

Is it possible that Shayla was never really killed? That the Nightmare Elf didn't choke her to death? Maybe he only choked her unconscious.

And what about Garth? Is it such a stretch to think he might've survived having fallen out the window? In the video, there was a close-up shot of an ax, but we never actually saw it come down on Garth.

I've been racking my mind for months, asking myself why the Nightmare Elf would've cut the scenes where he did— why he wouldn't have shown the characters' very last breaths. "They're here. Alive somewhere. Parker is too," I say, thinking about the box of letters in my bag.

"I just don't want you to be disappointed."

"They're here," I repeat, turning away to study the photos again. Shayla's wearing a pair of gray sweatpants and a big, bulky coat. Frankie's in a hooded sweatshirt; I can't see his legs. Neither of them is in the same clothes as on the night of the Dark House amusement park.

"Okay, but what if these photos were Photoshopped. Wasn't Frankie buried alive at the amusement park?"

"They never found his body," I remind her. "It'd been dug up. No one ever found any bodies."

"Okay, but didn't Garth fall like a kagillion stories out of a building?"

"Who knows how many stories it really was. The camera can and does lie."

"My point exactly."

I clench my teeth. Her words have blades.

"I'm sorry," she says, reaching out to touch my arm. "I can be an insensitive beetle sometimes. I guess I'm just preparing myself for the worst. That's sort of how I deal."

I take a deep breath, and suck up any tears. It's not like I haven't heard these doubts before—from police and people at the hospital, and even from Apple and Core.

Taylor wraps her arm around me. "Don't listen to anything I say. I wasn't even there. I was a coward, remember? I didn't get to meet the others."

"You met Natalie," I say, correcting her.

"Right. And why isn't her picture here? Or Parker's?"

I search the wall, as well as the photos, really wishing I had a clue.

"Look," Taylor begins again, "if you really believe that the people in these photos are the genuine, bona fide players, then I believe you."

"Except they aren't players." I turn to face her again. "They're people."

"Right, and *I'm* an insensitive beetle, remember?"

"If that were true, you wouldn't be here."

"Okay, so maybe only the beetle part is true. I mean, seriously? If someone like you can be so optimistic despite everything she's been through, then what the hell is my problem?"

"Let's just keep moving," I say. "Ticktock, remember?"

We continue down the hallway, passing by classrooms to the left and right. There's a door at the end of the hall. We go through it. Facing us is a mahogany stairwell that leads up and down.

"Should we try the basement?" I ask.

"Do you really think that prep school kids would agree to sleeping by leaky water pipes and mousetraps?"

"Maybe not."

"Now, if *I* were a dorm room . . . " Taylor taps her chin in thought. "Upstairs?"

"It's worth a try."

We hike up the stairs, two at a time. At the top there's another long hallway. Sheets of paper are sprinkled about the floor—fresh paper, the texture is crisp, the color is bright white. I trample over a couple of sheets before picking one up.

"What is it?" Taylor asks.

"'In a thousand words or less,'" I read aloud, "'describe your worst nightmare. By Jenna Adams.'"

"*Huh?*"

"They're contest entries," I say, shining my flashlight over pages and pages of nightmares—there has to be over a hundred of them. "Some of the people who didn't win, maybe."

Taylor nods, reading one of them. "This person dreams about the chicken in her freezer coming to life in the middle of the night and paying her back by pecking at her face."

"Except if it's frozen chicken, then its beak's been removed."

"Not necessarily." She grimaces.

While Taylor proceeds down the hallway, I poke my head into a few of the rooms. You can tell that the core of this building was probably once a mansion. Though set up with school desks and chairs, most of the rooms have hardwood floors, ornate pillars, and sculptured fireplaces.

I step inside an office, noticing a shiny red apple sitting in the middle of an ink blotter. I point my flashlight at it, trying to see if the apple's real. I pick it up. It's definitely real. I puncture the skin with my fingernail; the juice pulls away on my thumb. I go to put the apple back.

And that's when I notice.

The ink blotter is actually a calendar. It's set to April 1966. There's an illustration of storm clouds and rain droplets decorating the April heading.

"April showers," I whisper, flipping the page to May. Daisies and daffodils frame the page. *Bring May flowers.*

A giant *X* is marked over May 9th.

"Will you help me?" a male voice whispers, from behind, making me jump.

I turn to look.

A girl with swollen dark eyes stares back at me. Her lips are chapped. Her cheeks look sallow and sunken.

I take a step closer, suddenly realizing that the girl is me— my reflection, my ghostly appearance, my ratty hair. I'm looking in a full-length mirror. The words SAVE THE DATE are scribbled across my image. I reach out to touch one of the letters. A smear of red comes away on my finger.

"Knock, knock." Another voice. It steals my breath, even though I recognize it right away.

I open the door.

Taylor's standing there. "What gives?" she asks. "And why do you look all Laurie Strode?"

"Laurie *who*?"

She rolls her eyes. "From *Halloween* . . . Jamie Lee Curtis's character. She always looked so haunted." Taylor continues to ramble on about some bedroom scene and the boogeyman.

I'm only half paying attention, trying to listen for that male voice—the one that asked for help.

"So, do you want to find room F or what?" Taylor asks.

I nod and move back into the hall, slamming the door behind me.

From the Journal of E.W.

Grade 7, August Preparatory School

WINTER 1972

"You'll die in here too," a voice whispered, over and over, eventually waking me up.

It was Ricky's voice, hours ago. I shot up in bed.

Ricky's face stared back at me in the window glass.

I blinked and rubbed my eyes, but the image of him wouldn't go away.

I got up and went to the door, turned the lock, and tried to get out. But the knob wouldn't turn, even when I moved the lock left and right.

I pounded on the door, flashing back to being locked in my room years before. "Somebody get me out of here!" I shouted, glancing back at the window. Ricky was smirking now.

Mother had been like that too.

Finally, Mr. Shunter came. He opened the door without a problem. By that point, Ricky had vanished.

"Can I sleep in your room?" I asked him. "I'll bring my blanket and pillow. I can sleep right on the floor."

"Go back to bed, Ethan," he said, turning away and going back down the hall.

I've been under the covers since, adding to my prayer cards. Here are a couple that I've been working on:

RICKY, GO AWAY

This is my fortress.
You can't touch me here.

Protection is all around me.
Within these walls, I have no fear.

The guardians are watching down.
The gods are listening in.

Go away, go away,
For you will never win.

YOUR MISERY EVER AFTER

You made your choice.
I can make mine.

Might as well stop haunting.
In my fortress, I'm divine.

I may never rest.
But you will never sleep.

How is that for irony?
A life in Limbo you will reap.

IVY

"WE NEED TO FIND ANOTHER PART OF THE BUILD-
ing," Taylor says, pointing toward the room numbers. "Nine,
ten, eleven, fourteen . . . "

I nod. She's right. "We need to find the lettered rooms."

We move down the hall. A sign for the dormitory points us
back downstairs. On the first floor again, I notice a door to
the left without a room number over it. I open it wide.

This isn't a classroom or an office. There's a narrow hallway
with a low ceiling and a ramp that leads downward. "Come
on," I say, wishing my flashlight beam were brighter.

The dormitory must've been added on. I picture us moving through a tunnel, into another building altogether.

"Talk about a claustrophobic's worst nightmare," Taylor says.

I'd have to agree. There are no doors or windows, and there's barely enough room for two people to pass through, headed in opposite directions.

"Where are you going?" a male voice stutters out.

I stop. And look back. Taylor shines her flashlight all around. But we don't see anything. There doesn't appear to be anyone.

We continue through the tunnel. The sound of footsteps follows us.

"I wouldn't go in there if I were you," the same voice whispers.

Someone screams. A female voice. A piercing blare that burrows into my heart.

I stop again. Taylor's right behind me. "Who was that?" I ask, my mind zooming to Natalie and Shayla.

Taylor shakes her head.

I turn back around, finally reaching the other side of the tunnel. There's a pocket door. I slide it open and then slam it closed behind us, trying to catch my breath.

There's a staircase that leads upward and a crude cement

hallway—cracked floors, visible overhead pipes—that goes to the right.

Taylor shines her flashlight over a sign by the stairwell, welcoming us to the dormitory and pointing us upstairs. "Jackpot," she says.

My adrenaline pumps as I move up the steps, finally reaching the top. There's another narrow space. A long skinny hallway. I search the room numbers. They're in alphabetical order.

The door to room B is open. There are two single beds, two dressers, and a small corner desk. Like the rest of the place, the windows have been boarded up.

"Room F," Taylor says. She's moved down the hall, standing outside the room.

"Welcome to the dormitory, Princess." The killer's voice is a soft purr; it stops me in my tracks. "Nice work finding Ricky's room. I made up the bed, especially for you. But don't get too comfortable yet. Don't forget about Ricky's note."

"Is he talking to you right now?" Taylor asks.

I nod, moving forward again. I stand by Taylor's side to peek inside the room. There are spotlights over the bed and on the desk illuminating the space. There are also candles lit on the dresser, several more on an overhead shelf, and a bunch of tiny ones on the windowsills.

"What's he saying?" Taylor asks, grabbing an earpiece to listen.

"Be sure to blow out all the candles before you lay down to sleep," the voice continues. "And turn off all the lights, including flashlights. It's important that things are completely dark for shut-eye, wouldn't you agree? Lastly, I'll need you to close the door, leaving Taylor outside. Do all of that now."

Taylor shoves her hand over the camera lens. With her other hand, she blocks the mic to muffle our voices. "Don't close the door," she whispers. "It's not like he'll know."

"Have you not noticed the thing on my head that you're currently blocking? It's not exactly a tiara."

"So, what if you close the door and then I'll wait a few seconds and open it back up? If you're laying down, your camera's focus will be at the ceiling. And even if there are other cameras, the focus is going to be on you."

"Okay," I nod, more than anxious to get this over with. I close the door behind me and move into the room.

I unfold the note and set it on the bedside table, beside a book with gold trim. If only Ricky had done the same years ago, maybe people would've found his note. Maybe it would've become public. Maybe we wouldn't be here right now.

"Everything okay?" Taylor shouts.

"Just dandy," I mutter, shining my flashlight all around. The inside of the room looks a lot like the first one I looked at, with the exception of two beds; this room is a single.

"Ivy?" Taylor shouts again. The knob jiggles back and forth. She can't get the door to open.

My heart tightens. The room starts to tilt. I move back to the door. "The knob won't turn." I try to twist it, pull it, and wrench it with all my might. But nothing makes a difference. The door won't open.

I take a step back, wondering if the killer's here somewhere, in this room, under the bed. Could he be using a remote control? I try to maintain normal breath, but it gets caught in my lungs. I press my forehead against the door and silently count to ten.

"Do you want me to go look for something to break the lock?" Taylor asks. "Or I can stay right here and talk to you the whole time. Just tell me whatever's best."

There's a broken-glass sensation inside my chest. I look toward the bottom of the bed and scoot down, shining my flashlight beneath it. But I don't see anything.

"Ivy?" Taylor calls.

"I'll be fine," I call back, suspecting what this is about. The door won't open until the killer gets this scene.

I blow out all the candles and click off both spotlights.

Sitting down on the edge of the bed, I close my eyes, preparing myself for the darkness. I breathe in the scent of the blown-out candles, trying to think of happier times, like my purple birthday cake two years ago and the wish I made for someone like Parker to come into my life.

I run my lips over his T-shirt bracelet, imagining that it still smells like him—a musky, salty scent. I click off my flashlight and open my eyes, almost unable to believe what I see.

There are numbers scribbled across the wall: 843.8, the call number for *Madame Bovary.* The digits glow in the dark. They're written all over—again and again and again—in different sizes, without spaces: 843.8843.8843.8843.8843.884 3.8843.8843.8843.8 . . .

Beneath a heading that reads BE CAREFUL WHAT YOU DREAM are the images that represent the nightmares of all of us contest winners: an eel (Parker), an ax (Garth), a bear (Taylor), a tombstone (Frankie), a broken mirror (Natalie), a noose (Shayla), and a pair of demon eyes (me).

There are more images too: a carousel with a possessed horse, and a boy and a girl holding hands at the entrance gate to an amusement park, separated by bars.

"Ivy?" Taylor shouts.

"Hurry up now, Princess. Be a good girl and get into bed."

My teeth clenched, I peel back the covers. There are

glow-in-the-dark words there too, scribbled across the sheet. *Ricky was here, but now he's dead. Nobody ever listened to a word he said.*

I wheeze—an air-sucking noise that doesn't sound human.

"Ivy?" Taylor's pounding on the door now. "Say something. Tell me you're okay."

"I'm fine," I try to shout, but the words are barely audible.

"Are you all snuggled up now, Princess? Snug as a bug in a rug?"

I lie down and reach for my flashlight, just to know that it's there. But I can't seem to find it now.

"If you haven't already guessed it, this was my room as well. I was the first student at August to be assigned to room F after Ricky. And so I slept in Ricky's bed, wrote in my diary at Ricky's desk, put my clothes away in his drawers, walked in his same path."

My mind zeroes in on the book on the night table. Could that be the diary he's talking about?

"It wasn't long before I became haunted by Ricky," his voice continues. "All because he wanted me to find his note. I'd wake up to the sound of Ricky whispering in my ear: *843.8, help me, find it.* I started to see flashes of that number everywhere: in class, on the radio, in phone numbers and zip codes. I'd look at the mirror and it'd be scrawled across the shower

596

steam. Then I'd blink and it'd be gone. Imagine what that was like for me, Princess—for a twelve-year-old boy to try to make sense of that madness: *843.8*," he whispers. *"Help me, find it. 843.8, help me, find it. 843.8, help me, find it. 843.8, help me, find it . . ."*

"Hello?" Another voice; it calls out over his whispering.

I sit up, like a reflex, and rake my fingers over the bedcovers, still trying to find the flashlight.

"Are you there?" the voice asks.

Shayla?

It sounds like it's coming from somewhere behind me or under the bed.

"Come out, come out, wherever you are!" a voice sings.

"Garth?" I climb out of the bed and get down on my hands and knees. I reach beneath the bed—as far as I can stretch—picturing a scene in one of the Nightmare Elf movies, when Annie's Chatty Cathy doll comes to life, hides in the middle of the night, and stabs Annie's searching hand with a pair of scissors.

"Hello?" Shayla says again.

I crawl out and squat down by the bedpost. There's glowing writing on the wall: 36 L. I touch the spot, running my fingers over a series of slats. This must be a heating vent. "Shayla?" I call, suspecting her voice is coming from the other side of it. "Can you hear me? Is Garth there too?"

"I'm downstairs," she says.

"Where downstairs?"

"Come out here and I'll tell you."

"What? Out *where?"*

A knocking sound comes from the other side of the room—against the wall, by the door; a hard, frantic pounding.

"Taylor?" I shout, wondering if the sound is from her.

"Your role has been cut, Ms. Belmont," the Nightmare Elf says, his voice coming from the heating vent.

A motor revs, making it hard to hear anything else. I recognize the sound. A chain saw. Like in *Nightmare Elf.* It's coming from the vent as well.

Shayla lets out a scream—a thick, throaty wail that rivals the rev of the motor and slices through my chest. *"No!"* she screams.

A few moments later, the chain saw motor stops.

"Shayla?" I place my ear against the vent, desperate to hear even a breath. Instead, I hear music.

Instrumentals.

Song lyrics.

A woman's voice.

An old tune from an old movie: *"Baby, can I play for you? I'll dance and sing and play for you. Just pull my puppet strings, and I'll do anything. Oh, Baby, I can play for you."*

My nostrils flare. My lips bunch. A hand touches me from behind.

Taylor's hand.

Her familiar face.

I can see.

"Ivy?" she says.

Her flashlight shines, fading the glowing words.

"What happened?" she asks, kneeling at my side. She pulls something from the wall, by the heating duct. An envelope with the number 13 inked onto it. She tears the envelope open, revealing a tarnished key ring with two keys attached.

I don't speak. I don't have words. I just crumple into her arms and wait for the music to stop.

THE MUSIC HAS FINALLY STOPPED. IVY'S FACE HAS
lost all color.

"Shayla's here," she whispers.

"How do you know for sure?"

"I heard her. She spoke to me."

"Or it seemed like she spoke to you," I say, ever the bearer
of reasonable doubt. "What if it just *sounded* like her voice . . .
like if it was an actor or something, and the voice had been
prerecorded?"

"You just don't get it, do you? I heard Garth's voice too."

I bite my tongue and look down at the key ring in my hand. There are two keys attached, one bigger than the other. "Any guesses as to what these might go to?" I ask, dropping them into her palm.

"Maybe room thirteen," Ivy guesses. "Maybe that's where the others are being kept."

I bite my tongue harder and peer around the room. Without the candlelight, or aiming my flashlight at the walls, I can see pictures and writing everywhere—done with glow-in-the-dark paint. The words WHY?, I CAN'T, and I HATE IT are splattered by the door.

"We need to go downstairs," Ivy insists.

"Okay," I say, getting up, checking my watch. Two and a half hours left.

"How did you get the door to open?"

I pull a hairpin from my pocket. It's been bent into a lightning bolt. "In the words of Sebastian Slayer from *Forest of Fright:* 'Easy as squeezy. I love bein' cheesy.' A little trick I learned in acting camp to sneak into the green room after hours."

"I think that's the clue," she says, nodding to the heating vent, not even listening.

I shine my flashlight over it, unable to see a thing. "Am I missing something?"

She points my flashlight away so I can see 36 L written across the vent in the alien-green paint.

"Okay, no doubts about it," I say. "This is definitely part of a combination code for a lock or safe: twenty-eight R, thirty-six L . . . but we still need one more number. I'm telling you, somewhere in this creepy-ass place, there's a padlock with our names all over it."

Ivy takes her notepad from her bag and adds the new clue to her list, as well as the date May 9.

"What's that for?" I ask.

"The day of Ricky's death. April showers bring May flowers . . . ."

"Oh, right, how silly of me." I roll my eyes, completely oblivious.

"We need to go down to the basement," she says, ignoring my sarcasm, refusing to explain. "We need to—" She stops short, touching her earphones.

"What's he saying *now*?" I scoot back down to listen.

"I haven't even told you how Ricky died yet, have I, Princess?" he says. "Let me assure you that he made quite a statement. Awkward, introverted, did-all-his-work/never-sneezed-too-loud-or-laughed-too-hard/ate-every-last-morsel-on-his-plate Ricky chose center stage for his death. On the night of his suicide, he went down to the locker room and took a hot shower. If you haven't already seen signs for the locker room, it's two floors beneath you."

"Downstairs," Ivy says, her eyes wide with hope, no doubt imagining finding Shayla and the others. "Are *you* thinking what I'm thinking?"

"That I'm going to need serious therapy after today?"

"He seems to know a little too much about Ricky's death . . . since he was a student here *after* Ricky, I mean. He wasn't even around for the suicide."

"Are you kidding? Rumors that potent stay alive for years. For instance, there was this one girl who'd attended the same arts camp as me. Rumor had it that after rehearsals for the *Wizard of Oz*, she skipped down the yellow brick road with both the Tin Man *and* the Scarecrow . . . if you know what I mean."

"Not really." Ivy makes a confused face.

"The point is that even though her attendance at the camp was years before my time, the story was still legendary."

"Rumors in such detail, though?"

"He could just be elaborating."

"Or he could be Ricky himself."

"Except Ricky's supposed deadness puts a wrench in that theory, wouldn't you say?"

"Maybe it was only an attempted suicide."

"And maybe we should get going. Ticktock, ticktock," I say, reminding her. Our flashlights in hand, we scurry out of the room.

From the Journal of E.W.

Grade 7, August Preparatory School

SPRING 1972

I haven't written in a while. I've been too busy doing research on Ricky Slater. There are so many rumors about him—about what he did on the night he killed himself, and how he did it, and what he had with him. Kids say that Ricky was really weird and that he said strange stuff—like if they were talking about a cute girl, Ricky would try to fit in by saying how much he loved boobs. And he talked about the characters in books like they were real people, mumbling about their problems, and acting all concerned about the choices they were making.

Some kid whose mother works in the library said that the teachers didn't like him either, that his mother used to come to school and flirt with the old headmaster, spending hours in his office—even though they were both married.

Ricky's mother killed herself too, less than a year before his own death. Does suicide run in families? Word has it that after her suicide, Ricky got weirder, even giving the teachers the creeps. Kids say he stared too hard, lingered too long, and grinned at inappropriate times.

I saw a movie about ghosts the other day—about how this one ghost was haunting a girl because he wanted her to find a special coin he'd hidden while he was alive. After she found it, the ghost went away. If I do what Ricky wants, will he go away too?

Did Johnny leave Mother alone after she burned down the house? Part of me hopes that he didn't—that he'll haunt her until she dies. Another part wonders if maybe Mother was never being haunted at all. Maybe the ghost of Johnny was just an excuse to torture me.

IVY

WE MOVE THROUGH AN EXIT DOOR AT THE END OF the hall. There are tiny spotlights positioned in the corners of the ceiling, highlighting the stairwell.

Music starts playing. A peppy piano tune. A wiry male voice. *"Wanna play dress-up, little girl, little girl? It's time for your makeup, little girl, little girl. Blanched-white skin, like the dead. Lie still in a satin bed. Dark-red lips, be still your breath. Little girl, little girl."*

"Where's it coming from?" Taylor asks.

It sounds as if it's far away—in another part of the building. Meanwhile, photos of me—from age twelve until just last week—hang on the walls. Dozens of photos that show me walking home from school, getting on a bus, playing tennis off a wall, reading on my front porch.

"Holy hell!" Taylor shouts out, shining her flashlight on my eighth-grade graduation photo—with my full-on braces, bright orange hair (an attempt to transform my chestnut tresses into blond ones), and wire-rimmed eyeglasses.

"It's like he's in love with you," Taylor says.

"Not in love, just . . . "

"Starstruck?" she asks, finishing my thought, pointing at a crudely drawn star outlining my MVP soccer photo, done in green crayon.

I nod, thinking how in some twisted sort of way—despite the obvious creep factor—seeing all of these photos feels somewhat cathartic, because it helps explain the constant sensation I felt of being watched. Dr. Donna believed it was pure paranoia and prescribed pretty little pills to blot out what I was feeling. But here's proof that I wasn't being paranoid.

A locker room sign at the bottom of the stairs points us straight ahead and to the left. We're right near the tunnel. I peer down the hallway—the same one we passed before going upstairs, the one with the visible pipes. There are no spotlights here, nor one single candle. The music sounds even farther away now. "Shayla!" I shout.

"Holy darkness, Batgirl," Taylor says, moving down the hall, several steps in front of me.

Something squeaks. Taylor lets out a yelp. I shine my flashlight along the floor, suspecting there must be mice.

But instead I find something else.

A shoe.

Someone's leg.

I angle my flashlight upward, able to find a pair of eyes. I let out a gasp.

"This way," Taylor calls. Her voice is coming from a good distance away, but I have no idea where she is; I can no longer see her flashlight beam.

A door creaks open at the end of the hall and then slams shut. My pulse races. My legs start to tremble. I angle my flashlight to see who the eyes belong to.

Danny Decker.

I recognize him from the amusement park, as well as from *Nightmare Elf II*. His brother Donnie stands beside him. Dressed in tuxedos, the ten-year-old twins have slick black hair, ghost-white faces, and dark, dilated eyes that stare straight back at me.

"Taylor!" I shout.

She doesn't answer. She must've gone into the locker room.

Danny and Donnie's noses are bleeding. The blood drools over their lips and down their chins. "I'm so glad you've come to join us." They smile—red teeth, bloody tongues. "We've been waiting for you all day." They move to stand in the center of the hallway, blocking my path.

Piano music starts to play—the tune to "Three Blind Mice."

They sing in unison: *"One blind mouse, one blind mouse. See how she runs, see how she runs. She thinks she's so much smarter than he. But he has a better plan, you see. Keep finding his clues, and you will be, one dead mouse. One dead mouse."*

I grab my knife and start to move past them, slicing through their image, the blade cutting through the air.

I hurry down the hallway. There are two doors at the end, one on each side. A locker room sign hangs crooked above one of them; it's been scribbled in red crayon, just like the WELCOME TO THE DARK HOUSE sign from the Nightmare Elf movies.

I go inside. Dim spotlights hover over rows of metal lockers, as well as a long wooden bench.

"Taylor?" I shout.

A trickle of something rolls toward my feet. I squat down to see what it is. At the same moment, there's a banging sound—a series of loud, hard clamors that stop my breath.

I turn toward the sound, covering over my ears. The locker room doors clank open and shut, open and shut. Meanwhile, the trickle on the floor rolls between my feet. It's red, like blood.

I go to get up, using the bench for leverage. My legs are

shaking. My heart is pounding. I catch myself from toppling over, my hand smacking down on the floor—into the stream of red.

"Taylor," I shout again, trying to yell out over the clamoring. I shiver at the sight of my palm—at the deep red color and its slimy consistency.

Finally, the clamoring stops. The spotlight overhead blinks. There must be a loose connection. I wipe my palm on my pants and look over at the rows of lockers. One of them has a lock. I approach it slowly, suspecting it must be number thirteen. With trembling fingers, I fish the key ring from my pocket.

The number thirteen is scratched and faded, but still it's clear. I push one of the keys into the lock. It turns with a click. I open the door latch.

A picture frame sits on the top shelf. It looks vaguely familiar, but it takes my brain a beat to process what it is.

As well as who it's of.

And where it's from.

It had sat on my real father's bedside table for years, but I hadn't thought about it until now. The killer must've taken it on the night of the murder. When the police went through their room, taping it off as a crime scene, I hadn't noticed that the picture was missing.

I take it from the shelf. A picture of me sits in the middle. I'm six years old, wearing a pink tutu for Halloween. The word "Princess" is printed at the top in pink bubble letters.

"Anything look familiar, Princess?" His voice crawls over my skin. "Just a little souvenir from your childhood home, but I thought you might like it back."

I clasp my hand over my mouth to hold back a cry. I couldn't hate him more.

"I'm sure that Ricky's very pleased with you so far . . . setting the note where it should've been placed to begin with, and now walking in his shoes. Slippers, actually." He snickers. "Ricky had been wearing slippers on the night of his death."

Next to the framed photo, there's a pair of slippers inside the locker, as well as an orange, a set of pajamas, and a thick roll of roping. I touch the pajamas; the flannel is stiff. The pant legs are faded and frayed. The initials on the shirt tag read R.S. Is it possible that these were really his?

"Who knows what Ricky had been thinking that night," the voice says. "Why did he have an orange? What possessed him to take a shower? Was it some sort of symbolic gesture of rebirth? A washing away of his sins? Did he simply want his body to be clean when found? Or perhaps the warm rush of water made him feel safe? I must admit, the answer has plagued me for years. But perhaps you can figure things out. Go find his shower stall now—the one in the far corner, against the wall."

The sound of glass breaking gives me a jolt. It came from the other side of the locker room.

Someone laughs—a high-pitched cackle that ripples down my spine.

I slip the picture frame into my bag and move around the corner. Ricky's stall is unmistakable. A spotlight shines over a series of dark red words dripping down the ceramic tile: WHY?; I CAN'T; I HATE IT.

"Of course, I've taken the liberty of re-creating the way the shower had looked that night," the voice continues. "But if you get real close, you can still see the marker he used. There's a trace of it on the tile, despite how hard the cleaners scrubbed. Go ahead and have yourself a peek."

I step inside the shower and bring the flashlight close to the tiles. He's right. Some of the original letters are still visible. I run my fingers over them; they're faded cries for help.

"I used to shower in the corner too, whenever the stall was available," he continues. "I'd imagine Ricky standing there, the water rushing against his face, and wonder what he'd been thinking—why he'd chosen those particular words."

I can't help wondering the same. What couldn't Ricky do? What was the answer to why?

"Stand beneath the faucet, Princess. And turn on the water. Let the warmth pour over your skin."

The inside of my mouth tastes like lead. The sound of glass breaking again cuts into my core.

"Remember, failure to follow my instructions will result in never seeing your co-stars again. Is that clear?"

It's as if he can read my mind.

I turn the faucet on, bracing myself for a gush of water. But it doesn't come—not even when I twist the valve all the way.

I look up at the spout. It's bone dry, not a drop of water. He's playing with me. I should've known better. Why would an abandoned building have running water to begin with?

"You'll find a marker on the soap dish," he continues. "Use it to add your own thoughts. What would your last words be?"

I take the marker and press the tip against the shower tile. A series of words and questions floods my brain, but the one phrase that screams the loudest is the one that I write down: GO TO HELL.

The high-pitched giggle repeats. It sounds as if it's coming from around another corner. I head in that direction—into the bathroom area. The mirrors are broken. Glass lies in the sinks and on the floor.

All of the bathroom stalls are open, except for the fourth one; the door is partway closed. I take a step toward it, noticing blood dripping onto the floor.

"Hello?" I call.

A pair of feet appears—clunky boots, dark tights. The person steps down from the toilet seat.

A whining sound comes from the door hinge, and yet the door doesn't move; it remains half-closed.

Natalie comes out. There's a wide smile on her cut-up face and a piece of glass in her blood-soiled hand. Her image wavers slightly as she brings the glass up to her face and makes a sideways slit. Blood drips down her neck, over her clothes, and onto the floor. "You know that I don't like mirrors, right?" Her voice sounds exactly as I remember it.

She moves over to the mirror and pounds her fists against the glass, producing the familiar shattering sound. "Seven years of bad luck," she says, grabbing another piece of glass. She turns in my direction, staring out into space. "You've had seven years of bad luck too, haven't you?" There are two pieces of glass in her hands now. She rubs them together, as though sharpening knives; there's a slashing sound. Then she moves back into the bathroom stall and climbs up on the toilet seat.

I wait for the scene to repeat—for her to come back out, so that I can go in. Once she does, I open the stall door wide. There are words above the toilet, written in bloodred lettering with someone's finger; I can see the fingerprint marks: RICKY WAS HERE BUT NOW HE'S DEAD, NOBODY EVER LISTENED TO A WORD HE SAID.

I search the stall: under the seat and in the toilet paper dispenser. I even remove the lid of the tank, knowing there must be a clue somewhere.

The sound of glass shattering startles me.

"Seven years of bad luck," Natalie repeats. "You've had seven years of bad luck too, haven't you?" Her voice is followed by the slish-slash sound as she rubs the blades of glass together.

She comes back into the stall. And climbs onto the seat. Frantic, I reach through her image—right into her gut—to pull up on the seat. She blinks her eyes; they're exactly as I remember them: light blue, dark makeup, a mole on her lower lid.

When she gets up again, I can see something sitting at the bottom of the toilet bowl. I reach in to grab it, but it jumps from my hands, moves deeper into the hole.

I pull up on my sleeve and reach in farther, my fingers grazing a box—plastic, the size of a cell phone. I pull it out and open it up. There's a slip of paper inside. I turn it over, my fingers trembling. It says 41R.

Forty-one Right?

The giggling starts up again. It's louder now. A piercing shrill. It sounds so familiar.

Music starts to blare—a guitar, drums, cymbals. I recognize the tune: "Wipe Out" by the Surfaris.

My heart quickens to the beat. I move out of the stall, passing right through Natalie, racing to get away.

TAYLOR

THIS CLEARLY ISN'T THE LOCKER ROOM. A LIGHT-bulb fixture with an extension cord attached hangs down from a ceiling with exposed beams. It's like I've just walked onto the set of *Night Terrors III*—in the scene where high school junior Reva Foster plays hide-and-seek in an old, abandoned paper factory and ends up getting sliced and diced by a super-size paper shredder.

There are boxes of books everywhere, and random school supplies: a chalkboard, a photocopy machine, one of those rolling skeletons from bio class, and a human brain encapsulated in some jellylike substance and kept in a glass tank.

The room is long and narrow. I walk a little farther, spotting a lit candle on the floor. It highlights the word RICKY, written in big black capitals on the cracked cement, and crossed out with a giant *X*.

The candle sits in the center of a bunch of other items—a ceramic statue of the Virgin Mary, a string of rosary beads, a chalice, and a big chunky crystal.

I squat down in front of the candle, and a tendril of smoke floats up my nose. It smells like beeswax.

There's also a deck of index cards held together with a rubber band. The cards have yellowed with age. The corners are torn. The ink is smudged. I remove the band to take a closer look. It's hard to tell what they are. Poems? Chants? Prayers? I start to read one of them, but then the lightbulb blinks. There must be a loose connection. I stand, just as there's a knock on the door.

"Ivy?"

The knocking shifts to the back of the storage room. I look in that direction. There's writing on the chalkboard. The letters *Y* and *O*. It wasn't there before. The letter *U* is forming now, like phantom writing.

I scan the room, trying to find an explanation, in lieu of pissing my pants. Meanwhile, the phantom writing continues. I watch the words form, imagining myself on the set of a movie. *This is only for entertainment's sake,* I tell myself. *My role is to act scared.*

I blink hard, and then look back up at the board. It now reads YOU WILL . . .

. . . *be sorry you ever came here?* (Too late, I already am.)

. . . *wake up and discover this was just a nightmare?* (Could my subconscious be that cruel?)

. . . *piss your pants?* (Totally possible, though I'm dehydrated and starving to death.)

The light flickers again. I look up. The bulb seems brighter than before, blinding me, making me feel off balance. I glance away and try to refocus on the board. The message becomes clear: YOU WILL NEVER GET OUT.

My stomach sinks. My skin starts to sweat. The writing continues. The letters *L* and *O*.

I take a deep breath, spotting something move out of the corner of my eye. A shadow. A flash of light.

The bulb flickers again.

I look back at the chalkboard. Beneath the message are the words LOVE, RICKY.

I close my eyes a moment, channeling Neve Campbell's Sidney Prescott from *Scream*, in the scene where Sidney's on the phone with the killer, acting all ballsy, only to discover that he's actually inside the house, hiding in the closet, ready to pounce.

"Is someone there?" I ask, just as the light goes out altogether. I squat back down, searching the floor for my flashlight. I put it down when I was checking out the index cards.

There's a bulb flashing sound. And a big burst of light. Someone's here, taking pictures.

"Who's there?" I shout, shielding my eyes from the blow of light.

Flash.

Flash.

Flash.

I creep forward, on my hands and knees, toward the door. I reach upward, searching for the knob, pounding my fists against the door panel. "Ivy!" I shout.

Footsteps move in my direction. There's a deep-throated giggle.

Flash.

Flash.

My back up against the door, I face the room, trying to mentally prepare myself for what comes next.

"Who's there?" I call again, my heart racing. There's a spray of colors in front of my eyes.

A moment later, I fall backward. The door's whipped open, and I tumble onto my back, into the hallway.

Ivy's there. She must've heard me.

"Someone's in there," I tell her, able to hear the fear in my voice.

Ivy points her flashlight inside. I move to stand behind her, making sure the door doesn't close. Her flashlight shines over the skeleton, the brain, the religious stuff.

The chalkboard is clear now—no writing. The candle's been extinguished. And I don't see a single soul.

"Your flashlight," she says, nodding to it, on the floor by the brain tank.

I hurry to snatch it up and then I shut the door behind us.

Ivy

"WHAT THE HELL WERE YOU DOING IN THERE?" I ask.

"Let's go," Taylor says, speeding past me down the hallway.

I hurry to keep pace beside her. "What happened?" I insist.

She doesn't answer. She just keeps on moving—past where I saw the Decker twins and back through the tunnel. Eventually, we're spit out into the hallway we first entered—the one with the snapshots of Frankie and Shayla.

"Taylor!" I shout, talking to her back.

Finally, she turns to face me.

"Are you going to tell me what happened?" I ask her. "And what you were even doing in that room?"

"Clearly not my nails." She angles her flashlight over her chipped green polish. "Look, I'd really rather forget the last twenty or so mortifying minutes of my life, but suffice it to say that I want to go—like now. Are you with me? This is an old building. There's got to be a way—a crack, a hole, a balcony window that I can jump out."

"You know I can't."

She grinds her teeth. Her eyes roll up toward the ceiling. And she balls up her fists.

"I'm sorry," I tell her, but only for disappointing her, not for wanting to stay. "But I need to see this through."

"This is insane. You know that, right?"

I shrug. My heart sinks. "My whole life has been insane. But yours hasn't. That's the difference. I understand if you want to go."

"Okay, fine," she says, after a five-second pause. She takes a deep breath and looks directly at me again. Her eyes are watery. Her upper lip trembles. "I'll stay. But when this is all done, you owe me big time. I see a major spa day in my future, and not just a measly mani-pedi either. I'm talking facial, brow wax, salt scrub, the works." There's a smile on her face, and yet tears streak down her cheeks.

"Are you sure?" I ask her.

"About the spa day? Yes. About enduring another minute of this funked-up-crazy shit? Hell no. But I can't jump ship—not without you, that is."

I give her a hug. She quivers in my embrace. It feels weird being the brave one—empowering and unsettling at once.

Instead of going back to the lobby, we move through the door at the end of the hall.

"Where are we going?" Taylor asks.

I lead her down the stairwell, headed for the basement.

There's a steel door at the bottom of the stairs. I shine my flashlight over it, noticing a metal box above the knob with a blinking red light.

"What's that?" she asks.

There's a keypad on the box. I try the knob; unsurprisingly, it doesn't turn. "We need to enter a code."

"One that we're bound to get on one of these crazy-ass challenges. I really think we need to get all of our ducks in a row first."

"Excuse me?" She sounds like a grandma. "You hardly strike me as a planner."

"You're right." Taylor sighs. "I'm a fly-by-the-seat-of-my-pants kind of girl, but still that doesn't change my mind."

Except we're running out of time. I focus back down at the keypad and type in the words *Nightmare Elf*. A red *X* appears.

Too easy. The code word needs to be something more clever. I try Dark House, Parker Bradley, Ivy Jensen, my old name (April Leiken), my parents' names (Sarah and Matthew Leiken). I go to type in Ricky Slater, but the keypad doesn't work. The buttons no longer push.

I'm cut off.

My chest tightens.

I slam my fist against the door, hoping to get another shot—that I'm only allowed a certain number of tries, within a certain amount of time, before the keypad locks up.

"I hate to say *I told you so*, but . . . " Taylor chides.

I rest my forehead against the door. "They're in there," I whisper. "Shayla's in there. I heard her. Natalie called me."

"On the phone? I thought your cell was dead."

"Before, I mean. In the parking lot at the police station." I don't have time to explain. I need to crack this code. I take out my notebook and scribble down the new clue. "Forty-one R," I say aloud.

"It obviously supports the locker combination theory."

"How are we doing for time?"

"An hour and a half left."

"We need to get to the theater," I tell her.

"How do you know?"

"Because after Ricky took his shower, that's where he went. Center stage."

"Upstairs," Taylor says. "I saw a sign for the auditorium."

We race back upstairs, down the hall, and through the lobby. As we pass by the library, I'm able to hear the familiar music—the piano playing and Denise Kilborn's voice.

"That way." Taylor shines her flashlight over a double set of doors. A sign for the theater/auditorium hangs over them.

We step inside. It's dark, but a light clicks on, illuminating the center stage. A noose hangs from the ceiling, wavering back and forth, as if someone just touched it.

"It's show time, Princess," his voice whispers into my ear. "Go have yourself a seat. I've reserved the front row just for you."

Taylor takes my hand and gives it a squeeze. Slowly, we walk down the aisle, toward the stage. I keep my eyes focused on the noose, imagining a body hanging from it: feet dangling, eyes open, limbs pooled with blood.

"There," Taylor says, bringing me back to earth, pointing to the front row. A bouquet of dead roses rests on one of the seats.

I move closer, noticing two cardboard buckets tucked beneath the seats, filled with movie snacks—popcorn, soda, Sno-Caps, Jujyfruits.

"I wonder if he can hear the growling of my gut." Taylor plops down in a seat and starts digging into her bucket o' crap, like it's a Saturday afternoon and we're here to see a movie.

"Do you like your view of the stage, Princess?" the voice

asks. "Ricky hung himself during his sophomore year. I'd see his body throughout my school day—in the shower, out the window, in the corner of every classroom. Dangling, swaying, eyes open, mouth arched wide. You know a thing or two about being haunted, don't you, Princess?" There's amusement in his voice.

A screen drops down in front of the noose. The lights go out. My skin starts to itch.

Parker and I appear on the screen. We're lying in bed, facing one another—me, beneath the covers; him, on top of them.

"Holy shit," Taylor mutters.

A lump forms in my throat.

"I'm assuming that's at the Dark House," Taylor says.

"It is." I nod.

She doesn't say anything. Meanwhile, I can't help feeling everything: angst, frustration, sadness, regret.

On the screen, Parker swipes a lock of hair from in front of my eyes. The camera angles on his face, highlighting the upturn of his lips. *"You're pretty cool, you know that?"*

The sound of his voice sends a shockwave through my body.

"You're only saying that because you feel sorry for me," I tell him.

He makes a confused face. *"What's to feel sorry for?"*

"You're kidding, right?" I smile and roll my eyes. My hair's draped over the pillow, and there's an unfamiliar glow on my face. I look so happy, despite where I am.

"I'm not kidding," he says. *"So take a compliment, okay?"*

"You're just being nice to me because I'm the biggest scaredy cat ever . . . not to mention because I made a mistake by coming here."

"Ivy . . . "

"Parker . . . " I say to mock him.

"You're braver than you think. I mean, you made it here, didn't you?"

"I guess."

"And as for this being a big mistake . . . I'd like to think that it wasn't a mistake at all." He ventures to touch my forearm.

I remember the moment distinctly—the swelling sensation inside my heart, the warming sensation swimming through my veins.

"Now, on to more important topics," he says.

"Like what we'll be doing tomorrow?"

"Like best movie kisses." He smiles, sneaking a glimpse of my lips.

I sit up straighter in my seat, anticipating what comes next. But the scene fades to black.

The room goes dark again.

"What happened?" Taylor asks. "Things were just getting good."

I want so badly to replay the scene—to see his crooked smile when he says the word *kisses,* to hear him say my name, to watch his mouth as he tells me about Spider-Man and Mary Jane.

"No wonder," Taylor says, snagging me from my thoughts.

Her flashlight's on. How long has she been watching me?

"No wonder?"

"Why you're here, I mean. You guys really had something special, didn't you?"

Before I can answer, numbers flash across the screen— from ten down to one. "It's starting again," I say, reminded of our first night at the Dark House, in the theater room, when Midge disappeared.

A loud, blaring buzzer sounds. The number one flashes on the screen.

Taylor swivels in her seat, pointing her flashlight toward the back of the auditorium. "Wait here," she says.

"*Why?* Where are you going?"

Without a word, she stands and moves out into the aisle, aiming her flashlight upward, where there's a balcony with a projector.

"Did you see something?" I ask her.

She doesn't answer. She just keeps on moving farther away, closer to the exit doors.

"Taylor!" I shout, remembering Harris's unfinished warning: *Don't let her out . . .*

"I'm going to find some answers," she says.

. . . of my sight?

"Taylor, *no!*"

"I'll be right back," she says, disappearing up the aisle.

From the Journal of E.W.

Grade 7, August Preparatory School

SPRING 1972

The headmaster pulled me into his office yesterday and said that teachers have told him I'm not doing well in classes and that everybody's worried. He called my grandparents, but they told him I was just fine if not a little homesick. I know this because Gramps called me right after and said that if I don't start shaping up, he'd lock me up in the funny house with my mother.

Kids have stopped sitting with me at lunch. They don't want me to be on their teams at recess or to sit with me in the library. But I don't really care. I don't need any of them. I have movies to keep me company. They show one every Saturday night in the rec room. Even if I don't like the movie pick, I'm happy just sitting there in the dark, where nobody else can see me, guessing at the director's choices for casting and camera angles. I analyze the story, asking myself questions about motivation and plot. Sometimes I even take notes.

Jarrod told me that everyone's comparing me to Ricky, saying I'm weird, different, spooky, strange. Jarrod asked why my eyes are always so red, why I don't dress neatly, and why I've been mumbling to myself.

"Who are you always talking to?" he asked.

"Nobody," I told him.

"Well, tell Nobody to shut up." He laughed.

I had to hold myself back from smashing him in the face. And I did, because I wanted to know: "Hey, do you still hear that knocking on the walls of your room?"

It took him a second to remember what he'd told me, and when he did, a grin appeared on his face. "I was just playing with you, man. Nothing like that ever happened for real."

"Then why did you lie?"

"Why not?" He laughed again. "To keep the legend going. It makes this place a lot less boring."

I hated him for that. I hate everyone here now. And I hate Ricky the most. I'm not like him at all. I'm smarter and more in control—maybe even a little like Mother. Once I do what Ricky says and find his suicide note, he's in for a big surprise.

NATALIE

"GET UP," THE ELF TELLS ME.

I do as he says, but not too quick—slow, slow, slow—imagining that my limbs are filled with lead.

"You need to appear weak," Harris says.

The Elf reaches through the bars. There's a cup in his hand. The tips of his glove are dirty. From chimney soot? Or filling stockings with coal? Is it Christmas already?

"Drink this," he tells me.

I take the cup, imagining eggnog.

"Don't," Harris says.

I nod—to Harris—holding the cup at my lips, allowing only my teeth to touch the liquid. I tilt my head back just enough for this to look real. There's a sweet taste: lemon and honey. My tongue really wants it. My throat croaks to get it. It's so hard not to gulp it down.

When the Elf turns his back to pour a second cup, I dump the liquid inside my coat. I'll be on Santa's naughty list for sure.

I smack my lips, make a soft "yum" sound, and picture a snowy day, wanting to pull so bad. In my mind, I grab a clump of hairs behind my ear, where it's been growing real good, and give a nice yank.

I twitch. My pulse races. My insides feel jumpy.

"Go sit down," Harris says.

"Okay."

"Okay?" The Elf turns back to me. His eyes find mine from behind his mask. He presses his face against the bars of the cell. "I'm just a turn of the key away."

His singsongy voice sends chills down my spine, but I pretend not to be affected. I'm too weak and tired to be affected. I imagine warm teabags on my eyelids, while trying to hold my eyes open.

I move to the back of the cell and melt down against ground, as if there's no other logical choice—as if I'll collapse if I don't get down fast.

"Very nice," Harris compliments me.

I love making him happy.

TAYLOR

I REACH THE BACK OF THE AUDITORIUM, DESPITE Ivy's pleas for me to stop and turn around. As I suspected, there's a stairwell that leads upstairs to the balcony. It's tucked in the corner, behind an American flag.

I proceed up the steps, using my flashlight to guide the way. I didn't want to say anything to Ivy, but I could've sworn I saw some curtains or drapes flapping up there, as though in the breeze. If that's the case, then there must be an open window.

I reach the top step. It's dark, but there are candles sprinkled about the space, making my stomach churn. This is a setup.

I haven't uncovered the secret cave that houses the precious jewel.

Still, I point my flashlight toward the billowing drapes—a good fifteen feet away. They hang from a giant window, with no bars and no boards. It appears wide open.

A trick? A trap?

I peer over the balcony, searching for Ivy, but she's no longer standing at the front of the theater. She must've moved backstage.

I point my flashlight toward the window again, able to see the darkening sky. It's gray out. It must be approaching dusk.

Slowly I begin toward the window, aiming my flashlight all around—in all corners, along the walls, at the ceiling, and even behind me—but I don't see anything suspect, aside from the candles and the window itself.

Is it possible that the candles are part of a scene he's staging for later? And that he left the window open simply to get some fresh air? What are the odds that he'd guess I'd see the curtains flapping and venture my way up here?

Just a few feet from the window now, the cool, crisp air blows against my cheeks. I breathe it in, able to smell the promise of snow, wondering how far up I am.

I take another step, just as my body falls forward. I drop downward. My chin smacks down against a ledge. My teeth clank together. I tumble onto my side.

A trick floor.

I'm in a hole.

Three feet down.

My flashlight still gripped in my hand, I shine it all around. There's a blue tarp lining the hole. It makes a crunch sound as I move to sit up, trying to get my bearings.

Footsteps move in my direction. I can hear the sound of the floor creaking. I scoot back against the wall, able to see someone's shoes; the tips inch out over the hole.

He's holding a lantern in his bright green glove. It dangles right above me. I shield my eyes from the light.

"Hello, Ms. Monroe. Thanks so much for *dropping by*." The sound of his voice makes me wince. "Some things never change, do they?"

"Change?" I ask; the word comes out shaky.

He peeks down into the hole. He isn't wearing a mask. A bad sign—the *worst* sign. I'm going to be sick. The killer only shows his face if he knows the victim will die.

"You were going to escape, weren't you? By sneaking out the window? Thinking only of yourself again, leaving Ivy on her own?"

"No," I say, shaking my head. "I was only going to look—to check the window out, to see how far down it was. I wouldn't leave without Ivy."

"Tell that to poor Natalie and the other Dark House Dreamers."

"Please," I beg. "I'll do whatever you want. You're the director," I say, as if he needs a reminder. "You can make it look like I died, but then it could be a trick. You could have me come back for the next movie—to round out the trilogy. I could be the perfect plot twist."

He stares at me—a wrinkled face, a scar down his cheek, the tiniest eyes I've ever seen. There's a curious smile across his lips, as if he might actually be considering the idea.

"I'm a scream queen," I continue to beg. "I was made for this stuff, trained by the very best. How about if I go back downstairs—back to Ivy? I'll tell her anything you want. She trusts me. Use that, use *me*."

His curious smile grows bigger. "That's a very generous offer, but no one likes a traitor, especially not in horror movies. They're often the first to die. Now be a good girl and shut off your flashlight."

"Please," I beg.

"Now, Ms. Monroe."

I do as he says and click it off. At the same moment, I see the glimmer of a blade.

"No!" I shout.

"I'm very sorry, Ms. Monroe, but your role has been cut."

The lantern goes out. My world turns dark. The last sounds I hear are the crinkling of the tarp and the screaming of a voice.

Ivy

THE BUZZER STOPS. IT'S MORGUE SILENT. I STAND and shine my flashlight around the theater, looking for Taylor.

A thwack sound cuts through the silence: The doors at the back of the auditorium slam shut.

"Ivy?" Parker's voice.

I turn to look, my pulse racing. There's a tunneling sensation inside my heart.

Parker's there, on the screen. At first I assume it's more footage from the Dark House weekend. But then I see what it really is: Parker sitting in a dark room, mostly hidden in shadows, much like the video of Natalie.

I can tell that it's him from his silhouette—his wavy hair, his broad chest, his long legs, and the muscles in his forearms. I recognize his sneakers too—black cross-trainers with bright green stripes.

"I've been told that you're coming here," he says. "I hope that isn't true. You've been through enough." He leans forward slightly, and I'm able to see his strong jawline and a flash of his blond hair. "There's a lot I want to tell you, but so much that I can't say." He rests his hand on his knee. There's something wrapped around his wrist. A rope? A chain? He moves his leg and the image becomes clear.

A narrow, cylindrical shape.

The bottle pendant charm. My aromatherapy necklace. It dangles against his kneecap, sending chills all over my skin.

"Please be careful, Ivy. Please know that nothing's worth your safety. I have a—"

His voice is cut short, cut off.

My hand trembles over my mouth. What was he trying to say? What did he want to tell me?

Is it a coincidence that his words were cut off in the very same spot as my mom's? Those were her very last words before the killer took her life. "*I have a . . .*"

The screen fades to pale gray. There's the shadow of someone on a swing now: a billowy dress, clunky boots, a mass of hair.

"Natalie?" I shout.

I move closer to the stage, trying to see if the person swinging is behind the screen. But there's only about a six-inch gap between the floor of the stage and the bottom of the screen. I don't see feet, nor do I see the shadow of anything moving behind the screen.

The silhouette continues to swing, back and forth. Whoever it is turns her head; a massive bubble blows out her mouth.

A moment later, the bubble pops, and I hear the snapping-sucking of bubble splat as she takes the gum back into her mouth. The noises sound live—like they're happening in real time and not part of any film.

"Who's there?" I ask.

"I'm not allowed to tell you," a voice says from behind the screen.

"Natalie?" I repeat; my heart throbs. It sounds just like her voice—same tone, same crackling quality.

"I can't talk right now." She jumps off the swing. The motion of the shadow matches the thump sound.

I rush up the stairs that lead to the stage. There's no one behind the screen. There's no swing either.

Only the noose is there. It dangles under a spotlight. "Natalie?" I call, even though it probably wasn't her; it was probably just a trick. My voice cracks the silence, causes my blood to stir.

I grab my knife and move closer to the stage curtain. There's a tiny hallway that leads backstage. A shuffling noise comes from that direction. I follow the sound, unable to stop shaking. The knife tremors in my grip.

Just then, a blast of air punches me—blows against the side of my face—and I let out a wail. It came from a wall vent.

"Back here." Natalie's voice.

I move in deeper, feeling my body turn to ice.

A body hangs down from the ceiling. Ricky Slater's. The image of his naked body wavers back and forth. His skin is gray. His eyes are rolled upward. The veins in his feet are swollen.

I stand, frozen, noticing a trickle of blood running from his nose, onto the towel beneath him. More blood trickles from his ear and down his neck.

I start to back away, just as his head tilts forward and his eyes refocus.

He looks right at me. "I'll haunt you for life," he whispers.

I take a few more steps back, bumping into something from behind. Six feet tall, freckled face, short blond hair, and dressed in a schoolboy uniform; a mannequin of Ricky stares straight ahead.

My face only inches from his chest, I second-guess myself that it isn't real. But I can't detect a breath. And his eyes have yet to blink. I reach out to touch the face, just as his arm flies up.

Like a reflex, I jam my knife into his gut. The arm continues to move, bending at the elbow.

I tear open his shirt, where the knife made an incision.

The body's plastic. There are screws and bolts.

"Ivy!" Natalie's crying now; I can hear it in her voice.

I pull the knife free and move farther behind the stage. There are more dolls here, against a wall—at least a dozen of them. Mannequins with made-up faces, wearing elaborate costumes. A king and queen, a pauper, a knight, a man with a horse's head, a couple of prep school girls, a swamp creature with webbed feet.

"I'll haunt you for life," Ricky repeats.

His voice is followed by whispering. I can't tell where it's coming from. By the image of Ricky hanging? Behind the mannequins somewhere? I turn round and round, keeping a firm grip on my knife, trying to find the source.

And that's when I see him.

Out of the corner of my eye.

The Nightmare Elf.

Blood rushes from my head, makes everything feel dizzy, desperate, dark, vacant. Was that a grin? Did he mouth the word "Princess"?

I try to breathe through the stifling sensation, but the air gets caught in my lungs. A gasp escapes from my throat.

I blink hard, wondering if I'm seeing things, unable to even find him now. He was behind the queen, wasn't he? There was an ax in his hand, wasn't there? I shine my flashlight over the mannequins' plastic faces. Their eyes gape open, as if staring out into space. Their mouths are parted as if they have something to say.

I strain my eyes, wondering if he might be tucked behind the queen's dress. I aim my flashlight at the floor, trying to spot his boots, unable to find anything.

The whispering continues again, as does Natalie's crying. I stumble forward, beyond the mannequins. There's a narrow hallway to the right. It's lined on both sides with racks of costumes. I move slowly, angling my flashlight all around. The whispers get louder. My pulse is racing faster. The wings of a ladybug costume stick out into the aisle. I go to push them in, startled by what I see.

A red-haired boy, crouched on the floor, hiding in the costumes, holding a statue of the Virgin Mary. His body is transparent; he's almost hard to see. "Is it safe to come out yet?" he asks me.

I move past the boy, where the whispering seems more audible. There's a heat duct by the floor. I scoot down and press my ear up against it.

"You should read this, not that," a male voice whispers. "You should look up, not down. You should study harder, not longer. You should speak loudly and clearly. You should think twice before speaking at all. My life is an endless black tunnel of should."

It's part of Ricky's suicide note.

I listen until the end, wondering if I'll hear anything else. But instead the whispering continues. The note's read from the beginning: "I'm sorry for what I've done, but I couldn't bear listening to the voices anymore. They creep up on me in the middle of the night and sneak beneath my bedcovers to whisper into my ear . . . ."

I get up. My legs wobble.

A scream sounds, erupting in the space, rattling my nerves, causing the stage to vibrate. My mind tells me to hurry, but my body is stuck. Motionless. Color fades from in front of my eyes; my whole world darkens and swirls.

Another scream. Taylor's voice. I'm screaming too, but no sound comes out. Still, I try to remind myself: *I'm stronger than my fears. Bigger than this moment. What I need to accomplish is more important than being scared.*

I repeat this mantra inside my head until I'm finally able to move my feet. The static fades from in front of my eyes. I take a few steps, so focused on the stage curtain that I bump into the mannequin of Ricky again. It makes a shifting noise. I make a gagging sound.

Did someone just tug my hair?

"I'll haunt you for life," a voice plays again.

Back out on the stage, I don't see Taylor. I look upward, just as the overhead spotlights turn on.

Whoosh.

Whoosh.

Click.

The lights shine over the stage, the seats, the center and side aisles. The doors at the back of the theater are open again. The balcony, where Taylor was headed, is lit up as well. I can see a video projector and some other technical equipment, but she's nowhere in sight.

"Taylor," I shout, tears sliding down my face.

Ricky's whispering starts up again. It's louder now, coming from the speakers as well as from my headset. There are other voices too, all of them overlapping, making it hard to decipher whose voice goes with what's being said:

"There's a lot I want to tell you, but so much that I can't say."

"It looked like I died, didn't it? Like a giant piece of pointed glass fell on top of my head. But I was able to step back, thanks to Harris's warning. He has a warning for you too."

"What no one seems to realize is that I hate myself even more than they do, and that the voices in my head are the loudest ones of all."

"Are you there?" Shayla's voice. *"I'm downstairs."*

Holding the knife in one hand and the flashlight in the other, my first instinct is to move the headset away and cover my ears. But instead I stand at center stage. The noose is still there. There's something attached to it. An envelope dangles from the loop of the rope. Was it there before? Is it possible I'm just noticing it?

I take the envelope. The loop is at eye level. I picture it around my neck, imagine it squeezing my throat. I turn the envelope over. Scribbled across the front is #4B. I tear it open. There's a tiny candle inside, as well as a slip of paper. I turn the paper over to read the words, printed in black block letters: IT'S TIME TO PAY YOUR RESPECTS.

"What is that supposed to mean?" I shout. But my voice goes unheard, drowned out by all the others.

IVY

"TAYLOR!" I SHOUT, MOVING OFF THE STAGE. I scurry down the center aisle, shining my flashlight all around, looking for some sign of her.

Back out in the hallway, I call her name a dozen more times. My voice echoes off the ceilings and walls, producing little more than a throat that feels raw and bleeding.

I move toward the lobby area, thinking of it as our meet-up spot. On the way there, I check the numbers on all the doors, searching for #4B, like it said on the envelope, wondering if it might be a room number.

Room number 4 is a tiny space; it was probably once an office. But there's no adjoining room connected to it.

"Taylor?" I call, peering around the lobby.

She isn't here.

There's no sound.

Anxiety bubbles up in my gut. Tears streak down my face. I fold to the floor, feeling like I'm going to be sick.

"I hate you!" I scream at the top of my lungs, wishing he'd take me instead. I gaze upward at the cross on the wall, remembering church on Sundays with my birth parents. They'd had so much faith, put so much stock in God's word. We used to give thanks before our meals, and pray before bed too. Mom always said that everything happens for a reason—that even when something seems difficult or inexplicable, it's part of God's plan.

Was their death part of His plan as well? Was losing the others? Or coming here?

"Take me!" I cry out, over and over again, until my throat burns raw. But nothing happens and still I remain.

Alone.

Empty.

Guilty.

Nauseated.

I look up at the cross again, picturing Taylor in my

mind. "Please," I whisper, reminding myself how smart and resourceful she is, how she was the one who made it out of the Dark House, after all—the one who figured out, after barely an hour, that it wasn't a safe place to be. *Please, be okay*, I repeat inside my head, hoping that someone is listening, feeling entirely responsible.

If it weren't for the killer's obsession with me, the others would all be safe.

If it weren't for my obsession with the case, Taylor would never have come here.

I tuck myself into a ball, barely able to move, unsure if I can breathe. After several moments, I'm finally able to reach into my bag for my bottle of water.

My hand finds my container of pills first. I'm supposed to take the green one every day, as well as three of the peach, and the tiny yellow ones as needed. The white ones are for sleepless nights.

A whole rainbow of barbiturates.

It's been days since I've had even one.

I go to shake a green one onto my palm, but two of them come out instead, along with a peach and two yellows. I pop them into my mouth and chase them down with a swig of water, hoping to get a grip, desperate to numb this ache.

It doesn't take long before I start to feel the effects. My

stomach's empty. I haven't slept. I picture the capsules dissolving inside my gut, the contents absorbed inside my veins. The chemicals warm me up like toast, filling all of my cold, dank spaces.

Is the knife still clenched in my hand? Or did I put it back in my bag? I go to check, but something distracts me.

Footsteps?

Music?

What was I checking for?

Am I supposed to blow out all of the candles? Switch off all the spotlights?

I'm so unbelievably tired. My eyelids feel heavy.

"Don't fall asleep," a female voice says.

Taylor? My eyes won't open.

"April, honey." Mom's fingers cradle my palm.

I feel sick. I'm going to yack. Did I eat Miko's stuffed waffles?

"You've been through a lot." Dr. Donna's voice. *"Post-traumatic stress disorder can do that; it can impair your ability to distinguish what's real from what isn't."*

"Do you want to be an actress?" Parker asks me.

"Apparently I'm not a very good one if you're onto me already," I say. *"Can you keep a secret? I hate horror. Like, I really hate it. I don't get what the appeal is . . . why someone would ever want to be scared."*

"Please, April. Get rid of it. Use your fingers; stick them down your throat." Mom rubs my back; a warm, comforting sensation.

"You're one of the chosen, here for the party. Stay for the rolling credits, why don't you?" Garth?

"Ready, Princess? It's time to pay your respects."

I picture my fingers inside my mouth, inching toward my throat. Is it really happening? Am I really doing it?

There's a rumble in my gut and an acidic taste in my mouth. My mind says sit up and yet I'm still lying on the ground. My head aches. My mouth fills; I spit onto the floor.

My stomach lurches again. More liquid spews out—again and again and again—until nothing is left except the reflex of purging and the sound of my retching.

My eyes are watery. My nose burns. No one else is here. But still I can still feel my mother's hand on my back, as though I'm suddenly not alone.

IVy

I SIT UP AND GAZE AROUND. THE LOBBY APPEARS AS it did before—the lit candles, the evil-children-reading statue, the cross on the wall. There's a sickly sour smell in the air.

I start to get up, but my head feels woozy and my limbs are heavy. How much time remains on the clock?

I make sure that everything's still in my bag, and then I stumble out of the lobby, hating myself for taking those pills.

It's time to pay my respects. I remember having spotted the chapel from the courtyard; it was on the right side of the building. It looked as if it'd been added on; the stone didn't match the rest of the building.

I proceed down the hallway, past the library and auditorium, still looking around for any sign of Taylor and the others. It's quiet again—there's only the crunching of my feet as I walk over broken floor tile and the beating of my heart; it reverberates inside my ears.

"Come on," a male voice says.

I shine my flashlight at the ceilings and walls, unable to tell where the voice came from—not from my headset or from any overhead speaker. Was it just in my head?

There's a narrow door at the end of the hall. I move toward it, wondering if the voice might've come from the other side of it.

"Better watch your back," the voice says.

"Frankie?" I ask. There's a ringing in my ears.

"Come on," he says again; his voice seems louder now, as if it's definitely coming from behind the door. Is he locked up? Or talking to someone else? Or maybe this is a trick. Or probably this is a trick.

I stop a couple feet from the door and grab the sides of my head. *"What do I do?"* a voice asks. It takes me a moment to realize that it's mine—my voice, my doubt.

But what if it really *is* him? What if something good will happen? What if I lose it right here, right now?

"You can't stop living," his voice says.

"Frankie?" I ask again, reaching out to touch the door handle, wanting so badly to believe it's him, and not another trick. And not my imagination.

The knob turns. The door opens. My heart sinks.

No Frankie.

No anyone.

There's another dark tunnel; it must join the two buildings.

I hold my flashlight high. The walls are blank. The ceiling looks cracked. "Frankie?" I shout; the blare of my voice makes my head ache.

I begin toward the door at the end, but then I feel myself fall. My foot plummets through a hole. The floor collapses beneath my step. My knee lands hard against a jagged edge.

I shine my flashlight over the damage. My pants are ripped. Blood covers my knee. About two feet of flooring has caved in.

On my hands and one knee, I climb out of the hole to get onto a solid surface. At the same moment, the door slams shut behind me. I pull a scarf out of my bag—the wool one I used to hide the knife—along with a tiny bottle of tea tree oil. I douse the scarf, hoping the oil's antiseptic qualities will be good enough for now. Then I wind the scarf around my knee—tight—to stop the bleeding.

I begin down the tunnel again, cautious of each step. A crackling sound stops me.

A child's voice begins: *"Now I lay me down to rest. I pray my guardians will protect me best. But if I die at Ricky's will, I pray that I'll do worse than kill."*

I shine my flashlight behind me, above me, on the floors, at the walls. I'm still alone. There's no one else here. Breathe in, breathe out. It's just a scare tactic—an audio track piped through a speaker.

The prayer repeats over and over as I move toward the end of the tunnel. Once there, I open the door. The smell of burning candles and something else—sandalwood incense—hits me in the face, makes me feel nauseated.

I've found the chapel. It's tiny—ten rows of pews, maybe. The altar is piled with flowers. A podium stands in the middle.

I walk down the center aisle and take a seat in the first pew, noticing the arrangement of candles. A tall, thick candle stands in the center of what looks like hundreds of smaller ones.

I bow my head to play along, while thoughts and questions fog my mind. Was I dreaming about my mother in the lobby?

Was it her hand I felt on my back? "April showers bring May flowers." Was that the purpose of that clue—to get me to turn the page in the calendar? To see that Ricky killed himself on May 9?

May 9. I picture the big black *X* over the date, feeling my body chill.

I get up, still playing by the rules, to approach the altar. I fish the candle from my pocket and light it from the flame of the large center candle.

At the same instant, I see it.

Stuck to the dripping wax, like a bright shining star.

A gold key.

I grab the candle. Hot wax drips onto my trembling fingers, searing the skin, making me wince. I dig my thumb into the wax, trying to pluck the key free. Finally it falls into my grip and I'm able to run for my life.

From the Journal of E.W.

Grade 7, August Preparatory School

SPRING 1972

I found Ricky's suicide note. He hid it in his favorite book. He wants me to share it, but that would mean letting him win, and I'll never let him win.

What Ricky doesn't seem to get is that I'm in control of my life. I decide how the scenes play out. Unlike Mother (if she was really being haunted by Johnny) I will never bow down to the enemy. To be a star means to face the demon and to slay him in the end.

So I'm keeping the note. I'm not going to show anyone. Ricky can rot away in Purgatory for all the misery he's caused me. I don't even care if he continues to haunt me. I'll just use it as inspiration for my movies. The movies I'm going to make one day.

IVY

I HURRY BACK THROUGH THE TUNNEL, HEADED FOR the other side of the building. In the lobby, I stop a moment to catch my breath, to take out my notebook, to make sure that I have everything.

I flip open to the page with the clues and read over the list—the padlock combination, the April showers riddle, the 4B number—suddenly realizing that I don't even know what 4B means.

A wave of panic storms my body. I touch my T-shirt

bracelet, thinking about Parker. He's down there. I know he is. I have the code. I need to try.

Ticktock, ticktock. I recheck my pocket. The key ring (with the two keys) and the gold key are still there. This is still real. The air feels colder somehow.

I strap my bag across my body and move down the hallway. The photographs of Shayla, Garth, and Frankie are no longer here. I should've taken them earlier—should've stuffed them in my bag.

My heart pummels with each step toward the door at the end of the hall. I push through it and move down the staircase, wondering if the *B* in 4B might stand for basement.

At the foot of the stairs, I try the knob—just in case. It's still locked. The red light continues to blink. I type May 9 onto the keypad.

A red *X* appears.

I try again, picturing the desk calendar in my mind: 05-09-66.

A buzzer sounds. A green light flashes. The hairs at the back of my neck stand on end. I try the knob; it turns.

I open the door. A long corridor faces me. There are spotlights along a ceiling with exposed pipes and overhead ductwork. The lights shine over life-size cardboard cutouts.

The first one is of me, wearing the purple sundress from the

Dark House weekend and holding the bottle pendant around my neck. My face is full of uncertainty—my brow furrowed, my lips pressed together.

Behind my cutout are those of Parker, Shayla, Frankie, Garth, and Natalie. Shayla's wearing the same tracksuit that she arrived to the Dark House in, with the cropped jacket that showed off her navel piercing. She's smiling—a wide, contagious grin, as if caught in a laugh.

Parker's cutout is just behind hers. His mouth is open in angst. His eyes are red with tears. He's standing in front of the exit gate, trapped inside the amusement park.

"Parker?" I shout, trying to be strong. "Taylor? Are you down here?"

I continue past the cutouts, noticing doors on both sides of the corridor; they're numbered with the letter *B*.

1 B.

3 B.

5 B.

4 B.

A weathered gray door. A combination lock holds it closed. The lights go out. I'm in the dark. I hear an evil giggle; it steels me in place.

"I'm so glad you decided to return to the Dark House, my Princess." The killer's voice, inside my ear.

I press my back against the wall, trying to breathe at a normal rate and feel stable on my feet.

"Well, I, for one, had no doubts," he says. "I know a shining star when I see one, and you certainly don't disappoint. We have so much in common, you and I. Though I was initially terrified by Ricky's hauntings, my own desire to win trumped my fear. You're terrified of me, and yet you're here, determined to win as well. Sometimes it's the things that scare us most that offer the greatest lessons. Don't ever lose sight of that, my Princess."

I scoot down to be at eye level with the lock. I angle my flashlight over the numbers. My hand is shaking. My mind is racing. I turn the dial to the right, to #28, but then my flashlight drops and rolls across the floor. I scurry to retrieve it by the foot of Natalie's cutout—her clunky black boot.

I pick the flashlight up; the beam catches her cardboard face: her cut-up lips, her eyes focused at the floor.

I try the lock again—28 to the right; 36 to the left; 41 to the right. It doesn't work, even when I pull, yank, and wrench the lock with all my might. I tumble back on the floor, landing smack on my butt. I get up and try again, slower this time.

My hand continues to tremble, but I'm able to get to 41 Right once more. I hold my breath and pull.

The lock opens and clatters to the floor. I pick it up, stuff it into my bag, and open the door. The hinges whine.

There's a large, open cellar area with crude cement walls. It's dark except for a dim light in the far corner. It shines over an antique-looking trunk. The rest of the space appears empty. The stench of mildew lingers in the air. Acid travels to the back of my throat.

I cross the room to open the trunk. The lid lifts up with an unsettling creak.

My bottle pendant lies on top, making me feel sick. Why doesn't Parker still have it? What does this mean?

Sitting beside the necklace is Frankie's infinity bracelet—the one that his mother gave him. There's a handful of sterling-silver jewelry too: a skull necklace, a clunky bracelet that connects to a snake ring. Garth's jewelry.

And Natalie's scarf—the one that she lent to me, the one I used for Parker's wounds. The bloodstains are still visible. Taylor's cell phone is here too. I'd left it behind at the amusement park; it's still in its leopard-print case.

I continue to pull things out: sheet music from Frankie, Shayla's square black glasses, Natalie's feather-capped pen—the one she used with her stationery. I reach in a little deeper, spotting something dark at the bottom of the trunk. I grab a piece of it, almost unable to digest what it truly is.

In my hand.

Between my fingers.

The jet-black color.

The coarse texture.

Natalie's wig.

It's like when someone dies at war—when they send home the remains in a box.

Tears run down my face. I slip the pendant necklace around my neck, hoping that, somehow, it was indeed my mother's touch I felt earlier, that she's watching over me somewhere, that she can give me the strength I need.

IVY

I STUFF SOME OF THE ITEMS FROM THE TRUNK INTO my bag. And then I get up and shine my flashlight along the walls, spotting an open doorway. It appears to lead downward, deeper into the ground. There's a dripping sound somewhere—leaking pipes? Creepy sound effects? I grab my knife again. My hand wrapped tightly around it, I move down a stairwell—rock slabs—feeling my pulse race.

The walls and ceiling are dirt, held in place with wood strapping; it's as if a tunnel's been carved out of the earth.

Candles light up the ground, guiding the way, affirming the obvious: I'm supposed to be here.

There's a door at the end of the tunnel. I try the handle; it's locked. With trembling fingers, I pull both the key ring and the gold key out of my pocket. I try the gold key first and go to unlock the door, but I drop the key in the process. It falls to the ground. I scramble to pick it up, my fingers raking over the dirt. The key gripped between my fingers, I try again.

A second later, I hear it: a piercing scream that stabs right through my heart, nearly bringing me to my knees.

Taylor's scream.

The key's in the lock.

I get the lock to turn.

Where did her scream come from? Behind me? Beyond the door?

"Taylor?" I shout.

The door cracks open. There's a light on inside—another spotlight, maybe—but I'm unable to see much. Walls on both sides of the doorway block my view. I take a few steps to the end of the wall, finally able to look beyond it.

My heart hammers. My entire body tingles. The breath stops in my lungs.

Parker's here. In a cell. Lying on the ground.

His face is pale and gaunt. It doesn't look like he's breathing.

He's wearing someone else's clothes: baggy sweats, a red T-shirt.

"Parker," I cry, but no sound comes out.

The room starts to spin. I hear a shifting noise behind me. I turn to look.

Natalie's face is pressed between two cell bars. She's staring straight at me. Her eyes are red. Her cheeks look hollow. Her wig is gone, leaving coarse, uneven hair: half a bang, lopsided length.

My mind reels with questions. Is it possible that the joke's on me? That her image will fade in a matter of moments? I blink hard, but still she remains.

She's real.

I'm here.

"You were warned," she mumbles; her voice is shallow and weak. "Harris warned you. He told me. I told you." She stumbles over her feet, seemingly unfazed by my presence. "Don't let her out of your sight. Is it true what Harris has been telling me, that Taylor came here too, that she's missing now as well? That she's not going to make it?"

"No," I whisper, shaking my head. "She's fine. Taylor will be fine."

Natalie covers her ears with her hands, as if Harris is speaking to her at this very moment.

"No," I repeat, studying her eyes. Beneath the redness, her pupils are dilated; there's only a slim ring of blue. "Were you given something?" I ask her, assuming she must've been sedated or tranquilized.

"Not as much as him." She nods to Parker. "But Harris warns me about that too—about which foods to eat and how much to drink."

It takes me a second to notice the lock at the front of the cell. I fish a key out of my pocket—the gold one again—and jam it into the lock, suspecting that it won't turn.

But it does. The lock clicks. The cell door swings open.

I hurry over to Parker's cell, fearing the key won't work, dropping it once again. It lands inside the cell. I scoot down and reach in, between the bars, but I can't quite get it. I need a few more inches. I struggle to reach in farther, my shoulder jammed against the bars, my cheek pressed against the dirt.

Finally, I'm able to grasp it. I get up and stick the key into the lock. It turns.

I'm in.

I rush over to Parker's side.

"Hurry," Natalie shouts.

I shake his shoulder and call out his name over and over. At last, I can tell he's breathing—can feel the air exhale out of his nostrils.

"He's been like that for a while," she says, joining me inside the cell.

I reach into my bag, retrieving a small tin box filled with lemongrass and peppermint tea leaves, along with a bottle of eucalyptus oil. I unscrew the cap off the oil, pour a few droplets over the leaves, and mix it all up with my finger, releasing the scent notes.

"What are you doing?" Natalie asks.

I place the tin in front of Parker's nose and wait for him to breathe it in. After a few moments, his eyes open.

He sees me.

His lips part.

He blinks a couple of times, perhaps thinking that this is a dream.

I pinch his forearm. "It's real," I tell him, leaning in to kiss his forehead.

Parker labors to sit up, lifting himself with his elbow and then his hand. His eyes are dilated too. "Ivy," he whispers; his voice is frail.

"Don't try to talk."

He reaches out to touch my face. His fingers are cold; they tremble against my skin. "You came back."

I nod, desperate to hold him, to touch him, to never let him go again.

He squeezes my hand. I recognize the fit of my palm inside his grip.

"We need to go," Natalie insists, looking toward the doorway.

Parker tries to get up, stumbling back, uneven on his feet.

"Stay close to me." I stand and take his hand. "We're going to get through this, but I need you to be strong for me."

We move down the tunnel and up the slab steps. Parker's gait is slow and clumsy. Back in the open basement area, something catches my eye—over to the side. There's something reaching out from the bottom of a closed door.

I move closer, my mind almost unable to grasp what I see.

Fingers.

Chipped green nail polish.

Taylor's hand.

There's a puddle of blood seeping through the crack at the bottom of the door, gushing beneath my shoes.

I try the knob. It's locked. The gold key doesn't work, neither do the keys on the ring. "Taylor!" I shout.

"She won't answer you," a voice says.

I look back at Parker and Natalie, standing a few feet behind me. But the voice didn't come from either of them. It came from someplace else—across the cellar, hidden in the shadows. I hear the scuffing of his boots.

"Hello, Princess," he says, stepping into the path of my flashlight beam.

The sight of him evokes a visceral reaction in my gut. I grab the knife from my bag.

"Taylor isn't the only one who didn't make it. Those who aren't currently present were properly disposed of long ago."

"No." I clench my teeth and shake my head.

"I couldn't let her get away twice, after all. You, Parker, Natalie—you three are my survivors. For now, anyway." He giggles.

He looks exactly as he did at the amusement park, wearing an elf mask (rosy cheeks, darted brows, and a perma-smile) and dressed in a bright red suit, floppy hat, and green gloves.

He cocks his head. His tongue peeks out through the mouth-hole in the mask. "It's very nice to see you."

I lunge for him, knife first, picturing the tip of the blade puncturing his neck. I go to stab him, aiming for the area just above his collarbone.

He grabs my arm and twists it behind my back—a stinging, wrenching pain.

I bend forward, trying to break free and unwind from his grip.

"Feel nice?" he asks; I can hear the smile in his voice.

Parker comes at him, swinging at his face, hitting him

square in the jaw. I topple to the floor, landing on my side.

The killer is quick to rebound, securing his mask, and then pushing against Parker's chest.

Parker nearly loses his balance, taking a moment to regain stability. He blinks a few times, confused.

"You're in no condition for such heroics," the killer says to him, pulling something from his pocket. A needle, with a syringe.

I charge him, wielding the knife above my head. But the killer trips me, winding his leg around mine, grinding his elbow into my spine. I hear a loud crack.

He shoves me, face-first. I land against my chest. The camera flies from my head. My nose hits the ground. The knife jumps from my grip. I go to retrieve it, blood pouring from my nose.

Parker jumps at the killer once more, throwing his weight against him, trying to knock him down. The killer staggers back a few steps, but then regains his footing. He thrusts Parker—hard.

Parker falls headfirst to the floor. He tries to get up, but the Nightmare Elf kicks him in the side—again and again and again—before jabbing the needle deep into Parker's thigh.

Parker lets out a sharp, piercing wail that stabs through my heart.

"No!" I scream.

Parker looks at me with a pleading expression—his eyes wide, his mouth parted. But, not two seconds later, those same eyes go vacant.

His legs stop twitching.

His body lies still.

"This is turning out better than I anticipated," the killer says, zeroing in on me again.

Still on the floor, I look around, searching for Natalie, but she's nowhere in sight. Where did she go?

The killer turns to face me, his head cocked to one side. "Your turn?" he asks, taking out another needle.

I get up and meet his eyes, noticing the motion of his chest as he breathes. He's slightly winded. His feet—work boots—are pointed toward me, ready to charge.

I wait for his first move, conjuring up various lessons I've learned in self-defense class: eye contact is key; timing is essential; more than half of all defense begins in the mind as we await the opponent's vulnerability.

I'm done being the vulnerable one.

He comes at me, the needle clenched in his fist, angling down toward my neck. I take a step back, watching the needle in my peripheral vision—just six inches from my heart now—anticipating the opportune moment.

I plunge the knife deep into his gut. The needle drops to the floor.

He retreats, but then unzips his coat, revealing a layer of protective padding strapped to his body. My knife's stuck inside the padding.

"Nice try, my Princess." He laughs. "But I'm always one step ahead." He grabs the handle of the knife and twists it left and right, trying to pry it out.

I run before he can, as fast as my legs will take me—hating myself for each stride I take toward the door, leaving Parker once again.

NATALIE

I BACK AWAY—SLOWLY AT FIRST—KEEPING MY EYE on the fight.

Parker and the Elf.

Ivy and the Elf.

My fight is with Harris.

"I can't just leave like this," I tell him, able to hear tears in my voice.

"There's no other choice," Harris says. *"Not unless you want to be killed. A slice to your neck, in front of a mirror, so you can watch."*

Is he saying that just to scare me? The mirror detail is suspect, but I don't want to chance it.

When I get to the doorway, I turn and run down the stairs, headed for the bulkhead exit. I know it's here somewhere.

The hallway is dark, lined with candles along the ground, positioned every few feet. I grab a candle for light and then move in the opposite direction of where the prison cells are located, turning left and then going right, trying to stay focused on Harris's voice.

"There," Harris says, referring to a weathered door just a few feet away.

I remove the wooden brace across it. The door creaks open. A set of stairs faces me, but it's too dark. I can only make out two of the treads.

There's a slamming sound in the distance. It blows right through me, like a gunshot to my heart.

"What are you stopping for?" Harris asks.

I move up the stairs, into a black hole. My head hits something hard. Am I trapped? What's happening? Harris, are you still here?

I set the candle on a step and reach up. My fingers rake against something cold, hard, metal—like a ceiling above my head. I push upward, feeling a little give. My muscles quiver. My head whirs. I slip down a step. I don't think I can do this.

"You can," Harris tells me.

Using all my strength, I push harder. The bulkhead doors part open. A funnel of cold air blows against my face.

But then my muscles give. My arms jitter. I let out a wild animal cry.

Harris whispers in my ear: *"This is your only hope, your only chance."*

I take a deep breath and push upward again, punching against the metal, popping the doors open. They start to close once more, but I punch them again, feeling a rip in my skin. The doors splay open.

I climb up the rest of the stairs and take a step outside. The cold air kisses my face, finds the bald patches on my head, reminding me who I am.

But still, I'm out, I'm free.

"Not yet," Harris says.

Ivy

I CAN HEAR HIM COMING AFTER ME—THE CLOBBER of his boots, the panting of his breath. I hurry down the hallway, my nose still bleeding, my shoulder aching from when he twisted my arm. I scan the walls, still looking for the photos of Frankie, Garth, and Shayla, as if they might possibly reappear.

In the lobby, there's a chair positioned dead center. Two dolls sit on it—a mama with a little boy. Both have cracked porcelain faces. The mama only has one cheek and half of a forehead. Their eyes are white, the pupils faded. The boy doll looks sad, its mouth turned downward. There's a tear inked onto its cheek.

"Leaving so soon?" the mama's voice squeaks out. *"I was just in the middle of telling a bedtime story."*

Facing the exit door, I feel a rush of adrenaline inside my veins, but I know that I can't leave—not now, not yet. I turn away, just as the killer appears. He stands in my flashlight's beam.

"Leaving so soon?" he asks. "The story isn't over yet."

"I want to see your face."

He's got the camera strapped to his head now. The shadow of a candle flame flickers across his mouth.

"Show me," I tell him, trying to be strong, hearing a quiver in my voice.

He shakes his head again. His tongue sticks out through the hole in the mask. He waggles it up and down, teasing me, taunting me.

Keeping my eyes on his, I take a deep breath, noticing the knife gripped in his hand, down by his side.

"Leaving so soon?" the doll asks again. *"I was just in the middle of telling a bedtime story."*

The killer comes at me with the knife, slicing through the air, releasing a maniacal scream.

I duck and pivot to the side. The knife punctures the door.

I smash him over the head with my flashlight—so hard that the flashlight falls from my grip, crashes to the floor.

Using both hands, he tries to pry the blade from the wood. At the same moment, I kick him—hard—my heel plunging into the back of his knee. He collapses forward, losing his grip on the knife. But still he rebounds quickly, catching himself on the floor.

He goes for the knife again.

Meanwhile, I grab and twist the door handle, tearing the door wide open, smacking it against his head. I shiver at the impact—a deep clunk sound.

He lets out a howl. I hear him stumble back.

I snag my flashlight and plow down the front steps—three at time.

It's dark out. The chill in the air moves across my skin, waters my eyes. I run through the courtyard area, past the water fountain, headed for the woods, hoping the darkness can swallow me whole.

It's quiet behind me. Is he still in the building? Watching me from afar? I wind through the mazelike bushes and get back on the trail, moving forward, feeling as if I've gotten a decent lead.

I stop, click off my flashlight, and crouch down behind some bushes, desperate to know where he is, tempted to go back.

My pulse races. My body shivers. I don't hear him anywhere. I can't see a thing in the dark. Does he have a flashlight too?

After several moments, I stand and take a step. There's a loud snap. It echoes inside my bones, freezes me in place. It takes me a beat to realize that the sound was from me; I stepped on a stick.

"Leaving so soon?" a voice squeaks out, cutting the dark silence. It's the doll's voice, right behind my ear.

I let out a scream. Hands wrap around my neck. The knife is pressed against my throat. I can feel his chest against my back, can feel his breath against my skin.

"You'll always be my princess," he whispers, running the blade along my neck.

I swallow hard, my mind reeling, my heart pounding, waiting for the right moment. Wind rustles through the trees, sending shivers all over my skin.

I press my back closer to his chest. The motion takes him aback; I'm able to feel his sharp inhalation. Before he can blow it out, I pound him—hard—in the groin, with the flashlight.

The knife drops. He lets out a grunt and doubles over. I kick him again, plunging the heel of my shoe into his hip. He topples over, leaving me a window to run.

I grapple through the brush. Branches scrape my face, pull at my hair, slow me down. But I continue through them as best I can in the dark, keeping my bag in front of my eyes as a shield.

A good seven or eight strides away, I bump into something hard—a tree trunk. There's brush all around it. I maneuver past and take a few more steps.

"Come out, come out, wherever you are," the killer sings.

I stop in place, able to hear him moving toward me—the crunch of his boots over dirt, the sound of twigs snapping beneath his feet. But he isn't using a flashlight either, so I can't see him anywhere.

I crouch down, and wait, and listen. After several moments, his footsteps seem to veer off in another direction; I hear the sound of twigs snapping at least several yards away.

I click the flashlight on, keeping the beam angled low, searching for the path. I don't see it anywhere. I turn the flashlight off and venture to stand. It's quiet again; he must be standing still too.

There's a rustle in the brush; it sounds as if it's coming from a distance. I click the flashlight on again—for just a second—hoping to finally find the path.

Instead I find him—his eyes.

No mask.

My parents' killer.

He holds a flashlight at his chin, highlighting his face. "You got your wish. It's been a long time since you've seen this face, hasn't it, Princess? Did you miss it?" He's standing only a few feet away; we're separated by a sprawling bush.

I recognize his silver hair—thick and wiry. I picture him standing over my bed seven years ago—his dark gray eyes, his crooked teeth, the stubble on his chin, and the scar down his face.

"I would've stayed to tell you a bedtime story that night in your room, but our time was cut short, wasn't it, Princess?" He begins toward me again, the camera still strapped around his head, recording our every move. Part of me wants to charge right into him, but I try to bolt instead.

I barely get two steps before I feel myself pulled back. He yanks me by the hair, giving me a sharp tug, dragging me into some brush. There's a knife—a new one, with a jagged edge—pressed against my neck.

He's crouched behind me. I'm on my back. Razor-like branches poke beneath my clothes, cutting into my skin.

"I'd have told you the story about little Johnny and the burning house." He points the tip of the blade below my ear and makes a tiny incision. He draws the knife downward, toward my chin. I can feel a trickle of blood, can see a star-filled sky.

"Once upon a time," he begins, "a little b—"

There's a loud, hard thwack. Something metal. He lets out a wail and releases his hold on me. The knife falls from my neck.

I scramble to turn over, hearing the thwacking sound again.

Natalie's there, with a shovel in her hand. The killer is down on the ground. I shine my flashlight over a trickle of blood running from his forehead.

Natalie takes the killer's flashlight and points it beyond the brush, zeroing in on the path. "Come on," she says.

Together we run, swiping branches and brush from in front of our eyes. Eventually, after what has to be a couple miles, we get to the lake. The boat's there. We untie it from the stump and climb in. I grab the oar. My arms ache as I paddle.

Natalie keeps the flashlight pointed toward the dock on the other side of the lake. With her other arm, she paddles, as we steer in that direction. It feels like we're going nowhere. I can't paddle fast enough.

There's a giant splash sound. Natalie sits up straight, pulls her arm out of the water. Did he jump in? Is it another trick? I paddle harder; my arms move faster.

Finally on the other side, I scramble to climb out, nearly losing my balance. Already on the dock, I hold Natalie's forearm, and we struggle our way across the field.

I can tell she's weak, can see it in her gait. It's labored and clumsy; she's staggering from side to side. Her adrenaline's running out.

Her knee buckles slightly and she lets out a yelp. I secure her arm to catch her from falling. With each step, our pacing gets slower, heavier. We still haven't reached the rock wall. There's so much more distance to run. My wounded knee is aching.

"I can't," Natalie whines. She stops short, all out of breath, placing her hands down on her knees.

"You *can*," I insist, still holding on to her forearm, giving her a tug forward. "It's just a little bit farther," I lie.

But Natalie won't budge. She shakes her head and sinks to the ground. Tears run down her cheeks. I pull my water bottle out of my bag and kneel down beside her. I place the spout at her lips.

She takes a few sips, but then ends up hacking up. "Go without me."

"No. We've come too far."

She curls up on the grass. "Just leave me here to die. I don't really care. I miss Harris too much anyway."

"Harris won't be waiting for you," I tell her. "Not if you quit."

She looks at me, her eyes enlivened. "Has he been talking to you too?"

"He has," I lie. "Now, come on." I help her up, and we begin forward again, my knee throbbing with each step.

At last, we reach the rock wall. We climb over it and continue across the second field, not stopping until we get to the road where the bus let me out. My breath is visible—a long-winded puff of air. A mix of emotions stirs inside my heart: sorrow, failure, loss, relief.

I look down both sides of the road, spotting a car moving toward me in the distance. I flag it down. Natalie's sitting on the ground.

There's a young couple inside. A tiny black dog.

"Could you give us a ride to the police?" I ask, keeping a firm grip on my bottle pendant.

I think they say yes. Maybe I respond with a thank-you.

The couple asks us questions: if we're okay, what happened. Too much to answer. Way too much to think about.

Natalie opens the car door. There's a sweet tobacco scent inside the car. She scoots in to make room for me.

But I don't move. And I can barely breathe.

"Ivy?"

I look at the driver. She reminds me a little of Shayla—dark skin, pretty smile.

"Come on," Natalie says, patting the seat beside her.

"I can't," I tell her, shaking my head.

"Ivy—"

I close the car door and head back toward the field.

PARKER BRADLEY

INT. BASEMENT, ABANDONED GOTHIC
BUILDING—NIGHT

A large open space with cracked cement
floors and overhead ductwork. It's dark,
except for a spotlight that hangs in the
far corner, several yards away.

ANGLE ON ME

I lie on the ground in a pool of my own
blood. My head is bleeding. No one else is
here. I've got to leave too.

I manage to sit up, but I can't move my leg.
I can't even feel it.

Using all my strength, I prop myself up
on my elbows and slither across the floor,
toward the doorway that'll lead out.

I let out a GRUNT. My bones ache. My muscles
twitch. Drool drips down my chin.

En route to the doorway, there's a puddle of
blood on the floor, seeping out from a door
to the left.

CLOSE ON DOOR

A hand sticks out from beneath it, palm
facing up. The nails have chipped green
polish.

I go to reach up for the knob, but my elbow
buckles and I nearly fall on my face. I try
again, sitting up. The door is locked, as
before. The wood is thick and heavy. I'd
need to be able to stand to bust it open.

I POUND on the door.

                    ME
          Hello? Can you hear me?

I touch the fingers. The skin is cold. I
apply pressure to the thumb, looking for a
response. There isn't one; no movement—even
when I pinch the skin.

I continue to POUND on the door, shoving my
weight against it as best I can in a seated
position, continuing to SHOUT for whoever's
inside to hear me.

A door SLAMS somewhere. I stop pounding
and drop down to the ground. On my elbows
again, I slither along the floor, working my

way to the doorway. The skin on my forearms burns.

There are FOOTSTEPS in the distance. I'm just a few feet from the doorway now. A trickle of sweat runs from my forehead.

I wrestle my way down the slab steps, landing face-first. My chin hits a rock. My teeth clank together. Blood runs from my nose. I drag myself onto the dirt floor; it's lit up with candles that lead the way back to the prison cells.

I move to the left, through an open doorway. My shirt rolls upward. The skin on my stomach scrapes against something sharp—a tearing, singeing pain—and I wince.

It's completely dark here. No lights, no candles. I continue to crawl forward, my fingers raking over the dirt. My fingers are raw and bleeding.

The ground feels suddenly colder. I must
be getting closer. A door hinge WHINES
somewhere. There are other sounds too:
CLANKING, BANGING, CLAMORING, the RUSTLING
of bags.

I keep moving forward, unable to see a
thing. I should've grabbed a candle. It's
too late to turn back now.

I hit a dead end—a dirt wall. I move in the
opposite direction. Another dead end. The
FOOTSTEPS move in my direction. I don't know
where to go. I back up against the wall,
praying that he won't find me.

Ivy

I RUN ACROSS THE FIELD AND CLIMB BACK OVER the rock wall, wondering how much time has passed since I left Parker. It has to be well over two hours (no less than forty-five minutes in the woods with the killer; another ninety minutes, at least, getting to the street with Natalie; and now an additional hour to get back). There's a cramp in my side. It bites below my ribs, nagging me to stop.

Finally I get to the lake, but the boat has floated away. I can see it in the distance—too far to swim. The oar has floated off as well—in the opposite direction than the boat.

I kick off my shoes, not knowing what to do with my flashlight. I search inside my bag, pulling out the Ziploc I use to store my mix of tea leaves. I dump the tea onto the ground and then slip the flashlight inside the bag. It doesn't fit. The handle's about two inches too long. I zip the bag up as best I can and fasten a rubber band around it. Then, I toss my shoulder bag to the side.

Keeping hold of the flashlight, I dive in. The water chills me to the bone, shocks my entire body. I begin my way across, trying to swim as fast as I can without making too much of a splash, but the other side of the lake looks so far away. My stomach aches. There's a gnawing sensation in my shoulder.

Treading water, I pause a moment to catch my breath, angling my flashlight at the other side of the lake. I'm only about halfway there.

I continue to paddle for several more minutes. My body feels like lead. My fingers are numb. I struggle through the water—flailing, kicking, swiping—trying to move as fast as I can while keeping the flashlight up. But for all the work, I can't get there quickly enough. I'm making too much of a splash. And my flashlight's getting wet.

A few strokes later, something stops me in my path. A thick, slimy substance. I try to get through it, but it's all around me, weighing me down, twisting around my ankles—ribbons of something slippery—pulling at my feet.

I struggle forward, flashing back to Parker's nightmare—the eels that swarmed him. But whatever this is, it doesn't seem like it's alive. Could it be algae? Do lakes have their own form of seaweed? Did the killer dump something into the water?

I fall beneath the surface, still struggling to hold the flashlight upward. Water fills my nose, my ears; it leaks between my teeth. Something gritty slides down the back of my tongue. I make my way upward, able to see something floating all around me; it catches in the light. Thick bands of something dark.

I splash forward, concentrating on the muscles in my legs, channeling more mantras from self-defense: *I'm stronger than what weighs me down. I can get past that which tries to anchor me.* I thwart the slime to the side. It catches on my arm. I shine my flashlight over it. A dark olive goop. It doesn't look real.

The other side of the lake is still several yards away. I continue to paddle toward it, finally free of the muck. At last I reach the bankside. Breathing hard, I climb out, collapsing to the ground. My wounded knee stings.

My flashlight blinks. The inside must've gotten wet. Angling it outward, I get up and run down the path that cuts through the woods, my bare feet trampling over dirt and rocks. Branches and brush cut into my face, pull at my hair. I'm shivering. My teeth chatter. The flashlight continues to blink.

I trip and fall forward again. My cheek lands against

something sharp. I touch the spot. The wound is open. I can feel a gash in my skin. Blood comes away on my hand.

I go to rip a piece of fabric from the scarf on my knee, noticing the blood that's seeped through the fabric. It's sopping wet.

Meanwhile, blood runs down my neck. My fingers quiver over the spot. A whimper escapes out my mouth.

I bring the collar of my sweatshirt upward to catch the blood. Then I continue to move forward again. The school must be close.

I wind through the maze of bushes, panting the whole way. Is the killer still in these woods? Is he watching me? Did he go back inside? Am I already too late?

I stumble forward, over a rock, but catch myself before I fall. Still, I step down on something pointed. A ripping, burning pain sears my skin and radiates up my calf.

Wind whirs through the trees, rustles the branches. Sticks break somewhere behind me. I turn the flashlight off, squat down, and wait, and listen.

"Ivy?" a male voice whispers.

I grab a sharp stick and try my best to stand. My foot aches. My knee stings. My head feels dizzy as I struggle to my feet. I grip the stick hard, confident that his voice is coming from an area to my left.

I click on my flashlight, ready to strike out. The beam blinks a couple times before I'm able to see.

His eyes stare back at me in the light, taking my breath.

He's lying on the ground. Blood runs from his forehead.

Parker.

I race to him. His face looks pale. He's shivering uncontrollably. "Just hold on," I tell him, using the hem of my shirt to blot his wound. "Do you think you can walk?"

"My leg," he croaks out. "I can't move it."

I touch right above his knee. His leg twitches in response. I do the same to the other one, but nothing happens. "Is that the one he injected?" I ask, putting the pieces together.

I blanket myself over him, placing my hand over his heart. I can't feel a beat, but his breath is at my neck. "We're going to get through this." I kiss his cheek. His skin is cold. I look in the direction of the school. It must be so close now. "I should go back for the others too."

"There aren't any others." His eyes close.

The flashlight goes out completely.

"Just hold on," I tell him, my mind scrambling, trying to decide what to do. Go back to look for Taylor? Run to get help?

I take his hand to feel his pulse. At the same moment, sirens sound in the distance, giving me breath. I collapse onto his chest, praying that by some miracle Taylor will be okay.

PARKER

ONE DAY LATER

FADE IN:

INT. HOSPITAL—THE FOLLOWING DAY

A typical hospital room with stark white
walls and a TV that hangs from the ceiling.

ANGLE ON ME

I lie in bed, attached to all sorts of machines and monitors that ensure everyone that I'm okay. There are stitches in my head and bandages all over my body. A bag of fluid is being fed to me intravenously.

I look like shit—sallow from lack of sunlight and thirty pounds skinnier than I used to be, pre-Dark House weekend.

PULL BACK TO REVEAL IVY

She sits by my side, resting her head down on my chest. I squeeze her hand to let her know that I'm awake.

She looks up. She's wearing a T-shirt and sweatpants, her hair's pulled back in a long ponytail. She looks unbelievably amazing.

                    IVY
     How are you feeling?

                         ME

        I could ask you the same.

She's a patient here too, and has been
bandaged up accordingly—knee, foot,
shoulder, chin. And while I'm pretty sure
visitation for me only includes family, the
rules have been bent for those who risk
their lives to save people they barely know.

                        IVY

        As well as can be expected, I guess.
        Without Taylor. Without the others.

                         ME

        You saved my life. You saved Natalie's
        too. You brought the police closer to
        finding the killer.

She nods, listening to the words, but I'm
not sure she truly hears them. There's a
sadness in her eyes, an absence in her
whole demeanor.

                    IVY

Apple slept by my bed last night. Your
parents are on their way too. Someone
said the plane landed about an hour
ago. It must be pretty surreal . . .
the idea of seeing them after all this
time.

                    ME

The whole thing's surreal.

                    IVY

You still haven't told me how you
managed to get out of the basement.

                    ME

With only one working leg? Imagine a
snake with elbows.

                    IVY

Through the front door?

I shake my head.

                              ME
      Through a side door he liked to use—
      sort of like a bulkhead. I used to sit
      in my cell, tensing when I heard the
      bolts unlatch on his way in. And then
      I'd hold my breath, waiting to hear
      him lock back up: the cold, hard clank
      of metal against metal.
                       (looking away)
      I don't really want to think about it.

My heart monitor speeds up. I take a deep
breath, trying to put stuff out of my
mind.

                              IVY
      The police will be asking you.

                              ME
      Someone was in already. They said I'll
      be getting released soon. I can hardly
      wait to fly back home, see the rest of
      my family, my friends . . .

                    IVY
              (faking a smile)
That's great.

                    ME
But I'm coming back, Ivy. That's *my*
promise to you. I want us to begin
again.

                    IVY
You don't have to promise anything
right now.

                    ME
I want to. The time we've spent
together . . . I know it hasn't been
much, but I feel you know me in a way
that no one else ever could.

                    IVY
I suppose I do.

                              ME

     So, then will you let me come back?

     You don't have to say anything right

     now. Because I know you've probably

     moved on, met new people, got your

     life back on—

Before I can finish babbling, Ivy leans

forward and shushes me with a kiss. My

heart monitor speeds up again. But instead

of trying to tame it, I pull her closer,

confident that I'll never let go.

CUT TO:

NATALIE

My parents shake their heads at the sight of me, lying in my hospital bed, in my hospital gown and bandages. I feel like I've been away for years, traveled over a million miles, and yet they still look at me as they always did—like I'm their biggest disappointment.

"I told you that contest was a bad idea," my father says, standing at the foot of the bed. "You could've gotten yourself killed."

My mother props an extra pillow behind my head. Her eyes linger on my patchwork scalp. I want to pull out more hair, but

I hold in the impulse by taking a deep breath and focusing on a blotch on the ceiling.

"It must've been so scary for you," she says.

"It was, but I had Harris to keep me company. I would never have survived without him."

"Harris is dead," my father barks. "His body was buried inside the ground."

"No, he's alive." I shake my head. "His soul is cradled inside my heart."

Dad turns his back, unable to look at me now. Meanwhile, Mom remains on the sidelines—mute, pretty, obedient—in her pale blue dress, with the matching bag. But still her eyes look swollen, like she hasn't slept. And I'll bet those are unspoken words on her parted lips.

"You haven't learned anything, have you?" Dad asks me.

"I've learned that I don't need others to believe me—to validate what I know in my heart to be true." I take another big breath, focusing again on the blotch, breathing through the impulse to pull.

"I wish you really believed that," Harris says. *"Hopefully, in time you will."*

Mom opens a bag she's brought along. Butternut squash soup, my sister Margie's favorite, which means that I must like it too.

"Where's Margie?" I ask.

"She couldn't get away," Mom says. "Too busy with her studies. She made highest honors this term."

Dad sighs. Because I never made honors? Because my being here means he had to take time off from work, and pay for airfare and a hotel? "How long do they want you in here?" he asks.

His question makes my eyes fill. He doesn't seem happy to see me. And I can't live in this hospital forever, where the nurses call me a hero. I'll be released in only a couple of days.

Mom takes the cover off the soup and sets it down on a tray. "Eat this," she says, as if it could possibly make everything better.

There's a rap on the door. A woman with dark purple hair appears. "Natalie?" she asks, glancing at both of my parents, silently asking permission to come in. "I'm probably breaking the visitation rules, but . . . my name is Apple. I'm Ivy's mother." She bypasses my parents when they don't respond, and sits down on the chair beside my bed. "You must be thrilled to see your daughter," she says to them.

Mom musters a polite smile, as if this moment is at all smile-worthy, while Dad merely clears his throat.

"Mom and Dad love you," Harris says. *"They just don't know how to show it."*

Apple takes my hand. Her fingers are warm. She smells like oranges. "You saved my daughter's life. Ivy tells me that if it weren't for you, she'd have never made it out of there." Her eyes locked on mine, tears of gratitude trickle down her cheeks. She leans in to kiss my forehead. Her palm glides over the crown of my head. "Thank you," she says, without a second glance to my hair.

I want to tell her how strong Ivy is; that if it weren't for her, I wouldn't be here either. But I'm crying too hard to speak. Her kindness is too much to bear.

I peer over her shoulder at my parents. My tears have made everything blurry, but somehow, despite the blur, things are starting to look a whole lot clearer.

IVY

TWO WEEKS LATER

THE DOORBELL RINGS. IT'S APPLE AND CORE,
bringing me bags full of groceries. They've been stopping by
at least a couple of times a day to check on me. I can't really
say I blame them. My apartment is under twenty-four-hour
surveillance, because I saw the killer's face—again.

I've been racking my brain as to why he might've revealed
it. Was it because he thought he'd won—because he was

convinced he was going to kill me? Or maybe it was his twisted way of trying to reward me for a job well done.

Whatever the reason, I don't think he's going to come after me—at least not for a while anyway. The killer spent years of his life studying me—my choices, my psychology. But I'm no longer the same person. These past several months have changed me. If he wanted to come after me again, he'd need to discover this new person I've become.

"How are you doing today?" Apple asks, sitting across from me on the sofa. Her crumpled expression tells me that she already knows the answer.

"I'm okay," I lie. "I want to go back to work."

"Are you sure?" Her dark eyes narrow. "Maybe it's best to wait a few more weeks."

"I'm ready." I need the money. I need to appear normal. I need to show the killer that he didn't get the best of me.

"Miko's been asking about you." She runs her hand over her freshly cut hair spikes. She recently hacked off more than ten inches for Locks of Love. "I think he might have a crush."

"I wouldn't be so sure." Most people are calling me crazy for going after a killer with little more than a knife. Others are calling me selfish—myself included—for getting Taylor involved. I'm not sure how I'll ever forgive myself for letting her come along.

"I wouldn't be so *unsure* either." Apple winks.

I love Apple, and I know she means well, but the fact that she thinks I can move on after everything that's happened just distances us more.

After Parker and I were saved, the police scoped out the August Prep building, but they couldn't find any traces of Shayla, Frankie, or Garth—aside from the items left in the trunk. The blood I saw seeping through the door crack in the basement indeed belonged to Taylor, but, like the others, she was nowhere to be found.

What they *were* able to find? A bunch of the audio and video equipment, but none of the footage from that day. The killer had obviously been in a rush, but he knew just what to take. And, in the end, he got what he wanted—his sequel, right down to the final chase scene where the heroine faced her opponent.

The school's become a crime scene, not to mention a hot spot for Dark House series fans seeking a little thrill, eager to learn more about the legend of Ricky Slater. The good news: Though they won't reveal his identity, the police assure me that they know who the killer is. Now it's just a matter of finding him.

The police also have Natalie's testimony—for whatever it's worth. She claims that Parker was the only other survivor she saw during her time in captivity, and that, according to Harris, the bodies of Frankie, Shayla, and Garth are buried in a sinkhole somewhere in South Dakota. "Taylor's body will be dumped too," she told police. "That is if you don't find it first; Harris doesn't think you will."

Even though, so far, Harris has proven correct on pretty much all accounts, I'm still holding on to hope, praying that the others are somewhere out there still.

Core lifts a pot of something heavy onto the stove. "Apple and I stopped by the diner earlier," he says. "Miko made you a batch of his famous chicken gumbo soup."

"I'll have to call him to say thank you." I force a smile—and not because I don't think the gesture was incredibly sweet. I'm just not sure I'm capable of spontaneous smiles anymore.

"Dr. Donna called the house earlier," Apple says. "She'd love to start seeing you again."

"I'll call her too." I smile wider. The irony: I was never into acting before, but ever since the Dark House weekend, it's become a way of life—a means of survival even.

I move to the kitchen table and eat a bowlful of soup, forcing down each bite, hoping I'm playing a convincing role.

Once they finally leave, I head into the bedroom. Beside my bed is the box of letters from Parker. After the police found Parker and me in the woods, I asked an officer to go back to the lake for my bag. I gave the officer the items I took from the trunk: Garth's skull necklace, Shayla's glasses, Frankie's sheet music, Natalie's scarf and wig. But I kept Parker's box of letters for myself, because I didn't want it to get taken away.

Parker has my letters too—the ones I wrote to him and mailed to myself. I packaged them all up before he flew back home. We've been talking every night since he left, and texting a few times a day. He says he can't wait to get back here and see me again. Part of me can't wait either—the part that still holds on to hope.

I sit down on the edge of my bed and run his bracelet over my cheek, remembering our first kiss—on the deck, holding hands, facing one another; the warmth of his breath against my skin, a hot buttery heat spilling across my thighs.

I gaze at the wall—at the giant, mural-size posters (cityscapes of Paris and Nice) that hang from a curtain rod I was able to rig. I get up and unclip them, revealing hundreds of pieces of paper—maps and charts and graphs I've made; a wall covered in conclusions I've drawn, questions I have, facts I know, pictures I've found, hours I've spent trying to get into the mind of a killer.

He may be a step ahead right now, but he won't be for long. The heroine always wins in the end.

The End

EPILOGUE

SPRING

IVY

I'VE TAKEN UP RUNNING AS A WAY TO CLEAR MY head—perhaps the very best form of therapy. When I'm running, there's nothing else. My thoughts clear. My worries flee. With the wind combing through my hair and the warmth of the sun against my cheeks, I imagine myself like an animal—wild, free, unstoppable.

My birth mother often joins me on my runs. I know that probably sounds crazy, but sometimes I'm even able to catch a hint of her lilac perfume. She may've passed on seven years ago, but she's never far from my side—I know that now. The

Nightmare Elf was right about one thing: sometimes it's the things that scare us most that teach us the biggest lessons.

I inhale the smells around me—of freshly cut grass, morning rain, tree bark, and lilacs—and I listen to the birds chirp. It's only when I feel my legs betray me that I start to head back.

I'm just about home now. My aunt's car is parked in the driveway. She hasn't left for work yet. I slow my pace, moving up the walkway, noticing a large envelope sticking out from my mailbox. I take it. My name and address are printed across the front. It was postmarked in Canada, but there's no return address.

I unlock the door to my apartment and then lock it back up—three bolts, plus a chain, and a chair propped beneath the knob.

I unload the pockets of my jacket first—chewing gum, pepper spray, a knife, my cell phone—and then I sit down on the edge of the couch and tear the envelope open.

There's a book inside. It's navy blue, hardcover, with a torn spine and gold trim. My heart begins to pound, because I've seen this book before—in Ricky's room, on the bedside table, when I left the suicide note.

There's a tiny lock for a key.

I reach into my bag and search for the key ring from that

night; I've been keeping it tucked inside a zippered compartment. I pluck it out and insert the smaller key into the lock. It turns. I open it up. The words THE PROPERTY OF E.W. GRADE 7, AUGUST PREPARATORY SCHOOL are printed on the inside cover.

The doorbell rings.

I look toward the windows. The blinds are drawn. Apple and Core are at work. My aunt is going to be late if she hasn't already left. Who else could it be?

My pulse racing, I stuff the book beneath the sofa and go to the door. I peek through the peephole, almost unable to believe who's standing there, suitcase in tow.

I remove the chair, unlock the bolts, retract the chain, and open the door wide.

"Hey," Natalie says.

"Hey." I smile—probably my first genuine one in weeks.

Natalie looks the best I've seen her yet. Her eyes are no longer red and swollen; they're a brilliant shade of blue, made more dramatic with inky-black lashes. Her hair is different too. It's been cut super-short, about an inch long all over.

Without another word, I move closer to give her a hug. Her arms wrap around my shoulders, and we melt into each other's embrace. There's so much I want to say—so much I need to know. Aside from a couple of texts back and forth to share our contact info, we haven't seen each other or spoken since the night of our escape (and our brief overlap at the hospital).

Our embrace breaks. Our eyes lock.

"What are you doing here?" I ask her. "Over a thousand miles from home."

"They just don't get me. I guess they never did. But that's okay." She shrugs. "I mean, I'll be okay."

I bite my lip, remembering calling her house during the Dark House weekend. Natalie's mother picked up, and when I told her how troubled Natalie was and asked for her understanding, all she gave me was anger and resentment.

"Do you think I could maybe stay here for a while?" The words come out shaky. Her face turns bright pink.

Maybe, like me, she isn't used to being vulnerable. And maybe, like her family, I don't understand her either. But still we share something pretty significant in common, and maybe that's more than enough for now. I take her bag and invite her inside.

WELCOME TO THE DARK HOUSE

ACKNOWLEDGMENTS

A VERY SPECIAL THANK-YOU TO CHRISTIAN Trimmer, my brilliantly talented editor of five years. I'm so grateful to have worked with you. Thank you for acquiring this project and beginning its editorial journey with me.

Huge thanks to Tracey Keevan, who continued with me on that journey, working round the clock, cheering me on, and pushing me harder—my very own literary personal trainer. This book is so much stronger because of you.

Thanks to Kathryn Green, agent extraordinaire. I'm so grateful to have you in my corner. A million thanks for all you do.

Special thanks to music guru Frankie Price for answering all of my guitar- and music-related questions. Any related errors found within this novel are mine and mine alone.

Thank you to all of the friends and family members who offer to read drafts of my work and who give me time to write as well as cups of fresh coffee (black, no sugar).

And lastly, a very special thank-you to my readers, who continue to support my work and cheer me on. You guys are the absolute best.

RETURN TO THE DARK HOUSE

ACKNOWLEDGMENTS

I would first like to thank my editor, Tracey Keevan, for her invaluable feedback and continuous enthusiasm for my work. I'm so grateful for her keen insight and enviable superpower of knowing just the right questions to ask. This book is so much stronger because of her.

A million thanks to my amazingly talented agent, Kathryn Green, for her literary guidance and advice, and for her willingness to discuss reality TV with me. Eleven books together later, I'm enormously grateful for all she does.

Special thanks to Scott Olson, my psychological guru, for answering all of my questions pertaining to mental health and therapy. Any related errors found within this novel are mine and mine alone.

Thanks to friends and family members who are a constant source of support, who give me the time to write, offer to read drafts of my work, and who don't mind if the house gets messy or if I declare take-out night for dinner because I'm too busy working.

And lastly, a very special thank-you goes to my readers, who continue to support my work and cheer me on from near and afar. Thank you for reading my books, entering my contests, attending my workshops, sending me letters and artwork, coming to my events, and making book-inspired videos. I've said it before and I'll say it again, and again, and again: I'm eternally grateful. You guys are the absolute best.